Man, she should have jumped his bones ages ago. The idea nearly drew a giggle from her.

Apparently he felt it because he pulled back a little, letting her catch her breath. "What's funny?"

She could feel her cheeks heat. She hoped he thought it was the heat from the fireplace, although it wasn't that warm. "It's silly," she said, sounding as if she had to force the words out.

"Oh. That's okay. I always thought you were the most wildly beautiful woman I'd ever seen."

Wildly beautiful? Her heart slammed and began a rapid tap dance of delight. "I was just thinking..." She drew a breath and blurted it. Truth for truth. "I was just thinking I should have jumped your bones a long time ago."

The smile that spread over his face would have lit the arctic night brighter than the aurora. "Oh, I do like the sound of that."

With a gentle hand, he cupped her cheek and drew her in for another kiss. "Jump away," he murmured against her lips. "Any time."

DEADLY SEARCH

NEW YORK TIMES BESTSELLING AUTHOR

RACHEL LEE
& ADDISON FOX

Previously published as *Missing in Conard County*
and *Colton K-9 Cop*

ISBN-13: 978-1-335-45483-6

Deadly Search

Copyright © 2020 by Harlequin Books S.A.

Missing in Conard County
First published in 2018. This edition published in 2020.
Copyright © 2018 by Susan Civil-Brown

Colton K-9 Cop
First published in 2017. This edition published in 2020.
Copyright © 2017 by Harlequin Books S.A.

Special thanks and acknowledgment are given to Addison Fox for her contribution to The Coltons of Shadow Creek miniseries.

Recycling programs
for this product may
not exist in your area.

This edition published by arrangement with Harlequin Books S.A.

For questions and comments about the quality of this book, please contact us at CustomerService@Harlequin.com.

Harlequin Enterprises ULC
22 Adelaide St. West, 40th Floor
Toronto, Ontario M5H 4E3, Canada
www.Harlequin.com

Printed in U.S.A.

CONTENTS

Rachel Lee was hooked on writing by the age of twelve and practiced her craft as she moved from place to place all over the United States. This *New York Times* bestselling author now resides in Florida and has the joy of writing full-time.

Books by Rachel Lee

Harlequin Intrigue

Cornered in Conard County
Missing in Conard County
Murdered in Conard County
Conard County Justice

Harlequin Romantic Suspense

Conard County Witness
A Secret in Conard County
A Conard County Spy
Conard County Marine
Undercover in Conard County
Conard County Revenge
Conard County Watch
Stalked in Conard County

Visit the Author Profile page
at Harlequin.com for more titles.

MISSING IN CONARD COUNTY

Rachel Lee

Chapter One

Day 20

The forecast called for a severe winter storm to move into Conard County, Wyoming, in the next two days, so animal control officer Allan Carstairs was out hunting for strays. By nightfall, the temperatures would be dropping rapidly, and while the storm itself wasn't moving fast, the cold was stampeding down on them. Subzero temperatures weren't good for animals that were used to warm homes and not used to dealing with Arctic weather. Al had seen cats with badly frostbitten paws and ears, and he would never forget the dog that needed a leg amputated. Nor would he ever forget the animals he had found frozen to death.

So when the weather was about to turn dangerous, he roamed the area outside town looking for strays, as well as a family of felines that a trucker had reported dropped by the roadside. A lot of people let their cats roam free, and any cat that didn't sense the changing weather as a reason to get home would be looking at trouble, even death. Then there were the dogs. The leash law didn't always keep them from escaping and having so much fun racing the countryside that they often didn't seem to realize danger was closing in.

At that moment he already had three annoyed cats in cages and a miniature schnauzer that appeared to be sad because he couldn't keep chasing a prairie dog.

Then he spied Misty. A beautiful golden retriever with a distinctive prance to her step, she seemed to be running in circles about a hundred yards inside the fence line of the Harris family ranch. He was surprised to see her so far out here. The Avilas had always been careful owners who tried not to let Misty slip her leash, but she was an accomplished escape artist. With the weather turning so bitter, perhaps one of the kids had let her out in the backyard without watching and she'd burrowed under the fence. Regardless, at the times she proved to be Houdini's reincarnation, Al usually picked her up within or near the city limits.

Al pulled his van onto the shoulder, grabbed a slip-knot leash and climbed out. Misty had never been a problem to round up, so he expected her to come immediately when he called. Just after he slid off the seat and his feet hit the ground, he felt a light weight land on his shoulder and hang on. Regis, he thought, and smiled.

He closed the vehicle door so the animals would stay warm and gave thanks that the wind hadn't really started yet. Just the faintest of breezes to chill the air, and a tang that hinted at coming snow.

For the first time ever, Misty wasn't in a cooperative mood. As she raced around, she tossed some kind of toy in the air, and although she occasionally glanced at him when he called her, she kept right on playing, pausing only occasionally to paw at the ground before returning to her private game of catch.

"Hey, Misty," Al called. "Come on. Don't be a pain. Seriously."

Just then a sheriff's SUV pulled onto the opposite shoulder of the road. It bore a rack of lights and Conard County Sheriff painted in green on the tan background. K-9, Keep Your Distance was also labeled on the side. By that, before she even climbed out, Al knew it was Kelly Noveno.

She had apparently taken in the situation before she pulled over to approach him, and grinned as she climbed out. "Having a problem, Al?"

He had to grin back. Kelly was a wildly attractive woman to his way of thinking, but what he most liked about her was her sunny nature and readiness to tease. He also liked her dog, a Belgian Malinois named Bugle for his slightly strange bark. Kelly left Bugle in her vehicle, however, and sauntered toward Al, her khaki uniform and jacket looking scarcely heavy enough to withstand the chilling air. "Misty giving you trouble?"

"She's in a mood, all right," Al agreed. Apparently, Kelly had had her own run-ins with the dog.

Kelly whistled, but Misty barely spared her a glance as she tossed her toy in the air and caught it.

"What in the world is she playing with?" Kelly asked.

"I've been wondering. Rawhide bone? Heck, she knows I wouldn't take that away from her."

Kelly chuckled. "She's teasing you." Then she turned to look at Al. "What in the dickens is that on your shoulder?"

Al didn't even have to glance. "That's Regis."

"That's a *squirrel*! You can't keep them for pets."

"I don't. Regis decides for himself. Sometimes he likes to ride shotgun. What can I tell you, Kelly? The squirrel has a mind of his own."

Al felt her staring but heck, what could he do about it? He'd rescued Regis as an abandoned baby, fed the animal until it was strong enough to take off into the woods and live the squirrel life. Except Regis kept coming back to visit.

"Now I've seen everything," Kelly muttered. "Someday I want to hear this story."

While Al wouldn't have minded spending the next day or two chatting with Kelly, there was still business to attend to. "Misty, get your butt over here now." This time there was an edge of impatience to his voice and Misty didn't miss it. She froze, looked at him, then came trotting over with her toy.

Al squatted down, ready to reward the dog with a good scratch and rub, but as Misty drew closer something inside him began to feel as chilly as the day.

"Kelly?"

"That's not rawhide," she said too quietly.

Al didn't answer. He waited until Misty snaked through the fence and came to a halt before him, dropping her toy and looking at him with a proud grin.

Al reached out, scratching her neck automatically as he looked down at the "present" she'd placed before him.

"Tell me that's not human," he said.

"I can't," Kelly answered, her voice unusually taut.

Their eyes met and Al knew they were both thinking of the same thing: the three high school girls who'd gone missing nearly a month ago.

"I'll get an evidence bag while you put the dog in your van," Kelly said. But he noted she walked to her SUV with a leaden step. All her natural vivacity had seeped away. She'd be calling for help, he thought, to try to learn where the dog found the bone. Before they were even certain.

"Yeah," Al said, speaking to the icy air. "Yeah." Then he stood, slipping the loose leash around Misty and leading her to the back of his truck.

"God," he told the dog, "I hope it's from a deer."

But he was very afraid it was not.

Chapter Two

Kelly Noveno rolled over in her bed with a groan, wishing she could knock the ringing phone off the hook and go back to sleep. Being a sheriff's deputy, she knew she couldn't do that even though she'd worked graveyard.

The night shifts ended in the wee hours with her being too wound up to sleep immediately. Inevitably while she worked she drank far too much coffee, and by the time she reached her snug little house near the edge of Conard City, she was wider awake than an owl. She unwound with recorded TV or music, and often didn't fall asleep until late morning.

Thus, no one should bother her this early. She'd made that much clear to the dispatcher. She and her dog, Bugle, must be allowed to sleep.

Right then Bugle, who was lying beside her on her rumpled queen-size bed, lifted his head and made a sound somewhere between a groan and a yawn.

"Yeah, me, too, boy." Except that as she pushed herself upright, she caught sight of the digital clock. Three in the afternoon was hardly early. If she were on shift tonight, she'd be getting up soon anyway.

"Hell," she muttered and stood in her red flannel pajamas, shoving her feet into warm slippers. "It's getting cold, Bugle." Even inside. The heat must be straining to keep up.

The phone jangled again, telling her it wasn't going to let her run away. Pushing her bobbed, straight black hair back from her face, she reached for the receiver and lifted it to her ear.

"Noveno," she answered, trying to sound alert and not groggy.

"Kelly, sorry to wake you," came the gravelly voice of the sheriff, Gage Dalton. She guessed her attempt to sound alert hadn't worked very well. "You found a car in the ditch along the state highway last night, didn't you?"

"Yeah." She closed her eyes, remembering. "About eleven o'clock. A trace on the tag said it belonged to Randy Beauvoir. I called and got no answer. Figured someone had picked the occupants up because it was so cold. No sign of any trouble, appeared to be a simple loss of control. I tagged it for tow because the rear end was dangerously near the edge of the traffic lane."

All of which had been in the report that she had typed at five that morning. Holiday weekend, lots of activity and lots of people not home. New Year's.

"I know you're probably still tired, but we need you

to come in. Three girls are missing, last known to be in that vehicle. Their parents called us half an hour ago."

"Oh, God," she breathed. "I'll be there right away."

SHE FILLED BUGLE'S bowls with kibble and fresh water, then while he filled his belly she hurried into a fresh uniform. Which girls? The thought ran around inside her head like a hamster on a wheel.

Beauvoir. She didn't know the family well, but she'd met Randy and May's daughter briefly last fall during one of those "don't drink and drive" demos they put on every two years, showing the graphic aftermath of an accident. The girl, woman really, had been pretty and engaging and full of questions because she said she wanted to become an EMT. Eighteen and full of promise.

"Oh, God," she said aloud once more.

Bugle looked at her, forgetting his food.

"Go ahead and eat," she told him. "Who knows when this day will end." Or how.

SHE GRABBED SOME dry cereal from the cupboard, poured milk on it and ate it too quickly. A couple of power bars wound up in her jacket pockets after she donned her utility belt and gun.

Time to go.

Anyone who'd grown up here should know better than to wander away from a vehicle on a cold night. It was easy to get lost out there on those open expanses, and people ought to be aware how fast the cold could become fatal. She couldn't believe three high school women wouldn't be aware. It was possible, but she was more inclined to believe someone had offered them a ride.

It would have been considered criminal by most folks around here to leave someone with a broken-down vehicle in such cold.

But if someone had offered a ride, who? And where had the girls gone?

Her stomach kept taking one plunge after another as she drove to the office. Bugle whimpered in his caged-in backseat as if he felt her anxiety.

"It's okay, boy," she said, trying to sound calm. Okay? Less and less likely.

THE SHERIFF'S OFFICE was a beehive of activity, with barely enough space to move around other personnel. Conversation was quiet, weighted with gravity. It looked like the entire department's staff was here, along with the city police department under the direction of Chief Madison.

Before she heard a word, she recognized that a search was about to get underway.

"Kelly?"

Sheriff Gage Dalton waved her back to his office. She wormed her way through the crowd with Bugle, greeting everyone with a nod. She knew them all but there was no time for conversation, not now. Bad things were afoot.

Once inside the sheriff's office, she closed the door at his gesture and took the seat facing his desk. Every time Gage moved, pain flickered across his scarred face. The result of a long-ago bomb when he'd been with the DEA. While he tried to give the pain no quarter, she didn't mind his manual suggestion that she close the door herself. Why would she?

Bugle promptly sat beside her, ears pricked, at attention. He sensed something.

"Okay," he said. "You know we don't usually respond to a missing person report this quickly, especially not when the missing are legally all adults. Any one of those young women has the right to skip town and disappear."

She nodded. "But not right before high school graduation. Five months before college and vocational schooling or whatever."

"Exactly. Plus, how likely is it for three of them to pull a disappearing act and take nothing with them? One might, but not all of them. So we're going to start looking immediately. You found the car last night around eleven. We're not quite eighteen hours into this. Maybe a little more. I figure the first thing to do is start looking along the state highway. You said the car was facing west in the ditch?"

"Mostly. It might have spun out, I can't be sure, but I had the impression it was on its way back toward town. I also didn't see any tire skids, but that doesn't mean much as dark as it was. I didn't spend a whole lot of time looking, because there was no injury and no damage."

Gage nodded. "I've sent some people out to look at the highway for any kind of marks. So what have we got east along that road that might attract three young women on a holiday weekend night?"

Kelly was sure he knew the answer. "Rusty's Tavern. You want me to take Bugle out there?"

He nodded. "They'll be opening soon enough. Maybe one of the bartenders will remember them. Regardless, Bugle will know if they've been there."

He sure would, Kelly thought. "So what made their parents worry?"

"They knew the girls were going out last night. Each of their families thought they were staying at one of the other girl's homes. Apparently nothing definite had been arranged except a pajama party at one house or the other. By the time parents started worrying and calling each other, it was late and they all figured it wasn't that…simple."

It was so unlike the sheriff to hesitate over a word. She guessed he was as worried about the young women as anyone. As certain this wasn't going to end well.

"There's still hope," she said, rising as she realized he was done. "I'll head straight for the tavern. Do we have a target for my dog?"

"The parents are each bringing some clothing. Guess you'll have to wait until they get here."

"Or Bugle could smell the car interior. It's in the impound lot now, right?"

"He might get more scents than the girls."

She shook her head. "The parents aren't going to pick up a piece of their clothing without touching it. He's going to get multiple scents. One of the wondrous things about him is that he doesn't get them mixed up."

He put up a hand. "Whatever you think best." Glancing at the old wall clock to his right, he added, "Another half hour at least before anyone will be at Rusty's."

"I'll be there when they are." She paused. "We've got photos and personal data?"

"Not enough. Ask Sarah Ironheart. She may have been able to pull a digital copy of the yearbook. It won't be printed for another two months. Otherwise we're waiting for photos and all the rest from the parents."

She didn't want to meet the parents. Cowardly of her, she supposed, but right now all they could do, once they provided necessary information, was slow her down.

It wasn't that she didn't care. It was that she would care too much.

Sarah Ironheart sat at a desk near the front of the office, images scrolling across her monitor. A woman in her fifties, partly Native American, she had features that had worn the years well. Her long black hair, now streaked with gray, was caught in a ponytail on her neck, and the collar of her uniform shirt remained unbuttoned.

There was a chair beside the desk, and Kelly slid into it, waiting for Sarah to reach a pause point. "Damn it," Sarah said finally.

"What's wrong?"

"The yearbook editors haven't organized much of this file. I don't know how they'll get it finished in time to print it and put copies in students' hands by the end of the school year. Heck, some items aren't even in the total file yet, but in separate pieces."

Sarah leaned back in her chair. It was old and groaned as it tipped backward. "Coffee," she said as if it were the answer to everything.

"Want me to run across the street?"

Sarah cocked a dark eyebrow at her and smiled. "Trying to escape?"

Kelly half shrugged, feeling rueful. "I'd like to avoid the parents. Guess I can't."

"All of us should be that lucky. You still need a target. They're bringing them."

Kelly didn't even try to argue. Yeah, Bugle could pick up the girls' scents from the car, but they'd be much stronger on items of clothing. "Stay," she ordered Bugle. He waited, still as a piece of statuary, while Kelly stood. "How do you like your coffee?"

"Black. Thanks."

"No problem." The coffee bar was against the back wall, a huge urn that simmered all day long. The coffee was famously awful, but it carried a caffeine charge. What amused her, however, was that just in the time she'd worked here, she'd watched the addition of about seven types of antacids to the table behind the foam cups.

Velma, the dispatcher who had been with the department since the dinosaurs had roamed the earth, still smoked at her desk despite the no-smoking sign right over her head and made the coffee. No one ever complained. But now there was that row of antacids. Velma ignored it.

Kelly smothered a smile at the incongruities but poured Sarah her coffee. She'd like some herself, but she'd wait until she could get something that wouldn't hit her stomach like battery acid.

Sarah thanked her as she returned and handed over the coffee. Then she rubbed her neck once and returned to scanning the images on her screen. "It would help," she said quietly, "if all these photos were labeled by name. Or sorted by class."

"Still early days, huh?"

"For the yearbook, evidently."

Just then the front door opened and a blast of cold air could be felt all the way across the room. Kelly immediately recognized Allan Carstairs, the county's animal control officer. Although he was loosely attached to the sheriff's department, he seldom wore a uniform. Today a dark blue down parka with a hood covered him to below his narrow hips—funny that she could see those hips in her mind's eye—above jeans. Thermal long johns, she guessed. A staple for everyone during parts of the year. Like the insulated winter boots on his feet.

She watched him ease his way through the room, pausing to talk to some of the gathered deputies. At last he approached the spot where she sat with Bugle and Sarah.

"How's it going?"

"I guess we're going to see," she answered.

He nodded, his expression grim. Sharp angles defined his face, giving him a firm look that rarely vanished, even when he smiled. Gray eyes met hers, but right now the gray looked more like ice. It wasn't a warm color.

"Which three girls?" he asked.

Sarah spoke. "Jane Beauvoir, Mary Lou Ostend and Chantal Reston."

Kelly felt her heart squeeze. Jane had been the only one she'd met, but still. So young. So entitled to a future.

"Hell," said Al. "Chantal volunteered with me last summer."

"We need to get the rest of the K-9 units in here," Gage suddenly called from the hallway that led to his office in the back. "Where the hell is Cadel Marcus? Jack Hart? What kind of search can we run without the dogs?"

"A sloppy one," Kelly muttered. Bugle eyed her quizzically.

Impatience grew in Kelly. She wanted to get on with it, find out if the girls had been seen at the roadhouse last night. If so, there might be a clue about who had picked them up. Or might have. At this point, however, it had clearly been no simple offer of a ride home.

The door opened again, this time for longer and letting in more icy air as the fathers of the three girls arrived. Randy Beauvoir entered first, followed by Kevin Ostend and Luis Reston. Kelly knew all three of them by sight, but only vaguely as she'd never had any business with them or their families.

She rose to her feet just as Gage reappeared and greeted the three men. They looked tense, worried, even a touch fearful. "Come back to the conference room," Gage said. "You've got the pictures? The clothing?"

The men nodded and Gage turned. "Kelly?"

"Coming."

Velma's scratchy voice suddenly penetrated the murmur of quiet voices. "Boss? Connie Parish says they need some help with crowd control. Word is getting around and folks are gathering near where the car was found to start their own searches."

Gage cussed. "Send ten men out there before they trample any evidence. Get ten volunteers. I got some business here first, then I'll go out there, too."

"I'll go," said Al Carstairs. He might be the animal control officer, but he had the physical stature to be intimidating, and the military bearing to go with it.

Velma looked around. "Nine more?"

Before she could see who went, Kelly and Bugle were being ushered into the conference room. In the relative quiet once the door closed behind them, the room filled with a different atmosphere. Fear. Worry. Even some anger. These fathers were like rifles that didn't know where to point.

"We're helping with the search," Randy Beauvoir said.

"I never thought you wouldn't. But I need Deputy Noveno here to give Bugle his target scents, and I want pictures of your daughters to go out with her, and with damn near everyone else. We're going to digitize the photos. They'll be on every cell phone in the county, okay? And TV, as well. But first things first."

A SHORT WHILE LATER, after a quick stop at Maude's diner to get a tall, hot latte, with her truck heater blasting, Kelly and Bugle headed east out of town with evidence bags holding part of the girls' clothing and photocopies of the full-size portraits. Even as she was driving she heard her cell phone ding, and figured it was probably the digital photos with background info.

It was beginning to hit her. She'd found the vehicle that had been carrying the girls only last night. Shouldn't some instinct have kicked in? Made her look inside the car, study the ground around for signs of a scuffle? Anything?

But the scene hadn't struck her that way. Once she knew the occupants were gone, that even their purses had vanished, there seemed to be nothing to worry about. No one injured, because if they had been they would have been on their way to the hospital and her radio should have been crackling with information.

It had been quiet, dark. People misjudged and went into ditches all the time, especially on cold nights where even a small patch of black ice could cause loss of control. She hadn't seen or felt any ice, but that didn't mean it hadn't been there when the car ran off the road.

But without any damage to the car or any obvious sign of foul play, there was really nothing she could do except get the vehicle towed when she couldn't get ahold of the owner.

Randy Beauvoir and his wife had been in Laramie for the weekend. They'd come home midday today, Randy had told her and the sheriff. They'd received Kelly's voice mail but hadn't immediately worried. No messages suggested the girl was in trouble. Probably at a friend's house for the night, as discussed. They'd get the car out of impound later.

But then Chantal's family had phoned, and the dominoes started tumbling. The girls weren't at one of their houses. Their families had no idea where they might be. Kelly's message about the car had suddenly struck them as a blinding warning flare.

The early winter night had begun conquering the landscape. Bright floodlights warned her of the approaching accident scene. She felt ill to the pit of her stomach. As she passed the cordoned-off area where the car had been found and crowds were beginning to gather, all she could hope was that somebody at Rusty's would give her a clue.

THE GRAVEL PARKING lot was clear of all but one vehicle, an aging pickup truck. Neon signs in the windows didn't yet shimmer with life and wouldn't until Rusty officially opened his doors.

She knew Rusty. She'd been called a number of times to help when some customers grew rowdy. Rusty did a better job than most of keeping it under control, but sometimes even he needed help. Roadhouses farther out had more problems, but here only ten miles out of town, the clientele seemed less likely to want to tussle, especially with the law. Most nights people came, drank and danced to local live music, and peace ruled, if not quiet.

This was the place that drew the patronage of local couples as much as local cowboys, and while she doubted anyone would think it wise for an unescorted woman to come here, three teens should have been safe. Older folks would have kept an eye on them, and Rusty would have served them soft drinks.

The door was unlocked. She pulled the tarnished brass handle and the ancient entry squeaked open. Inside the lighting was dim. The table candles in their squat hurricane lantern holders hadn't been lit.

Rusty was behind the long bar, polishing it with a rag. Directly across the large room from him, across the big dance floor, was a stage still holding band equipment.

"Hey, Rusty," she said as she and Bugle entered. "How's business?"

"Pretty good, but it always is on a holiday weekend. Tonight we'll be damn near empty. Can I help you, Kelly?"

He was a tall, lean man who always looked as if he needed to eat more of his own sandwiches. A gray moustache curled around the corners of his mouth.

"Have you heard about the three girls who've gone missing?"

Rusty's watery blue eyes widened. "No. Is that why you're here?"

She nodded and opened the brown envelope she'd brought with her, the one that held the eight-by-ten photos of each girl. She recited their names as she pulled them out. "Jane Beauvoir, Chantal Reston and Mary Lou Ostend. All high school seniors. We found their car in a ditch about five miles west of here just last night. No sign of them anywhere."

"Jeez," Rusty said, leaning toward the photos as if his old eyes needed some magnification. Reaching up with one hand, he turned on a bright light over the bar. Kelly blinked.

"Anyone else here yet?" she asked, even though it didn't feel like it.

He shook his head. "We don't open for another hour. Not much to do before then." He picked up the photos one by one and studied them.

"They were here last night," Rusty said slowly. "Seems like they might have showed up a little after eight. Early. I hardly noticed because we were already full. Holiday," he said again as if in explanation.

"All three?"

"I do believe so."

"They hang out with anyone?"

He shook his head. "They sat at that table over there—" he pointed "—and drank enough diet soda to float a battleship." He lifted his gaze. "No alcohol, I swear."

She nodded. "Can I let Bugle sniff around while we talk?"

"Go for it, although how he's going to smell squat over the stale beer and fried chicken beats me."

She didn't argue or explain, but squatted down and pulled the three evidence bags from her pocket. One by one she let Bugle sniff them, then said, "Seek." He was off.

Straightening again, she pulled out her cell phone and hit the record button. "I'm taping this, okay? Just in case you mention something that winds up being important to us. All right by you?"

"Happy to do it," he answered. His gaze had wandered over to the table where he said the girls had been sitting. "Damn it, Kelly, they're so young and were just having fun. Haven't heard that much giggling since my own school days."

Then he paused and looked at her. "I didn't pay close attention, though. I wish I had. I'm sorry. We were busy. All they were doing was sitting and drinking cola. Oh, yeah, and they ordered a BLT to share. That was it. I didn't see anything wrong so I wasn't staring."

She nodded. "I understand. Anything at all catch your attention? Did one of them dance with anyone?"

He scratched his head and closed his eyes, pondering. "Dance? I think I saw two of them dance together. Line dancing. Nobody feels awkward if they don't have a partner, you know?"

"I know. So that was it?"

"Maybe not," he said after another minute. "They're pretty. I saw some guys wander by to talk with them, but they didn't stay." His eyes popped open and met hers intently. "My opinion, if you want it…"

"Everything you've got."

"Those girls weren't looking for trouble of any kind. Now, I've had people their age in here before, skating the line of being unwise. Trying to get someone to buy them a beer, wanting to dance with anything in pants. It happens. These girls were different. It was like they were having a private party and everything else was background."

Kelly tipped her head a little. "Unusual?"

"For that age. I was impressed. Must have good mamas."

Kelly wouldn't know about that. Turning, she saw Bugle sitting patiently upright beside the table Rusty had pointed out. Yup, they'd been there.

"Seek," she told him again. Then the trail became more winding. It wandered out onto the dance floor, approached the bar, headed down the hall to the ladies' room, then back to the table. "Find," she urged him, envisioning the evening the three girls had spent here.

He lowered his head and wound up at the front door. They'd left.

She looked again at Rusty. "So…nothing concerned you. You didn't feel like getting out your baseball bat?" She'd seen him swing that thing once. It put a quick end to most arguments.

"I wish I could tell you something. Nothing got me concerned enough to really pay attention. Nothing raised my hackles. But I'll keep thinking on it. Dang, those poor girls. If the car was in the ditch I don't suppose they ran away."

"They didn't get far if they wanted to." Reluctantly, she turned off the recorder and slipped the photos back into the envelope. Then she passed him her business card, needlessly since he certainly knew her and how to call the department. It just made her feel like she was actually doing something. "In case," she said.

"In case," he agreed. "Can I post some photos?"

"They should be on everyone's cell phone soon, but if you want some copies to put up, I'll let the office know."

He nodded slowly. "Maybe someone saw something I didn't. I'll tell everyone to check their phones tonight."

"And I'll get you some posters. It's early days yet, Rusty."

"Forty-eight hours, isn't that what they say?"

Her nod was short, wishing she could deny it.

"You never know," Rusty called after her as if to be reassuring. "They could be somewhere safe."

"Sure. Thanks for your help. Someone else might come round." Because they were all going to get dizzy running in circles trying to find these young ladies. Every step would be retraced a hundred times.

Damn!

Chapter Three

Day 1.5

Al Carstairs stood by the roadside as the crowd grew around the yellow police tape. Nobody was wanted inside that sacred circle yet except the crime scene techs.

The ground beside the road, apart from being winter-hard and covered with bits of sprayed gravel, wasn't going to yield much, he thought. Even the grass in the ditch, long since in winter hibernation, could present only broken stalks.

But nothing was going to be overlooked. If they could find any sign the girls had been picked up, or if they'd wandered off into the night, they had to locate it.

For his own part, he stepped back and began to walk along the pavement. Not even rubber skid marks to indicate the girls had tried to stop in a hurry, or swerved to avoid something.

Squatting, safely within the orange cones around which light traffic was being directed by cops wearing bright yellow vests, he scanned every inch of pavement.

He couldn't imagine why the driver hadn't tried to stop. Ice? Possible, but then the shoulder should have been torn up by the locked tires.

Something wasn't right. Then it struck him.

He stood and wondered whom he should talk to. Then he saw Kelly Noveno's SUV headed his way. Kelly. She was a smart one, and he trusted her judgment. He knew damn near everyone in the sheriff's office, but not in the same the way he knew Kelly. His animal control job often brought them together because of Bugle. Yeah, there were others he trusted as much or more, but none of them were out here right now.

How could a car go off the road without the driver trying to stop it? How could someone abscond with three high school girls? Rudolph the Reindeer's nose couldn't have blinked more brightly in his mind.

Kelly pulled over, inside the cones, then climbed out and approached him. "Nothing?" she asked, waving at the crime techs.

"Not from them yet. Kelly… I had a nuts idea. Tell me I'm crazy and I'll shut up."

She tilted her head. A tall woman, she didn't have to look up very high to meet his gaze. Dark snapping eyes. Full of vigor.

She nodded slowly. "Talk to me, Al. So far I'm coming up dry. Rusty thought they were the most well-behaved teens he'd ever had in his tavern, not even remotely looking for trouble. He said they seemed to be having a private party among the three of them."

Al nodded, but felt anxiety running along his nerve endings. So the girls hadn't been looking for trouble. That didn't mean they hadn't found it. It just meant it had been harder to find.

"What are you thinking?" Kelly pushed.

"No skid marks."

"Black ice."

He shook his head. "They still would have braked, and if they'd been braking to try to avoid going in the ditch or to avoid an obstacle, the shoulder would be torn up. Frozen as it is, it would have shown some tire marks. So they didn't brake."

He saw realization dawning on her face. "You're suggesting they weren't conscious? At least the driver?" Then she paused and swore. "Rusty said some guys passed their table briefly and chatted with them."

"Enough time," he answered.

She nodded, her expression growing even grimmer. She squatted to take a look at the pavement for herself, then straightened to study the shoulder once again. "Okay, I'm heading back to the tavern. Maybe Rusty knows who some of those guys were."

"I'm coming with you."

Animal control was part of the sheriff's department, but Al wasn't a standard deputy. It wasn't exactly pro forma for him to go along on an investigation, but everyone else was busy at the moment, and Kelly thought extra brains could always be useful.

"Let's go."

Despite the traffic hang-up around the scene, they got through quickly and were soon whizzing toward

Rusty's. Bugle, in his backseat cage, knew Al so didn't seem disturbed by the addition of another person.

"It makes sense," Kelly said, although she didn't want to believe it.

"That someone could have drugged them? It's a wild hair, Kelly. It just popped into my head and wouldn't let go."

"I get it, but it still makes sense. Some guys stopped by their table to talk. And frankly, Al, considering these were young women out on a holiday weekend for some fun, they left Rusty's awfully early. I found the abandoned car just before eleven. When you were that age, did you call it a night that early?"

"No," he admitted. "Never."

"Exactly. No one was waiting for them, it was New Year's, all the parties would have been the night before. It's entirely possible that someone slipped something into their drinks and when they started to feel odd they decided to go home."

And that was crossing a lot of bridges with very little evidence, she thought. But it *did* make sense. She had to at least find out what guys were talking to them, if Rusty knew. Then she could interview them to see what more she could learn.

"Anyway," she said more to herself than him, "I didn't think of trying to track these guys down when Rusty mentioned them because he made it seem like it was all brief and in passing. I think I ought to kick my own butt. I should have gotten suspicious right then."

"Cut yourself some slack," Al said. "Three girls together at a table. A lot of men would stop by, get the brush-off and move on. Normal behavior. Nothing to stand out."

"Except the girls are missing." She clenched her teeth until her jaw ached, and when she turned into Rusty's parking lot she sprayed gravel.

She climbed out, leaving Bugle in the car with a cracked window and the heater on. Ten minutes. If this took longer, she'd come out and get her dog.

She slammed the SUV door emphatically, glanced at the watch on her wrist and marched toward the door, hardly aware that Al was on her heels.

Just then she was feeling awfully stupid. Stupid, and cold as the night nipped at her cheeks and the wind tossed her hair. She hoped the missing young women were safe and warm.

But she seriously doubted they were.

A COUPLE OF people had evidently showed up for work. A woman of about forty, wearing a leather fringed skirt, was making her way around the tables, lighting the hurricane lanterns. A younger man used a push broom on the dance floor, clearing off any remains of last night's revels.

"Already?" Rusty said, arching a brow as he pushed a spout into the top of a whiskey bottle.

"Some thoughts occurred," Kelly said. "Al?"

Rusty looked at him. "I know you. The animal control guy. What's up?"

Al unzipped his jacket halfway. Rusty didn't keep the place overwarm, but warm enough that winter gear could be suffocating. "Al Carstairs. I've got just a couple of questions, if you don't mind."

"You looking for these girls, too? I'm not surprised. Half the county will be out there tomorrow. Wish it wasn't so late right now. So, what can I do you for?"

"There's a chance the girls, or at least the driver, were unconscious when they went off the road."

Rusty straightened until he was stiff. He looked toward the table where the young women had been sitting just the night before. "Yeah?" he said hoarsely.

"Not sure," Kelly hastened to say. "Just an idea we're looking into."

Rusty nodded. He turned his attention again to Al. "What do you want to know?"

"You said some men stopped by their table. Do you remember who?"

Kelly had turned on her cell phone recorder and placed it on the bar so Rusty would know she was recording. He looked at it briefly.

"I gotta think," he said. "Like I told Kelly, I wasn't paying close attention. There was nothing that made me think anything was going on except three kids drinking soda together and having a great time. Two brunettes, one bottle blonde."

"Chantal," Al interpolated. "The blonde. Turned eighteen two months ago. Hard worker. Never heard a complaint out of her about cleaning my kennels. She did love the animals, though. Talked about wanting to be a veterinarian."

Kelly drank in the facts, but wondered why Al felt it necessary to add them. To make Chantal seem more real to Rusty?

Maybe it had worked, because Rusty's frown turned really dark. "Yeah, she stood out. The other two were cute, too. Having a great time together."

"Jane wanted to be an EMT," Kelly volunteered.

Without another word, Rusty leaned his hands on the bar and looked down, eyes closed. He appeared to be straining to remember the night before. After a minute, he looked up and called, "Martha? Those teen girls who were here last night?"

The woman, carrying her electric match, came over to the bar. Her fading red hair was caught neatly into a netted bun, and the harsh sun and wind had given her a few wrinkles around her eyes and mouth. "Blonde and two brunettes? Youngest gals in here? Yeah. They was cute."

"Some guys talked to them. I can't remember who. Maybe one was Don Blevin?"

Martha shook her head. "I saw a couple of guys. Let me think. Dang, Rusty, we had so many folks in here last night."

"I know," he answered heavily.

Martha's eyes suddenly widened and she looked at Kelly's uniform. "Is these the girls what's missing? Oh my God…"

"That's why it's so important that you tell us everything you can remember," Kelly said. "Everything. How did they get their drinks? Who talked to them? Did anything seem…off?"

Understanding dawned on Martha's face. "You think they coulda been drugged?"

"We're just theorizing here," Al hastened to say. "Call it a wild idea. We don't know. We *can't* know."

Martha nodded, her expression as sober as a judge's. Then she turned her head a bit. "Jack, you got a minute?"

Shortly they were joined by the young man who'd been pushing the broom.

"Jack knows the younger set," Martha explained. "Who was them guys who stopped by the table of the three teen girls who was sitting over there last night. You know the guys?" She pointed at the table.

Jack's forehead creased and a lock of greasy hair fell over his forehead to make a small curl. "Sure. First it was Hal Olsen."

Kelly had pulled out her patrol book and wrote quickly despite recording all this. "Tell us about Hal?"

Jack shrugged. "He ain't nothin'. Maybe thirty. His wife left him two months ago and he's pretty much been living here. He likes to get hisself a dance with the pretty women. The girls didn't want any so he walked away."

"And after that?" Al asked.

"He got hisself a dance with Margot Eels. Pretty enough so I don't think he was feeling dissed."

"Who else?" Al asked.

Jack worked his mouth as if it would help his brain to think. "Art Mason. He's another regular. Drinks too much sometimes and Rusty has to cut him off, but I don't think he was sober when he talked to them gals." He flashed a faint smile. "Was kind of weaving. The gals laughed a bit after they sent him on his way. I think he landed in a chair near the dance floor. Then there was Keeb Dustin. Everybody knows the guy. Got hisself the service station east of town."

"Never causes trouble," Martha agreed. "He comes one night a week, either Friday or Saturday. He occasionally hits on someone, but not in a way that makes them complain."

"Anyone else?" Al asked.

"Don't know," Jack said. Martha shrugged.

"How'd the girls get their drinks?" Al asked.

"I brought 'em," Martha said promptly. "Fill up my

tray with drinks at the station there, then pass them around to the tables. Keeps the bar from getting too crowded."

Kelly looked at Al for the first time. She saw awareness in his gray eyes, too. "Martha? You ever set your tray down with drinks on it?"

"Have to," she answered. "Gotta rearrange those bottles and glasses so I don't spill them all over anyone."

"But you're watching it every minute?"

"No," Martha answered. "People wanna talk. That's part of my job."

Kelly's stomach sank like a stone. So it was possible the girls had been slipped a drug. "How about," she said slowly, "you three make a list of everyone you can remember was in here last night. I'll pick it up tomorrow."

All three were agreeable, but Rusty looked positively dour. "I can't keep my eye on everything," he said to Kelly.

"Of course you can't, Rusty," she said reassuringly. "You folks have been a ton of help. And as for this suspicion, it's just that. Keep it quiet. We don't know that anything happened here at all. We just need every bit of information we can find."

Outside in the cold night, hearing Bugle call to her from the slightly open window of her truck, Kelly tried to keep her step steady as she walked toward him. Other cars were arriving now, but the flow wasn't heavy. Most of the interest would be down the highway around the crime scene. Folks had gathered to help, or out of curiosity. Who could say? But the crowd, the tape, the lights would draw attention. Wetting one's whistle could wait a short while.

When she laid her hand on the door of her vehicle,

however, she froze. Then she tilted her head back and looked up at the amazingly clear star-filled sky.

She hoped that somewhere out in those desolate spaces there weren't three young women looking up at the stars with dead eyes.

Al was suddenly beside her, touching her arm. "Nobody would go to all that trouble just to kill them."

She lowered her gaze to his face. "Maybe that's even worse."

"Then we have to keep going, push as hard as we can."

"Yeah." Her answer was short, but she squared her shoulders and shook off the despair that wanted to overtake her. They had to find them as quickly as possible. Somewhere there had to be an essential clue.

She just wished she knew where to look beyond this tavern.

"Let's go," she said. "We have at least three guys to track down and get someone out to them for interviews."

The car felt too hot when she climbed in, but a glance at the dash thermometer told her it was sixty-eight. A good temperature for Bugle. He woofed a welcome.

As soon as Al was in the passenger seat with the door closed, she reached for her radio. Velma's scratchy voice answered.

"Hey, Velma," Kelly said. "Is Gage around?"

"Yeah, in the conference room working out a plan for tomorrow's search. You need him?"

"Please." She waited a couple of minutes, then heard the sheriff's gravelly voice.

"What's up, Kelly?"

"We were talking to employees at the tavern. I need someone to hunt up three guys and question them about the interactions they had with the three missing girls last night at Rusty's." Flipping open her notebook, she read the names to Gage.

"Slower," he said. Then, "Okay, got it. I know two of them. I'll send some deputies out to talk to them. Thanks, Kelly. Good work."

"Thank Al Carstairs. He's been a great help."

"I will. Are you coming in?"

"Absolutely. We need to talk in person." No way was she going to put the drug theory on the air. God knew how many police band radios would pick it up. The names of the men she wanted questioned didn't worry her. They'd come up at the tavern and she was sure they were about to be shared with the evening's early customers.

Gage's laugh was dry. "See you shortly."

Kelly looked down at the tall cup of latte she'd allowed to grow as cold as the interior of the truck. "I think I'm going to take a brief break. I need some coffee to get through this night."

"I'll join you," Al answered. "It'd make some good time to run over what we just learned."

Bugle seemed to quietly woof his agreement.

Yeah, they needed to do that, Kelly thought as she put the SUV in gear, swung a wide circle and drove back onto the state highway. Time to think it all over. You could get only so far just by picking up the puzzle pieces. Sooner or later you had to try to put them together.

She glanced sideways at Al, and out of nowhere came the unbidden wish that this would be a social coffee. Nope. They could be friends but they had to remain professional or risk making a mess. If he was even interested.

Besides, the only thing that mattered tonight was three missing girls, girls who might be terrified out of their minds. Girls who might be suffering.

Girls who might be dead.

THE CROWD AT the accident scene had thinned out. She paused long enough to let Al jump out to get his truck while she surveyed the faces that looked so odd in the arc lamps. It was getting later and colder, and evidently people thought nothing more would happen tonight. Overhead the county's two choppers were flying a search pattern with bright spotlights sweeping over barren fields.

Fifteen minutes later, she pulled into a parking spot in front of the City Diner, also known as Maude's, and through the diner windows scanned the interior. Al pulled in beside her and climbed out, coming over to her window. She opened her door halfway but didn't get out.

"No discussion here tonight," she remarked. The place was jammed full.

"I'll run in and get the coffee, then," Al said. "Nobody will badger *me* with questions. Think Gage would like some? And if so how does he like it?"

"Are we going to offend Velma?" she asked almost absently. Her thoughts were far away, reaching out into the frigid, empty night, trying not to imagine horrible things.

"Do we care? Gage."

"Yeah, he always wants his black, I think."

"You?"

"The biggest hot latte Maude makes."

"I'll see you at the office, then."

She listened to her door squeak as she closed it. The thing always squeaked when it was cold. She glanced over her shoulder at Bugle and figured he was probably starting to get desperate for some room to move. He tolerated the caging part of the job, but he was naturally very active.

Smothering a sigh, she threw her truck into gear and drove it the half block to the sheriff's offices. Across the street was the courthouse square, where Bugle could run a few laps and deposit his business. She let him out, then grabbed a plastic bag to clean up after him. He was good about that, always doing his business near her so she didn't have to run around needlessly.

When he was done she dumped the bag in the trash can, then turned to cross the street to the office. She saw Al just about there carrying a tray and a big brown bag with handles from the diner.

"That looks like more than coffee," she remarked as they met at the door. Since his hands were full, she reached out to open it.

"Maude's clearing some things out for the night. I hope everyone likes pie."

"Maude's pies? I think half this county would crawl across hot sand to get to one."

He gave a short laugh. Relief. They needed something to leaven the horror.

Inside, the office was much quieter than it had been earlier. Only four officers sat at desks. Probably a great many deputies had been sent home to rest up for a search tomorrow. Any others might be out protecting the crash site. Even Velma had vanished, a very rare thing.

Al lined up four pies on the table near the coffee. They were going to make plenty of people happy in the morning. Right now, he cut into an apple pie and served himself the wedge on a paper plate. "Hey, guys," Al said to the others, "help yourself to the pie. What would you like, Kelly?"

For the first time in hours she remembered that all she had eaten was a bowl of cereal.

"There's apple, blueberry, mincemeat and cherry."

The thought of any of them made her mouth water. "Apple would be great."

Gage had apparently heard their voices because he came out of the back, thanked them for the coffee and dug into the mincemeat pie.

He led them to the conference room, where maps covered the table. "Planning for tomorrow," he said as he eased into a high-backed chair. "Now, what's going on with these three guys—who are being interviewed right now, I believe—and what didn't you want to mention on the radio?"

"I'll let Al tell you," Kelly said. "He thought of it."

"A wild hair," Al said yet again.

"It didn't sound so wild after we went back to the tavern and talked to Martha. Go on." She spooned a small bit of apple pie into her mouth, to make it clear she wasn't talking, and wished only that she could savor it as all of Maude's pies deserved savoring. Right now, as knotted with worry as she was, it might as well have been ash.

"Well," Al said slowly, "I was looking at the highway and shoulder. Everyone thinks the girls skidded."

"And you don't?" Gage asked.

"Not likely. If they'd braked, even if they didn't leave tread marks on the pavement because of black ice, they'd have chewed up the shoulder, frozen or not. That car is too old to have anti-lock brakes, so there should have been some sign."

Gage swallowed a mouthful of mincemeat, followed by some coffee. "You're right, and at last report from the scene, they're not finding any clues as to why the car went off the road." He paused, his dark gaze intent. "That doesn't mean they won't."

"I know. I'm not a crime scene tech. Hell, I'm only half a deputy."

"I beg to differ, but go on."

"Well, it was like a light going on in my head. Why wouldn't they brake when going off the road? Maybe they were unconscious or seriously drunk on soft drinks."

Gage sat up a little straighter and put his paper plate and plastic fork down. Pain rippled across his face but it didn't remain. The frown did.

"You think they were drugged? Before they left the tavern?"

Al shook his head. "I don't know. I can't prove it."

"But," Kelly interjected, "Martha, who served their drinks, said she often puts her drinks tray down, either to rebalance it or because people want to chat. In other words, nobody watched those girls' drinks every second between bar and table."

"Nobody would think it necessary," Gage murmured. He'd forgotten his pie and his coffee and rubbed his chin. "The problem around here is that people know one another. It wouldn't occur to them to question the trustworthiness of a neighbor. Over time, they've some-times had to, but by and large those are considered iso-lated incidents, nothing to worry about. Most people still don't lock their doors. We've grown, it's no longer a place where everyone knows everyone else, but the attitudes are still mired in an earlier time. We don't even imagine anyone would drug three young women. And yet, it's entirely possible we've got a sicko running around. As the old sheriff, Nate Tate, liked to say, 'This county's going to hell in a handbasket.' Not really, but change has been happening for a while."

He fell silent for a few beats. "Drugs. Damn it all to hell, I can see it and it would explain a lot."

"They left the bar early, too," Kelly said. "Kids that age don't end their partying around ten o'clock. I imag-ine they started to feel unwell."

"Probably so." He shook his head, then reached for his coffee. "Okay, then. Things just got even more com-plicated. If they were drugged, it had to be someone who didn't stand out at Rusty's place or we'd have heard about him by now."

He eyed Kelly. "In short, one of our neighbors."

Twenty minutes later, Gage sent them both on their way. "You need to rest up for tomorrow. It's going to be a long, cold day."

"I want to know what kinds of answers we get from those three guys," Kelly argued.

"Unless one of them confesses, it'll hold till morn-ing. Besides, we've got a team going out there to try to speak to everyone who was at the bar last night. You might as well get your sleep. If anything breaks, I'll let you know."

Kelly had to be content with that. She really didn't know what else she could do out there.

"Tips should start coming in," she remarked. "I can man the phones."

"There are already four deputies out there doing exactly that. Take Bugle home."

Out of arguments, Kelly obeyed. Al walked out with her but only around the corner to where she was parked. He needed to collect his vehicle from down the street in front of the diner. Kelly watched her breath blow clouds, and couldn't help but notice it was growing colder. Of course it was. It was night.

And the young women…

She truncated the thought. Running it ceaselessly through her head wasn't going to improve anything. With the rising sun at least they could search, maybe stop to ask questions at homesteads that weren't too far out.

Right now…right now they just needed to wait for word to spread. Then would come the tips, mostly useless.

But at the moment… She just shook her head.

Al spoke as they neared her vehicle. "You going to be okay?"

Her head snapped around and she stopped walking. "Why wouldn't I be?"

He faced her directly. "I'm a combat vet, Kelly. I know about second-guessing, delayed reactions and sometimes shutdowns. This has got you upset and worried. You give a damn. You're not just going to go home and turn on the TV to some romantic comedy or suspense movie."

No, she wasn't. Everything inside her was knotted

with frustration and worry. She probably wouldn't sleep worth a damn. "Sometimes you just have to endure. Get through it."

He nodded. "I know. I'm just saying…" He turned his head away. "Forget it. You need an ear, I'm available. This is probably going to eat you alive until we find those girls."

She figured it probably would. She just hoped they found the young women soon and found them unharmed.

Then she and Bugle headed home for what she anticipated was going to be a very long night.

Chapter Four

Day 2

Bugle found the first scent. At the scene of the accident, he nosed the ground and followed it to the highway's edge. There he stopped.

It wasn't a good sign, but everyone hoped Bugle was wrong or that some kind person had picked the girls up.

Or at least everyone *tried* to hope. If the girls had been given a ride by a friendly person, surely they would have called home by now. The silence had become terrifying for their families, and for everyone else.

Despite Bugle's following the scent to the road, no one even thought of calling off the search. They might have walked down the pavement, the cold might have weakened their scents. Regardless, there was no way they'd stop this search, whatever the dog might indicate.

Cadel Marcus, part-time deputy and dog trainer, joined Kelly at roadside with his K-9, Dasher. "I'm with you. Those girls didn't wander off over the fields. No scents on the far side of the road either."

"We still have to look. Someone could have left them farther along."

"Maybe." He nodded to Al, who joined them. "How's the dog-catching business?"

"I get most of them home. Say, if you want a shepherd mix to train, I have one whose owners are apparently fed up with his wanderlust."

Cadel nodded slowly. "Wonder what they're doing to make him run. Yeah, I'll take a look at him later. See what kind of potential he has."

Al's voice turned dry. "He's working on a teddy bear right now."

That drew a laugh from Cadel and even a very sober Kelly smiled.

The helicopters flew above again, having taken off as soon as the light was good enough to see the ground below. The searchers, civilian and police, were divided up into about ten groups and spaced out along both sides of the highway, on either side of the wreck scene. Between the rough ground and brush, they had to move slowly in order to avoid missing something important.

At this point few of the searchers hoped to find the girls. Now most of them were hoping for a clue. An item of clothing, a shoe, a purse, anything that might indicate the direction in which they had disappeared.

To Kelly's dismay, Bugle didn't seem particularly interested. She knew that he could pick up a scent from quite a long distance, either on the ground or in the air

above his head. His boredom was as loud as a paid in-
fomercial.

No girls around here.

Her gloved hand tightened on his leather leash, and
she had to force herself to pay attention anyway. Scents
were harder to detect in the cold, she reminded herself.
Bugle might need to get closer.

But at that point, she didn't know if finding the girls
out here after a long cold night would necessarily be
a good thing.

Damned if they did, damned if they didn't. Never
had that phrase seemed more apt.

THE GROUND SEARCH was called off for the night. Not a
thing had been found. Kelly dragged herself back to
her snug little house on the edge of town, a place that
needed far more attention than she gave it. All her plans
for fixing it up had kind of washed away in the reality
of being a deputy covering so much territory for such a
relatively small department. Oh, they had enough people to cover the routine, and even a group of investiga-
tors and a crime scene unit, but when something blew
up, it was all hands on deck.

Something had blown up.

She fed Bugle some extra kibble and treated him to
some chicken livers she boiled for him from a frozen
stash she kept. He'd had a long, cold day, too, and grate-
fully scarfed it all down.

For herself she did nothing but make a pot of coffee
because she needed something hot, fast. Then she collapsed in her easy chair, pinching the bridge of her nose
to try to stave off a headache. The sense of hopelessness seemed beyond defeat right now. Occasionally she

caught the sound of distant helicopter rotors as the two choppers kept up a search by spotlight in areas farther away from the wreck. The frigid dark made a continued search dangerous for people on foot, but the choppers kept up their valiant duty.

They had long since passed the limit of how far the girls could have walked, so now they were in the territory of a possible body dump. Or an out-and-out kidnapping, although no one seemed willing to say the word out loud.

In fact, no one seemed willing to consider the possibility that it might be too late for the three women. No one. A whole lot of determined people had spent a very long, very cold day hunting in the brush and gullies.

Just as the coffeepot blew a loud burst of steam to announce that it had finished, she heard a sharp rap on her door. Sighing, she rose and went to answer it, trying not to hope it was good news about the missing women. Good news, however, would have crackled over her radio or come by phone.

She opened the door, half expecting to see one of her neighbors with questions about the day's search. Instead she found Al Carstairs. His cheeks were still reddened from the cold, and he was carrying two big brown bags with handles and a tray of tall coffee cups. "Don't know about you, Kelly, but I'm starved and I don't feel like cooking. Care to join me for dinner?"

She couldn't possibly have refused the offer. Not only was it kind, but she really didn't want to be alone with her thoughts. Weary or not, she smiled. "Come in. I just made coffee, though." She reached to help with the cardboard tray.

"I bet it isn't a latte."

Despite all, she laughed. "It sure isn't."

Once inside he carried the bags to the kitchen counter. Small as this house was, the living area and kitchen were a single room, divided by a small bar. Bugle evidently had taken a liking to Al, because as soon as his arms were empty, the dog nudged his leg, then sat expectantly with his tail sweeping the wood floor and displacing a colorful rag rug.

Al obligingly squatted and gave the dog a good scratch around his ruff. Then he straightened and smiled at Kelly. "Bugle's a great dog. Anyway, dinner. I hope you like steak sandwiches. They're the most filling thing on Maude's menu and after today I think we both need calories."

"A steak sandwich sounds wonderful," she said, meaning it. "As many hours as we were out in the cold, I could probably eat a whole one."

The sandwiches were famous, and their size was always huge. Maude had always catered to hardworking ranchers, and people with more sedentary jobs made use of doggie bags. Kelly usually thought of a steak sandwich as two meals for the price of one.

Not tonight, though. She had a feeling she could polish one off in its entirety.

Al began pulling insulated containers out of the bags. He enumerated as he went. "Steak sandwich, steak sandwich, tossed salad, extra rolls for the extra hungry and another pie. I think Maude hopes that if she stokes us all on sugar we'll find those girls."

"Energy will help," she admitted. "I'm worn out. The cold absolutely drained me today."

He smiled her way. "Probably because we never took a break to warm up."

Bugle's nose reached the countertop, and he sniffed, making a hopeful little whine.

"You already had a huge dinner," Kelly said to him.

"He's apparently got good taste, though." Al's great smile seemed to leaven the entire room.

They decided to eat at the bar right out of the foam containers. "No dishes tonight," said Al. "We've got another long day coming up."

She agreed, and felt no need to apologize for failing to retrieve any of her limited quantity of plates, bowls and utensils.

She'd known Al for several years, but didn't really know him. It was odd, when she thought about it, but his work in animal control didn't often cross with hers as a deputy.

"You have a kennel out behind your house?" she asked him after she had swallowed the first juicy mouthful of the steak sandwich.

"Oh, yeah. Insulated metal building with twenty cages. More like a barn. I seldom need that much room but occasionally it happens."

"But don't the owners want them back?"

"First I have to identify the owners, and that's not always easy. When dogs slip out, they sometimes lose their collars and all too often they're not microchipped. Then there are the dumped dogs."

"Dumped?" She turned her head to look at him. He held up a finger as he finished chewing and swallowing a mouthful of his sandwich.

"Dumped," he repeated. "God knows why, but some idiots think their dogs are equipped to become self-sustaining. Now, mind you, these are animals that haven't had to hunt for a meal in their lives and are used to human care. Most of them, anyway. Some folks hope a rancher will find the animal and take it in. I hate to tell you how often that turns bad."

She nodded. "Why?"

"I've been called out too often by a rancher who's found a dead dog. He could just bury it, of course, or leave it for the vultures, but most ranchers care about animals more than that. So they call me, hoping I track someone down to tell them what happened to their animal. I wish I could. I wouldn't be polite about it."

"Nor would I," she admitted, feeling sickened by the thought of what those animals must have endured. "What a cruel thing to do!"

"Especially when you consider they could have turned them in at any vet's office if they didn't want to hunt up a shelter. The lucky ones get found and fed while a rancher waits for me to show up. They don't need another dog. Mainly because dozens are getting abandoned."

Kelly urged herself to eat more, and felt her appetite returning. "What do you do with the survivors?"

"Kennel them. The vet, Mike Windwalker, does his best to help get them adopted, but it's not like we're short on dogs around here. Or cats for that matter. But cats are better at looking after themselves, especially if they had some time with an older cat who taught them to hunt. And most of our ranchers and farmers don't exactly mind another barn cat showing up. They're useful."

"But the dogs aren't?"

"Not without a lot of training. Cadel Marcus takes some to train them as K-9s or service animals, but there's a limit to what he can do, too."

"It sounds like a serious problem."

"It is." He polished off his sandwich and some of the salad, then encouraged her to eat more. "Another long day ahead."

She didn't want to think about it. Not until it arrived. Reminding herself that she'd been famished, she focused on savoring her dinner.

At any other time, she realized she would have been feeling content. A pleasant, handsome man dining with her, and excellent dinner, Bugle pretending to sleep near the foot of her stool but alert for any falling crumbs.

"That fireplace work?" he asked.

"I believe so. I haven't given it much of a workout because I'm gone too often."

"Wanna try it?"

She shrugged as she was about to put the last bit of sandwich in her mouth. "Sure. It worked fine the one time I used it."

Shortly after she'd taken the job here, having moved from Laramie County. It had been a big change for her in terms of a smaller department serving fewer people overall, but that's what she wanted. Community policing. She'd certainly found it here, and after five years had no desire to move on.

There were dry logs stacked in a box near the fireplace, and he laid them on the grate with some twisted newspaper beneath them. They'd probably light good and fast as long as they'd been sitting there. Then he reached in to open the flue and an empty bird's nest fell out onto the stack of wood.

"I hope that's the only one," he remarked.

"So do I." She'd never had that chimney cleaned and

if it was packed with stuff like that, it'd become an interesting evening.

Grabbing a poker, he shoved it up inside the chimney and didn't even loosen any creosote.

"Well, here goes," he said, pulling a butane lighter out of his pocket and holding it to the paper. "If the flame and smoke don't head straight up, I'll put it out."

"Okay." She couldn't even work up any worry about it. Instead she began to gather up the remains of their dinner and put them away in the fridge. Except for the pie. That would be fine on the counter and she had a strong feeling both of them would want a piece before the evening was over.

She looked over and saw the flames were standing straight up and that no smoke was escaping. "I guess it's okay."

"Right as rain." He remained squatting for a few more minutes while she finally settled into her recliner. There was a gooseneck chair on the other side of the battered side table. Oh, it was apparent that she entertained a whole lot. Yup.

Mainly one girlfriend at a time.

Al straightened, brushing his hands on his jeans. "I guess I should go. I've imposed..."

"You haven't imposed at all," she interrupted swiftly. "Get comfortable. There's still that pot of coffee and..." She trailed off.

"You don't want to be thinking about those girls tonight."

"Not if I can avoid it," she admitted.

"Me neither."

The lattes were long gone so he hunted up two mugs from her cupboards and brought a couple of cups of coffee to set on the end table. "You want anything in yours?"

"Black is fine," she answered. "Thanks."

A silence followed after he settled into the gooseneck chair. She knew why. They were both thinking about the same thing and neither of them wanted to talk about it. Even distractions hardly worked. Three young women were residing at the corners of her mind and wouldn't go away. The second night.

They could be looking only for bad things now.

THREE TEENS HUDDLED beneath a ragged blanket in a dank basement that even during the day had barely let in a crack of light. A pile of protein bars had been dumped in with them along with a bunch of plastic bottles of water.

Their winter outerwear was gone, as were their shoes and phones. In trembling voices, they'd talked about finding a way to escape, but knew in the dangerous weather outside they wouldn't get very far in their thin clothes and bare feet.

All they could do was huddle together beneath a smelly blanket and wait. They tried to buck each other up, but young though they were they knew no good could come from this.

Over the last twenty-four hours, hopelessness had begun to settle in. Tears had been frequent, terror had been constant, and at one point Mary Lou had even suggested they stop using the blanket and huddling and just freeze to death.

The other two girls had gotten upset with her. Chantal pointed out tearily that they had hope only if they stayed alive.

They grew quiet for long spells, feeling wearier and

wearier. No protein bar could stave off the fatigue of constant fear.

They sat in the dark, as close as they could get, while their nerves crawled, their bodies ached and their minds ran rampant with horrible ideas.

They had no idea how they'd gotten here, nor any idea of who had put them here, but they knew there was no good reason for it. None.

EVEN COFFEE COULDN'T keep Kelly from dozing briefly in her easy chair. Sounds drew her out of an unpleasant nightmare and she saw Al putting another log on the fire.

When he turned around, he saw that her eyes were open, and he gave her a half smile. "Want me to leave so you can get to bed?"

She shook her head. She wasn't a coward by nature but this event had disturbed her more than many. "I'm still feeling guilty."

"For what? I saw your report. No damage to the car, no occupants, no reason to think anything except a passerby picked them up to get them out of the cold. It was too dark to look for tire skid marks. I mean…"

She nodded. "I know all that rationally, Al. It's the irrational part of me that's having trouble."

He pulled the gooseneck chair over until he was close enough to offer her his hand. She couldn't help but reach over and take it.

Bugle, finding this something entirely new in his experience, came over to investigate as if he weren't certain anyone should be touching Kelly.

"It's okay, Bugle. Relax."

The dog sniffed their joined hands, then settled on the floor between them.

Al grinned. "He's still feeling protective, I see."

"Always. My buddy." But her mind wasn't on Bugle, and she needed to distract herself or she'd get no rest this awful night, but she had to be bright and ready for the morning. A quiet sigh escaped her.

"Where are you from?" Al asked. "Someone said you used to be with the Laramie police, but I'm sure that wasn't your entire life."

She summoned a smile. "No. Hardly. I've moved around. My dad is Puerto Rican and I was born there. My mom worked as an executive for one of the companies that had a business there, but she died five years ago. Cancer."

"I'm sorry."

"So am I, but given what she went through in the end, her death was a relief." She shook her head a little. She didn't want to go down this road. "Anyway, they moved to Florida when my mom was transferred. My dad was a police officer and he took a local job."

"So you followed in his footsteps?"

"So it seems. I can't remember ever wanting to do anything else, but I essentially won the lottery when I was tapped to be a K-9 officer. I love dogs. Dad wanted me to stay in Florida, but I wanted to come up here. I visit him when I can. At least living in Florida, for him, means people don't look at him suspiciously."

His brow rose. "Why would they do that?"

"He's Latin, Al. With a bit of Indio in him. I get cross-eyed looks, as well. A lot of folks still think I'm a foreigner. Many people seem to have a hard time believing Puerto Ricans are US citizens."

He was frowning faintly. "I hope you don't run into a whole lot of that around here."

"No more than the indigenous people. Maybe less. I have a badge."

At that he laughed quietly. "That does help."

The smile felt awkward on her face, but it lifted her spirits a bit. She needed that. There wasn't a damn thing she could do right now. She was about to ask him his story when the landline rang.

Forgetting everything, nearly tripping over Bugle in her eagerness, she ran to get the phone. It was Gage Dalton. "I'm sure you're wondering about those guys we questioned."

"Absolutely. Al Carstairs is here. I'm sure he wants to know, too. Speaker?"

"Go ahead. Just don't give me a reverb."

She punched the speaker button, then sat on one of the bar stools. "You're on, Gage."

"Hi, Gage," Al said.

"Howdy. Okay, the long and short of it is that our three interviewees were put off by the way the girls dismissed them. Including our infamous drunk, Art Mason. Judging by what some of the other patrons said, he was in no condition to cross a room, let alone get down a highway. Jack, the janitor, said they wouldn't let Art leave until he'd drunk a pot of coffee. Way too late for the accident. As for Keeb Dustin, he appeared so appalled by the idea he'd be interested in girls so young that the deputy believed him. Anyway, he only stopped by the table because they were laughing and he liked hearing they were having a good time. Warned 'em to avoid anyone who showed them too much attention, then moved on to the bar, where most folks saw him nursing a few longnecks until after midnight."

"So they're clear," Al said.

"Well, hold on," Gage answered. "At this point I'm not clearing anyone, but yeah, neither seems likely. The place was busy. I'm not sure anyone would have noticed if one of these guys left for a while. Then there's Hal Olsen. Always on the lookout for a pretty woman. Apparently he scored that night because Lydie Dern says he went home with her about eleven or so. In the other direction, so they didn't see anything on the road."

"Dang," said Kelly, who only then realized just how much she'd been hoping they'd get a good clue.

"We'll keep an eye on them, of course," Gage continued. "I've got a couple of men working the tavern tonight, to see if anyone remembers anything unusual about last night, but so far no go. It seems many of them weren't there, and those who were had more important things on their minds."

Kelly chewed her lower lips for a few seconds. "Gage? Were the girls involved in anything that might have drawn attention? What have we got on their backgrounds now?"

"Been working on that. Three young ladies, all with high grades, members of the soccer team and the debate club. If it weren't for the fact that Jane Beauvoir was a member of the chess club, I'd have said the three of them were joined at the hip. Families all attend Good Shepherd Church, no one seems to think they had any enemies, either the teens or their parents…although that can always be a mistaken impression. Enemies don't always announce themselves."

"True. You're saying we don't really have anything."

Gage snorted, audible through the speaker. "I'm saying we haven't found it yet. Abducting three young women from the side of the road before eleven at night is a bold thing to do. It's also stupid, because no matter how smart they think they are, perps always leave something behind. You remember that rule."

Kelly nodded even though she couldn't be seen through the phone. "The perp takes something away but he always leaves something behind."

"We've just got to find it. Anyway, you two catch up on your sleep. Tomorrow's going to be another long day."

Kelly disconnected and sat staring at the phone as if it might have something else to offer. The ugly truth was that it wouldn't. It was like being inside a dark bag without a ray of light.

Maybe like those girls.

She passed a hand over her eyes as if she wanted to erase her thoughts, then looked over at Al. "It's still early," she said, surprised as her eyes grazed the wall clock. Not even nine yet.

As long as she'd lived up north, some part of her still lived where she'd been born, when night didn't fall so early even in the winter.

"Yeah," he answered. "Not a very helpful call."

"Maybe, maybe not. Weeding things out counts, too. But listen, don't you have animals to look after?"

"Not really. All the pets have been taken home. The rest have enough food to look after themselves tonight. Minks, by the way, don't make friendly pets."

But he was standing and pushing the chair back to its original position.

Crap, Kelly thought. He'd brought her dinner, she'd

asked him to stay just a short while ago and now he was apparently taking her question as a dismissal. She slid off the stool, saying, "Al."

He glanced at her. "Yeah?"

"I was asking about the animals, not hinting for you to leave."

"You should get some sleep," he answered. "You heard Gage."

She hesitated, then said, "What makes minks bad pets, and would you like some of that pie you brought?"

He laughed then. "Minks are hard to tame, even if you start when they're still kits. It takes a lot of patience. And that's just the start."

She pulled the aluminum foil off the pie and retrieved two small plates from the cupboard. A knife would have to do for cutting slices. "What's the rest?"

"They prefer a semiaquatic environment, not easy to do at home around here. They can be really aggressive and you can't let them out because they'll kill other minks if any are around, and foxes would love to dine on them. They should be solitary except during mating, and these folks made the mistake of keeping two. They weren't exactly getting along."

"Wow. Worse than ferrets?"

"Depends. They're part of the same family of carnivores, *Mustelidae*. There you've got ferrets, skunks, weasels, even otters. But as long as you get a ferret young and give it plenty to entertain itself, it'll be little trouble. Plus they can be truly affectionate. These minks?" He just shook his head. "Someone will think they're adorable. Someone always does."

"So what will you do with them?" She passed him a slice of peach pie that smelled richly of cinnamon.

He thanked her and slid onto a bar stool.

"Coffee?"

"With this?" he asked. "Absolutely. Maude's pie can make my teeth curl."

That drew a laugh from her. "Lots of sugar. One of the reasons I don't eat them often." She cut herself a slice, then poured coffee for both of them from the waiting pot. It really hadn't been that long ago that she'd made it. This day had been endless.

Well, until now, anyway. She was enjoying Al's company. "The minks," she reminded him.

"Oh, I'm looking for a facility to take them. A zoo, a rescue organization. We'll see, but since they've been fed ground meat by humans since they were tiny, I'm not sure they could make it on their own even if they survived predators."

"Probably not," she agreed, sliding onto the other stool. "I don't know that I'd want to take them on."

"You'd need the facilities to survive it. They're nocturnal but awake a lot in the daytime. They're carnivores. They don't like each other unless they're mating."

"Sounds like some marriages."

For the first time she heard his full-throated belly laugh.

"Well," she said, "it *does*."

"That's what made me laugh. Anyway, I'll find someone to take the minks. As for other animals…we're quiet at the moment. I keep an eye out for strays when the weather's dangerous like this, but most of them go home immediately. No pets have been dumped recently, at least none that have been found and reported to me."

The pie was an amazing combination of tart and sweet. She felt her mouth pucker and revel all at once.

Closing her eyes, she gave herself over to the wonderful flavor.

Al fell silent, too, and she could sense he was enjoying the pie as much as she was. It should have felt sinful, with those girls out there in some kind of terrible trouble, but somehow it didn't.

She couldn't spend every minute worrying and thinking about it or she'd soon be no use to anyone. She'd learned a while ago that the toughest part of her job was trying not to get so involved her emotions began to rule her. Separation was essential. Even if she had to go to the ladies' room and cry about it for a while until she could restore her balance.

God knew, she'd seen some awful stuff that still lingered with her.

"Did you grow up here?" she asked, once again seeking a diversionary train of conversation. Although, she admitted, she wanted to know more about Al.

"Yeah, I did. Family's gone now, though. The two of them operated a music store that mostly catered to students who wanted to rent instruments or take additional lessons. I used to love listening to my dad play the oboe. It's such a beautiful, haunting sound, but put him and my mother together on a pair of saxophones and the place would rock."

She smiled. "That sounds wonderful. You musical?"

"Me? Nah. I was at the wrong age to want to do anything my parents did. Bad enough I had to work at the store and sell sheet music and reeds. I used to go nuts sometimes watching a high-school-aged clarinetist try out a bunch of reeds before settling on one he or she liked. No thought to the cost of those discarded reeds, and sometimes I was never certain they could really tell the difference."

Kelly laughed. "I'm sure some could."

"Oh, yeah, but not all of them. I got the feeling it was a thing to do if you played a woodwind. Anyway, my folks didn't mind it, so who was I to get annoyed?"

"What made you leave?"

"Did you know you can die of a broken heart? For real?"

She turned on her stool until she faced him directly. He seemed preoccupied with reaching for another piece of pie. "Al?"

"It's true," he said, his tone changing, growing a bit sorrowful. "Dad took a road trip to Denver to get some supplies. Unfortunately, he was mugged and killed for fifty dollars and a credit card."

Kelly's breath snagged and her chest tightened, aching for him.

"Anyway," he went on, "Mom died two days later. Broken heart syndrome, they called it. It had a fancier name, of course, since it was discovered by some Japanese doctors, but whatever. Her heart stopped beating right, and she thought the pain was grief and…too late. She was gone."

Kelly instinctively reached out to grip his forearm. "I am so sorry, Al. So, so sorry."

"It was a long time ago." At last he turned his head and gave her a faint smile. His eyes were dry. "Still hurts a bit, but it *was* a long time ago. After I recovered from the shock and two funerals, I put the shop up for sale and went looking for the Marine recruiter. I needed to get out of this town."

She squeezed his arm, then let go. "I can imagine."

He shrugged slightly. "I turned tail, but at the time I was glad I did. Boot camp gave me a whole lot of ways to focus on something else and expend a bunch of anger."

To her it sounded like one rational solution to an overwhelming loss. Somehow she couldn't imagine him trying to run his parents' store after that, and feeling angry every time someone tossed aside a half-dozen reeds before finding the perfect one. He might have let them know what he thought.

That drew a quiet sound of amusement from her.

"What?" he asked, digging into a second piece of the pie.

"I was just imagining you dealing with the students who tossed aside reeds after all you went through."

That brought the smile back to his face. "It sure wouldn't have been pretty. For a while there I was one angry young man."

"Understandably. I was pretty angry after my mom died, but it wasn't as if there was anything she could have done. She had a particularly aggressive form of cancer. Oh, well." Thoughts kept getting dark, probably because of all that had happened in the last twenty-four hours.

Her mind kept wanting to wander out into the icy darkness outside, but she couldn't let it. What was she going to do? Race out into the night and run wildly around?

No, she had to wait for morning, for the briefing, for all the details that had been undoubtedly gathered today by various teams. Wait and hope for a major clue.

God, she hated this! She squeezed her eyes closed and battled all the feelings about what those young women might be experiencing, trying to put them away into a box until there was something she could actually act on.

"You care."

Al's voice reached into her dark thoughts and she opened her eyes. "Don't you?" she asked almost truculently.

"Very much. Thing is, being in the military I eventually learned to put things away until I had to deal with them. Once you've made your plans, done your end of it, there's nothing more except to wait for the fallout. If you can't sleep, if you're gnawing holes in your own stomach, it doesn't change a damn thing."

She knew he was right but didn't know how to get to that pinnacle of detachment. It wasn't as if she'd ever had to deal with anything like this in her policing career. "I deal with accidents, robberies, even a rare murder…not abductions, Al. It's different."

"Of course it's different. Worse, maybe, because at this point we can't even be sure those girls were abducted. Maybe they *did* hitch a ride, get dropped off at someplace closer to home and just never made it because of the weather."

She sat up a little straighter. "That's possible." Then she started crashing again. "There's still the fact that they went off the road without even braking."

"Maybe we'll find out otherwise. Those crime scene techs could pull a needle out of a haystack. Let's wait for the morning briefing. We could well learn something hopeful."

He was right, of course. That didn't change the ugly, dark roiling inside her. Finally she gave up on her pie and covered the pan with the slightly crumpled aluminum foil. "You take this with you when you go," she said. "It's more temptation than I can stand and I need it like poison."

His gaze grew inscrutable. "Okay," he said after a few beats. "Are you going to be okay, Kelly? Seriously? You want me to sleep on your floor? Or you want to come to my place?"

His words made her acutely aware that she wasn't behaving professionally. This was a case, like any other she had worked. It was always tougher when the victims were young, but you had to wade through it. Do the job. Not let it overwhelm you. She was in danger of drowning, not a usual state of affairs for her. She prided herself on being a good cop, not a mess of tangled emotions.

"This is really getting to me," she admitted. "More than things usually do. But I've got to deal, Al. I can't use you as a crutch, no matter how kind your offer is. Call it my learning curve. Especially if I want to stay in law enforcement."

He nodded slowly. "It's learnable. This is just a rough case. Rougher than usual."

She fixed her gaze on him again, turning outward from her inner turmoil. "I can't imagine what you've had to deal with. You were in combat, right?"

"Unfortunately. You make contact once or twice, and you learn how useful a shell can be. You just can't afford to brood about it. The next mess will always come. All you can do is maintain optimal readiness. Consider this your first contact."

"But I've done other things…" She paused. "There was this crash of a light plane. I was among the first responders and…" Again she paused, squeezing her eyes shut. "You've seen it. It was more than a year before I could deal with raw chicken or spaghetti."

"I know."

She opened her eyes. "I've moved past it. Mostly. But you're right. This is so different it might as well be first contact for me. So I just have to push through."

"Take something to help you sleep. Got any melatonin?"

"That stuff is a natural hormone, right?"

"The same thing the body makes. I use it once in a while when memory starts bugging me. Best part of it is I can wake up and one coffee makes me alert again. No hangover."

"I'll keep that in mind." Right then her insides and emotions felt as if they'd been thrown in a blender. But she had to get through it. Tomorrow was another day, and she wanted to be able to help. To be useful in whatever way she was needed. "Thanks, Al. You've been great."

He glanced at the digital clock on her microwave. "I should go. We both need some sleep and I *do* have a few animals I need to check on."

She wanted to keep him longer but knew that clinging wasn't going to fix a damn thing. She needed to find her objectivity and put this case into the realm of other cases, a problem to be solved. There *was* always a possibility this would turn out well. Heck, they might get a call in the middle of the night telling them the girls had turned up at some outlying farmhouse.

As Al was leaving, he paused at the door, pie in hand, then surprised her by wrapping one arm around her and hugging her tightly for a brief few seconds. "You're strong," he said. "You'll make it."

She wished she were as confident.

As she latched the door behind him, it struck her that she was being terribly self-indulgent, giving in to useless feelings and allowing them to run her.

She needed to be thinking, using her brain or sleeping. Either one would be more useful and less selfish.

When at last she curled up in bed, Bugle stretched alongside her, closer than usual, as if he felt her distress. With her hand digging into his ruff, she closed her eyes and finally, finally fell asleep.

Chapter Five

Day 3

Once again the sheriff's office was crammed with deputies and city police, and plenty of other people waited outside, wondering where the search would head today.

Because they were going to search. Even as the first, very faint light of dawn began to appear in the east, the helicopters could be heard taking to the air again, to hunt with their spotlights until daylight aided them, cabin crews alert for any movement, or any color outside the norm.

Today they had more information about the missing, however.

"All right," Gage said, rapping on one of the desks for silence. "Micah here is going to fill you in."

Micah Parish, of clear Cherokee ancestry, had been

with the office since the days when Gage had first arrived in town. At first he had been greeted with old prejudices, but over the years he had knit himself into the fabric of the community.

"All right," he said, lifting a whiteboard and placing it on an easel. The photographs of the three missing young women stared back at them. "You know these are the young ladies we need to find. We learned something from the parents about what they might be wearing, so keep alert for colors of bright pink, royal blue and, unfortunately, light green. That won't stick out very well. But look for colors that don't belong out there at this time of year."

Murmurs and nods went around the room.

"You'll need to inform the civilians who are searching with us. Given our search area today, we'll have one deputy leading each group of searchers. We can divvy it up before you depart.

"As for other things, the enemies these young women might have…need I tell you that nobody has an enemy?"

A quiet laugh rolled around the room. Dark humor. The kind that kept cops, firefighters and soldiers sane.

Micah nodded in response. "We're going to be talking to some of their friends today, other kids at school. We may learn that there are a few people who actually don't like them, or that they've had a run-in with someone. Kelly?"

She raised her hand so he could find her in the crowd. "Sir?"

"I want you and Connie to do the interviews at school today. The principal is agreeable and will give you a private room. Kelly, I know Bugle is suited to other tasks but his presence may keep the atmosphere more relaxing for the students, okay?"

"Okay, Micah." She could see his point, and much as her body wanted to be outdoors moving, and much as she was sure that Bugle would prefer that, she knew he was probably right. Bugle always drew interested attention.

As THE FINAL bell rang for the day and students started piling out of the high school for buses and their own cars, Connie and Kelly sat back at the table they'd been using in a private room facing laptops and notebooks.

Kelly sighed.

Connie stretched and nearly groaned. "I'm getting too old for this."

Kelly laughed. "You're not that old. Don't make me feel bad."

"You know how I met my husband, Ethan?"

Kelly shook her head. "Before my time."

"Well, he's Micah Parish's son."

That snagged Kelly's interest. She twisted on the folding chair that could have done with a pillow and looked at Connie. "Yeah?"

"Yeah."

"I wondered because of the name but nobody ever told me."

"Well, that was an interesting story. Micah didn't know about him because his mother hadn't told him, so one day Ethan shows up at Micah's ranch with the news. But that wasn't the point of me bringing it up. I brought it up because years ago, when my daughter was about seven, I thought she was kidnapped."

"Oh my God," Kelly breathed.

"Ethan tracked her, believe it or not. We'd had days of this awful tension because a stranger had approached her on her way home from school. Deputies were crawling every street, parents were warned not to let their children walk home alone… The drill. You know it. Then my daughter disappeared during the night out her bedroom window. The thing was, Ethan's background in the military gave him the skills to track her. We found her up at the old mining camp…and the man who had taken her was her father, my ex. He'd just gotten out of prison."

"You must have gone through hell." Kelly couldn't begin to imagine it.

"I did. But it didn't last long and it turned out all right." Connie's mouth compressed, then she said, "It's not looking good, Kelly. Almost forty-eight hours now. The window's closing."

"I know. But it's not immutable." She needed to believe that. She *had* to believe that. Out in the fading afternoon light, dozens, if not hundreds, of people were hunting the countryside, knocking on every door, looking for any sign at all of the three girls. At some point they couldn't keep the search going at this level. Even with all the volunteers, there would come a time when they'd have to give up looking and start hoping for some other kind of clue.

How could three girls just vanish into the night like this?

Because someone had taken them.

She looked at Connie. "We need to start thinking about whether there's anyone around here who might be capable of this abduction."

"We're already thinking about that," Connie reminded her. "We just spent all day asking a bunch of high school students if they'd seen anything odd, if these girls had mentioned being afraid of someone or something, if anyone disliked them enough to want to hurt them. We're already doing it, Kelly."

"It doesn't feel like enough."

"Especially when we haven't learned anything that feels useful. Yet." Connie sighed and closed her laptop. "I need to get home, make dinner for the kids and Ethan, assuming he comes in from the search. I'm going to spend an awful lot of time thinking about what we heard today. You?"

"I'm not going to be able to think about anything else. Maybe somewhere in this shower of love is a needle."

Connie laughed wearily. "Exactly. It was creepy, if you ask me. Kids this age always have some gripes about one another. This sounded like a wake."

No one speaks ill of the dead.

"Yeah, it did. And that bothers me, Connie."

"Why?" Connie's gaze grew sharp.

"Because you'd expect people this young to be convinced these girls were going to show up. Instead they seem to have given up. Why?"

"Maybe because it's so damn cold out there they know no one could survive for long."

"Maybe." But Kelly had trouble believing it. "And maybe I'm overreacting. They're probably all scared about this and just as confused as anyone."

Connie nodded and stood, pulling her uniform parka on. "I'll pass all this non-news along to the sheriff on my way home. The students all have our cards. If they think of something, or suddenly want to open up about anything, they know how to reach us." She smiled wanly. "They'll probably call *you*. Bugle was a hit."

Indeed he had been. He'd even preened a bit, if a dog could preen. Kelly suspected he'd have been happy to stay even longer to enjoy all the pets and praise that had come his way.

But the fun part was over.

"Work," she said.

He needed to hear no more. He stretched and got ready to move. His tail even wagged a bit. He truly enjoyed working.

Which was more than she could say that particular day.

On the way home, she stopped at the diner to pick up dinner. On impulse, she bought enough for two and hoped that Al might be inclined to stop by when the search ended. She told herself it was a silly hope, but she needed something to look forward to, even if she was imagining it.

All this time, Al had never shown any interest in her. Well, occasionally she thought she caught a spark of heat in his gaze, but if so he masked it quickly. Probably she was imagining that, too.

She shook her head at herself as she carried home enough food for an army. No involvement, she reminded herself. She'd seen it happen, when two people in the same department got close, then broke up. The subsequent situation was often uncomfortable for everyone, and sometimes it could grow ugly.

Nope, none of that.

She fed Bugle, who'd lacked only food during the day because she had a special water bottle for him that opened to provide a tray for him to lap out of. No, he'd never go thirsty as long as she could refill that bottle.

He didn't seem especially hungry, however. He left nearly half his kibble in his bowl, causing her to wonder if she should heat some more chicken livers for him. But no, she didn't want him to expect that every day. It didn't take long for him to create a habit.

A hot shower helped ease some of the tension from her, especially her shoulders and neck, then she dressed in flannel pajamas and a bathrobe, wrapping her hair in a towel. As she emerged into the main part of the little house, she eyed the fireplace. The logs had long since burned out, but she wondered if she should make another fire just for herself.

She certainly needed something cheery after today. On the other hand, burning the wood for her own entertainment seemed wasteful and not especially good for the environment. Last night had been a true splurge but it had been so enjoyable.

The towel damp-dried her short bob quickly, so she went to hang it over a rack and run a bush through her hair. How many kids had they interviewed that day? She'd lost count at some point, although she could check it on her computer or her notepad, where each of them had been dutifully noted by name and age.

It still seemed odd that no one had anything negative to say. She hadn't been in high school for a while, but she easily remembered the cliques and the gossip and the way some of the students had avoided others like the plague.

These three girls were unusual in their pursuits. Not cheerleaders, the perennially popular, but nerds. Chess club? Debate club? Soccer, and not even first string? Either they'd become basically invisible or no one today had wanted to mention the petty kinds of comments students like them often drew.

She bet it was the latter. She'd seen their photos. Nerds or not, they were all pretty enough to attract attention at a hormonally driven age.

Sighing, she fluffed her damp hair a little with her fingers and decided she needed to eat before she took a complete plunge. This entire situation was so upsetting, and she'd never dealt well with the feeling of helplessness. Right now she felt helpless. Closing her eyes, she could all too easily imagine those girls out there somewhere, terrified out of their minds.

Someone had taken them. She believed that now after Al's recognition that the car hadn't braked before going off the road. And for all three of them to have been taken? Drugs.

She felt her heart lift a bit, leaving the worst of her despair behind when there was a rap on the door. She opened it and Al stood there. He spoke before she could even greet him. "I was thinking about picking up dinner for us if I'm not becoming a nuisance. You interested?"

"Already done. Come on in. There's plenty. How'd the search go?"

He was cold enough that when she stood near him she could feel his body sucking the heat from the air. He tossed off his gloves and parka and knelt before her fireplace. "You mind?"

"I was thinking about doing it."

"Then let me. I need it. You know, like a candle in the dark."

She felt her heart and stomach both plummet. "Nothing?"

"Not a damn thing. A glove? A shoe? A scarf? Nope. Not even that much. You?"

"If anyone ever had a mean thing to say about those girls, we didn't hear it today. Tomorrow we'll talk to some teachers, too, but I'm not sure it's going to make any difference."

The dry logs he piled into the fireplace started quickly. He tossed the match onto the flames and remained squatting, holding his hands out toward the fire, lost in thought.

After a few minutes, she asked, "Hungry?"

"Famished," he admitted. A couple of seconds later he stood and came to the bar to help her unload the bags. "You went all out."

"I was seeking comfort," she admitted. And hoping he might stop by, but she didn't want to tell him that.

"You don't have to explain that to me," he agreed.

Tonight she brought out dishes. They had a lilac pattern on them, leftovers from her mother's collection that she'd never bothered to add to. A few dinner plates, salad plates and bowls remained. Enough for two people, at a pinch maybe three.

She'd skipped the steak sandwiches and instead had asked Maude for containers of tomato soup and thick grilled cheese sandwiches. More comfort food.

"Ah, man," Al said, "I love Maude's grilled cheese. It's like eating Texas toast covered in melted Havarti. She seasons them, too. I hope you like dill."

"Love it. That's one of the reasons I decided to try them."

"It's a hit and I haven't taken my first bite."

The soup was rich and surprisingly good, Kelly

thought. She wasn't the biggest fan of tomato soup but Maude's might change her mind.

Sitting at the bar with Al, feeling the heat from the fireplace warming her back, it was almost possible to believe everything was normal.

It was not.

She ate quickly, trying not to think about whether the missing students were eating anything tonight, whether they were warm enough, whether they were being terrorized. Later, she told herself, forcibly squashing the thoughts. They could talk about all this mess after they finished eating.

One of her previous partners had scolded her for losing her appetite. "You owe it to the victim to keep yourself in the best functioning shape possible."

But sometimes it was hard. Sometimes her whole body and mind wanted to rebel at the idea that anything, *anything*, could be normal in a situation like this.

Al kept the conversation general and light. She gave him credit for that because her attempts to respond in the same vein weren't exactly stellar.

She looked at Al. "After Connie and I talk to the teachers tomorrow, I want to go back to Rusty's tavern."

He raised a brow. "Yeah?"

"Everything seems to have started there, doesn't it? And they said they'd make a list of everyone who was there that night."

Al nodded slowly. "I'll go with you, if you don't mind."

Why would she mind? If police work had taught her nothing else, it had taught her that two brains were often better than one.

Settled in her plan, she resumed eating.

CLOSER THAN KELLY would have believed, and yet farther than it seemed possible, two girls awoke in a darkened basement, chilled to the bone despite the ragged blanket that had been tossed over them.

A single movement, and Chantal cried out. "Wire," she said. "Oh, God, wire." Her wrists and ankles were bound and every movement of the thin, bare wire cut at skin. "Mary Lou? Jane?"

"Me, too," answered Jane, her voice thick as if she'd been crying. "He drugged us again. Chantal, I don't think I can go without water, but it must have been in the water bottles."

"Yeah." Probably. Chantal's mind recoiled, then seemed to stiffen. "Mary Lou? Mary Lou?"

"I don't think she's here," Jane answered, her voice breaking. "She was right beside me earlier. Now she's not answering."

Helplessly, ignoring the cutting pain in her wrists, Chantal edged closer to Jane. "She's gone?"

Jane seemingly didn't even want to answer. After a few seconds she said in a cracked whisper, "Maybe she got knocked out more than we did."

"Shh," whispered Chantal. "Hold your breath and listen."

But there was no other sound in the dank space, not so much as soft breaths. A tomb couldn't have been any more silent.

Mary Lou was gone. But to where and for what?

"Oh my God," Jane whispered. "Oh my God. What did we do, Chantal?"

"That's not going to help," Chantal whispered fiercely. "We've got to get our heads working again. There's got to be something we can do *now*." She *had* to believe that. Never once in her life had she simply given up, even when a situation looked hard. Like trying out for the soccer team. She didn't have any real athletic ability, but she'd wanted to do it anyway because it was the kind of activity that was good for college applications. So she'd practiced until she'd become good enough to make the second string. Because she refused to be defeated by her own mind.

She believed in her ability to conquer the difficult, and she was trying to believe she could conquer this, as well.

But the wire around her wrists and ankles gave lie to that. Hopelessness, as cold and dank as the dark room, settled over her.

REVE HAD HAD ENOUGH. Maybe taking the three girls had seemed like a good idea at the time, but the one he'd just dealt with… No fun at all.

Well, he'd have no more to do with her. He still had two more and if he was careful, they'd probably work better. But he was going to keep them tied up in the dark longer, and keep them a whole lot hungrier. By the time he got done, they'd think he was their savior. Yeah.

In the meantime, he needed to ditch this one. Driving down back roads in the dark with his headlights off wasn't a whole lot of fun, but he was wary they might resume the helicopter search. They seemed to have called it off at dusk, though. Giving up, he supposed.

He didn't go far out of town, maybe ten miles. He knew of some wide-open ranchland that hadn't been used in years, and it would provide the perfect place to dump whatshername. Trash. That's all she was now.

He didn't bother to wrap her in anything. The last

thing he wanted was for her body to be protected from the elements or scavengers. Nope, she'd come into this world as naked as a jaybird, and she was going out the same way.

The hard ground aided him, leaving behind almost no sign of his passing. When he got far enough from the road, he stopped.

Damn, she'd grown heavy. Or maybe he was just hurting.

Didn't matter. She was knocked out and would stay that way just long enough. With a grunt, he rolled her naked body into a ditch. Cold as this night was, she'd be dead almost before she woke up.

Then he dragged a couple of tumbleweeds over her, checking to make sure the ditch wouldn't let them blow away too easily.

In a week or so, she'd be nothing but bones. As for her clothes…he had a woodstove to burn them. No sign she'd ever been anywhere near his place.

As for the other two…that abandoned, run-down house was perfect, with a solid basement but everything else going to hell. Nobody ever went there. Not even kids looking for a thrill. In a few years there'd be nothing left of the house except the hollowed-out basement.

Turning slowly, he drove away, making sure he didn't leave any deep tracks behind him. He stuck to old tractor ruts, hard as rock in the dry winter. He wouldn't stir up anything noticeable, and once it snowed there'd be absolutely nothing to see.

The winter had aided him, he thought. Traditionally the area didn't get a whole lot of snow and what it did was dry and blew around. The last couple of years had been unusual with heavier snows, but not this year.

Here they had reached January with nothing but a few light flurries that hadn't stuck. That wouldn't last, but it had lasted long enough for this job.

Damn, he ached from that kick. He'd have liked to treat her to a bit of a beating, but he was trying not to leave evidence, and even if all they ever found were her bones, assuming the wolves or coyotes didn't drag them away, they'd be able to tell she'd been hurt before dying.

Nope, teen girl freezes to death in January on the high plains of Wyoming. Wouldn't be the first. No clothes meant only that the carrion eaters had pulled them apart and dragged them away. It kind of amused him to think of the hours that would be wasted seeking scraps of cloth.

He realized he was thirsty and decided to go to Rusty's for a beer or two. He went several times a week and no one would notice him, except maybe for Spence and Jeff, if they were there and wanted to play pool. He had a life.

And the life provided cover.

CHANTAL AWOKE SUDDENLY. The jarring movement reminded her of the wire cutting painfully into her wrists and ankles. She drew a long breath, steadying herself, letting the pain wash over her and then away. Beside her, Jane still slept, a quiet snore escaping her. This basement was causing her allergies to act up, uncomfortable for Jane when she couldn't even blow her nose.

But those quiet snores hadn't wakened her. She listened intently but heard only the lonely sound of the wind. If their captor had come and left more food and water, she didn't know. Not that she wanted any of it now.

A headache pounded behind her eyes, either from hunger or from the drug they'd been given…when? She didn't even know how long ago they'd been knocked out and Mary Lou had disappeared.

All of a sudden she understood why people would find a way to scratch hash marks for days into the walls of their prisons. Except in here she could not be sure what was night and what was day. There was absolutely no way to keep track of time. That could prove maddening, she realized. As maddening as the endless night that swallowed them.

She stared into the unyielding dark and tried to think of something they might be able to do. Some way to put an end to this. She knew well enough that without shoes and jackets they wouldn't make it very far in the Wyoming winter weather. But some other way, because right now escape looked impossible.

Then, out of nowhere, a deep sorrow welled up in her and as if she'd seen it with her own eyes, she felt the truth in her very bones.

Mary Lou was dead.

She had to stifle a cry, to bite her lip until she tasted blood. How could she know? How could it be?

But she knew. And she didn't want Jane to know.

MILES AWAY, Kelly jerked out of a sound sleep. Bugle, who'd been snoring beside her, lifted his head. The small night-light glowed, her protection against jumping out of bed in the dark for an emergency call and barking her shins or tripping. In that light she could see Bugle's focus. He'd become alert, very alert.

She listened, hearing nothing but the night wind and

the occasional crackle from the banked fire in the living room.

Then Bugle made a sound she almost never heard from him. It came from deep within him, a low groan, not a growl, and it sounded so incredibly forlorn that it seemed laced with sorrow. But over what? A bad dream?

Then he put his head on her belly and whimpered softly.

Knowledge crashed in on her. She knew what had wakened her so unexpectedly and what Bugle was trying to tell her. She knew why she felt her chest squeezing as if it wanted to silence her heart.

One of the girls was dead.

Chapter Six

Day 4

His phone rang well before dawn. Al was used to it. He had no set hours and folks knew they could call him if their animal escaped in this dangerous weather. He didn't mind at all. Saving animals was one way he could make up for a bunch of things he'd done that he never wanted to remember. Besides, he generally believed that animals were kinder than people. Certainly more forgiving.

He threw back the comforter, slapped his stockinged feet on the rough would floor and leaned forward to grab the receiver for the landline. "Animal Control. Carstairs."

"She's dead."

He recognized Kelly's voice instantly. "Who is? What happened?"

"I don't know. I just know one of the girls is dead. Bugle feels it, too. Damn it, Al, I'm going to smash something!"

He'd worked with animals too long not to respect their intuition. Plus, Bugle had a link to those girls after smelling their garments.

"Hell, I'll be right over."

"I'm not crazy!"

"I don't think you are. I'm on my way. Give me a few. I need to make sure everyone's got some water."

"Okay." Her voice cracked. "Okay."

He dressed as swiftly as he could, wishing he had more zippers and fewer buttons, then ran out to the kennels in the insulated barn. Two felines and one canine raised their heads curiously but didn't seem at all disturbed. The minxes were snarling at each other from cages five feet apart.

Yeah, they had water. Plenty of food in their automatic feeders. The dog yawned at him and went back to sleep. The cats merely stared enigmatically. The minks ignored him.

Sure that his charges would be all right for a while, he headed out to his truck. The light from the lamp he'd left on in his cabin silhouetted a squirrel in the window.

"Hey, Regis," he said. "What are you doing out at this hour?"

He'd never get an answer. All he knew was that squirrels tended to stay in their dreys at night with the rest of their squirrel families.

Crap, was the whole world suddenly going nuts?

A million questions demanded answers but he refused to ask them until he got to Kelly's place. All he needed to know for now was that she was clearly distraught and probably didn't want to call anyone from her department. He supposed he ought to feel complimented that she didn't think he'd dismiss her or label her nuts.

Still, the only evidence a feeling? Hers or the dog's? Yeah, he wouldn't want to explain that to most people, although he wasn't the sort to dismiss it.

He'd been in situations in Afghanistan where feelings of that kind had been all that saved his life and the lives of his squad. The sense that something was about to happen. That someone lurked and was ready to kill.

Easy to dismiss by telling yourself you'd picked up on some small thing in the environment that you hadn't consciously noticed.

This was going to be different.

At three in the morning there was no hope of finding any ready-made coffee unless he drove to the far end of town to the truck stop. That would take too long. Dang, he needed some caffeine as quickly as possible, but he was sure he could make it at Kelly's house even if he'd have to wait fifteen or twenty minutes. She'd probably need some, too, before this night was over.

The drive seemed endless, which it didn't usually, but eventually he reached her little house on the edge of town and pulled into the driveway, two strips of concrete that were wheel-distance apart. An old-fashioned driveway, the kind that had come about in the days of wheeled carriages and wagons.

No getting stuck in mud. Or snow. Or... He shut the stupid line of thought down. The lights were on in Kelly's small cottage. Another time they might have looked welcoming.

The instant he reached her door, the icy night wind whipping through narrowed streets like a hungry animal, she flung it open. She'd been worried over the last few days, but now she looked sunken, circles around her eyes. Bugle didn't even rise from the floor to acknowledge him but lay there looking as depressed as a dog could look.

She couldn't even speak his name, simply stepped back to give him entrance.

"Coffee?" he asked, deciding to start on safe ground.

"I didn't… My hands were shaking…"

This was not at all the competent deputy he'd come to know over the last few years. Not that he knew her very well. They hadn't become fast friends, just acquaintances. But he knew her well enough to realize she was in a place she'd never gone before, at least not in her job. That was saying something because he had a good idea of some of the things she'd seen and dealt with. Law enforcement was the pointy end of the stick in a lot of ways, first responders like firefighters and EMTs. Nightmares that clung.

"Sit if you can," he said quietly. "Get a blanket. I'll start the coffee and build up the fire again. You look like an icicle."

Indeed she did. If he hadn't known better, he'd have thought she'd been standing out in the cold for the last hour.

She needed warmth, maybe food, something to help with the shock.

"I'm not crazy," she said, standing her ground.

"I don't think you are. But let's take care of your immediate physical needs…and frankly mine…before we talk."

At last she settled into her armchair. Bugle unfolded himself and came to place his head on her thigh. Since she'd ignored his other suggestion, Al grabbed the afghan off the back of the chair and tossed it over her, careful not to cover Bugle's head. Kelly's hand dug into the dog's neck as if she were hanging on for dear life.

Her coffeemaker was about the same as his, so stacking it and starting it came automatically, with one difference. He made this coffee strong. Then he nosed into her refrigerator and found a frozen raspberry Danish on a plastic tray. He popped that into the microwave for a quick thaw. Sugar was a good antidote to shock.

It didn't seem like something she'd ordinarily eat, however. But then, what did he know? She had friends who probably came over on weekends. Most people did. Even him, the isolationist misanthrope. Sort of.

At last he got a mug of coffee into her hands, watching them shake a bit, but not enough to spill it. "Want a piece of Danish?"

"Not yet," she murmured.

There was an embroidered stool stuck in one corner, maybe for use as an ottoman. He had no idea, but he had use for it now. He pulled it over until he sat right in front of her with his own coffee.

"Feel any better?"

She gave an almost invisible nod of her head.

"Ready to talk?"

She chewed her lower lip until he feared that she might make it bleed. "I can't explain."

"Then don't," he said gently. "Just give me the facts of what happened. You don't need to explain them to me."

Long seconds passed before she tried to speak again. "It's nuts."

"Don't dismiss it. Just tell me."

She squeezed her eyes closed. "I was sound asleep. I woke up suddenly and it was like…like this tidal wave of despair, maybe anguish…it just filled me. And then I noticed Bugle had come to full alert and he made this groan… Oh, God, I hope I never hear him make that sound again. It was heartrending. Then he put his head on me and he whimpered."

She drew a long, shaky breath. "That's when I knew. Thought I knew. Hell, I don't know. I was absolutely certain that one of those girls had just died."

"I guess Bugle was, too."

She opened her eyes and looked down at her dog. Her real partner. "Yeah," she whispered. "He felt something."

Al rose, then returned with two small plates, each holding a piece of Danish and a fork. "Use your fingers if you want." He set it on her lap and Bugle sniffed at it but left it alone. A well-trained animal.

"The thing is," Kelly said, her voice still thin and a bit cracked, "I can't go to work with this. I can't even tell Gage. He might believe me, but what good would it do? We've still got to look for those missing women."

"I agree."

"I also don't need half the department whispering that I'm losing my marbles if someone overhears me. But damn," she said, her voice nearly a cry, "what can I do? I've got to do something. What if he's going to kill again? Or what if I imagined all this? The stress since the disappearance…"

He reached out and covered her hand with his. Even as she used her fingers to try to hold on to the plate he'd practically forced on her, he could feel her tremors. And the ice that seemed to be running through her veins.

"Eat. Drink your coffee. You're half the way into shock."

"From a feeling?" She looked utterly dubious.

"From a feeling. That's all it takes sometimes." He knew that intimately from his time at war. Shock could occur from an unexpected emotional blow. She'd had one, regardless of what it was based on.

She managed to swallow half the coffee. He went to get her another cup while she picked at the Danish.

"I don't know what to do." She was gathering her strength again. He could hear it in her voice.

"I'm not sure you *can* do anything," he answered, hoping he sounded reassuring.

"I hope it's not true. I hope I just imagined it because I've been so worried."

"We can hope," he agreed. He was glad to see her drink more coffee and eat a larger piece of Danish. He swallowed his own drink and felt his stomach burn in response. She wasn't the only one who was upset. Usually his stomach was cast iron.

"I must have imagined it," she said a little while later.

"Is Bugle into imagining things?" he asked.

Her head jerked a little as she looked at him. "He might have been responding to me. To my feeling."

"It's possible. I'm going to tell you a story, if you're up to it."

"Why wouldn't I be up to it?"

"Because it doesn't have a happy ending. You're not the first or only person to get feelings like this. They aren't always accurate, but when they are…"

She hesitated, nibbled another piece of Danish. "This was for church on Sunday," she said absently. Then, "Okay, tell me your story."

"Long time ago, a couple of kids I was in high school with went on a family camping trip. The oldest two were avid kayakers. They loved white water. Anyway, the daughter was helping her mother cook dinner when she suddenly looked at her mom and said, 'If I don't go home tonight, I'll never go home.'"

Kelly drew a sharp breath.

"Mom talked her into a better mood, my friend seemed to forget all about it…but the next day she and her brother went kayaking together, they overturned and both of them were lost. So what do you make of what she said to her mom?"

"I know I wouldn't want to live with it," Kelly said, her entire face drooping. "Oh, God, that's awful."

He nodded. "I couldn't agree more. But it's not the first time I've heard a story like that. So maybe I'm less skeptical than most. I've sure heard some stories about people who knew that someone in their family had died before they got the news. It happens. I can't explain it, but I don't dismiss it. However, in light of the fact that we have no concrete evidence, it won't hurt us to go on hoping your feeling was wrong."

"No, but right now that feels awfully hard."

"I'm sure." It felt hard to him, too. What if one of those missing girls had died? Why? What was the abductor trying to accomplish? To satisfy some ugly need to inflict pain and death? Why three girls, anyway? Seemed like that would make everything more complicated. One you could handle. Three all at once? Difficult.

"I'm sorry," she said unexpectedly.

"For what?" He couldn't imagine.

"For waking you in the middle of the night over something like this. I just couldn't stand to be alone, and I knew if I called one of my friends from the department they might wonder if I'd lost it."

"I don't mind. I'm glad you called, actually." He offered a smile. "And as you can see, I don't think you've lost it." He rose again, stretching muscles that somehow hadn't quite made the transition from bed to being upright, and went to get himself some more coffee. "I get called in the middle of the night often enough. People get worried when their pets go missing in weather like this. I don't mind."

He had settled again on the ottoman in front of her before she spoke again. "So you're a one-man animal rescue team?"

"Sometimes. Mostly the animals haven't gone that far and by the time I show up they're looking to be warm again. Easy enough to find. Although there was one black Lab who didn't give a damn how cold or wet it was. To him, playing keep-away was a big game. I'll never forget that huge grin he'd give me as he pranced out of reach."

She was smiling faintly, a good sign.

"That dog developed quite a reputation in his neighborhood. Jasper. Lots of folks recognized him and got a kick out of him."

"I can imagine."

"You never ran into him? I'm sure he was here during your time."

"Never had the pleasure."

He wondered how circumscribed her life was. Maybe nearly as bad as his own? Nose-to-the-grindstone serious? Of course, he was sure she wasn't the only person in the area who'd never gotten to know Jasper. For most people, if they'd seen that dog he'd have been nothing but a black streak passing by.

The fire was burning behind him, just a small one, but a cheerful sound. However, it was the only cheerful thing in this room. He could feel the cold, as if it had seeped in from the night outside, but it wasn't that kind of cold.

It was the inky coldness of death. There had been times when it had been his nearly constant companion. Now this.

God, he hoped she was mistaken, that the chill he felt had merely arisen from her description of her experience, but he feared it had not. If one of those girls had died, it hadn't been an accident. It had been murder. All that did was make him worry even more about the other two, and worry had already been doing a damn good job of peaking the longer they remained missing.

She'd utterly lost interest in the Danish and coffee he'd given her, so he took them to the kitchen.

"Rest if you can," he told her. "Morning will come soon enough."

He moved the stool back and took the chair near hers, watching her as she stared into the fire, kneading Bugle's neck, her expression both dark and fearful.

At last, however, her eyelids drooped and sleep found her. As soon as it did, Bugle burrowed in a little closer and closed his eyes.

Dog and man kept watch through the silent, terrifying hours of darkness.

A little while later, she stirred and spoke drowsily. "You were in the military, right?"

"Marines."

"How'd you get here, Al? Just because you grew up here?"

But he didn't think that was the story she wanted the answer to. She wanted something more intimate. Deeper. Not superficial answers. Clearly she needed something from him, but what? He couldn't imagine, so he hesitated, maybe too long because she withdrew her question.

"None of my business," she said without opening her eyes. "Sorry."

"No need. I was just wondering how to answer. The facts are simple. I was wounded. Considered unfit for duty. Medically retired. Nothing all that great there. Me and thousands of other troops."

"Yeah." She sighed, and her eyes fluttered open a bit to look at him. "Sad."

"It's the risk you take when you sign up," he said flatly. So true. Except who in the hell really knew what they were signing up for? That was the great secret until you were in the middle of it.

"Anyway, after a while I realized I wasn't dealing well with people. Too angry. Like a firecracker with a short fuse. Animals... Well, they're a whole different story. Being around them is soothing. Uncomplicated for the most part."

"Even minks?"

That drew a quiet laugh from him. "They're predictable, anyway. With time my fuse is getting longer. I guess I'm finally coming home."

He'd never phrased it that way before, but he could see from her expression that had struck her. She ought to be sleeping but here she was pondering his past and his overwhelmingly philosophical statements. Oorah. Good job, Al.

Chapter Seven

Reluctantly, the world resumed its normal course. The search was beginning to taper off. People needed to get back to regular work. The sheriff couldn't afford to keep such a huge manhunt going, and after five days it had become obvious that wherever the girls were, they needed more detective work than traipsing across the countryside.

The families were beside themselves, of course. From the next room, Kelly could hear the sheriff explaining that all they were doing now was shifting focus.

"We'll still be looking but we're not going to find them out in the open," he explained. "We've covered every inch of more than a thousand square miles with our helicopters and quite a bit of the ground on foot.

Everybody's been helping and everybody's on high alert for any sign of your daughters. Those girls have either left the county or are indoors somewhere."

"So what do we do now?" Kate Beauvoir demanded. "We can't give up!"

"I didn't say we're giving up," Gage said patiently. Kindly. "We're shifting focus to other methods that we believe will be more useful. The girls clearly didn't run away across open ground. They weren't left out there. So now we concentrate our efforts at a different level. Someone took them and we need to get some clues as to who."

Then the conference room door closed, and the conversation became private. Still haunted by her dream or premonition from two nights before, Kelly was grateful not to hear any more.

The office was too small to offer each deputy his or her own desk, so they shared them, using them as necessary when they were on shift or just coming off and needing to tidy up paperwork. Kelly's share of a desk sat near a window looking out at the courthouse square. The computer that filled a large part of it was an older model, serviceable but needing replacement. A small tray pulled out on one side to provide extra writing space as needed. Creating a sort of wall behind her were three overstuffed filing cabinets. Insofar as possible, records were being retired and placed on microfiche in the basement of the courthouse, but there was still enough paper to jam every drawer.

She had a list of names in front of her, names gleaned from Rusty and his staff, and a few other people who had come forward. The names of those who had been seen at the tavern the night the young women disappeared.

Going through them, she tried to design the most efficient route for herself. Today, she and Bugle were going to knock on doors and ask questions. It was always possible that someone had seen something that might have been suspicious.

Yeah, this was the next level of detective work. Shoe leather.

She heard a door open and instinctively looked up to see the families of the girls leaving. The women all had puffy, red eyes. The men weren't looking much better. Not a one of them seemed happy about the changes.

She couldn't really blame them, she thought as she dragged her eyes down to the paper in front of her. Of course they wanted everyone out there looking. The problem with that was at this point the returns were seriously diminishing. It was a virtual certainty that none of those girls was lying out in the open. Nor had the choppers picked up any sign of disturbed ground.

That meant they were inside somewhere or they were in another county, and Gage had already flashed alerts to every agency within a thousand or more miles. Those girls' photos were going to be burned into the minds of every law enforcement officer in three or more states. Two FBI agents were on their way in from the nearest field office, not that they'd be much help.

Hadn't the mention of the FBI helped the parents a little? Kelly simply couldn't put herself in their shoes. She had no idea how they were assessing all of this, whether FBI agents seemed like they would help.

Even the FBI needed evidence.

Rapping her pen tip on the paper in front of her, Kelly studied it while she listened to the front door close behind the agonized parents. God, she wished she had something to offer them. That anyone here could offer them hope.

But right now hope was fading, and even the parents must realize that. Too long. Too damn long. Even a ransom note would have provided a thread to cling to. But not even that.

Which meant the abductor was up to absolutely no good. None. And that was a whole new level of terrifying.

Much as she tried not to imagine things, she still suffered from the same imagination as everyone else. She'd read enough stories about what had been done to young women who'd been kidnapped and held, sometimes for years on end. Right now those news stories seemed very close emotionally, very personal.

She pulled out her satellite phone and used the GPS to enter all the addresses she wanted to visit today. Sometimes this county seemed empty, but when you looked at going door-to-door, it grew huge.

When she'd entered the last address, she scanned the map and made the best judgments she could for which order to visit the outlying ranches. The likelihood that anyone had seen anything out there was slender, but on the other hand, those were people who, if they *had* noticed something unusual, would have paid attention. In town, too many people passed through because of the state highway. Roads out by the ranches were an entirely different story.

Satisfied she'd done the best she could, she folded the list and put it in her inside pocket. Then she buttoned up for the cold day and picked up her tablet. Bugle was already moving impatiently. He'd been wanting to get on the road for hours.

Even after all this time and five years here, not to mention Laramie, the first step out the door into the frigid air always felt as if it stole her breath. Once upon a time, as a pup, Bugle had been fascinated by the clouds of steam that came out of his nostrils, but he'd long since learned to ignore it.

As she buttoned him into his caged backseat and climbed into the car that held not one bit of the warmth she had filled it with on her way over, she wondered what Al was doing.

Patrolling? Rounding up escapees in answer to calls? Someday, when she had the time, she thought she might like to go on a ride with him and see what exactly filled his days. It probably wasn't much different from what she did on a lot of days: patrolling in case she was needed. Answering calls that came in if she was nearby. Often the job wasn't exciting. Boring, even. Then there were the other times.

Domestic disputes were the ones she hated most, and they were reaching the time of winter when they ramped up in both number and savagery. Cabin fever, she often thought, was lousy for relationships.

Not knowing what she'd find when she drove onto each ranch and knocked at the door put her on heightened alert. Most people would be friendly, some would even want her to come in for coffee and cookies because they were so glad to see a fresh face.

Her anxiety eased a bit and she smiled through the windshield at a day that was sacrificing all its clouds in favor of bright sun. At this latitude the sun didn't get that high, not like Miami or Puerto Rico, but once the snow covered the ground it would be every bit as blinding.

Right now it was just turning into a beautiful day. She felt a twinge of guilt for even noticing.

She was a little over five miles out of town, driving slowly over a dirt road that was bad now and would be even worse come spring. Thank God it was frozen, but it was like riding on a rubbery roller coaster. To the west the mountains rose like dark sentinels, promising a safety she had never managed to feel. They were close here, and seemed to loom over the county below. The mountains to the east were farther away, beautiful but not quite as dominating. Or threatening. Odd thought.

Just then Bugle started barking his strange half howl, and he persisted demandingly until she pulled to the side on a grassy turnout and put the SUV in Park. "What the heck, Bugle?"

As if he could answer. She could see nothing at all in any direction but dried grasses, scrub and tumbleweed. Oh, and the nearby mountains that right now felt as if they were pressing on her shoulder, leaning in.

He hurried to the left side of the truck and pressed his nose to the window, still howling his fool head off.

She wasn't stupid enough to ignore it when her dog acted like a fool. Something had gripped his attention.

"Okay," she said. She reached for the gloves on the seat beside her and pulled them on, leaving the car to run to keep it warm.

One thing for sure, she was leashing that dog. If he wanted to chase a rabbit, *she* wasn't going to chase him. He waited impatiently while she opened the door and hooked the long leather lead to the ring on his collar. Then, without so much as a command, he jumped down and began to pull her back the way they had just come. To the point where he'd begun to lose his calm.

Well-trained K-9 or not, Kelly was well aware that he was still a dog. Before she let him pull her completely away from the vehicle, she grabbed a tennis ball, his favorite toy, and shoved it in her pocket. She might need it to get his attention, the way he was behaving.

But he'd raised his head, as if pulling something out of the air. She waited while he sniffed and then blew to clear his nose for a fresh sniff. Okay, maybe not a rabbit.

Then he lowered his head and began to pull her along the shoulder, weaving a bit as he went. The odor he pursued hadn't settled into a straight line, but neither had it behaved that oddly. An animal carrying something? But what? Or was he tracking a scent from something left beside the road?

If he hadn't been so determined, she might have called him back to her vehicle, but she'd learned to read Bugle well. He was onto something that to him was awfully important. Considering his training, what he believed to be important often turned out to be important to her.

She hadn't realized how long she had driven past the point where he started his frenzied barking. Nearly half a mile. With every step she grew more aware of the icy wind. She couldn't imagine what had gotten into the car, but something obviously had, and he was determined to get to it. With each few steps, he grew more focused. More intent. Her K-9 was on the hunt.

She pulled her snorkel hood closer around her face but didn't zip it into a narrow opening. As a cop she knew how important her range of vision was to her safety. Better to have a frozen nose than be blindsided.

Finally Bugle paused. He lifted his head again, turning it a little this way and that, then dived into the field beside the road. Not far. There wasn't even a turn-out here, just some sagging barbed wire. But when he dipped three feet into the runoff ditch beside the road, he stopped and sat. Then he looked at her and pawed at the ground.

She recognized the signals. He'd found his target. But what the hell was his target? Sudden worry made her heart accelerate as if she were running the last lap in the Kentucky Derby. She began to breathe more rapidly, which made her chest ache and her sinuses feel as if they were about to crack from the dryness.

Damn weather. Carefully she approached the spot Bugle sat facing. He reached out one paw, touching nothing, but seeming to point.

She saw a dark heap, small, unimportant. Until she got closer.

A glove. A man's glove. Nothing important. Something like that could have blown out the bed of any pickup truck.

It would have meant nothing at all except for her dog's intense interest in it. Target.

One of the missing girls? But none of them should have a glove like this. So if...

She didn't allow herself to complete the thought. She didn't dare hope, not anymore. Not after the last days. But hopeful or not, she had to treat it as evidence.

"Bugle, guard."

Now that he'd found the object of his fascination, she had absolutely no doubt he'd stay put. Not that she'd have had any doubt anyway. Bugle did his job with all the panache and dutifulness of the cop he was. Maybe better.

She trekked back to her vehicle and pulled out a

rubber glove and an evidence bag. The glove had been worn. There'd be DNA evidence inside it if the cold hadn't killed it. It might be important, or it might just be some kind of mistake. Heck, it could be a glove belonging to one of the girls' fathers. Bugle sure wouldn't miss that. Probably nothing, she told herself with each step as her nose grew colder. Probably nothing at all.

But she trusted Bugle's instincts and could not ignore them. She thought about driving back to pick up the dog and glove, then decided against it. She needed to scour the ground with her eyes to see if something else might be there. This was a very isolated part of the county, mostly grazing land, few houses, but someone could have come along this road and dropped something else. Or left a track, not that the ground was lately in any condition to take tracks.

She took the walk more slowly this time, forcing her attention to the shoulder right in front of her. It yielded nothing at all, and the rusting barbed wire appeared untouched. Somebody had some work to do, she thought. She didn't envy anyone who had to replace all that fencing.

Then she reached Bugle, who was still at attention but starting to shiver a bit. So much for a fur coat. As soon as she reached his side, she squatted, snapped on a rubber glove after removing her own insulated one and picked up the ratty old glove to insert in an evidence bag.

As soon as it was secure, she said to Bugle, "Search."

But he sniffed around a small area and seemed to find the exercise pointless. Okay, the glove was it.

Taking his leash in hand again, she joined him in a

quick jog back to the vehicle. He seemed glad to jump inside the warmth. For that matter, she was glad, too.

Dang, it was so cold. She wondered how the coyotes managed it, because she knew they were out on their rounds despite the weather. She received the occasional call to check out an injured animal. Personally, she thought self-respecting coyotes ought to join bears in hibernation.

Her fingers barely wanted to hold the marker as she scribbled the important information on the evidence bag: her name, the date and time, the location where the item had been found. Then she sealed it, and no one would be able to open it without leaving evidence of tampering.

So careful. She hoped like hell it would do some kind of good for the missing women.

Just a clue. She'd been repeating the words like a mantra at the back of her mind for days now. Just a clue. She hardly dared to believe this might be it.

THE REST OF the day was devoted to knocking on doors, drinking quick cups of coffee or tea as she talked to the ranchers, their families and their hired hands, if they had any. A pointless waste of hours, she thought as she pulled up to the last house on her list.

The road had taken her the long way around, but the ranch house itself wasn't that far from the outskirts of town. There just wasn't a direct road to it.

She had to knock twice, and her stiffening hands didn't appreciate it. She had grown so cold with all of this that her nerves burned when jarred. Just one more, then she could drive back in the heated comfort of her car and hunt up a hot drink and meal. Loads of coffee today hadn't done her much good. In fact, no good at all. She'd quit after a single sip because, while she didn't want to offend, she also didn't want to ask to use people's facilities. Her mouth felt as dry as cotton now.

Bugle had it easy, she thought wryly. Every time she let him leap out, he took care of business.

After her third knock, the door opened. A bleary-eyed man of about thirty-five stared back at her and shook his head a little.

"Sorry to bother you, sir, but you're Walt Revell, the current owner?"

"Uh, yeah." He looked at her again. "Is… What happened?"

"We've had three young women missing for nearly a week now and we're trying to find out if anyone might have seen something unusual that might help us out."

"Oh."

God, she thought, was this guy drunk or drugged? Or had he worked all night? Mussed hair, clothes that needed ironing… Well, according to records he lived alone. He probably wasn't good at looking after himself.

He shook his head. "Heard about that at the tavern. Damn shame. But I didn't see nothing."

She doubted he could see past the end of his nose. "Thanks for your time." She handed him her card. "If you notice anything that seems unusual or out of place, give us a call, please?"

"Uh, sure."

The door closed even before she finished turning away. Guy probably wanted to get back to sleep.

As she walked back to her vehicle, she saw that Bugle had his nose pressed to the glass. He was probably sick of being cooped up and wanted to be let out to play.

"In a bit," she said to him as she climbed back in and turned her truck around to head back out to the road. "Soon, Bugle."

He gave a low groan as if that answer didn't please him at all.

JANE AND CHANTAL hardly twitched a muscle. At some point, they had been drugged again, probably because it was impossible to go indefinitely without water. At least the wire bindings had been replaced with chain. Kinder to the flesh, maybe, but no less miserable or escapable.

They both realized that Mary Lou was gone for good. They just hoped she wasn't dead, although in the darkness and quiet they sometimes whispered about it. Neither of them any longer nurtured much hope that they would survive this. At their age, that was an especially difficult conclusion to reach.

They'd lived relatively sheltered lives in this out-of-the-way county where, yes, bad things happened, but not all the time. Living on a ranch, or living in town, they hadn't feared walking the streets in the evening or even felt it necessary to lock their doors. Companies that wired houses for security would go broke out here except for some of the businesses.

But that didn't mean they were totally insulated. The news got through, either in newspapers or on the evening television. They'd heard or read stories of what could happen to young women who were kidnapped by unscrupulous men. The questions floating around in their heads now were whether they were to be sex slaves or sacrifices. Both possibilities terrified them equally.

But they certainly didn't expect to be let go. That

left them only a need to fight to survive. No other motive existed any longer.

They huddled as close together as they could, giving in and sitting up to eat the food bars placed nearby, forced to drink water because their bodies demanded it. Sometimes the water knocked them out. Those were the merciful times.

It had gotten to the point where Jane told Chantal that she hoped one of those bottles would contain a lethal dose of whatever was putting them to sleep.

Chantal wanted to argue with her, but her arguments were growing wearier and weaker. To fall into sleep and never awake again was beginning to appeal to her, too, though she refused to admit it to Jane.

So cold. Under the ratty blanket, pressed close to each other, they still grew miserably chilled. Unfortunately, not chilled enough to never wake up. They ached from confinement, from cold, from the hard floor. They hated the smelly blanket that did little enough of what a blanket was supposed to do.

They pressed icy bare feet together, rubbing them to stimulate circulation. They switched sides trying to warm one half and then the other.

Survival drove them, but they couldn't even explain why. Giving up would have been so much easier.

Nobody would ever find them, Chantal thought. Ever. But even as she grew more dazed with time, she squashed that thought every time it occurred.

"You know this county," she said to Jane, her voice little more than a cracked whisper from a sore throat.

"Yeah. If we're in Conard County." Jane didn't sound much better.

"It doesn't matter. People around here won't stop looking for us. They won't. You know that."

"Then why aren't they here already?"

Chantal had no answer for that. Instead she said, "They'll come. They must be looking over every inch."

"So? We're buried in a basement."

Chantal couldn't argue with that, so she fell silent. But then Jane said, "You're right. They'll even look in basements."

To that they clung as much as they could.

"Just eat another food bar," Chantal said. "If the bastard shows up when I'm awake, I don't want to be too weak to give him a hard time."

So they choked down the dry bars and risked a few sips of water.

Keeping up some strength seemed to be all they had left.

NOT TOO MANY miles away, Al Carstairs had resumed his usual duties in animal control. Mostly. Like everyone else, he was knocking on doors asking if anyone had noticed anything unusual. Like everyone else he was getting a lot of negative shakes of the head.

How could this guy have been so invisible? How was it nobody noticed something odd about a guy pulling three girls out of a car and putting them in his? God, they must have been drugged, and as such Raggedy Ann would have seemed more like a human body.

But nobody had noticed?

Well, it was New Year's night, and he guessed a lot of people were either at home nursing hangovers, or sitting in the bars, roadhouses and taverns that dotted this county, enjoying the hair of the dog that bit them.

Rusty had said more than once that his tavern had been hopping.

The girls had left early, too. With the next morning being Sunday, most people who went out to enjoy themselves probably hadn't called it an early evening. So it was entirely possible that not one soul had driven by during the time when the car went off the road, and the abductor moved them to his vehicle.

What if someone had stopped? The guy could have said, "My sister and her friends had too much to drink. I need to get them home."

And if the person who had stopped wasn't from these parts, why would the individual mention it to anyone? Why even question it?

Kelly had apparently been the first person to come upon the car once the girls were gone. No one else had reported a car off the road. A dead silence seemed to have filled the county that night.

He cussed, which didn't please the stray black Lab he'd picked up. Molly, her name was, and while she had a loving home now, there was no question she hadn't always enjoyed one. She was the only dog he'd ever known that would cower at a cuss word, even one in passing conversation.

He'd have loved to find out who her first owners had been so he could give them a piece of his mind. But she'd been dumped at Mike Windwalker's clinic by a guy who said he'd found her beside the highway. And the guy didn't even live in these parts.

No help. Not that it mattered now. Molly had a good home; she just liked to run. Usually she'd run for a couple of hours and then show up at her family's door. This time she'd stayed out longer than usual and Al had been advised the family couldn't find her.

Well, she'd wandered farther than usual. Much.

Then there was a raccoon back there who'd gotten herself tangled in some barbed wire while attempting to heist the contents of a trash can. She needed to see the vet as well as get a dose of rabies vaccine. Mike would probably keep the animal for a while to make sure it wasn't already sick. Unfortunately, even though it was the wrong time of year, she appeared to be pregnant.

But while he was usually very focused on the animals he looked after, it was different now. Now all he could think about was the missing girls. Acid chewed at his stomach lining, his mouth tasted sour and a beer sounded too good to a guy who'd been dry for five years now.

Not that alcohol had ever taken over, but he'd become nervously aware a year or so after he left the service that it could easily become a favored crutch. That he *could* become addicted. So he'd quit on his own. Not another drop. It hadn't been that hard because he'd taken charge of it before it took charge of him.

But right now he seriously wanted a beer.

Those girls. Those poor girls. And Kelly. He knew she was out there continuing the pursuit but doubted she was having any better luck. He kept remembering that nightmare or premonition she'd had that one of them had died.

He couldn't dismiss it, much as he'd have liked to, and now all he wanted was to discharge these animals and find her, to see how she was holding up. Because this whole situation was not only horrifying, it was weird.

It was as if something supernatural had swept them away.

He dropped Molly at home with her family. The Clancy kids were thrilled to have her back. Molly had apparently tired herself out, because she collapsed at their feet and grinned.

Mike Windwalker took the raccoon, handling her with long leather gloves to avoid a bite, and agreed she needed rabies vaccine.

"Pregnant, huh?" Mike said as he looked her over before popping the angry animal into a cage. "Somebody mess up her clock?"

"I haven't a foggy. I take them the way I find them."

Mike laughed. "Yeah, me, too."

As he drove away into the fading light of early winter night, Al wondered where he could find Kelly. Then he remembered his damn radio. Duh.

"Actually," she answered, "I was just about to hit the truck stop for one of Hasty's burgers. You interested?"

"Save me a seat."

Maude made a good burger, but Hasty fire-grilled them. A whole different level.

For the first time that day, things seemed to be looking up a bit. A burger and fries. He smiled wryly knowing his doc wouldn't like it, but since he was fit as a fiddle except for certain lingering effects of a wound, he refused to worry about it. If a single burger had ever killed anyone, he'd never heard about it.

But riding his shoulder like a shadow was concern for those three girls. He hated to imagine what their families must be going through. Not knowing was bad enough from his end.

Hasty's truck stop was full of grumbling beasts as

usual. Inside the café, truckers were scattered around, most of them eating heartily and drinking lots of coffee. They were allowed now to drive only eleven hours a day, and most trucks had trackers on them. For reasons of speed and ease of driving, that meant most of these guys slept in their cabs by day and drove all night. Unless the weather was bad, in which case they reversed, wanting all the clarity of sight they could get.

Tonight was looking to be a long night before breakfast came.

Kelly was already there, at a table near a window. He liked that. He never felt quite comfortable without an open view. He knew it was a leftover from war, but knowing it didn't make it go away.

He slid into the booth facing her and smiled. "Want a pregnant momma raccoon who got herself tangled in some barbed wire? She was dumpster diving."

Kelly blinked, as if she needed to change her location in the world. "Really? Pregnant?"

"Seems way early in the season. I left her with Mike Windwalker. First on the list, treatment for rabies and antiseptic for scratches. Anyway, how'd your day go?"

"It went nowhere," she said frankly. "I must have stopped at twenty or so houses. Nobody saw anything that aroused their interest. At least not yet. I'm hoping that maybe someone has a memory jog and calls. There was one interesting thing, however."

The waitress came over and took their orders. Lots of coffee, two burgers for him, one for her, and a heap of fries. It was the cold. He always ate more. So, he guessed, did she. "So what was interesting?"

"Bugle. We were a little over five miles out on a ranch road when he started to go bonkers."

Al arched a brow. "Is that like him?"

"Absolutely not. He wanted my attention and he wasn't going to let me ignore him. He howled and barked until I thought I'd go deaf. So I pulled over and let him hunt whatever scent had caught his attention. About a half mile back down the road he found a glove. A ratty man's work glove, and he wouldn't budge. I gave it to the sheriff before I came here."

"That's strange," he said, thinking it over. He knew a lot about dogs. The idea that Bugle might have caught the scent of one of the missing girls didn't escape him. He leaned back to let their dinners be served, then leaned in again, keeping his voice low. "They're going to test it?"

"Damn straight. I don't know if it'll tell us anything at all, but it's worth a try."

"Definitely." He lifted his burger, his mouth already watering. "You know how amazing dogs are, Kelly. You don't need me to tell you that if he caught a whiff of one of those girls he'd recognize it even after all this time."

"I know," she said quietly, almost sadly. "I don't know whether to be hopeful or not. I mean, it was in the middle of nowhere. It could have blown off the back end of a pickup truck, and there's no way to know where it would have been headed. So…"

"You're afraid it might be false hope."

"Yeah." She stared down at her burger, then picked it up with obvious reluctance. "I guess it's better than nothing. What if we can identify the DNA? Some guy with a record. That'd be a fantastic clue."

"But you're afraid it won't be."

She raised her gaze. "I somehow think I don't need to tell you about the tightrope between hope and despair."

"No," he admitted. "Come on, eat. Your eyes are so sunken right now they might fall out of the back of your head."

That at least brought a smile to her face.

"Bugle out in your truck?"

"Yeah." She motioned toward the window. "See him?"

He did. The SUV was obviously running to judge by the steam coming off the hood as a gentle swirl of snowflakes fell.

"I'm going to get him a couple of burgers, too," she remarked. "Please don't go sanctimonious on me about a proper diet for him."

At that she drew a laugh from him. "I'm sitting here eating two burgers myself. I'm going to get sanctimonious?"

Her smile widened. "He likes a few fries, too."

"Then let's save him some. I'm betting he's salivating out there, smelling everything that's cooking in here."

At that she finally laughed. "The aromas that pour out all the vents and ducts in this place call to human stomachs and noses for miles. Why should he be different?"

The rest of the meal passed amiably, and apparently the waitress knew the drill when it came to Bugle, because along with their separate checks came a couple of cardboard containers holding burgers and even a few fries.

"No ketchup," said the waitress. "I know he loves it, but you'll never convince me it's good for his stomach."

"I don't want to find out," Kelly agreed as she put a twenty on the table. Plus another five she tucked in the waitress's apron. "You didn't see that happen."

Al laughed and followed suit. They were halfway out the door when his radio began to squawk.

"Carstairs," he answered as they descended the steps into the parking lot. Bugle, in the wise way of all canines, was already standing at the window, his tail wagging like a flag in gale-force winds. He knew a treat was on the way.

Al listened, standing still, while Kelly opened the back door of her truck and put the burgers and fries in for Bugle. The cardboard went into the nearby trash can while the paper wrappers remained with the dog. He knew to lick them, not to eat them.

"I'll be right there," Al said. His voice had lost all cheer. He signed off and shoved the phone onto its belt holster.

"What's going on?" Kelly asked him, disturbed by his change in tone.

"A neighborhood problem dog just burrowed under a fence and menaced a four-year-old girl. Gotta go."

"Can I follow?"

"Sure, I might need you to help me legally confiscate the animal. Bugle could be a help, too."

"Where are we heading?"

"Downy Lane. Four-oh-nine."

Kelly radioed dispatch as she followed Al's van down the road. Velma, on duty again, cracked a laugh. "I heard the call. Bet Al needs you and Bugle more than himself."

"Now, Velma…"

Velma laughed again. "He's good with animals. This one is not a good animal. There's a difference. Only reason that dog ain't gone is pure neighborliness."

The listed address wasn't that far away from the

truck stop, maybe eight blocks on the far side of the railroad tracks that rarely saw any traffic these days.

It was a shame, Kelly often thought, that railroads had been replaced by trucks. However, given the mountains around here, maybe the trains couldn't be loaded as heavily as the trucks without becoming unsafe. What did she know?

The house in question was old but well cared for, a late-nineteenth-century structure built in the old "shotgun" style. With a narrow lot, every room added on had been added to the rear. The term came from the saying that you could walk in the front door and hit everybody in the house with one blast of a shotgun.

She was glad times had changed in that respect.

She pulled up against the shoulder—no curbs in this part of town—and waited while Al approached the house. Bugle had wolfed down his treats and was now noisily licking his chops.

The front door opened and a man's silhouette appeared. He was clearly upset and waving his arms. Instinctively, Kelly climbed out, leashed Bugle and approached, standing far enough back that she wouldn't seem like a threat.

"—don't know," the guy was saying, his voice raised. "Do I have to put bars and special locks on every door and window to make my daughter safe? She's *four*! I thought she was in bed. It's basically early, though, and I guess she got tired of watching TV or saw the snowflakes… I dunno. But she went out in her own backyard—a fenced backyard I might add—and suddenly I heard her shrieking and that beast from next door growling and damn, I never came so close to shooting an animal in my life!"

"Was the dog on your property?"

"You better believe it. Not two feet from her, crouched with his teeth bared. I've had it. That damn dog has threatened people before. Especially her. This isn't the first time I've called you, if you remember. It's time to listen."

Al nodded. "I'm sorry, Mr. Jakes. I think we're past issuing warnings now. Is the dog still out back?"

"I don't know. Fences won't hold him. He could be anywhere by now. But just tell me, Al, who the devil buys a dog to keep it outside all the time? I don't think that hellhound has been indoors once since they got him. Doesn't matter. What *does* matter is that my child ought to be able to play safely in her own backyard!"

To a point, Kelly thought as she listened. There were snakes, raccoons, foxes…but she let the thought go. She could understand Mr. Jakes's fury. Whether the dog would attack the child was irrelevant. What mattered was that no child should have to be threatened in his or her own backyard by a dog that should be properly confined.

"I agree," Al replied, keeping his voice calm. "Is your daughter safely inside now? No one else outside?"

"We're all inside, feeling like prisoners in our own house. Something has to be done about that animal or its owners. At this point I don't care which."

"All right. You all wait inside while we hunt for Cujo. That's his name, right?"

"Like some kind of prediction. Yeah. You got help? Because you're going to need it."

"Deputy Noveno and her K-9 will be helping. If we need more help, I can get it. Just relax indoors while we take care of this."

Still grumbling, Jakes went back inside, slamming the door for emphasis. Kelly really couldn't blame him. Apparently this Cujo had been a problem before.

Al came around to the back of his van and Kelly moved in close with Bugle. "Okay," Al said, opening one of the doors. "Time for long leather gloves. I'm going to give you a muzzle to carry in case we need it." Then he turned and faced her, and he didn't look at all happy. "While I don't advocate it, shoot if you think it's necessary."

Kelly looked down at Bugle. "I think a certain set of teeth will work better."

"I hope so. But I don't want Bugle to get messed up either. I don't know what this dog is capable of. Not yet. I know we've had complaints that he's killed pet rabbits and a couple of cats, but there was no proof to pin it on Cujo. So the owners have been slapped with warnings and some fines for not keeping him properly leashed. Here we go again."

They started by walking through a latched gate into the backyard of the Jakeses' house. It was obvious where the dog had dug his way under a wooden privacy fence.

"I wish the neighbors would put in some wire fencing about two feet down," Al remarked. "Most dogs won't dig that deep."

"What breed are we talking about here?"

"Rottie. Usually good dogs, but there are some…"

"There are always some," she agreed as they walked around the side of the house. She didn't know if it was lack of training or poor treatment. Or, if like some people, some dogs just weren't nice pets. They probably had all kinds of personalities.

The backyard proved to be a nice size for such a narrow lot. A metal swing set stood to one side, and what appeared to be a covered sandbox filled a corner. Large and small plastic balls were scattered about, along with a ragged stuffed doll. Al bent for the doll. "I guess Cujo had him some fun after all." He passed the doll to Kelly, who looked it over. The head had unmistakable teeth marks on it.

Bugle sniffed it and gave one quiet woof. He knew. Kelly just hoped the miscreant dog hadn't torn it from the little girl's hands. That would have utterly terrified her.

Al scanned the backyard, then walked up to the house and grabbed a shovel. He jammed it into the hole under the fence in such a way as to make it difficult for the dog to crawl under.

"Next door, now."

Kelly scanned one more time, looking and watching Bugle, but Bugle didn't seem to be much interested in the backyard after one sniff at the torn doll and a pass by the hole under the fence. Instead, he seemed more interested in pulling her back the way they'd come.

He'd be the best one to have a good idea of where Cujo was hanging out.

"You want Bugle to lead the way?" she asked Al as they passed through the gate in the other direction.

He eyed her over his shoulder. "Like I haven't done this before."

She flushed, grateful the darkness hid it. "I only meant he'll be able to smell the other dog."

"It hasn't rained shampoo recently," Al said wryly. "We'll *all* be able to smell Cujo."

He had a point there. Dogs weren't exactly odorless, even when dry.

The house next door was nearly a carbon copy of the Jakes place. Lights gleamed from the window, so someone should be there. Once again, Kelly stood back near the sidewalk. She knew that her presence might cause trouble if whoever answered the door felt belligerent. Best to let Al handle it. He knew these people.

Belligerence was definitely waiting for him. Before Al could say a word, the man who answered was on a tear.

"Bet that damn sissy Jakes called you. Look, a dog's a dog, and they do things like dig under fences. They get out and run. I don't give a damn. That man has been after Cujo since he was a pup! He just wants me to get rid of him!"

Kelly felt Bugle growing tense beside her, ready to spring into action if need be. She made no effort to calm him down. The way that guy was gesticulating, things could get ugly at the drop of a hat.

"Mr. Hays…"

But Hays didn't wait for Al to speak another word. "My dog ain't doing a damn thing but being a dog. Like anyone else's dog. If that sissy next door didn't have a bunch of cats, he'd understand better. He needs some schooling and I might just give it to him."

"Mr. Hays, are you threatening…"

"I ain't threatening nobody. I just want him to leave my damn dog alone."

At that moment the ill-famed Cujo decided to come running around the corner of the house. He didn't go sit placidly beside his master. No, he bared his teeth and growled at Al. Worse, his hackles were raised. That dog was ready to fight.

Kelly tensed but didn't want to intervene unnecessarily. This was Al's job and he probably knew a whole lot more about how to handle this.

"Call your dog off, Hays," Al said. His voice held the sharp edge of command, a voice that said he was used to being obeyed.

"Why? He ain't hurtin' you and *you're* the one trespassing. I'd be within my rights to sic him on you."

Not exactly, Kelly thought, but bit her lip. *Stay out of it.*

"Mr. Hays," Al said, his voice suddenly as cold and hard as steel, "either control your dog and get him to settle or I'll deem him dangerous and put him out of everyone's misery. Are you hearing me?"

Al, still wearing the elbow-length leather gloves he'd put on, reached to his hip and for the first time Kelly noted he was carrying a collapsible baton on his belt. He pulled it off. That baton could put human or dog out of commission without killing either. With a pointed snap, Al extended it.

Bugle sidled forward, as if he wanted to take action, but the gentlest tug on his leash caused him to settle quietly beside Kelly.

Something must have gotten through to Hays, because he snapped, "Cujo! Here!"

The dog, still snarling, obeyed, standing beside his master, facing Al.

"Leash him," Al said in the same steely voice.

Cussing a blue streak, Hays obeyed. Kelly was grateful to see that Cujo's leash was a chain. She figured he could chew his way through leather in no time at all.

"Now," said Al, "we're going to talk. Unless you want me to take Cujo tonight."

Some kind of sullen mumble emerged from Hays.

"You have been repeatedly warned about failing to keep your dog under control. He is to be leashed any time he's outside your front door unless confined by a fence. Your fence out back isn't doing a damn bit of good to judge by the way he tunnels into the Jakeses' yard."

"He's just a dang dog…"

"A dang dog with a mouthful of teeth and a bite powerful enough to break bone. And the Jakes have a four-year-old daughter who has as much right to play safely in her backyard as Cujo has to be in his…as long as he stays in his own yard. Is that clear?"

"They oughta watch her…"

"And you ought to watch your dog. Quit arguing or I'll get really angry. I'm only halfway there."

For halfway to angry, Kelly thought Al seemed remarkably calm. Although his voice still sounded like honed steel.

"Now, listen carefully because I'm through repeating myself. Cujo crawled under the fence and menaced a little girl…"

"He don't menace nobody!"

"He was just menacing *me* and I'm not four. What's more I've got Deputy Noveno as a witness. Clear?"

Finally Hays stopped arguing and just nodded.

"If Cujo had so much as scratched that little girl, I'd be taking him to have him put down right now. This is not a joke. Are you hearing me?"

Hays nodded glumly.

"Unfortunately," Al continued, "a lot of people want

rotties because they're tough and dangerous. But the most dangerous dog is one that's thoroughly trained. You hear me? Ask the K-9 officer there if you don't believe me. Regardless, I'll give you two choices. The first is give the dog up to me tonight. The second is, tomorrow morning take him to Cadel Marcus to be trained. If Cadel can train him, you'll have a dog that won't give you any heartburn but will still protect your family. But if you can't do that..."

Finally Hays spoke. "Heard that Marcus guy is good."

"The best. But Cujo needs to be trained, not running wild. And I don't just mean that he sits and stays. There's a lot more to a well-trained dog than that. So those are your choices. In the meantime, you get a citation for animal at large, and you owe the little Jakes girl a new doll."

Hays cussed again, but didn't argue.

Al pulled his summons book from his jacket pocket, tugged off one leather glove, which he tucked under his arm, and began writing. "Okay," he said as he ripped the summons off the pad and handed it to Hays. "You know the drill. Pay the fine by the date listed and you don't have to go to court. But I'll give you one more warning."

"Yeah?"

"Yeah. If Cadel tells me you haven't left Cujo for him to train by ten tomorrow morning, I'll take the dog. No more chances, Mr. Hays. Not one. The life of a four-year-old girl is still worth more than a rottweiler. Clear?"

A couple of minutes later, as they were about to get into their vehicles to leave, Al came to stand beside

Kelly. "I hate to put a dog down," he muttered. "I hope that jackass pays attention this time."

Kelly understood. "I wouldn't want to either, but that little girl…"

"Exactly. Listen, if you don't have other plans, want to come to my place? I know it's a ways out."

She smiled, her heart lifting a bit. How did he do that to her? "My place if you'll be comfortable. I've got an early call."

"Your place it is. Want me to grab some coffee from Maude's on my way over?"

"That would be super."

Chapter Eight

Day 17

Chantal and Jane had passed the point of caring much anymore. The cold was gripping them constantly, and their bodies demanded that they eat. They gobbled down food bars without a thought for what might be in them, and when a big package of sandwich cookies showed up, those disappeared in record time.

They'd even stopped worrying about what was in the water bottles. Survival had come down to instincts they could no longer ignore. With chains holding them, they huddled close and were even grateful when a second blanket appeared with the food while they were sleeping. Sleeping or knocked out. They didn't know.

They felt they were being watched sometimes, but were past caring about that, too. They struggled to get the second blanket wrapped around them with the first. It, too, stank, but it smelled like an unwashed body.

"He never met a washing machine he liked," Chantal said, a weak attempt at humor. She couldn't see Jane at all, but heard what sounded like the breath of a laugh.

They'd stopped asking why. They couldn't imagine why they were captive, and they'd given up hope that Mary Lou wasn't already dead.

Chantal, though she'd never said so to Jane, remembered that moment when she'd felt as if Mary Lou had said goodbye. If she was dead, at least she was out of this. Safe. Free of the cold and the terror.

The food warmed them temporarily, as did the extra blanket, and this time when she started to fall asleep, Chantal thought it was natural sleep.

At least she hoped it was.

WALT REVELL, Reve to his friends, came back from a pool game and a few beers at Rusty's Tavern and pulled off the road. It was dark, the moon dropping behind the Western mountains, but there was still enough light to see by. Grabbing a backpack out of the rear of his truck, he began the trek to the collapsing cabin where he was keeping his girls.

Day by day he could see he was winning them over. They talked less, they ate without trying to avoid the food or water. They'd become his creatures, without will of their own.

Not much longer now. He just had to decide which one seemed most ready to behave herself. He wasn't going to ask much, after all. Some cooking, some cleaning, a little sack time... Not much at all in exchange for continuing to live.

Oh, yeah. No talking. He'd hit 'em into next week if they gave him any lip.

He counseled himself to patience. He'd been too quick with the first one, thinking terror alone would control her. It had been a waste, but he still had two left. He just had to wait until they forgot how to hope.

And from what he could see, hope was beginning to desert them.

When he was sure the drug in the water had done its work, he unlocked the metal door and descended the steps into the basement. He dropped more food and water beside them, a roll of paper towels to let them know that if they behaved they might get more comforts from him.

He hesitated over the cookies, then decided it was too soon to give them yet another reward. Let them eat the dry food bars and drink the water.

When he kicked them lightly with his foot, they barely stirred. Just a few more days. Not much longer.

Already the cops were near to giving up. The female deputy who'd shown up at his door hadn't been especially inquisitive. He could feel her dismissing him mentally. He was a nobody. She probably thought he was stupid.

Good thing she'd left her dog in the car, though. He was scared of what a dog might smell.

Terrified if he were to be honest. Maybe it was time to suffer through another shower and throw some of his clothes in the rickety machine.

Smells could give him away. He didn't want to risk that, not when he was so close to achieving all he wanted.

Over two weeks had passed since the girls had gone missing. A feeling of despair was beginning to settle throughout the entire department. Kelly felt it when she went into the office nearly every day. The girls, they had begun to believe, had been taken far away from here. How else could there be no trace of them or their abductor?

Kelly supposed that at this point they'd give anything for a ransom note, but it was getting too late for that. Way too late. For all anyone knew, the girls were already being moved underground by some trafficking outfit, long since out of the county and maybe out of the country.

Kelly couldn't bear to think of it. Nobody wanted to say it out loud, but she was sure they all feared the same thing. The girls' families were at the end of their rope. The FBI agents who had promised to show up were acting on the idea that the women were no longer in the county and thus they were operating out of Denver.

They might be right, but it scalded everyone in the Conard Country Sheriff's Department to feel that the FBI considered them to be too useless to even talk to.

Each day as each shift set out, every single deputy was determined to find something that would help locate the girls. Despairing or not, they certainly hadn't given up. They all feared that some pervert had them in his clutches and was treating them like slaves and whores.

When they could, the helicopters took to the air for an overflight, but had found nothing. Everything out there on the open expanses of wintry range looked as it always had.

And they still didn't have the DNA analysis back from the glove yet but were expecting it hourly. If it would answer any questions, no one knew.

Kelly started visiting Rusty's Tavern on the weekends. Al joined her. A beer, a chance to watch everyone without being obvious. Bugle resented being left at home, but Kelly didn't want to take her departmental SUV. It would be like walking in in full uniform, and her personal vehicle didn't have accommodations for leaving Bugle for long periods. All she wanted to do was watch, anyway.

As if, as Kelly had told Al at one point, the kidnapper was going to be wearing a sign around his neck.

Leaving no stone unturned had begun to take on a new meaning. Martha knew why they came. She didn't mention it, but she once said in passing, "I'm paying attention."

Kelly believed her. If one person did anything suspicious, they'd be facing Martha, who looked perfectly capable of breaking a beer bottle and using it as a weapon.

Rusty greeted them with a nod, as if to say he was keeping an eye out, as well.

After two weekends, Kelly and Al were both beginning to recognize the regulars. Some of them Kelly had questioned in the days immediately following the abductions, like that Revell guy. Watching him play pool, she wondered if he'd ever learned to color inside the lines.

A silly, useless thought, but a couple of other guys at the bar seemed to like to play with him and bet him a dollar at a time. Nobody was going broke or getting wealthy.

Al talked her into line dancing the second night they were there. All of a sudden her body felt awkward, as if parts wouldn't move right.

"Just relax," he said. "Nobody's watching, everybody's too busy watching their friends."

He was probably right, but she'd never felt comfortable dancing. He slipped his arm around her waist, showed her the simple steps and murmured in her ear, "Treat this as undercover work, a chance to watch people."

Well, that darn near worked like magic. Forgetting about what she was doing, she stumbled only once and Al steadied her. But he was right about watching people. Standing in line with other dancers, facing yet another line, sometimes wheeling around the floor, gave her an excellent chance to take in faces without being obvious about it.

Not that a face was going to tell her anything, but she could hope.

"This is a waste of our time," she said as they returned to their table, the bowl of nuts and two sweaty beer bottles.

"Maybe so. You're the cop. But we're reasonably certain our guy had to find our gals here. Whatever he did, he might try it again." He gestured with this bottle. "See that table over there in the far corner? Take a peek but don't zero in."

She took a quick look and felt her heart slam. Seriously? Two teen girls were sitting over there? They hadn't heard what had happened?

"Indestructible," Al remarked. "At that age, they all believe it."

Won't happen to me. Kelly could almost hear herself saying that from her high school days.

"Anyway," he continued, "unless you have an objection, I figure we'll stay until they leave and maybe follow them at a reasonable distance."

"That's a great idea." She was embarrassed not to have thought of it herself. But then, she'd failed to be observant. That was part of her job. Al had picked up on those girls.

"I must be getting too tired," she remarked. "I should have noticed them."

"Maybe so, but I had a lot of years where I couldn't afford to overlook so much as a misplaced pebble."

That snapped her thoughts to him. "You never talk about it."

"Most of us don't. Nothing like war stories to ruin a mood, ruin friendships or convince folks we're totally crazy."

"I don't think there's any way I could believe you're crazy."

"You haven't seen some of my finer moments." He turned the beer bottle in his hands, and she noticed not for the first time that he seldom drank any of it. He held it like a prop.

"War takes a toll on everyone," he said presently. His voice was pitched so as not to travel. "Some guys come home and put on a veneer that fools everyone. They're okay. Or so everyone thinks, and that makes it easy on the people who care about them. Some can't do that. They need help dealing with what they saw and did. Me, I was somewhere in the middle for a while. Now I'm on the smooth veneer side."

"But is that good for you?"

He shrugged. "Whatever works. I consider myself lucky that I don't have to wallow."

"I doubt I'd think of it as wallowing."

He smiled faintly. "I didn't use that word seriously. I just mean I'm lucky that I don't have to dwell on it all the time. Animals are my medicine. I love the critters."

"Even rotties? By the way, did that dog ever get to Cadel?"

"Cujo is in boot camp right now. And I made sure Cadel knows the situation. Cujo isn't going to get an easy graduation because he doesn't have an easy owner."

That was one way of thinking about it, Kelly decided. The dog was probably going to be more responsible than his owner. That could create an interesting set of problems.

When she thought about Bugle, however, she had some idea of a dog's capabilities absent someone to tell it what to do. "Did I ever tell you about the time that I caught one suspect and Bugle chased down the other?"

"What?" The word came out on a laugh.

"Yup. Pulled a car over. I was getting the data on the registration when the driver climbed out, hands up. So Bugle and I both exited our vehicle. Then for some unknown and unexpected reason, the passenger jumped out and took to his heels. So there I was with the driver at gunpoint and my dog haring off into the woods after the passenger."

Al laughed. "I can just see it."

"Wasn't much to see except his hindquarters and tail. Well, I knew the driver was under the influence but with a backseat full of Bugle's cage, there was no place to put him. Certainly not in the front seat of my vehicle."

"God, no!"

"So I handcuffed the guy and made him run with me as we chased Bugle. Not a happy suspect, I can tell you."

"I imagine not."

"Got lots of body cam footage of him complaining he was tired and could we please take a break. Me, I was worried about getting to Bugle before the other guy could hurt him. For all I knew he had a gun or a knife. Anyway, by the time I'd followed Bugle's bark, and caught up, Bugle had the other guy on his knees with his hands over his head. Never laid a tooth on him."

Now Al was really laughing. "I wish I could have seen that!"

"It *was* quite some scene. And not exactly what I expected. Bugle undertook to make an arrest on his own initiative. Very cool."

"Was it a good arrest?"

"Absolutely. The guy he chased couldn't quite ditch all the cocaine in his pockets before I got there. And there was more in the car. I'm glad to say backup wasn't far behind because at that point we might have been stuck there for a little while, two suspects and no place to put them."

Al smiled. "I love stories like that about animals."

"So you're really crazy about them?"

"Let's just say I think the world would be a better place if we took a few lessons from dogs and cats. They pretty much live in the moment, their spats are never designed to harm one another in any serious way. Think of wolves."

"Wolves?"

"Yeah. They create family groups and take care of each other. Yes, there's a hierarchy, and the omega may have to eat last, but she *will* get enough to eat. And her job is to be the family clown, basically. The social grease that prevents things from growing tense. And as near as anyone can tell, they don't bear grudges."

"We could all do with a few less grudges."

"The girls over there are getting ready to leave,"

he remarked. Before she could move, he threw some money on the table, then sat back and watched.

Finally he said, "They're out the door. Nobody seems to be watching or paying attention."

"Okay." She rose and he followed suit. Together they eased through the crowd. Kelly bumped into a guy she didn't know. Right behind him was a man that she seemed to recall interviewing. Revell, that was it. This time he looked a little neater and a bit drunk.

"Deputy Kelly," the first guy said heartily. "Going so early?"

"Cut it out," said Revell, looking nervous as if he expected trouble. "Jeez, Spence, not every woman on the planet wants you to take a pass."

Al slipped his arm through hers, his face smiling but a tightness around his eyes. His entire posture seemed to turn into a warning or a threat as he eased her toward the door once again.

It struck her, as they eased their way out toward the door, that their cover was useless. Spence or whatever his name was had made her as law enforcement. So sitting in this damn tavern was probably a waste of time. Hell. Sure, they were trying to make it look like they were dating, but how many believed that?

"Hey," Spence called after them, "you ever find them girls yet?"

At that instant the bar grew immediately silent. Even the live music from the small stage trickled away.

Kelly felt herself stiffening, wanting to turn around and give the idiot a piece of her mind. Those missing girls were no joking matter. Not even for a drunken jerk. Still, she refused to yield to her baser impulse.

"Pretty damn bad," said Spence, "when the law

can't find three girls. Bet they're right under your noses somewhere."

"Let it go," Al said quietly.

Oh, she didn't want to let it go. The anger that had been growing in her in response to weeks of worry wanted to erupt into vesuvian proportions, to flatten the guy's face just for the pleasure of wiping that smirk away.

But Al kept her moving toward the door. "We've got some girls to watch," he murmured.

"Dammit, Spence," she heard Revell say from behind. His tone still sounded a little nervous, but few people wanted to argue with the law. "You tryin' to get yourself in trouble? You're still on probation, remember?"

"So announce it to the world," Spence said angrily. "Just pointing out that cops shouldn't be out havin' a good time when them girls is missing. Get off my case, Reve."

Kelly focused on the door and the girls they were going to keep an eye on. They mattered, not some drunken blowhard who couldn't resist poking at a cop. Almost as if on cue, the band on the stage burst into a rowdy rendition of "Friends in Low Places," singing it about as well as anyone could except the original artist. Which meant poorly.

She drew a steadying breath of icy air as they left the stale beer and noise behind them. Without a word, Al hustled her into her car in the passenger seat. When he held out his hand, she gave him the keys. He hadn't been drinking and frankly, given her response to the idiot back inside, she wasn't at all sure how much she'd put away. Two bottles? She usually had her temper on a tighter tether.

Al wheeled the car around and started down the state highway, following the only visible taillights, the ones that must belong to the young women who'd just left the bar. At least no one else had tried to follow them. Not yet, anyway.

"That Spence guy was right."

"No, he wasn't. He thinks we were there having fun. Far from it, and you don't need me to remind you of that."

"No," she admitted. "But we still should have found *something* about those girls by now."

"This situation stinks," Al announced.

"No kidding."

"You're certainly tied up in knots. I'm getting there."

She twisted in her seat to better see him in the light from the dashboard. "It's not like I can forget those girls. I'm positive my imagination has been doing its worst."

"It has for all of us." He surprised her and reached out, covering one of her hands with his.

She watched the taillights ahead of them, then squeezed her eyes shut briefly. "You know, I've been a cop for nearly ten years now. I'm good at separating the job from the personal. Usually. This time I can't do it, Al! Those girls are haunting my every waking moment. Yeah, I'm still doing my job, but I'd like to be a whole lot busier. Instead I spend a lot of time driving back roads hoping for a glimpse of something useful. Anything. And I keep praying the girls are alive and all right."

For long minutes he didn't speak. The car ahead of them reached the edge of town, turned down a street, then pulled into a driveway. Clearly these young women were getting home safely tonight.

"Job accomplished," he remarked before turning onto another street and heading for her place. "What's getting you wound up," he continued, squeezing her hand, "is that it's been so long and the outcome is not at all promising. You didn't need me to say that, did you?"

No, she hadn't needed to hear it. She felt it in her bones. Since the night she'd wakened from a dead sleep to sense that one of the girls had died, she hadn't been able to believe this would end in any way other than tragically.

"I guess I'm begging for closure," she said after a pause.

"We all are. I can't imagine the hell those parents are living. Our share of it is nothing by comparison."

At that she felt embarrassed. "I'm being selfish."

"I didn't say that. I'd be worried about you if you didn't care this much. We aren't robots, Kelly. We do what we do because we give a damn, you know? There'd be something wrong with you otherwise."

She remembered her dad speaking about a case that had tormented him for years. "Maybe you're right. My dad had some cases that haunted him."

"Let's just hope this one doesn't have to haunt us. There *is* still hope."

But not much, she thought grimly. "The glove didn't tell us much." Their one clue. Basically useless.

"Well, we know it touched one of the girls. Bugle was right about that. But whoever wore it…"

Whoever had worn it wasn't in the database anywhere. So no criminal history, at least not since law enforcement had started to keep such records. "Useless," she said aloud.

"Not if we find the guy. The DNA can tie him to the girls, right?"

"To one of them, at least. Yeah, that could be useful." But only if they found the perp.

She sighed, thinking this was very unlike her. Hope was usually the last thing she tossed overboard when the seas grew choppy. Yet here she was, arguing with every possible strand of hope Al tossed her way.

"I need an attitude adjustment," she said. "Some separation and a tighter focus on solving the crime."

He didn't argue. He turned into her driveway and switched off the engine. "Shall I stay or go?" he asked.

"Stay. Please. Talk me down."

He gave a mirthless laugh. "Maybe you can talk me down, too."

Once again she felt embarrassed. She'd been so busy thinking about how she felt that she hadn't given enough thought to how he must be feeling, as well. The idea that men didn't feel anything...well, her own dad had raised her to realize otherwise. No stoic stiff upper lip for Hector Noveno. He was a man who hadn't been afraid to shed a tear.

As soon as she opened the car door, she knew something was wrong. She could hear Bugle barking, something he rarely did, and he sounded...seriously disturbed.

She hit the ground running, then realized Al had the keys. Had she locked the front door? She didn't think so. She heard the pound of his feet right behind her.

"He doesn't usually do that, does he?"

"No. No." He was upset and communicating it in the only way he could.

She was sure she'd left the front porch light on, but it was off now. Burned-out bulb? Maybe. Criminy, she'd come out for the evening without most of her usual gear, not even a flashlight. Only her service pistol rode on her belt, hidden by her jacket and a bulky sweater. But the streetlight offered almost enough illumination to see the door and try the knob. If they needed the key they'd probably need the car headlights, as well.

But the knob turned under her hand and she threw the door open only to have Bugle launch himself at her and push her backward.

"Is someone inside?" she asked as she staggered back and regained her footing.

"He doesn't want you in there," Al agreed. "All I've got is my baton."

She lifted her jacket and tucked it back. "I'm armed." Unsnapping her holster, she drew her Glock. "A flashlight could be useful."

But that would take time. She had plenty of them inside, and a couple of good Maglites in her official vehicle, but how long would it take to get them?

"Bugle."

The dog immediately came to her side. "Find."

Well, that didn't get his attention. "Seek," she commanded.

She could have sworn he shook his head but marched forward. Something in the way he moved told her the threat was gone but that something else had seriously bothered him. As soon as they were inside her small foyer, which gave a view of everything on the ground floor except her bedroom, she flipped the overhead light on.

Then she saw what had upset her dog, and wondered how someone had managed to do that without Bugle latching onto him.

A stuffed toy rabbit lay on the floor, and wrapped around its neck was a ragged piece of pink cloth. She didn't want to think about where the cloth had come from. "Time to call for help." Her voice had flattened with tension.

Then she moved slowly back through the house while Al called for reinforcements. She saw the damage before long.

Bugle had been in the bedroom, the door closed. Yeah, she must have done that. He liked to sleep on the bed while she was out, and closing the door was an almost automatic response on her part to dampen winter drafts.

But someone had taken advantage of that, and now her bedroom door had been clawed until Bugle had managed to get free. Long after the miscreant was gone.

Then she set the safety on her gun and sat in her armchair with her hands dangling between her legs, staring at the toy rabbit.

A message? A taunt? A threat? But why?

INSTEAD OF COOKIES, Reve's next reward to the girls was slipper socks. He worked weekends at the hospital as a janitor and had access to plenty of them. He also had access to the drugs he was giving the girls, but nobody would notice such small amounts missing. He didn't need much; it wasn't like he was going to perform surgery.

Anyway, he'd been hearing their complaints about how cold their feet were and it finally dawned on him that neither of them would be very useful or attractive without feet.

He'd seen a gangrenous limb at work once, and he was absolutely positive that he wouldn't want it in his bed. Besides, it would stink.

It was a good thing he'd decided not to let Spence in on his plans because after tonight it was obvious the guy couldn't keep his yap shut. Taunting a cop? That was a good way to get arrested and maybe worse.

The wrong cop, too. People thought Reve was dumb. He kept his head down, didn't say much and often pretended not to hear even when he had. He made himself invisible.

But Spence had drawn attention his way, however indirectly. And that cop Noveno with the dog…she wasn't giving up on the girls. He saw her prowling even when she wasn't on duty, crisscrossing the county like she hoped to spy something.

It might be necessary to get rid of her, he thought as he popped the top on another beer and settled at his own creaky kitchen table. Nearly everyone else seemed convinced those girls were long gone, vanished into some shadowy trafficking organization.

Which, now that he thought about it, might have been a good way to make some money. But no, he wanted those girls for himself. The guys with money could get plenty of girls to enjoy, but Reve…he didn't have the money. He had to find and catch his own or do without.

The catching part had come to him only lately, but after some thought and planning, he'd thought he'd done pretty well. Only one girl lost, and that was because he'd grown too impatient.

He'd learned something and was putting it into practice right now. A few more days, a week maybe, and those girls would be putty, willing to do whatever he said to get out of that basement, to get warm, to eat real food. Yeah. It was working.

But Spence had better just keep his mouth shut. He didn't want that cop's laser gaze trained his way. He swore that Noveno woman had the evil eye or something.

Regardless, if she started hanging around too much, he wouldn't hesitate to eliminate her. See, he wasn't dumb. He knew words like *eliminate*, and that's exactly what would happen to Kelly Noveno if she started hanging around this end of the county too much.

For that matter, Spence, too. He'd better just stop giving the cops a hard time. No need for that crap. Reve had waited too long to fulfill his dream. He wasn't going to let anyone get in his way, including Spence.

Damn, what had possessed the man, anyway? It was almost as if he was taunting Reve rather than the cop. But Spence didn't know what was going on, so how could he?

Reve rubbed his head, trying to ease a growing headache. Maybe he ought to just stay home for a while, avoid the tavern. Maybe he ought to let the girls be for a couple of days. They had enough water. Didn't matter if they didn't eat for a few days.

Yeah, time to lie low.

Chapter Nine

Day 18

Having the crime scene team crawl all over her house wasn't the most enjoyable experience in the world even though Kelly understood it all. It had to be done. The furry bunny with the odd bow had long since been bagged, but someone had entered her house and perhaps left traces behind them.

She patiently answered questions, but there were no real answers. Al stuck around and explained, too. They were hanging out at the tavern on weekends like a dating couple—two whole weekends, thought Kelly. Some dating—and keeping an eye out for anyone acting strangely.

Which led to the overwhelmingly huge report that they'd watched over several girls, making sure they'd returned home safely. Gigantic effort. Maybe they'd get a medal for valor.

Ah, damn, she thought, letting her head fall back in the recliner. As a cop she was messing up. Her stakeout at the tavern wasn't helping a damn thing. She was too emotionally involved, so much so that a piece of evidence could possibly walk right under her nose without attracting her attention.

And what was with the stuffed rabbit? Somebody's bad idea of a joke?

Gage had dragged himself out of a warm bed to come over here and keep eyes on things. He'd headed up the CSU before he'd been elected sheriff when Nate Tate retired, and he probably knew damn near as much as anyone in this room.

"The rabbit," Gage said, pulling the stool over to sit on.

Kelly came to herself. "Want this chair, Gage? You've got to be miserable on a stool."

"I'm probably less miserable than you are right now. The rabbit."

"Yeah, the rabbit. I have no connection with rabbits, Bugle doesn't especially want to chase them, and…" Suddenly she looked at Al. "There was that guy we spoke to about his rottie. You mentioned the dog had killed some pet rabbits."

Al nodded and shrugged all at once. He was perched on a bar stool. "If Spencer Hays wanted to make a statement about that, my place would make more sense."

"I was with you when you talked to Hays."

"And you stayed well out of it. No, this is something else. Damned if I know what."

Gage bent, wincing as he did so, and picked up the

rabbit now safely encased in a clear plastic evidence bag all marked up for the chain of evidence. He stared at it, turning it over a couple of times. "That ragged cloth bothers me. It's impossible to tell if it's supposed to be a bow, or a noose."

Kelly felt her heart skip. "A noose?"

Gage didn't answer her, but instead looked at Al. "How well you know this Spencer Hays? Had many dealings with him?"

"Not many, unless you count the number of times I've had to warn him to keep his dog under control. The dog, by the way, is with Cadel Marcus right now. Time for some decent training before a little girl loses a hand or her face."

Gage nodded thoughtfully. "Well, we'll take a closer look at Mr. Hays. If he thinks you two have been going to the tavern together often, this could be his round-about way of getting to you, Al. I can't see any other reason to leave it here."

"I've been spending quite a few evenings here," Al said. He didn't offer an explanation, for which Kelly was grateful. He *had* been spending a lot of evenings here when she wasn't working, but she didn't place much importance on it except they were growing a friendship. A very special friendship, she believed, closer than she'd enjoyed in a while. But still just a friendship. How could anyone hope to get at him through her?

After a moment, she decided to bring up the scene at the tavern. "Hays did have something to say to me tonight about not having found the girls yet. He was loud and noisy about it. But I can't imagine when he could have left the rabbit."

"He had time," Al said. "While we followed those

girls home. How long do you suppose he needed to dump a stuffed toy here? Was your door locked?"

"No." So maybe he *did* have time. "It still doesn't make sense. It's hardly a threat. A taunt? But why?"

Gage spoke quietly. "Or just to say he knows how to get to you."

Aw, hell, thought Kelly. Aw, hell. "But why?"

The answer to that was a ringing silence.

It was nearly one in the morning. Kelly needed to be on duty at seven. She ought to be sleeping but sleep appeared to be far away.

Al examined her bedroom door. "Gotta hand it to Bugle. You're going to need a new door."

"I'm not surprised."

He sat cross-legged on the floor and looked across the room at her. "You're a beautiful woman, Kelly Noveno."

She caught her breath, morose thoughts flying away to be replaced by astonished wonder. "What brought that on?"

He smiled. "I've been thinking it for ages."

She shook her head a little. "You've avoided me for ages. Come off it, Al."

"Sorry, lady. Been avoiding you because I'm a bad bet for a relationship. But that didn't mean I didn't notice. Anyway, sometimes I'd see you and it was like I lost my breath. But…beauty isn't a foundation, and my foundations are shaky anyway."

"You keep saying that. Or versions of that. Just what do you think is wrong with you?"

"If I can't trust myself, why should anyone else trust me?"

He shook his head and stood. "I don't want to leave you here alone tonight."

"I have Bugle," she reminded him.

He nodded slowly. "You're on duty in the morning?"

"Yeah. I hear there's a storm coming so I'll probably be doing welfare checks most of the day." Looking in on older residents who lived out of town, who might need a better place to stay for the duration or who might need some help stocking the larder, in which case she'd give one of the volunteer groups a call.

"Okay, then. I'll see you around."

A moment later he'd disappeared out the door. *See you around?* Had she offended him? All she'd done was ask what he thought was wrong with himself.

Well, if he was going to react that way...

Shaking her head, she climbed into bed wearing her thermal underwear, with Bugle's warmth snuggled up against her beneath the quilt.

A dog was more reliable than a man any day, she thought. She should have figured it out years ago.

But as she drifted into sleep, she had dreams of a rabbit wearing a noose, of a girl in a torn pink jacket, of Bugle with his teeth bared.

Bugle stirred nervously beside her but didn't wake her. His eyes never closed, though.

IT TOOK A hell of a lot of effort. Chantal was past worrying whether she cussed in the silence of her own mind or if she did it out loud so Jane could hear. It didn't seem to bother Jane, anyway.

They were chained so that their hands could reach their mouths, but not much beyond. Her wrists were sore, so sore that she was sure they must be scabbed over. Every movement hurt, but she steeled herself to ignore it. Their ankles were tethered to some kind of ring in the floor, giving them a few feet to move around in, but no more.

Her body felt as if it were crawling in filth. It had been so long since last she'd been able to get clean. Living worse than an animal.

The man hadn't been back in a couple of days, but she was sure he'd return. He wanted something from them and she was certain it was nothing good. They had to find a way to get out of here, except there was no way out except by the stairs that led to the metal door. A storm cellar, she thought. An ancient storm cellar, except over her head was the remains of a window. That seemed odd, so maybe it had been mostly a root cellar.

Whatever it was, it was boarded over with just the slightest cracks that sometimes let in some pale, watery light. Not enough to illuminate the room, but enough to sometimes tell her whether it was night or day.

The nights and days had all run together, though, and she no longer had any idea how long they'd been here.

She just knew she couldn't take it any longer. She was past caring if she died.

She stirred a bit and felt her elbows touch her ribs. For the first time in her life, she could feel her ribs sticking out. To think she'd once wanted to be that thin.

If she ever got out of here alive, she swore she was going to eat herself sick on every kind of junk food she could get her hands on. Her mind played tricks on her now, and sometimes she was sure she could smell a hamburger. Or a French fry. Or even broccoli.

Broccoli? Man, that was desperation. Worse yet, sometimes she craved Brussels sprouts, what her little brother called cannonballs. She'd never liked them, but now she'd have traded a whole lot for a big bowl of something green.

It was dark again, and she could faintly hear a wind whistling. It seemed to be coming from the remains of the window above her head.

"Jane?"

"Yeah." Jane sounded flat, as if she'd totally given up. Chantal was on the edge of it herself, but not quite ready. She had to make at least one attempt, and out of the fog of hunger and darkness an idea had come.

"Can you reach that window above us?"

"You're kidding, right? That's no window, that's jail bars."

"I know, but there are these small cracks in places. You saw them when we talked about them a few days ago." Or whenever it had been. Time had ceased to have meaning.

"So?"

"What if I rip off a piece of my sleeve with my teeth? Do you think you could shove it out a crack?"

"What good will that do?"

"It's bright. If the wind blows it like a flag…"

Jane was silent for a long time. "If it'll make you feel better, I'll try it, but it's a waste of time, Chantal. If it blows away, it says nothing. Anyway, who's going to care about a scrap of cloth? I don't think anyone's been looking for us for ages. They probably think we're in Mexico or getting whisked away by a gorgeous European prince."

Chantal fell quiet for a while, then said, "Being in a palace sounds better than this."

For the first time in forever, she heard Jane laugh.

The noise was cracked, almost broken, but it sounded so good to Chantal.

"I like that," Jane whispered. "A big, rich, handsome prince who'll fall head over heels for both of us and treat us like priceless jewels."

"I think your mom was right when she said you read too many of those books."

Jane snorted. "Better than your cowboy stories. Didn't you ever want to get farther away from here? You don't really want some cowboy to lasso you, do you?"

"Depends. Not the cowboy who has us now."

Once again their mood darkened.

She felt Jane stir beside her. "I can just about reach the bottom crack," she said. "Give me that piece of cloth."

Of course, it wasn't that easy. The way Chantal's teeth felt right now, she wasn't sure they wouldn't all fall out of her head if she tried to tear at something.

"I want a hot shower," she murmured. "I want to be clean again, all over. I want to eat a double cheese-burger."

Jane was silent for what seemed the longest time. "Give me a piece of that cloth," she whispered finally. "If nothing else, it'll be a good grave marker."

Chantal caught her breath. "You think he's leaving us here to die?"

"How should I know? All I know is Mary Lou's been gone forever. If that guy ever wanted anything from us, it was probably before we looked like filthy scarecrows."

Chantal squeezed her eyes shut, holding back tears that couldn't fall anymore. It was as if she had gone dry.

"Come on," Jane said, sounding broken. "The cloth. At least it'll tell them who the skeletons are."

NOW REVE DIDN'T dare do anything about the girls. Not since Spence had opened his yap. He'd have to wait a few days, see if that damn woman cop homed in on Spence in any way.

Talk about skating near the edge. And Spence didn't even know what was going on. It was as if some evil demon had put words in his mouth, causing him to draw attention to the very thing that Reve wanted to keep buried.

Crap.

And that stupid man had actually entered the deputy's house to leave part of an animal skin, he said. To give her a scare, he said.

They'd been lucky her dog hadn't been able to break out of the other room. Reve had spent the whole time sitting in his truck wondering if he should just find a way to shoot Spence when he was out running his trapline.

Another stupid thing. Spence lived in town but thought he was some kind of mountain man. Setting traps for foxes and selling their pelts. Damn fool was lucky he didn't catch himself a bear. Didn't matter. Fox trapping was legal. Wasn't nobody who liked the vermin.

But still. An animal skin?. For the cop when it was the animal control guy he was mad at? So what if the two had started dating. Only a fool went after a man's woman.

Spence was a fool.

Sitting at his kitchen table again, Reve pondered what he was going to do about those girls. He didn't dare go near the place right now, not after the cop had been warned something was going on. What if she drove out here and saw him approaching that tumble-down shack. She might wonder. She might even think he had something to do with that damned toy.

Oh, he'd planned it all so carefully, but he hadn't counted on his friend being an idiot. Hadn't counted that foolish remarks might draw the wrong kind of attention.

Well, he'd better come up with a plan now. The girls had enough food and water for another five or six days. Then there was that storm moving in. If it was as bad as they were predicting, he might not even be able to reach them for a while.

They could die out there.

And right then that didn't sound like such a bad thing to Reve. He'd be shed of the problem and there'd always be another day down the road where he could try this again.

One thing for damn sure: he couldn't do anything from a prison.

Damn Spence all to hell.

THE MORNING BEGAN with an eerie light, a flat grayness that was still quite bright. No shadows fell anywhere, but the breeze, strangely gentled, still whispered of dangers to come.

Al stood outside, making a mental plan for the coming storm. They still had a couple of days, so it was too early to be worrying about wandering animals that might freeze, but he still had his regular tasks. At least they gave him an excuse to roam the county, hoping for a glimpse of something that might tell him what had happened to those girls.

Because he seriously doubted that if they were in this county that they were still alive. Hiding them from neighbors, even out on isolated ranches, would be hard to do for long. People visited, saw each other at church. Only someone who'd been a recluse forever would be overlooked for long.

Kelly had said she was going to be starting her welfare checks. Most of the deputies would be dropping by homes to find out if anyone needed heating oil or supplies, or to come to shelter in town.

So another blanket of searchers was going to be out all day, setting up things to help folks out, but still getting a good look at the entire county. Two days wasn't a long time to set up deliveries of heating oil if very many people were getting low. Impossible to know now, too, how long people might be shut in after the storm. Sometimes the wind blew the snow away like so much dry powder. Other times it built it into huge banks that covered houses until they were nearly invisible.

Only time would tell on that one.

And three girls, if they were out there and weren't being properly cared for, were probably already dead.

The thought darkened his mood considerably as he climbed into his utility vehicle, the one that had been modified to hold four cages comfortably in back. More than four and he'd have to bring them back to shelter.

Today he determined to head outside town, because any lost or abandoned animals were likely to be facing the most trouble out there.

As he bumped along the roads, however, he drifted into thoughts about last night. Spencer had been an ass, for certain, but the man always had been. At least he'd finally seen the light about his dog, Cujo.

But then there was that stuffed rabbit. What in the hell did that mean? That it was a threat was obvious, to him at least. Dismiss it as a toy, but it remained someone had entered Kelly's house without her permission in order to leave it. Not a friendly gesture at all. He made a note to check with her later to ensure she was locking doors and windows. She shouldn't need a reminder but there'd been no evidence of a break-in at her house last night. Someone had opened the door and just walked in.

If he were Kelly, he wouldn't be feeling terribly safe after that. But she hadn't wanted him to stay. Of course, she had Bugle. He was probably more useful than ten armed guards, but still, Al hadn't liked being dismissed in favor of a dog.

But she had Bugle. And he'd had to come home and worry about her.

Then there was that stupid moment when he'd blurted how beautiful she was. Holy cow, what had possessed him? It was like something had taken over his mouth and issued the words before he could stop them.

Then that stuff about how he wasn't good for a relationship. It was true, of course. He hadn't lied about that, but he could see the questions dancing in her dark eyes, and if a guy was going to say things like that, he ought to be willing to answer the questions.

He guessed he spent too much time with dogs and cats. The idea amused him, but it was true. A flick of a tail, a long look, a twitch of ears, those animals could communicate entire encyclopedias to each other.

Him, not so much. He needed to use the whole dictionary of words to make his points. He was out of practice, though. He'd come home from the US Marines, mustered out with a disability, and discovered he had more problems than some shrapnel-torn back muscles. Nope, he had a brain problem, a brain full of rage that could be triggered unexpectedly. He'd gotten better with time, but that monster still lay in wait, and he treated it with wary respect.

What woman needed that? Hell, nobody needed that.

Then, like a great big wheel, his thoughts returned to that damned stuffed rabbit. No mistaking it was a message, but what kind? Why would anyone want to scare Kelly? Yeah, she'd found the car by the roadside, but that had proved to be useless. No information there to explain how three young women could vanish from the planet.

He smiled into the brightening day, with its strange light that assured him the sun was rising somewhere, as he recalled a conversation he'd overheard the other day at Maude's diner. Two men were absolutely convinced the girls had been abducted by aliens.

Vehemently convinced, even to the point of arguing when another fellow had discounted it after overhearing them.

"Where else could they be?" one of the men demanded. "Not in this county, that's for sure. You ever tried to keep anything secret around here?"

Interesting question. If those teens had been taken by someone who lived here, even if he'd transported them out of the state, he'd managed to keep it secret. And the guy at the diner was right. Keeping a secret around here was nigh on impossible.

"Ah, hell," he said to his empty truck. "Just keep your eyes peeled. He had to have left a track somewhere."

Sure. Like he'd left traces they couldn't find in the car. The abduction had been well planned, no question. But to what end? He hoped like mad those girls were still nearby and could be found somehow. That at the very least one of them escaped to seek help.

But with each passing day that hope seemed dimmer.

So did the sky all of a sudden. Though he seldom cared to listen to the radio while he cruised around looking for animals that were out of place, he turned it on now.

Wicked storm on the way. It would hit full force by the day after tomorrow. No searching in the middle of that.

His radio squawked and he picked it up. "Animal control, Carstairs."

"Al," said a familiar voice belonging to an elderly lady outside town, "my Ruffles hasn't come home since yesterday. Not even to eat."

"I'm coming, Mrs. Jackson. Did she seem all right yesterday?"

"She was fine when I let her out yesterday afternoon. Just fine. And she knows how to hide from them coyotes. Heck, I think they're terrified of her."

"Maybe so," he agreed as he used one hand to execute a three-point turn. "I'll be there in fifteen minutes."

She thanked him, her voice wavering as it only could when a person was really upset.

He hoped to God he found Ruffles, an independent, stubborn, single-minded Maine coon that had plenty to say about how life should work.

Yeah, he wouldn't be surprised if that cat scared the coyotes. She was almost as big as some of them, big even for her breed. And while Maine coons were sweet tempered, this one had a temper.

She was also bred to withstand the kind of weather that was coming. Which was about the only good thing Al could say about it.

WHEN HE REACHED Mrs. Jackson's ramshackle ranch about ten miles beyond town, she was standing on the porch bundled up head to foot and calling Ruffles.

This was not good, he thought as he pulled his own jacket on and bundled himself. Ruffles had never run away this long before. A few hours, maybe, but overnight?

As soon as he reached the porch, he urged Mrs. Jackson back inside. She was in her eighties and like many older people she had grown thin and a bit stooped. No meat on her bones to keep her warm, winter-weather wear notwithstanding.

"It's too cold for you to stand out here. You wait inside. You know I always find Ruffles."

"Ruffles has never been gone this long before," she quavered.

He hated to imagine how long she had worried before she finally decided to call him. Several hours at least. "I'll find her," he promised. He just hoped he'd find Ruffles alive and well. "Say, are you set for the storm? Heating oil? Food?"

Mrs. Jackson lived alone, something he couldn't afford to forget.

"I got my heating oil last week," she answered. "I've got food."

"Well, I'll take a look at things in the house once I find the cat," he said. It wouldn't hurt to make sure her heater was operating correctly, and that her idea of food didn't amount to a single can of beans or soup.

She nodded, looking forlorn, and disappeared inside. She continued to peer out the front window, however, pulling the sheers back so she could see.

Okay, Al thought. *Where the devil would you be hiding, Ruffles?*

Something must have scared her good, Al reasoned. More than usual if she'd taken to hiding and didn't want to come out.

He walked around the house, peering at every possible place that cat could have gotten herself stuck. Troubling him, however, was that he didn't hear a single *mew.* If the cat was in trouble, it should be calling for help. They usually did.

A gust of wind caught him, reminding him the weather was about to turn bad and the cat must be found, Maine coon or not.

Sighing, he started to survey the area around the house. A culvert, maybe? But coyotes could get in there. Ruffles didn't seem like the kind of cat that would allow herself to be cornered.

Then he spied a big old cottonwood, bare of leaves for the winter, but still high enough to attract a climber. Giving a mental shrug because he'd never known a cat to get stuck in a tree—they always seemed to find a way down, usually by jumping—he started to walk that way anyway. He'd made a promise.

As he walked, he scanned the ground almost out of habit. He could read the tracks of animals that had wandered through here before the winter had hardened the earth to cement.

Yeah, lots of coyotes, he saw. A wolf? Maybe, although they usually came in packs. Probably someone's stray dog. Cat tracks, mountain lions. They didn't usually come down out of the mountains this far, but one of them would be big enough to give Ruffles a bad time.

Then he saw a scrap of pink cloth. Just a torn scrap,

but a different color from the one from last night's stuffed rabbit. Bending, he looked at it, then scanned the area around. Nothing for over a mile. Still...

First he took a photo with his cell phone, crouching close. Then, touching the scrap only with his glove, he picked it up and tucked it in a seldom-used breast pocket on his jacket. Screw DNA, he guessed, but if he left it here it would blow away. Probably a useless exercise anyway.

Standing again, he continued his trek toward the tree. It was beautiful in the spring and summer, when it was all leafed out. Worthy of photographing. Right now it looked like a bunch of skeletal fingers, something he didn't want to think about.

If that cloth in his pocket had come from one of the missing teens... No way to know. Pink fabric was everywhere, and where could anyone be out here? Mrs. Jackson would know what was in her basement, and she wasn't likely to be involved in a kidnapping.

Still, he'd bring it to the sheriff's attention. Maybe they'd want to look around more out here. In case.

And all the cases were ugly.

"Ruffles." He called for the cat, hoping to see a huge Maine coon come running out of the sagebrush. No such luck. A big tumbleweed came at him, though, brushing by before the wind died again.

It was then he thought he heard a faint sound. "Ruffles?"

Another gust snatched it away and he froze, waiting to hear it again. He needed to locate it, and one sound wasn't enough out here. Sounds, he'd long ago learned since moving here, could be terribly deceptive in the wide-open spaces. Almost as bad as when they echoed among the rocks of mountains.

He resumed his march toward the cottonwood but kept scanning the ground. Where there was one pink piece of cloth, there might be another. There might even be a trail.

Like bread crumbs in Hansel and Gretel, he thought with sour amusement. Yeah, they should be so lucky. Those girls should be that lucky. Damn near three weeks now, and he was holding out very little hope.

He'd had to stop by the Episcopalian church two days ago, a tiny little building, to help the pastor with a barn owl that seemed to be caught in the belfry. While he was there he'd seen Jane's mother lighting a candle. Lighting a candle. It was enough to tear out a man's heart.

But hope endured, somehow. That woman hadn't given up but by now she must be wondering if God was even listening.

He reached the foot of the cottonwood and saw the ground had been ripped up. Coyotes. Then he heard another, faint *mew*.

Looking up, he saw Ruffles, her flecked brown coat blending well with the tree branches. Well, that explained a lot, he thought. Coyotes had treed the cat and she was afraid to come down. Must have been a pack of them or she'd have used her claws and teeth and sent them packing.

"Hey, Ruffles," he said in a soothing tone. "Rescue has arrived. Wanna come down?"

Because he sure didn't want to climb that tree. Winter slumber had probably made a lot of branches brittle, and there didn't look to be many really strong limbs positioned for a man to climb.

But the cat, like most cats, had a problem. She couldn't back down the tree. Cats just wouldn't do that. They had to see where they were going.

"Come on," he said. "You don't want to be the first cat I've ever seen who couldn't get out of a tree. I bet there's a can of food waiting for you right now. Aren't you cold?"

Talking to a cat. Okay, he was crazy, but at least it was harmless crazy. Anyway, hearing his voice, Ruffles appeared to be relaxing a bit. No coyotes were going to come if the man was here. He just hoped she realized that.

He was also glad this wasn't their first encounter. Ruffles knew him so she had no reason to fear him. He wasn't a stranger. Given the solitude in which Mrs. Jackson lived, there probably weren't a whole lot of people whom Ruffles knew and would trust.

"Come on, sweetie. Did those mean coyotes scare you? I wouldn't have thought they could tree you like this. You prefer life on the ground, don't you?"

Maine coons were definitely not tree cats, preferring to be on the solid earth, but Ruffles must have been terribly scared to perch herself up there.

Not knowing what else to do, he unzipped his jacket and spread his arms invitingly, ignoring the cold and hoping he looked like a safe landing place.

Ruffles looked in every direction, assessing threats, he assumed. Then her green eyes fixed on him again. Much to his relief, she started to ease her way down. Not easy, headfirst, and she froze often, as if uncertain of her purchase.

Then, in one daring leap, she jumped down on him. He just managed to catch her, feeling her claws trying to dig in through his sweater, and hold her close. Those green eyes stared at him, then a purr told him most of what he needed to know.

Good. He grabbed a flap of his jacket and wrapped it over her. Then he spied some flecks of blood, almost invisible on her mottled coat. Hell, those coyotes had gotten a piece of her.

"I'll get you fixed up," he told her soothingly. "Bet you'd never guess I have a first aid kit for animals in my truck, would you? But I do. Some safe antiseptic. If you get to licking your coat, it won't sicken you. I think of everything, don't I?"

Ruffles's purr grew louder. Happy cat. All was well. For the cat and Mrs. Jackson at least.

RUFFLES HAD SOME scratches and had lost a few tufts of fur but no apparent bite marks, even though he and Mrs. Jackson went over every inch of her. Of course, that thick coat of hers had probably protected her from worse. Once he'd put the antiseptic on her, Al went down into the basement and checked out the heater. Everything appeared to be in working order, and the battery in the carbon monoxide detectors both in the basement and upstairs appeared to be reasonably fresh. He found some new ones in a drawer and changed them out anyway.

Her cupboard wasn't exactly overloaded with food, but she had considerably more than a can of beans. She'd be able to heat food on her propane stove.

Then, as she sat in her rocking chair with a now-happy Ruffles in her lap, he squatted before her.

"The storm is going to get very bad, Mrs. Jackson. No one can say for sure how many days you might be cut off from the world after it passes through. Would you rather I take you and Ruffles to the church shelter?"

She shook her head. "I'm fine. Besides, I was born in this house and if I'm going to die, I'd rather do it here. Been through bad storms before, Al. We'll do all right."

He nodded. "Just call if you need anything. I'll find a way to get here. Promise me?"

"I promise."

He had to be satisfied with that, he supposed. Then he hit the road again, wondering if he should take the scrap of cloth directly to the sheriff or wait until he finished his rounds.

Damned if he knew what use it would be, but maybe he ought to just turn it in. It felt almost as if it were burning a hole in his breast pocket.

So at the end of the driveway, he turned back toward town. The eerie light had changed and become purely leaden.

Winter was about to do her worst.

Chapter Ten

Day 20

"That piece of cloth has been gone for more than a day," Jane remarked wearily. "I told you it wouldn't do any good."

"I think we should try another one."

"You would. Don't you *ever* give up?"

Chantal struggled until she could reach her friend's hand. "What's the point in giving up?" she asked, her voice raspy. "At least we're trying everything we can. Better than just waiting to die."

Which was what they seemed to be doing. As far as they knew, the guy hadn't come back. The water supply was diminishing. The food bars had become a smaller pile. Jane mentioned rationing what they had, but neither of them had the brainpower left to figure out how.

They just resorted to sharing the food bars when they absolutely *had* to eat and taking only small sips from the water bottles.

"You haven't given up either," Chantal said. "If you had you'd finish the water or food."

Jane was silent for what seemed like a long time. "It's night out there," she said finally. Her voice sounded rusty. "Night. You hear the wind? Bad weather."

Indeed Chantal could hear the wind. Whatever cracks this place possessed often whistled from it.

"That's why the cloth blew away."

"Then let's try a piece of my sweater instead of my undershirt. It's thicker. It'll jam in better."

"And unravel."

"God, don't be so down. I can tie off the threads. I'm a knitter, remember? I made this darn sweater."

"At least it's bright green."

"Most visible color in the spectrum," Chantal mumbled, remembering her physics class. "Chartreuse. Okay. It might take me a while, but I'll unravel enough to stick in the crack."

"Better than doing nothing, I suppose."

Yeah, it was, thought Chantal. She was so weary she had to struggle to keep her eyes open, and she couldn't seem to stop shivering. Shivering was a good thing, right?

She twisted, crying out once as her wrists screamed, but she got hold of the bottom of her sweater near the seam. She'd made that seam, she could unmake it.

Then they were going to fly another little flag.

Reve thought of the girls in the cellar a mile or so from his house, but with the storm coming and the roads covered with cops doing welfare checks, he decided it would be smart to leave them alone. They'd either make it or they wouldn't.

Since Spence had shot off his fool mouth, though, Reve had been questioning if he'd been wise to abduct those girls so close to home.

He'd had his eye on them for a while, of course. Bright shiny faces, youthful healthy bodies. He saw them in church when he felt like going and then he'd heard they were planning a New Year's get-together at the tavern.

It had seemed like a golden opportunity to stop dreaming and start enjoying his fantasies in real life. He was good at planning, too. He'd even managed to slip them just enough of the drug that they'd been able to get out to their car and start driving home.

It would have been hopeless if they'd passed out in the bar. Instead they had grown cautious because they weren't feeling well and finally had drifted off the road as easily as they fell asleep.

A great plan, one leaving no tracks that would lead to him. But the first one had proved to be a mistake, and now the other two had been in that basement for so long that the smell was sour when he opened the storm doors.

He wasn't sure he even wanted them anymore. Yeah, they could shower, but that wasn't going to put meat back on them. At his last check a few days ago, they'd looked almost like skeletons.

He didn't find them attractive anymore. What was he going to do? Drag their submissive, weakened butts out of the hole and fatten them up again? Hoping they'd be grateful to him? That they wouldn't act like the first one once they got a little energy back?

Much as he hated to admit it, despite everything he'd done right, he'd messed up. He should never have taken all three at once. He shouldn't have done it so close to home, not when a so-called friend like Spence was going to shoot off his mouth.

He tried to tell himself that Spence had merely diverted attention with his behavior. After all, no cop would expect the kidnapper to draw attention to himself.

But maybe that wasn't true. Maybe the guilty often liked to needle the cops. Hell, he'd read about how many guys had been caught simply because they couldn't avoid going back to the scene of the crime to watch. To enjoy their own handiwork.

He for sure wasn't that dumb. Hence finding a place far enough away, long enough abandoned, that it didn't look as if anything could possibly live in there except some rats and ground squirrels. It wasn't even on his property. No one could conceivably know that he'd shored up the root cellar to make a small prison.

He hadn't even had to buy any materials for the job. His long-gone family had left enough crap in his barn that he could probably build an ark for Noah. The thought amused him while the TV, with a snowy picture as usual, blathered on about how bad the storm was going to be.

At least he didn't have to go to work at the garage. His boss, Keeb Dustin, had told him to stay home. After the storm they'd probably work around the clock trying to jump-start dead batteries and repair bent fenders and snapped belts. The cold, this kind of cold, was cruel to cars.

And then there'd be the tows. A lot of people might

well get stuck trying to get out of their own driveways, especially outside town. Or stuck in ditches because it was a strange fact that every single year people needed to learn to drive on snow all over again, and this would be the first snow this year.

So yeah, he'd be plenty busy for a few days after the storm. He might even pick up a few hours driving a plow if they got really buried.

Which left the girls. And leaving them was just about what he'd convinced himself to do. Too much trouble. Try another time. Learn from this and move on.

Hell, the cold from this storm would probably kill them in a few hours, and damned if he was going to drag them out of their hiding places and bring them here. Just his luck some cop, like that Kelly Noveno, would stop by to check on him and one of those damn teens would start screaming her fool head off.

Leave them, he thought. Let nature take care of them.

There were plenty more where they came from.

AL TURNED IN the scrap of cloth he'd found while rescuing Ruffles and Gage slipped it into an evidence bag with tweezers before looking it over. "Did you record where you found this?"

Al pulled out his cell phone and showed him the information. "I got it all, including the GPS, but I don't know what good it does us."

"Maybe nothing yet. Maybe nothing ever. But one of those girls was wearing a pink parka when she disappeared and this appears to be the right kind of nylon fabric. Then look, did you see the teeth marks?"

Astonished, Al leaned forward for a closer look. "It was chewed," he said.

"Yeah, it was. Which is an odd thing to do with one's parka, I have to say. Looks like it was deliberately ripped off."

Al's heart stuttered to full speed. "Maybe I should look around some more near Mrs. Jackson's. I didn't see any buildings anywhere near but…"

Gage nodded. "Wind," he said. "It's lightweight." Then he motioned Al over to a wall map of the county, one that was decorated with pushpins. "Here's Mrs. Jackson's place. Nearest structure is probably…five miles? There might be some old line shacks out there, but nothing that's occupied. Wouldn't hurt to look around some, if you feel like it."

Then Al's radio clamored for his attention. A family of felines had been dumped by the state highway, spotted by a trucker who couldn't stop for them. "I've gotta go," he told Gage.

"Yeah. I'll think about this," he said, indicating the swatch of fabric. "Maybe something will come to me."

"It better come soon. That storm is supposed to hit tomorrow night or the next morning."

Gage merely nodded. Because, of course, he already knew.

KELLY WATCHED THE sky thicken with threat and was glad she was out doing the rest of the welfare checks. The predictions for the storm had grown so much worse that sometimes entire families were telling her they were moving into town to stay with relatives and friends, or at one of the church shelters.

Few wanted to be caught out here if something went wrong. One grizzled rancher wanted a few minutes of conversation and she was happy to provide it.

"Can't go into town," he said. "I got me some forty cows in the barn I gotta look after. Thank the good Lord I could get them all in."

"Can someone stay with you?"

He laughed. "I'm moving in with the cows. They'll keep me warm as toast and I'll have ice cream fresh from the tap."

She joined his laughter. "It *is* going to be bad."

"I reckon." He looked up at the sky. "You can laugh if you want, Deputy Kelly, but I'll tell you anyway. Spent my whole life out here. This ain't normal weather we been having, not for a few years now. And this storm? Nothing like it ever before. Them folks can laugh at climate change all they want, but I'm living close to it and I see it. It's not the same, not the way it was. So let 'em tell me it's just one storm and doesn't mean a hill of beans."

They probably would say exactly that, she thought as she drove away with a wave. Not everyone, but some. She'd been listening to the arguments for a long time now. She did, however, listen to her dad.

"Streets are flooding all the time down here, Kelly. Never used to see that. Houses that were safe except in the worst hurricanes are getting flooded at high tide, especially if we've had some rain. Streets undrivable. Things are changing. I'm glad you're up there."

Things are changing. Maybe that was the only thing people would agree on. But behind her Bugle let out a low moan, reminding her she hadn't given him a chance to take care of his business for a while now.

"Bad, bad Kelly," she said aloud. In the rearview, she could see Bugle cock his head inquisitively. "Next turnout," she promised him. It'd give her a chance to give the binoculars on the seat beside her a good work-out. At every opportunity she'd scanned the surrounding country because she couldn't stop hoping she'd find some sign of the missing teens.

The rabbit in her house seemed like a minor thing compared with that. So somebody wanted to make her uneasy. Big deal. They probably also didn't want to mess with Bugle. She didn't need the Glock on her hip to feel safe.

But unless those girls were being held somewhere right around here, hope was nearly pointless. They were gone, one way or another, maybe not even in this county anymore. And if someone was holding them prisoner somewhere around here...well, something should give him away soon. A trip to a store, a pharmacy, extra food...if he had to care for three teens, he was going to need supplies. Supplies that wouldn't be on his usual shopping list.

Maybe.

But so far nobody had come to the sheriff remarking that they'd noticed something unusual. The most unusual thing had been that dolt Spence poking at her, and that hadn't been the first time she'd run into a jerk who liked to give a cop a hard time.

In fact, given the kidnapping, she was surprised that she and other cops hadn't suffered a whole lot more from impatient, angry people. They must seem like total failures.

And from Kelly's perspective, she felt like one. It seemed next to impossible that someone could have taken those girls and left no evidence behind. That was one of the almost unbreakable rules of crime scene in-vestigation: take something, leave something behind.

But if he'd left anything behind, they didn't know what it was. They might stare straight at it and not know it. That glove was all they had. It linked to one of the girls, but not to the perp. No help until they had someone to charge.

Sometimes she found that the most frustrating part of police work, to be able to develop a mountain of evidence that you couldn't link to anyone specific until you put hands on the guy.

How many men in this county—assuming it was a man—might be enough of a pervert to take those girls? Did any of them have families they were hiding this from? Or did they all live alone? How many of *them* were there, solitary men?

Plenty, unfortunately. Women seemed more eager to leave this town and county than men by far. They wanted something more than the smell of cow poop and skunk in the morning.

She found a turnout and let Bugle out without a leash. He needed to run off some energy. Then she pulled out the binoculars and began to scan the countryside from east to west toward the mountains. A tumbledown line shack that looked like it should have collapsed long ago. No houses immediately in sight, but yeah, she thought she could see one farther out. A couple of miles? Possibly next on her checklist.

The mountains, for all they had prepared for winter, still looked dark and forbidding, probably because the sky was trying to work itself into an early version of night with lowering clouds.

The air felt oddly warm, though. Strange, but maybe it was an effect of the approaching cold, sucking heat toward it from somewhere else. Her weather knowledge was miserable, but as she stood there studying the barren countryside and a few cattle that really needed to be on their way into a barn, she wondered if she should have majored in meteorology.

Following in her father's footsteps had seemed like the thing to do for so many years, but how often had Hector tried to talk her out of it?

"You don't know, *muchacha*," he'd say to her. "The things we have to see. I'm not talking about risks. Sure there are risks but it's more dangerous to cut down trees or catch crabs. No, I'm talking about what we *see*. Things that get stamped in the brain and never go away. Why would you want to do that?"

Because that's what he had done and she admired the heck out of him. He'd been right about the things stamped in her brain, however. Absolutely right. At least she saw a lot fewer of them here in Wyoming than she had during her brief stint in Fort Lauderdale.

When Bugle apparently felt he'd run off enough energy, he came back to her with his tail wagging, ready to go on patrol again. It seemed he hadn't noticed anything untoward, and only then did she realize how much she'd been hoping that he'd find another piece of evidence, like that glove.

No such luck. She put him back in his cage in the backseat and wondered absently how soon it would get so cold that she'd need to put his quilted vest and booties on him. Not yet, anyway.

By comparison with the last few days, the air felt almost balmy.

Before she pulled back out onto the road, her cell phone tweeted at her. She almost laughed. She thought she'd been out of range for a while.

"Hey," said the now-familiar voice of Al Carstairs, "how are your rounds going?"

"Nearly done, for today at any rate. You?"

"Couple more houses. I'll be out on 581 for the next half hour or so. Listen, when you want lunch, look me up. I've got a story about a Maine coon for you, and I found a scrap of pink cloth that even Gage isn't sure means anything."

"Pretend you just heard me sigh. Okay, I'll see you on 581. Maybe an hour?"

"I'll be there. I'm running back to my cabin first, though. Some people call me on the landline and talk to my answering machine. Can you believe it? An answering machine in this day and age."

She laughed. "Hey, you heard of voice mail?"

"County won't pay for the additional service. Nope, I'm a tape man. Play and erase. See you shortly."

A Maine coon and a good story. Sounded like it might be a nice lunch break. Plus a piece of fabric. Her heart did one of those nervous little skips it had been doing ever since this case exploded.

She closed her eyes a few moments, sending a prayer for those girls winging heavenward, then pulled back onto the road.

She believed in a benevolent God. Absolutely. But she also figured the human race had him or her so overworked that single prayers might get lost in the tsunami.

"We make most of our own problems," her father had told her once. She wasn't sure if he was speaking as a cop or a dad, nor did it really matter. They'd just come out of Mass, and she'd donated her babysitting money to the poor.

"What do you mean?" she'd asked him.

"People don't starve because God wants it. They starve because other people are hard-hearted."

That philosophy had stuck. So maybe her prayer was useless. A bad guy was involved in all this. He had made this problem. Unfortunately, entirely too many people were in the perp's class, harming others for their own satisfaction.

But that didn't keep her from saying yet another prayer as she drove.

BACK AT HIS CABIN, Al got word of two missing cats, and he still had the ones dropped by the roadside to worry about. Kittens. If he hurried up, he could grab them and get to 581 with the missing cats who'd been out since last night.

Cats were a piece of work, he sometimes thought. He loved them as much as any animals, but cats could be especially difficult. Somehow, they'd managed to keep their own minds and wills intact. They could be cuddly companions one minute and troublesome isolationists the next.

As he jumped back into his truck, ready to rescue the local feline population, he felt a light weight land on his shoulder.

"Regis," he said, twisting his head to look at the gray squirrel. "You really don't want to come along to look for cats."

But Regis, like the cats, had his own mind. He chittered, then settled into the space between Al's collar and shoulder.

And that, thought Al, was what he got for rescuing an infant squirrel last spring and nursing him to health before releasing him. Regis still had a bit of human in him.

FIFTEEN MINUTES LATER he'd rescued the family of cats, the kittens no more than a week old, and placed them on a towel together in a cage in the back of his truck. Mama immediately wrapped herself around them, protecting them. The two other missing cats showed up on their home porches, so he erased them from his mental list.

Once he approached 581 he saw Salty, a schnauzer from an outlying ranch that shouldn't be anywhere around here. So Salty was placed in a cage a distance from the cats and began to whine. Of course. He'd probably been having a great time chasing a ground squirrel, had indeed chased it so far he was too far from home.

At last he turned onto 581, looking forward to seeing Kelly. She was occupying a whole lot more time in his thoughts than was probably good for him, but he was past caring. There were enough bad things to think about.

Kelly was like a bright shining oasis in a world full of ugliness.

Then he spied Misty. A beautiful golden retriever with a distinctive prance to her step, she seemed to be running in circles about a hundred yards inside the fence line of the Harris family ranch. He was surprised to see her so far out here. The Avilas had always been careful owners who tried not to let Misty slip her leash, but she was an accomplished escape artist. With the weather turning so bitter, perhaps one of the kids had let her out in the backyard without watching and she'd burrowed under the fence. Regardless, at the times she proved to be Houdini's reincarnation, Al usually picked her up within or near the city limits.

Al pulled his van onto the shoulder, grabbed a slip-knot leash and climbed out. Misty had never been a problem to round up, so he expected her to come immediately when he called. Just after he slid off the seat and his feet hit the ground, he felt Regis dig in his claws. He had to smile.

He closed the vehicle door so the animals would stay warm and gave thanks that the wind hadn't really started yet. Just the faintest of breezes had begun to chill the air, starting to vanquish the unusual warmth of the last few hours, and now held a tang that hinted at coming snow.

For the first time ever, Misty wasn't in a cooperative mood. As she raced around, she tossed some kind of toy in the air, and although she occasionally glanced at him when he called her, she kept right on playing, pausing only to paw at the ground before returning to her private game of catch.

"Hey, Misty," Al called. "Come on. Don't be a pain. Seriously."

Just then a sheriff's SUV pulled onto the opposite shoulder of the road. It bore a rack of lights, and Conard County Sheriff painted in green on the tan background. K-9, Keep Your Distance was also labeled on the side. By that, before she even climbed out, Al knew it was Kelly.

She had apparently taken in the situation before she pulled over to approach him, and grinned as she climbed out. "Having a problem, Al?"

He had to grin back. Kelly was a wildly attractive woman to his way of thinking, but what he most liked about her was her sunny nature and readiness to tease. He also liked her dog, but Kelly left Bugle in her vehicle and sauntered toward Al, her khaki uniform and jacket looking scarcely heavy enough to withstand the chilling air. "Misty giving you trouble?"

"She's in a mood, all right," Al agreed. Apparently, Kelly had had her own run-ins with the dog.

Kelly whistled, but Misty barely spared her a glance as she tossed her toy in the air and caught it.

"What in the world is she playing with?" Kelly asked.

"I've been wondering. Rawhide bone? Heck, she knows I wouldn't take that away from her."

Kelly chuckled. "She's teasing you." Then she turned to look at Al. "What in the dickens is that on your shoulder?"

Al didn't even have to glance. "That's Regis."

"That's a *squirrel*! You can't keep them for pets."

"I don't. Regis decides for himself. Sometimes he likes to ride shotgun. What can I tell you, Kelly? The squirrel has a mind of his own."

Al felt her staring but heck, what could he do about it? He'd rescued Regis as an abandoned baby, fed the animal until it was strong enough to take off into the woods and live the squirrel life. Except Regis kept coming back to visit.

"Now I've seen everything," Kelly muttered. "Someday I want to hear this story."

While Al wouldn't have minded spending the next day or two chatting with Kelly, there was still business to attend to. "Misty, get your butt over here now." This time there was an edge of impatience to his voice and Misty didn't miss it. She froze, looked at him, then came trotting over with her toy.

Al squatted down, ready to reward the dog with a good scratch and rub, but as Misty drew closer something inside him began to feel chillier than the day.

"Kelly?"

"That's not rawhide," she said too quietly.

Al didn't answer. He waited until Misty snaked through the fence and came to a halt before him, dropping her toy and looking at him with a proud grin.

Al reached out, scratching her neck automatically as he looked down at the "present" she'd placed before him.

"Tell me that's not human," he said.

"I can't," Kelly answered, her voice unusually taut.

Their eyes met and Al knew they were both thinking of the same thing: the three high school girls who'd gone missing weeks ago.

"I'll get an evidence bag while you put the dog in your van," Kelly said. But he noted she walked to her SUV with a leaden step. All her natural vivacity had seeped away. She'd be calling for help, he thought, to try to learn where the dog found the bone. Before they were even certain.

"Yeah," Al said, speaking to the icy air. "Yeah." Then he stood, slipping the loose leash around Misty and leading her to the back of his truck.

"God," he told the dog, "I hope it's from a deer."

But he was very afraid it was not.

Chapter Eleven

Days 20–21

An hour later, Cadel Marcus showed up with four of the K-9s he was training, and Jake wasn't far behind with his dog. Soon deputies began to congregate, filling the shoulders of the road, cutting it off to traffic.

The only thing they knew for sure was that a doctor at the hospital had said it was definitely a human thigh-bone, the growth plates hadn't fully hardened and he wouldn't be surprised if it belonged to one of the missing girls. The bone was now on its way to a forensics lab, but there was no time to waste.

Gage was blunt about it. "Figure we've got twenty-four hours max," he told everyone. "We've got to find the scene, find the body, find the evidence before this storm makes working impossible, or buries the remains again."

And none of that meant they'd find the perp.

Al had used the time to take the animals in his truck home or leave them in his kennels, and now he was ready to take one of Cadel's dogs to aid in the search.

"Same commands you've heard Kelly use with Bugle," Cadel told him. "Except these dogs are trained to hunt for cadaverine."

Cadaverine. The odor of death, something dogs could sniff even if it was way more than six feet underground. "Bugle doesn't do that?"

"Around here, not much call. Three of these dogs are in training for other police departments. One body hunter is probably all we'd ordinarily need in this county. Today is different."

Different in so many ways, with a severe storm moving in that could hide evidence until much later in the spring. That would give scavengers more time to devour it and disperse it. Important traces, like cloth and hair, could vanish in a strong wind. Even teeth…

Al drew himself up short. He'd seen it in Afghanistan. He didn't need to think about all the stages of decay.

Kelly approached him, her face drawn. "I'd like to miss this day entirely."

"I think we all would," he agreed. "I'm sorry. I had funny stories to tell you."

"Where's that damn squirrel of yours?"

"Being smart. When I got back to my place, he headed for his drey. I don't know if he made himself a family yet, but I'm sure he's got other squirrels to hunker down with."

"I definitely want to hear that story."

"You will."

As if they were hunting for someone buried in a landslide or avalanche, they all carried long, thin metal poles to stick into the hardened ground. It wasn't easy, but they were thin enough to penetrate with reasonable effort. Even so, Al felt it all the way through his injured back.

But what they all really wanted was for the dogs to alert. To give them a narrower area to search.

They set out almost shoulder to shoulder, heading toward the area where Misty had been playing with the bone. Unfortunately, Misty had probably found it somewhere else and had carried it with her while she played.

Cadel had spread his dogs out with other deputies so they covered a much wider area. They offered more hope than rods and eyes right now. At least they still had visibility, but it seemed like the winter night was moving in even faster than usual. Al wished he had some night vision goggles. Detail was beginning to vanish as the light grew flatter by the minute.

Even if they found remains, all they could do was cover them until morning and hope it didn't grow too cold for the crime scene folks to gather everything in the morning light.

But mostly Al thought about the girl that bone had belonged to, about all three of the missing girls. How awful all the way around, from their disappearance to their parents' hoping and praying they'd be found alive to this.

He doubted anyone wanted to tell the parents about the bone. It might not belong to one of the girls. It could have come from somewhere else. Why terrify them any more than they were already terrified. Why steal the hope they had been depending on for weeks now.

Not without damn good reason.

But for him, as for many of the searchers, he suspected, hope was clinging by one last, thin thread after the bone. No reason to think only one of the girls had been killed. That would make no sense at all.

Not that any of this made any sense.

The wind was picking up as the last light faded from the day. They were done until first light in the morning. The dogs hadn't even signaled, and Al was quite sure they'd long since passed the spot where Misty had been playing. The question now was where she had found it.

They marked the place where they stopped looking with pin flags, then tramped dispiritedly back to the cars. For some reason, a hope of another kind had been born in the searchers: hope of closure. Even that was denied to them tonight.

Back at his car he saw Kelly loading up Bugle. He turned his charge back over to Cadel and headed her way.

"Say, Deputy," he said. The wind tried to snatch his words.

She looked at him, her expression sober, her hand on the driver's door latch.

"Come to my place tonight," he said. "It's a good night for not being alone."

To his amazement, she nodded. "I'd like that. Bugle, too?"

"I can't imagine you without that dog. Of course he comes."

She smiled lopsidedly. "Do you need me to bring anything?"

"Yourself and your dog. The pizza place is on the way if that agrees with you."

"I love pizza. Any kind, except anchovies. They're too salty for me."

"Done. See you there shortly. And oh, by the way? I have food for Bugle, too, so just bring something warm to hang out in. I have a feeling the temperatures tonight will make the North Pole seem balmy."

In fact they were already headed that way, he thought as he climbed into his truck. He really needed to check the weather so they'd know what they were facing tomorrow.

Of course, the weather was going to be only a small part of it.

KELLY PACKED HER usual flannel pajamas, slippers and robe, as well as a fresh set of silky thermal underwear for the morning, a clean uniform and Bugle's tug rope. From the way the air was feeling outside, she wasn't sure this storm was going to wait until the day after tomorrow.

So when they started in at dawn, they were going to have to give the search a massive effort. If only Misty could show them where she'd found the bone. Of course, any carrion eater could have dragged it away from the rest of the body. Whoever the poor victim was, he or she could be scattered over acres by now.

The pressure of time rode her like a goad. The coming storm could hamper them so much, could blow away evidence, could even bury things and freeze them so hard that the best dog might have trouble picking out a scent.

Maybe that had been part of their problem this afternoon. The body had been frozen, had lost a great many of its scents, those scents had been overlaid by whatever animals had torn at the flesh…

Cold as it was, a corpse should have been preserved, but not in the open where coyotes, bears, mountain lions and even wolves could get to it. Food was in short supply and high demand in the cold of winter. And bears, while they hibernated, often emerged from their dens in the course of the winter to hunt for food, as well. If there were easy pickings…

She didn't want to think about it. They couldn't do much until morning. At this point an air sweep probably wouldn't find a thing. Why should it? It hadn't directly after the girls had gone missing. No brightly colored clothing had given them away then, so why expect it now when the elements and the animals had had their way?

With her carryall packed, she hesitated, looking around her little house for anything she might have forgotten. The heat was on, the water was dripping so pipes wouldn't freeze, and she could think of nothing else she needed.

She and Bugle climbed into her official vehicle, which she'd left running, and a blast of warm air from the heater thawed her cheeks, which had started to freeze on the way out the door. Colder and colder.

Cold weather was nothing new here, but this was going to be a killer cold if the forecast was correct, maybe hitting thirty or forty below. That wasn't a regular event. Sure it happened sometimes in the winter, but compared with places farther north, this part of Wyoming was usually much gentler.

Regardless of what was *usual*, the approaching storm

was going to be a winter beast and would curtail them in their search for a body and evidence. Every minute tomorrow was going to count.

Al's cabin and kennels took up a couple of acres about five miles away from town along a paved county road. A big wooden sign, deeply carved and recently painted, announced that this was Conard County Animal Control, Chief Allan Carstairs. Two phone numbers, in smaller lettering, filled the bottom.

His driveway was in fairly good shape, given the time of year and that it was gravel, and soon she was pulling up to his front door and parking beside his van and his truck with the high cab on the bed to make room for cages.

Sitting out front was a cute wood cutout of a dog and a cat looking welcoming. She wondered if Al had created them.

The cabin itself, while looking like a leftover from the frontier days, was in great shape and the light pouring from windows was inviting. Smoke, caught in the gleam of her headlights, rose from a chimney. He must have built a fire.

It was almost as if all the bad things that had been riding her shoulders lifted and drifted away. There was nothing to be done tonight except enjoy time with a man she had come to like a whole lot more than she probably should.

Plus, tonight she wouldn't have to sit in her own house counting on Bugle's protection. Because whether she wanted to admit it or not, the stuffed rabbit had unnerved her. Someone had entered her house for no discernible reason and left behind a toy that might have been wearing a bow but might also have been wearing a noose.

She'd have to be made of steel not to be uneasy about that. Nor could she imagine any possible reason for it. Who the hell did *she* threaten?

Well, she had a night off from that, too. Maybe when the whole case got sorted out, she'd find out what that rabbit meant along with all the rest of it.

Then Al opened the front door, a powerful silhouette against the light behind, and waved her to come in.

For the first time in hours, she genuinely smiled. Sight for sore eyes, she thought. Bugle even gave a woof of approval.

Yeah, they'd made the right decision to accept his invitation.

REVE CAME BACK from checking on the girls. It would be his last check. He figured the coming cold would kill them, but since he wasn't entirely heartless, he'd left them some more water and food bars. Lucky the cold had put them to sleep or he wouldn't have left them anything.

Then he headed back to his place, headlights out as always, beneath a sky that had been blotted by clouds until he was practically driving into a black hole. Only once he was on the county road again did he turn his lights back on.

Nobody flying tonight. Nobody searching tonight. He felt free as a bird.

Until he got home and his landline rang. It was Spence.

"What do you want?" he asked irritably. Spence was an okay friend to have at the tavern, but Reve didn't much care for socializing in general. He'd go to church once in a while, smile at a few old ladies and grab some baked goods. The baked goods were free and were always delicious, and the old biddies pressed him to take loads because he was so thin.

Lean and mean more like, he always told himself. But he wouldn't turn down a whole pie, or an entire plate of brownies.

But friends? They had to be kept in their proper places, and Spence's proper place was at the tavern, at the pool table. Besides, he was mad at Spence for giving that deputy a hard time.

Cripes, a man on probation ought to know better.

"Hey," said Spence, "you see all the excitement of them looking for those gals this afternoon? Did you hear about the bone?"

Now Reve no longer felt like hanging up. Spence had piqued his attention. "What bone?"

"Story is some dog found it and was playing with it. Deputy Dawg took it to the hospital and they identified it as a human thighbone. You should have seen the show. They were out there for hours this afternoon with searchers and dogs. Didn't find anything."

Reve tried to decide if that was good or bad. "Sounds bad," he said finally, though he didn't mean it.

"Well, I had my fun."

"What fun?"

"You know the cars them gals was drivin'? Before Deputy Dawg came along I found it. Nothing inside. I was hoping for a wallet. Instead I found a damned stuffed rabbit. I brought it home to give to my dog for a toy, then decided to have some fun."

Reve's stomach had begun to knot. "What kind of fun?"

"I left it at the deputy's house. Only seemed right. They can't find them missing gals, and after the look she gave me at the tavern when I said something about it, I thought I'd give her a little fright."

"You said you'd left part of an animal skin!"

"Fooled ya," Spence laughed.

Reve swore. "Let me guess. You left your fingerprints all over the toy and her house!"

"Man, I ain't no fool. Had too many brushes with the law. Nah, I wore gloves. Jeez, it's cold out there. Everybody's wearing gloves. Like I'd grab something like that with my bare hands, or use them to leave it at Noveno's house. Give me some credit, Reve."

Oh, Reve gave him credit, all right. Credit for being the biggest fool to ever walk on two legs. Taunting the deputy hadn't been enough. No, he had to go drop a big fat threat at her doorstep. "If you get picked up again, blame yourself."

Spence snorted. "No way on earth they can find out it was me. Wish I'd got to the car earlier, though. I wish I'd seen what happened to those girls."

You're lucky you didn't, Reve thought as he hung up his phone. Although at this point he was wondering if Spence wasn't a liability he needed to get rid of, the sooner the better.

But how?

He sat at his table, oil and whetting stone in front of him as he followed his monthly ritual of sharpening the kitchen knives. The process soothed him, and he enjoyed seeing how the blades had worn away with time, becoming narrower but no less sharp. When he finished each one, he would wipe the oil from it and test his arm to make sure it was sharp enough to cut the hair from him, like a razor. Better than a razor.

For now, he forgot about the girls. They were rapidly passing into the rearview mirror of his life, little to interest him, soon to be gone. Their bones might be found in a century or two.

But the other one, the one he had taken out to the gully and covered with tumbleweed. A bone. So the animals had done their work, but that meant that the cops had renewed their search.

And Spence had just put his ham-fisted "joke" in the middle of it all. Damn, if those cops started taking a close look at that rabbit, they might find something from one of the girls on it. A hair. Whatever. And Spence in his absolute idiocy had thought it would be funny to try to scare the deputy with it, sure in his folly that no link would ever be made to anything.

The regular grating sound of the metal on the whetting stone created a comforting rhythm, but Reve wasn't comforted at all. Damn Spence, he might have created a serious problem for him. No, there was nothing that should link Reve to the girls, but the rabbit… How had he overlooked the rabbit when he pulled everything out of the car? What if it had *Reve's* hair on it? Just because he'd been wearing a watch cap didn't mean strands of his hair weren't elsewhere, ready to fall off him like mini grenades.

Crap, that thought really disturbed him. There he'd been trying to be so careful and only *now* did it occur to him that there might have been a stray hair or two on his jacket or jeans?

Not that it mattered unless they caught him. He'd

never been arrested, nobody had his DNA that he knew of...

He twisted on the chair, putting the knife down, and reached into the fridge for another longneck. He was worrying too much. The girls would be gone, nobody would find them for a hundred years. Think how much harder he'd have made it on himself if he'd tried to bring them here and make them behave. Nah, that first girl had taught him a lesson. He just hadn't taken it far enough.

Next time, he'd know better how to accomplish this. And he'd start with one girl at a time.

AL'S LIVING ROOM was hardly any bigger than her own, and it, too, had a kitchen in one corner, except he didn't have a bar as a divider.

A fire burned warmly on a fieldstone hearth, adding cheery light and warmth. As he took her bag and leaned it nearby against a log wall, she turned slowly to look. Yes, it was a log cabin, but the whole feel of it, dark wood and all, made it seem so cozy, much more so than her house, which she had already thought was cozy.

Then she spied a small white Christmas tree in the corner near the front door and wide window. She couldn't help smiling.

"I know," he said, as if reading her mind. "It's still there. But some nights I just like to light it up and watch it change colors. It's fiber optic with one of those color wheels."

"Red and green?"

"Nah. More pastel. If you like, I'll show you later. But while the pizza is still warm..."

He'd gotten a pie with everything except anchovies.

Maybe he'd made the store put extra veggies and pepperoni on it, because she couldn't remember seeing one loaded with so many green peppers, onions and mushrooms.

Two plates sat beside the box, and he served her a piece, inviting her to sit on his sofa. He actually had a sofa. But before he served himself, he opened a kitchen cupboard and pulled out a rawhide bone for Bugle. He looked at Kelly. "Is it okay for me to give this to him?"

She appreciated his understanding of the bond between her and Bugle that had to be protected, but it didn't need to be protected every single second.

Bugle knew exactly what Al was holding, and sat at attention, his mouth framing his version of an eager smile.

"Bugle, okay." At once the dog trotted over to Al and quickly accepted the gift. Al grinned.

The dog decided this place was okay and the offering pleased him. Soon he was sprawled on a colorful area rug, gnawing intently and happily.

Al joined her on the sofa with his plate. "TV might be hard to come by. They never ran the cable all the way out here, but I have a dish. I use it mostly for internet, but I can get a few stations if you're in the mood. Otherwise I have a collection of movies that ought to embarrass me."

"Why?"

"Because every time I think about how much I've spent on DVDs, I think how much healthier my bank account could look."

She laughed, then took a bite of her pie. "This is great. What magic wand did you use?"

"A credit card that was willing to pay for extra toppings. I mean, I like the sauce and cheese well enough, but it's the toppings I'm really after."

"One piece will be an entire meal!"

He winked. "For you, maybe." Plate in hand, he rose from the couch and walked over to his little Christmas tree. It wasn't very large, just over three feet, but when he flipped a switch it became a gorgeous panoply of slowly changing lights. To her delight, she thought the nearly pastel colors were prettier than the usual Christmas colors.

"There," he said, returning to her side. "A little ambience. We could sure use some. Today was tough."

In so many ways. The bone, a virtual guarantee that at least one of the girls was dead. As for the other two…

Kelly sighed and closed her eyes. A moment later she started as she felt a weight on her thigh. Opening her eyes, she saw Al's hand.

"Don't stop eating. I shouldn't have mentioned it. Even on the battlefield we took breaks when we could. Otherwise you go nuts or become useless."

He probably had a point, she thought. It was hard to shed the feeling of wasted time, of guilt, but there was nothing they could do out there tonight. It was dangerously cold. How many people did they want to put in the hospital from frostbite or hypothermia when they didn't even have a definite place to look?

If only they could ask Misty where she'd found that bone, but the dog wasn't likely to learn to talk. Then she had a thought and sat bolt upright.

"What?" Al asked immediately.

"Misty," she said. "What if we took her back out there? She might want to find another bone to play with. If they were close enough, she might be able to guide us to others."

He nodded slowly, evidently thinking about it. "It might work. She was sure having fun with it, and a dog would remember where there were others."

"I never had a dog lose a rawhide bone. Hide it maybe, lose it never."

"I think we should try it. I'll give the Avilas a call in the morning and ask to borrow Misty. Better clear it with the sheriff, too, I guess."

Her appetite was coming back and just before she took a bite of pizza, she said, "I think Gage would try anything that had even a remote chance of helping."

"I'd walk barefoot on desert sand right now. I think he's probably feeling about the same."

"I know I am."

She managed to finish the slice, but her mind was wandering down the rabbit hole again. What if she'd found the car a little earlier? What if she'd looked a little closer for some evidence? Why hadn't she been more suspicious?

That was really killing her, that she'd treated a car in the ditch as a matter of no importance once she found that no one was in it and hurt. While that might have been true most of the time, it sure as hell hadn't been that night.

God!

But even so, she wasn't sure what she might have done differently. She'd been beating her head on that wall since the instant she learned that three young women had been in that car and that all of them were missing.

What *could* she have done differently? She didn't

even know who was involved. She'd called the phone number on the registration and left a message when there was no answer. It wasn't as if she could have even done a thing to raise the alarm earlier.

Fingers snapped in front of her. Startled, she drew back a little and looked at Al. "What?"

"Come out of that hole you're digging. It's not going to help anything at all, Kelly. Beating yourself up is no help either. I should know."

She shook her head a little, but he wouldn't let her look away. He placed his finger beneath her chin and turned her head toward him. His gray eyes had grown distant and dark, like windows on hell.

"I was on a mission. Afghanistan. We were supposed to be training a local unit in mountain patrols. Unfortunately, we trusted the wrong people. I lost two men. Two. Our supposed allies turned on us, right when we were vulnerable because we were supposed to be working together. You wanna know how many weeks I spent beating myself up over that?"

She drew a long breath, unable to look away now. He was sharing something deeply personal and painful, and deserved her full attention. Her heart felt as if it were squeezing in her chest. So much anguish, so carefully controlled.

"There should have been a clue, I thought. I should have seen some sign that they were plotting, that they weren't trustworthy, that they meant us harm. How in the hell could I have eaten with them, joked with them, traipsed shoulder to shoulder with them on that patrol and never, *never* picked up on any warning sign?"

"Al…" she breathed.

"Yeah," he said after a few beats. "I know that hole

you're digging. I've plumbed it all the way to the bottom. Thing is, I never got an answer. I just kept hating myself until another officer who'd gone through the same thing finally asked me, 'Are you supposed to be psychic? Prescient? None of us is that. None.' I got his point. It was a while before I could let go, and I still get angry, but I've had to accept I didn't do anything *wrong.*" His gaze lost a bit of its edge. "You didn't do anything wrong either. Get used to it. It'll never feel good, but the guilt is wasted. You did everything right."

She had a feeling it might be a while before she'd be able to believe that, but she could accept what he was saying about not digging herself into a deep hole. Beating herself up hadn't done a bit of good so far. Not one little bit.

He stirred, setting his plate aside on an end table, then scooted over until he could wrap his arm around her shoulders and draw her into a loose but comforting embrace. "I can't dictate the best way for you to handle this," he said quietly. "We're all different and I'm no shrink. But I honestly feel that you didn't do anything wrong. Not easy to live with, but not everything is easy. Especially stuff like this."

She placed her plate on the arm of the sofa and turned into him, enjoying the warmth and strength of his embrace, only in those moments realizing how *lonely* she'd been feeling in the past few weeks. His scents, of the outdoors, of man, filled her, touching her deeply in ways she hadn't felt in a long time.

Yeah, she was surrounded by comrades who'd joined the search, but she still felt alone, probably because she'd been the one to find the car. No one else had to deal with that.

But Al understood, and he was offering comfort. And while she tried to remain strong at all times, she could remember tears in her own father's eyes from time to time, and it didn't seem like weakness to accept the comfort Al was offering.

He tightened his arm around her shoulders just a bit, making her feel more secure, letting her know that she was welcome. Resting her head on his chest, she listened to his strong, steady heartbeat and watched the play of firelight and his silly little fiber-optic tree. It felt almost as if she'd stepped into some kind of dream.

Another world, one far away from her worries of the past few weeks. Could it be so bad to take a break for just one evening, especially when the temperature was dropping dramatically outside and no one could possibly continue the search?

The sight of Bugle happily gnawing on his rawhide added to the feeling of contentment that was trying to rise in her, offering her that break she probably needed. No reason to feel guilty. No reason to beat her head on the problem until morning. She said another prayer for the girls out there and hoped that they'd finally get a break in the morning. But until then…

Al murmured her name.

At once she lifted her head and looked at him.

"I'm no good at this," he said, brushing a strand of hair back from her face.

"At what?"

"I told you. Relationships. But…" Almost as if an invisible force tugged them together, their faces came close and their mouths met. At first it was a tentative kiss, a feeling-out, but not for long. Kelly reached up a hand to cradle the back of his head and draw him closer, to deepen the kiss that soon grew hard and demanding.

Oh, man, it had been too long, she thought. Entirely too long because of all her scruples about her job but all those scruples seemed to be vanishing before the force of her need for this man.

This one man, not just any man, she realized hazily as her body began to awaken to desire long suppressed. Man, she should have jumped his bones ages ago. The idea nearly drew a giggle from her.

Apparently he felt it because he pulled back a little, letting her catch her breath. "What's funny?"

She could feel her cheeks heat. She hoped he thought it was the heat from the fireplace, although it wasn't *that* warm. "It's silly," she said, sounding as if she had to force the words out.

"Oh. That's okay. I always thought you were the most wildly beautiful woman I'd ever seen."

Wildly beautiful? Her heart slammed and began a rapid tap dance of delight. "I was just thinking…" She drew a breath and blurted it. Truth for truth. "I was just thinking I should have jumped your bones a long time ago."

The smile that spread over his face would have lit the arctic night brighter than the aurora. "Oh, I do like the sound of that."

With a gentle hand, he cupped her cheek and drew her in for another kiss. "Jump away," he murmured against her lips. "Anytime."

She was falling into him, all wariness and reluctance fading away, her world becoming Al Carstairs. Everything else vanished as her body felt a new tide rising, a tide of need and longing, a tsunami of desire long denied. It was washing through her and over her and driving out everything else.

The world drifted away, the universe became this one man and their embrace.

She felt as if everything inside her were quivering, steadily working her into a rhythmic need that made her clench her thighs and start to roll her hips. Oh, man, she needed, wanted…

A woof startled her. She and Al separated quickly.

Hazy-eyed, with her lips feeling swollen, she turned her head and saw Bugle eyeing them quizzically.

"Oh, boy," said Al. "Jealous?"

"I'm not sure." She shook her head a little, trying to come back to reality, much as she didn't want to. She was, however, acutely aware of what this dog could do if he thought she was in trouble.

"Maybe," she said slowly, "it's his training. He's not supposed to let anyone touch me except casually."

Al snorted. "This could get fun."

"This could be maddening," she replied, regaining some of her sense of humor. "Now I've got to figure out how to let him know you're okay."

He laughed. "Are you sure that's wise?"

She liked the twinkle in his eyes, and the way he was taking this with humor. At that moment she wasn't very happy with Bugle. Interference at exactly the wrong time. Her body was still humming with the forces Al had awakened in her, but she had to deal with Bugle first. He probably wouldn't bite Al without a command, but he could easily insert himself between them as a matter of protection.

"Hmm," she said.

"Yeah," he answered.

"Bugle, it's okay."

He tilted his head the other way, as if trying to figure out this new and perplexing situation.

Kelly leaned slowly into Al's side and took his hand in hers. Bugle whimpered quietly. "It's okay," she said firmly.

He didn't budge, but his gaze was skimming over the entire situation.

"I should have asked Cadel for a command to tell him someone's a good person," she remarked dryly. "I could lock him in another room."

"I saw what he did to the door in your house. Nope, we gotta win him over. I have an idea."

He slid off the couch until he was on the floor. He reached out his hand, letting Bugle sniff him. "Now you come down here, too."

Kelly dropped to the floor beside him.

"Now start petting him like you're playing a little rough. When he seems happy I'll get in on the action with you."

Made sense, Kelly thought, but she never in her life would have imagined that she'd have to get her K-9's permission to make love. "Let me pull out his tennis ball, too. You can toss that for him a few times when he seems to be mellowing. That's his signal for playtime."

Al smiled. "He's not exactly *un*mellow right now. Just unsure."

She had several tennis balls in her tote, but brought out only one. She made a big ceremony of giving it to Al. Bugle was instantly engaged.

"Okay, big boy," she said, using both her hands to scratch around his neck, then playfully push him side to side. It took a minute or two, but soon he adopted the play posture, lowering his front legs until he rested on them. A happy woof escaped him.

She moved in for some more easy wrestling, and when Al joined her, Bugle didn't object. Soon he was bounding around the room and coming back to them both to nudge at them with his nose. Then Al threw the tennis ball.

And Bugle fell in love.

Kelly was laughing aloud at her dog's antics, and Al grinned from ear to ear. Bugle ran back with the ball and dropped it on Al. One more toss and he brought it back to give it to Kelly to throw. The bond was happening.

Eventually, Kelly fell back against the sofa, laughing, worn out from dog wrestling and ball tossing, as well as a long workday. She wasn't totally worn out by any means, but Bugle and Al had managed to ease her emotional turmoil.

Bugle could probably have kept at it for a long while, but he sensed the humans were done, so he returned to gnawing his rawhide as if it were all that existed on the planet.

Kelly looked over at Al and enjoyed the sight of him sprawled on his back on the floor. He seemed so relaxed now, the kind of relaxation she'd seen in him before only when he was helping animals. He'd reached his place of serenity.

His position also revealed his body in a way she'd never really noticed before. Oh, she'd always known he had a great build, but as he rested there, she could see how deep and powerful his chest was, how broad his shoulders and how incredibly flat his belly. Narrow hips, long legs with thigh muscles that showed even through his jeans…

He was a man in prime condition. Her heart fluttered, and the heat he'd ignited in her renewed. Every cell in her body quivered with anticipation. If only he would roll over, reach for her, touch her in places no one touched her. She lost her breath just thinking about it. His hands on her breasts, between her legs.

Oh, man, the bug had bit badly. She'd locked away her womanly impulses for so long, acutely aware that she was trying to make her way in a man's world. In Fort Lauderdale, in Laramie, there'd been plenty of guys ready to remind her that she was "just a woman." There hadn't been any of that here in Conard County, maybe because they'd long had female deputies, and two of them were closely related to one of their most prominent, Deputy Micah Parish. She was sure nobody wanted to ever get on Micah's bad side.

But Sarah Ironheart and Connie Parish were both related to him through marriage, one to his brother, one to his son. Nope, they were accepted, all right, and that acceptance seemed to have extended to her and the few other women on the force. Connie hadn't always been a deputy, she recalled, but after Ethan joined the department, so had she. Then Ethan had left to help Micah with his ranch and Connie had remained.

Micah, she sometimes felt, was easing his way out of the department, working fewer hours, spending more time at home with Faith and their family. But with Micah, it was hard to be sure of anything.

And why was she thinking of him and his family, anyway? He was a solid man, an excellent deputy, and as far as she could tell blessed with both a deep spirituality and strong compassion.

None of that had anything to do with right now except that she was trying to divert herself before she did something incredibly forward, like jump Al's bones.

Her cheeks grew hot as she remembered saying that out loud, but she'd said it, and she'd meant it. And he'd called her wildly beautiful. Wow. That compliment reached all the way to her very core. Never once in her life had she ever felt that way about herself, nor had anyone ever told her that. But Al had, lifting her self-image in a new way.

Her thoughts were starting to drift to the frigid night outside, and the missing girls. One maybe dead, but what about the others? She couldn't know. No one could. All they could do was hope and restart the search in the morning.

In the meantime, Al was right, she shouldn't dig herself into that hole. Right now it could do no good except ruin this entire night.

Al seemed to be watching the patterns the firelight and his Christmas tree made on the ceiling. The logs dulled the glow quite a bit but didn't entirely erase the dancing color. It all looked so warm.

And he looked so inviting.

Hardly aware of what she was doing, she pushed away from the couch and crawled across the floor toward him. She felt Bugle's eyes on her, then heard him resume his gnawing.

Al spoke. "If you're about to do what I think you're about to do, should we let the dog take a walk, first? He's already proved he has a talent for timely interruption."

He wasn't looking at her, but she could see the corners of his firm mouth twitch. In spite of the tension and excitement that filled her, she had to laugh. She loved that he could make her laugh.

"Probably," she answered, hearing the huskiness in her own voice.

To her surprise, he reached out and tugged her gently until she fell on his chest, then arranged her so she lay squarely on top of him. "I want you," he said boldly. "But the damn dog…"

Then he kissed her so hard and so deeply she felt as if he took possession of her very soul. Soon the niggling needs that had been tempting her with excited anticipation had become a wildfire of hunger.

"The dog," he said, tearing his mouth from hers. "Damn, do you feel good."

Then he rolled her gently to the side and rose to his feet in one smooth movement. "Bugle, walk."

Kelly tried to clear her throat and brain. "Business," she said.

Bugle at once dropped his rawhide bone and headed for the door where Al awaited him. A moment later he darted out into the frigid night.

"I bet he doesn't take long," Al remarked. "I think we've lost another ten or fifteen degrees. Must be on their way to Texas."

A thought that another time might have made her laugh, but right now impatience was riding her like a goad. If one more thing kept her from discovering what sex with Al was like, she might groan in frustration. She was hardly able to think of anything else at all. Unfortunately, he'd been right about the dog.

A few minutes later, a bark alerted them. Al opened

the door and Bugle trotted in, a few snowflakes dotting his coat like diamonds. Then something else followed him at top speed.

"Regis?" Al said, disbelieving. "What the—"

Kelly sat up instantly. A gray squirrel had darted across the floor, then turned around and set himself up in the tiny Christmas tree.

It was too much. Bugle looked befuzzled, Al looked astonished and there was a gray squirrel sitting in an artificial tree amid the fiber-optic lighting.

Kelly started to laugh. Maybe it was hysterical laughter, but it felt damn good, and she wound up leaning against the couch and holding her sides. "Regis? What?"

"Exactly. What?" Al squatted and studied this new conundrum. "You didn't really want to go to bed with me tonight, did you?"

"I did."

"Well, we seem to have a whole bunch of busybodies here."

"Bugle will behave."

"I'm sure," Al retorted. "But Regis? I may have hand-raised him when he was orphaned last spring, but he's never been what I would call trained."

"So he doesn't have a family?"

"How would I know? He's been pretty much living as a free squirrel since I was able to release him last spring, but whether he hooked up with other squirrels, or had a family of his own, I have no idea. He just shows up from time to time, like he wants to visit."

"Or maybe tonight is just too damn cold and you opened a warm door."

"Entirely possible." He sighed, then settled cross-legged on the floor. "I'd feel like a monster throwing him out if he's too cold but we *do* have a dog in here."

There was that inescapable fact. Just because she'd never seen Bugle chase squirrels or rabbits or anything like that didn't mean he wouldn't suddenly take a notion. "So you raised Regis, huh?"

"Well, I wasn't going to leave him to starve to death."

She was loving this view of Al. Hand-raising a squirrel? Letting the animal ride with him sometimes? The squirrel trusting enough to come inside even though there was a dog in here?

She looked at Bugle, who was still eyeing the animal as if unsure how to react. "Bugle, okay. Relax." *Relax* was a word she'd been using with him for the last few years and she had no idea if he grasped the concept. She was sure that dog understood more English than anyone realized, but she couldn't always be certain *which* words made sense and how he might interpret them.

Bugle shifted from one side to another, watching the squirrel, which seemed to be regarding him with at least some suspicion. He lowered himself slowly, reluctantly.

"Solution," said Al, rising. He walked out into his small kitchen and returned with a custard bowl full of sunflower seeds. "This'll keep Regis happy. As for Bugle…we could take him and his rawhide into the bedroom with us if you're still interested."

Still interested? She felt like a pot simmering on low heat, just waiting for the right time to boil. "Oh, yeah," she answered.

He smiled and held out his hand. "Not exactly the most romantic way to start out."

"I'm not looking for romance." And she wasn't. If there was ever to be any romance between them, it could come later. Tonight she wanted passion, fire and forgetfulness.

Bugle picked up his bone and followed them into the bedroom. Behind her, Kelly could hear the squirrel cracking sunflower seeds.

It was indeed as if she had entered a whole new world with Al, and when he drew her into his arms, she went with a leaping, eager heart. Had she spent all this time avoiding her attraction to him? Because it felt as if it had been deeply rooted in her forever.

Impatience was winning, however. They'd spent enough time dealing with dogs and then a squirrel. She wanted him and wanted him now before anything else happened.

He laughed quietly as she pulled at his shirt, and as their eyes met she saw both heat and delight in his gaze. He was as eager as she, and with every touch she seemed to lift out of herself until she felt she was floating in space.

Their clothes vanished, although she couldn't remember how and didn't especially care. At long last came the moment when they tumbled onto his bed in glorious nakedness, nothing left between them but bare skin.

The feeling of skin on skin was beyond compare, like nothing else in the world. She could feel the shackles of the everyday world letting go, could feel the freedom of being naked with a man and free to touch however she chose.

An amazing exuberance filled her, joining the growing heat that made her breasts ache and caused her to throb hungrily between her legs.

Running her hands over him, enjoying the way he

moaned softly at her touches, she felt scars and signs of old injuries but ignored them for now. Nothing, absolutely nothing, was going to get in the way now. There would be later.

His small nipples were already hard, as hard as hers seemed to be, and she couldn't resist tonguing them and nipping gently, causing him to writhe and grab her shoulders. So much here to explore and discover. Sliding her hand down over his flat belly, she reached for his groin and found him stiff and ready, jerking at her lightest touch.

Excitement rushed through her, stronger than ever. She had wakened this in him. The sense of power and delight overwhelmed her.

She held him, stroking his silkiness softly, teasingly while she continued to torment the small buds of his nipples.

Then he apparently had enough.

He rolled her over and suddenly he was above her on his elbows, and the drowsy smile on his face promised more tortures to come. Tortures for her.

His tongue trailed over her neck, at first making it warm, then a chill followed, a delicious shiver. She'd never guessed her neck could respond that way. She grabbed his shoulders, feeling as if she would fall over a cliff edge if she didn't hang on for dear life.

Evidently he was as impatient as she, because soon he trailed his kisses to her breasts, sucking gently at first, then so hard she felt as if he were going to consume her. With each movement of his mouth, he sent another wave of desire racing through her, making her feel as if electric wires joined her breasts and her loins. Like being strung on a welder's arc, she burned for him.

His fingers found the sensitive nub between her legs, and at his first touch she learned that pain and pleasure could be the same. He rubbed her, his touches growing harder until her hips bucked helplessly, and moans escaped her. She had become a mindless bundle of need and want and he seemed to know it.

Then, at last, he slid over her and into her, filling her until everything inside her clenched with pleasure. Yesssssssss…

His thrusts were powerful, each one causing another happy moan to escape her. She felt as if he were pushing her, driving her ever higher into a world of magic, a place where stars exploded and filled the night with wonder.

Then came one last endless, almost painful moment when everything inside her seemed to pause in an infinite time of anticipation, where she almost feared she wouldn't tumble over the edge into satisfaction.

But with one last thrust, he brought her more pleasure and pain, the ecstasy of completion. Her world seemed to turn white like flame, and satisfaction rolled through her whole body like a powerful wave.

A cry escaped her, then him, and she felt him shudder as he followed her over the cliff into completion.

The world had slipped away, leaving her spent and happy, and secure in his arms. Nothing could be more perfect.

Chapter Twelve

The night passed too swiftly, yet not swiftly enough. Kelly slept better than she had any night since the teens disappeared, but even before the sun was up the anxiety began to fill her. The storm would arrive later today or early tomorrow. If they hoped to get any forensic evidence from where Misty had found that bone, this might be their only chance for a while.

The girls' lives might hinge on their speed.

Al appeared to feel pretty much the same. They'd managed to put the pizza in the fridge last night before it could spoil, and now he pulled it out. "Cold pie okay? I wanna start calling."

"Absolutely." Instead of feeding herself immediately, she took her bag into the bedroom and pulled out her fresh uniform. Bugle, who had spent the night at the foot of the bed, behaving himself, at once became alert. He loved to work.

Once she'd dressed and straightened herself up in his small bathroom, she emerged to smell coffee, to see a squirrel watching the world from his artificial tree and to hear Al on the phone. Now he was talking to Gage.

"It was Kelly's idea. She's thinking that Misty might remember where she found the bone, and I agree with her. Dogs don't lose their bones."

Gage must have agreed, because a minute later Al was on the phone with Misty's owners. It was early yet, but not as early as it might have been with the winter sun rising so late. The Avilas were agreeable to sharing their dog. They didn't know exactly why, and she gathered that Al had never mentioned the bone to them. They were, however, glad to do whatever they could to help with the search.

Good. They didn't need to be feeling uneasy around their dog because he'd been playing with a human bone. He was just a dog, making no moral connection to the idea of not disturbing a corpse.

They scarfed the pizza down with unseemly speed, and Al filled an insulated bottle with the fresh coffee before turning the pot off. Then he opened the door. "Out, Regis. You can't stay inside all day."

"Will he make a mess?" Kelly asked.

"He already has with those seed shells, but that's not what I'm worried about. He needs to be out doing squirrel things or I'll start to feel like I've deprived him of a real life by hand-raising him."

Kelly flashed a grin even as her stomach turned over nervously in anticipation of the day ahead. "You made sure he has a life. Right now he looks pretty happy."

But Regis was still a squirrel at heart, and with the door open he dashed out into the cold day. A wind had begun to batter the world, heralding the coming bad weather.

"I hope this storm doesn't show up earlier than expected," Kelly remarked as she pulled on her gloves and her watch cap.

"We'll do what we can. I'll catch up with you once I have Misty. The place where we found her?"

"Best place to start."

He caught her at the door before she could slip out and pressed a hard kiss on her mouth. "Later," he said. "Tonight."

Oh, she had no problem with that idea.

Bugle leaped up eagerly into his cage, and Kelly closed him in. He was going to need booties and his quilted vest today, she thought as the wind turned her cheeks almost instantly to ice.

It was a relief to climb into the cab of her truck and get out of the wind. She suspected the heater would take a while before it started blasting. Worse, she saw that snowflakes were falling again. Lightly. Almost like a promise more than a threat.

She had to face something, she realized as she drove back to the place on the country road where she'd found Al trying to corral Misty: finding the remains might not tell them a damn thing.

She'd been hoping—she supposed everyone was still hoping—that they'd find the remains and find a clue. A clue as to what had happened, a clue as to who had done it. Would they? With a sinking stomach, she seriously feared they wouldn't learn a single useful thing, and maybe not in time to save the other girls even if they did. How long would forensics take?

No answers. They were racing into the teeth of a winter storm to gather evidence that might not save a single life. That might not help them find the perp.

This was the part of police work she most hated, finding evidence that didn't lead to the perp. Evidence that would be useful only once they found the baddie. Great in court, but no lighted road to the door of a killer or rapist.

Nor any guarantee that they would find something to lead them to the other girls, if the bone did indeed come from one of them. No guarantee they could save their lives.

No guarantees at all.

JANE AND CHANTAL huddled together beneath the stinking blankets. Upon awakening, Jane had remarked that there was more food and water. The thinnest stream of light that came through a crack in the boards over the window had become, for the girls, almost as bright as a midday sun. It was the only light they ever saw, and somehow they adapted.

They found, too, that they'd each had one hand released from the chains. They used the slightly increased mobility to double the blankets and give themselves a little more warmth in their cocoon as they downed the power bars with the aid of water. Neither of them cared anymore if the water was drugged. Sleep was now preferable to wakefulness.

"We're never going to get out of here," Jane said.

"We can't be sure." But in all honesty, Chantal figured she was going to die in this hole. All eating and drinking did was forestall the inevitable. But she didn't want to say that to Jane. Having both of them suicidally depressed would help nothing at all.

She pushed up as best she could to pick out the place where they'd stuffed strands of yarn from her bright green sweater. Only one strand appeared to be left in the crack. Not enough to be seen by anyone.

"Finish that bar," she said wearily to Jane. "We're going to unravel some more of my sweater, make a bigger flag to shove out there."

Jane merely sighed, as if an answer required more strength than she had. Minutes passed before she appeared to find energy to reply. "You tear down that sweater too much and you're going to freeze to death." She paused. "It doesn't matter, does it?"

"Of course it matters or I wouldn't be trying. We're going to make this as big as we can fit into that crack. This color ought to stand out like neon." The winter countryside now was so washed out with shades of winter brown and gray-green that any bright color ought to catch attention. She pulled at the yarn, trying to gather her exhausted thoughts into an idea of what to do with this to make it more noticeable. That crack, after all, wasn't very big. Long streamers had evidently been pulled out by the wind. So maybe a big ball to anchor them. She yanked more yarn out of the sweater.

Then Jane caused a new and different kind of chill to run through Chantal. "When he brought this last water and food, I saw his face. If we could get out, I could identify him."

Chantal stared blindly into the near darkness, her fingers growing still. If he hadn't concealed his face, he meant for them to die here. She'd begun to suspect it but facing the reality made her quail deep inside. She didn't want to die. She was only eighteen. There were so many things she had always wanted to do. A tear burned in her eye, but it was wasteful and she was almost perpetually dehydrated in the icy air, despite the water bottles. The tear never escaped and she sought to stabilize her reeling emotions. "Jane?"

"Yeah. I know. God help me, if I get a chance…"

"Who is he?"

"We saw him playing pool at the tavern with another guy. I could point him out. I could describe him. So could you. He was the shorter one."

Chantal flashed back to what had since become the last happy moments of her short life, and she did indeed remember. Ick. What a creep! Was she going to let him win?

Sudden strength infused her limbs and she started pulling at the yarn of her sweater once again. "We're going to get out of here, Jane. Our parents won't quit. They won't let anyone quit. We'll get out of here if I have to knit us booties for our feet with my teeth. But right now we need to poke out the biggest flag I can put together. Someone will see it because I swear they haven't stopped looking."

"Maybe not," Jane said tiredly. "Mary Lou…"

"We can't afford to think about her now. I'm afraid…"

"Me, too." Jane fell silent, then said, "Want me to try to braid some of those strands?"

"Good idea. The wind's probably getting strong enough to blow them around. Let's make them longer and fatter."

As she ruthlessly ripped yarn from her sweater into

long lengths, she sawed it with her teeth to separate it so Jane could braid it.

"I never imagined," Jane muttered, "that braiding my horse's mane for the county fair would come in useful."

Under any other circumstances, Chantal would have laughed. But some creep had stolen her laughter. She wanted it back.

THE CREEP IN question had closed the shutters over the windows of his ramshackle house to better withstand the coming storm. He pulled his pickup into the lean-to that would provide some shelter. He'd already stocked up on supplies, and even had extra thanks to all the energy bars and water he'd bought for those girls. So if he got snowed in and for some reason lost the use of his water pump, he'd be fine.

And they'd be dead.

Crazy, he thought. He'd wanted to make them his slaves, to whip them into line and make them serve him in any way he decided. Now they were going to die because of Spence's stupidity and a coming storm that would probably suck the last life out of them with its cold.

He ought to be furious. Instead he only felt two things: fear that he might have left evidence on that stuffed rabbit he'd overlooked, and a strangely warm feeling about those girls dying.

Odd, he'd been mad when he killed the first one. She'd infuriated him and gotten her just deserts. He hadn't felt then what he was feeling now: a kind of pleasurable delight not unlike sex.

Those two girls would die on his say-so because he refused to set them free. They were totally at his mercy, and he liked that. Although he could have let them out, he supposed. They'd die quickly enough in their thin clothes with nothing but slipper socks on their feet. He'd made sure that they had no warm winter gear for protection.

Once that storm started howling, he could throw them out into its fury and let it erase them until long after they were dead. By the time anyone found them, they'd probably be as chewed up as the one he'd already tossed aside. He kind of liked that image, too. On the other hand, forcing them to lie in that basement and just die because he *wouldn't* let them go appealed to him even more. *He* was the man in charge, in charge of something more important than shoveling manure and fixing old cars for the first time in his life.

A few nights ago he hadn't been able to resist visiting the body of the first girl. He wanted to see what the animals and elements had done to her. Bones had been tossed about, little flesh was left at all, and the only thing that caught his eye was a small gold necklace with a cross that he'd missed at the outset.

He considered taking it, then decided it didn't matter anymore if they identified the body.

They wouldn't be able to trace it to him. Let her family have that stupid keepsake…if they ever found the body.

He was sitting there, enjoying a longneck, patting himself on his back mentally, thinking just how smart he was.

Then there was a hammering at his door.

MISTY FOUND THE BONES, all right. At first she seemed to have no interest in helping, as if she couldn't understand what they expected of her. But then Kelly decided it was worth a try and retrieved the target bags. The bags containing pieces of clothing from the girls. Just maybe Misty would remember the scent and along with it the bones, although her hopes weren't really high.

"The cadaver dogs didn't find anything," she remarked to Al as she zipped the bags closed. "Why should Misty?"

"Maybe the cadaver dogs didn't get close enough." He shrugged one shoulder as Gage joined them. A line of searchers, already looking cold, edged the road again.

"I think," Gage said, "that it's time we got some luck on this. By the way, that rabbit left at your place? I sent it to the lab for forensics. Something not right about any of that."

"Tell me," Al said dryly.

"Okay, let's see what Misty can do for us. Maybe Bugle can follow the scent."

"I don't know," Kelly answered honestly. "Misty may remember she smelled it before when she found the bone. Bugle wouldn't be able to track it from here unless the victim passed this way."

"Good point." Gage shook his head. The last three weeks seemed to have aged him. "All right. Go for it, Al."

Misty suddenly became eager. Maybe she wanted to get back to her toys. Maybe she just wanted an excuse to run around the countryside. Only time would tell.

The rest of the searchers were told to keep back about twenty feet in case something turned up. They didn't want the scents to become muddied.

For a while it seemed as if Misty was prancing around the field as she had the day Al had found her with the bone. But Misty had her own methods of operation, and eventually the dancing gave way to a more directed movement. She *did* seem to know where she was going.

Kelly followed a little more closely with Bugle but was careful not to get in the way in case Misty made a discovery. Behind her, crime scene techs were ready to get to work, the sooner the better given the increasingly bitter cold.

Then Misty came upon the remains, over two miles in from a county road, in a gully now filled with tumbleweed. She jumped around, then wanted to dive in, but Al restrained her with a powerful arm.

Bugle walked a little closer and announced with a whimper that he recognized the odor. At once he sat at attention.

There was nothing left, Kelly thought as the team cautiously pulled away the tumbleweed. Nothing but some hair. Not even a scrap of cloth. Teeth and DNA would probably be necessary for ID, and the bones were pretty well scattered around.

Gage stood at the edge of the gully for long moments, then said, "My God, I recognize that cross." He looked up, closed his eyes and appeared to steel himself. "Mary Lou."

A HALF HOUR LATER, Kelly felt so helpless and hopeless she could barely stand it. Bugle kept pulling her west, toward another county road, as if he was after something. Finally, she decided to give him his head.

"Bugle scents something. I'm going to let him lead."

Gage nodded. "Go."

Al, who was still hanging on to a disappointed Misty, looked as if he wanted to go with her.

"Take Misty home," she said. "You'll be able to find me at the road out there. How far will I go without my truck?"

"Give me your keys. I'll bring it to you after I return Misty."

She watched him and the dog trot away, then looked at Bugle. "I hope you know what you're doing."

Because it was utterly unlikely that girl had gotten here under her own steam. If she had, there'd at least have been some patches of cloth left.

Bugle put his nose to the ground but after about five yards lifted it, indicating that whatever he was looking for was in the air.

It never ceased to amaze her that dogs could detect odors up to three hundred feet above their heads, and odors that might be weeks old, even in the air. The dang air was moving all the time, right?

But maybe he wasn't getting the scent out of the air. There was enough dry grass and brush around to have caught those odors and retain them even through the cold they'd been having. Or maybe some of the predators that had gotten to Mary Lou's body had left their own trail and he was following *them*.

Sometimes she really, truly wished Bugle could talk. She'd have loved to question him for hours about how he perceived the world.

But he was on a determined trek, and since she couldn't do anything back at the body, she might as well keep following. As the sky grew more leaden, and the wind stiffer, it occurred to her that once Al caught up to her with her truck, she could perhaps do one more swing of welfare checks along this road.

There'd been enough badness over the last few weeks. They didn't need people dying in this storm.

The hike was fairly long, well over a couple of miles before they reached the crossroad, but at least the quick pace of the walk was helping to keep her warm. She wondered if Bugle was glad of his quilted vest or if it annoyed him. But these temperatures must be as dangerous to him as to anyone else. In one of her pockets she'd tucked his booties in case it started to snow heavily. Right now he was okay, but if ice started to build up between his toes, he wouldn't be.

Not that there was any danger of that yet. Snowflakes were in the air, but so light it hardly seemed possible a killer storm was headed in over those mountains.

At last they reached the road, but Bugle wasn't done. He tugged her to the right and she followed, after closing the sagging ranch gate behind her. She just wished she knew what he was after. She guessed she'd find out when he discovered it.

So much of this county looked all the same—ranchlands and fences and wide-open vistas until you ran up against the mountains—that if she hadn't known which county road she was trotting along, she might have been anywhere.

But then something caught her eye. Something she remembered about the way the road looked. Too recently familiar. Hadn't she stopped here the other day? Somewhere just up ahead?

At that moment, Bugle came to a halt. Full stop. He sat, telling her he'd found it. She stared at him, then looked around, trying to figure it out until she remembered.

The glove.

The *glove*.

This was where they'd found that glove, and he'd tracked it from Mary Lou's remains. Her heart began to race and her stomach tried to flip over. A connection. No way to know what it meant, but it was a connection according to Bugle, and she absolutely couldn't afford to ignore it when he was doing his job.

She had yet to see him make a mistake when it came to his olfactory sense. This dog said that body was linked to this spot where the glove had been found.

Pulling off her own glove, she reached under her parka for her radio and called.

AL HEARD KELLY'S radio call shortly after he returned Misty to her owners and expressed his gratitude. He offered them absolutely no idea of the grisly task she'd been asked to perform; let them think she'd helped him round up another dog.

They wanted to talk about the storm, but he eased away from that, just warning them not to let Misty out off her lead.

"If she decides to go for a run, I may not have time to find her."

He looked at the kids, the usual aides to Houdini-dog, and they nodded solemnly with wide eyes.

He picked up Kelly's truck, leaving his own behind, and headed out to the county road where he'd promised to meet her. So Bugle had tracked the glove all the way from the remains. Although she didn't mention the body directly, only that he'd followed the trail from where she'd started her walk. Damn, dogs were amazing.

Not that this was going to tell them enough to find the other girls or the kidnapper. But it was still an essential link.

He listened to the chatter. Gage asked Kelly to flag the location and said he'd send some deputies out her way if she found anything else. Right now they were busy searching the current area for other signs.

"So far," Gage said irritably, "our dogs have found two raccoons and a fox. Yee-haw."

"Must have had a fight over the body," someone else remarked.

"Not on the air," Gage snapped. "How many police scanners do we have in this county? Keep it all under your hat. Face-to-face or shut up."

All that skirting around the word *body* and someone had blown it with one statement. Al might have been amused under other circumstances. There was nothing amusing about this.

When he caught up with Kelly, she was standing by the road and the pin flags she'd used to mark the spot Bugle had led her to. They might not survive the storm, probably wouldn't, but he was sure she'd marked the GPS coordinates and saved them. Routine for her.

He offered to let her drive as she piled Bugle into his cage and into the warmth of the SUV. She shook her head and climbed into the passenger seat.

"I am so *cold* I'm not sure my fingers could manage the steering wheel," she said as she fumbled at the seat belt clasp. "Dang, that dog dragged me quite a distance in this icy weather. Three miles? Maybe more? He seems fine, though."

"Well, he *does* have that quilted vest."

"It's not like I'm running around out here naked," she answered a bit tartly. "Damn, Al. The glove. The body. So they're linked but where do they get us?"

"That the glove fell off a truck and Bugle says it was near the body. That's good for something."

"You'd think. But *who*?"

Which, of course, was the big question.

He let the vehicle idle, blowing heat into the compartment, while neither of them said a word. He suspected they were both trying to figure out what this could mean. That the kidnapper lived somewhere along this road? Or that he'd just driven through here? Hardly a guided tour of his whereabouts.

"I was thinking of driving out along here for a final welfare check," Kelly said after a few minutes. "Might as well since I'm here. But could you drive? Slowly? I want to use my binoculars to scan the countryside. Just because I didn't notice anything a few days ago doesn't mean nothing is out there. I saw a tumbledown line shack that's probably empty, but there's another house up this way a few miles. Maybe the guy noticed something."

Without a word, Al put the SUV in gear. Unlike many vehicles, it proved to be capable of moving at five miles an hour. Kelly kept her binoculars pasted to her eyes. Big binoculars, the kind he used to carry. Those long lenses could see a long way.

"Just don't hit a rut," she muttered.

Yeah, it would jam those eyepieces into the bones around her eyes. An unpleasant experience.

Then all of a sudden she said sharply, "Stop!"

He obeyed, trying not to ram the binoculars into her

eyes. The instant the vehicle stopped rolling, she hopped out and resumed scanning the countryside.

He put the vehicle in Park and locked the brake before climbing out to join her. "What did you see?"

"I thought I saw something like chartreuse. There's nothing that should be that color out here."

"Where?"

She lowered the binoculars and pointed. "Believe it or not, near the base of the line shack."

"Oh, that's not a line shack," he said as he began to scan the area she indicated, adjusting the focus to make the building even larger to his eye. "Old ranch house. Man, somebody must have abandoned it two generations ago. It was tiny! Nobody could..."

His voice trailed off as his gaze fixated.

"Al?"

"I see it, too. It looks like some fabric poking out of a boarded-up window."

"Then let's go."

He lowered the binoculars, eyed the terrain and figured they might be lucky to have suspension after this drive. Lucky if their axles weren't broken. "It's going to be rough." It also might be a humongous waste of time, although at this point it was beginning to feel like wasting time was all they were going to do, anyway.

"All right, let's go. And put your gloves back on. You need those fingers."

He could sense Kelly's impatience in the way she leaned forward against her seat belt, but she didn't press him to a higher speed. She evidently was as aware as he that Bugle was in the back and didn't want him to be banged around inside his cage.

Steadily, with plenty of stomach-dropping dips and jaw-jolting rocks, they approached the shack.

And there was no question but what something green was fluttering from a boarded-up window. Detritus blown there by the wind? Maybe, but it looked more purposeful.

This time Kelly leaped out before the vehicle fully stopped and ran toward the fluttering green strands. She leaned her face toward it and called loudly, "Girls? Are you in there? Is anyone in there?"

The wind almost snatched her words away, but he heard the response of faint cries.

"We're coming in to get you out. Sheriff."

Well, that settled that, Al thought. He couldn't even begin to describe the feelings that twisted up his insides. Good. Bad. Relief.

God help them. He feared they'd find nothing good.

Going round to the other side of the shack, he found the cellar doors, heavy steel, chained and padlocked.

"Kelly," he said, "I'm going to use my gun. Call the sheriff to send an ambulance and more help while I open this up."

Then, standing to one side and hoping a ricochet merely bounced away into the weeds, he fired at the padlock.

He heard faint screams from inside, but he had to get this damn thing open. If he'd had his own truck, he'd have had bolt cutters. But he didn't, and his gun it was going to have to be.

"One more time," he shouted, hoping that was all it would take.

Kelly came round. "Help is on the way. We could wait but I'm not sure…"

He agreed. More than anything, those girls needed to be freed. They probably needed a lot of other things, like medical help, but primarily they needed to know they were safe now.

He leveled his gun again and took another shot at the lock. This time, probably with the help of the cold, it shattered and released the chain.

Kelly beat him down the steps. He listened to girls sob. And he waited for the sirens.

They had the teens. Now they just had to find their tormentor. He went to Kelly's SUV and hunted up the blankets he was sure she must carry for use at accident scenes. When he found them, he took them downstairs and fought back a wave of fury as he saw the girls' condition. Scarecrows. Filthy scarecrows.

It had been a while since he'd killed anyone, but he wanted to kill right now.

Then he heard Chantal's friend say, "I know who took us."

Chapter Thirteen

Day 22

Walton Revell tried to blame the kidnapping on his friend Spencer. There was the stuffed rabbit, after all. Jane defeated him, however, because she'd seen him.

And when he was arraigned before Judge Wyatt Carter and looked into the black gaze of Al Carstairs, he knew he was peering into hell. For the first time it occurred to him that he might be safer in prison than in walking away from the sheriff.

He was remanded into federal custody for the kidnapping, but there were also charges of murder and attempted murder, and a whole bunch of other things that added up to false imprisonment and torture. Maybe some other stuff, too, but the feds would put him away for life, whether the state decided to pursue the other charges. His public defender, who looked as if she'd be happy to kill him herself, didn't hold out much hope.

Not even a plea bargain.

Finally, Walton Revell began to wonder what had possessed him and why he'd ever thought this would be a good idea. All he'd done was end his own freedom, not make slaves out of the girls.

Now he'd be a slave to someone inside the pen. *Great thinking, idiot.*

At least he had the pleasure of seeing Spence have to explain why he'd put the rabbit in Kelly Noveno's house. "She was taking too long," Spence answered simply. "They weren't finding them girls. I admit I took it out of the car when I saw it along the road, but I got mad when she wouldn't answer my questions about the investigation and I decided to give her a scare. Speed her up."

He got a B&E for entering her house. The county attorney said there might be additional charges, like interfering with evidence, but no one seemed in much of a rush to hang Spence. No, Spence was all too eager to hang Reve, ready to talk about how they'd often discussed what it would be like to have some women as slaves.

He thought they were just kidding around.

Apparently, Reve hadn't been.

LEGS AND HANDS SHACKLED, Reve was led out toward a cell. The FBI would be coming to get him as soon as the blizzard passed. Yeah, the same FBI who hadn't shown much interest until they got word the arrest was made.

"Better late than never," Kelly remarked.

"Well, we didn't have a heckuva lot to go on when

we first contacted them," Gage said. "I'm more interested in what they'll do now."

The storm had arrived. The outside world looked dangerous and bleak, but Al insisted Kelly and Bugle come to his place. He could tell she was dragging anchor, as if someone had let the air out of a balloon that had been overinflated.

He had some idea of how she'd been beating herself up, but now that could stop. The girls' families were with them at the hospital, and he told Kelly they'd go visit once the storm passed and it was possible to move around again.

She simply nodded. He was sure she was thinking of the lost Mary Lou, but there wasn't a thing that could be done about that.

At his place he barely unlocked the door before Regis darted in, but he didn't come alone. He had a bunch of smaller squirrels with him. His kids? Who knew. He brought out a bigger bowl of sunflower seeds and a small bowl of water and let them take up residence in his Christmas tree.

Bugle found his rawhide bone, ignored the squirrels and settled down to a happy chew. Kelly was the only one who couldn't seem to settle. She changed from her uniform into a set of flannel pajamas, a royal blue fuzzy robe and slippers and looked comfortable.

But nothing about her felt comfortable.

He made coffee, pulled out the leftover pizza and a Danish he'd bought a couple of days ago, and motioned her to eat something.

"I've got cereal and soup, too," he offered.

"This is fine." She took a mug of steaming coffee,

then sat and ate two whole pieces of cold pizza. The weather and stress had made her hungry.

Heck, everything was making him hungry, too. Without apology to himself or the world, he pulled out a package of chocolate chip cookies and opened it, dumping them in a bowl. Then he sliced himself a huge piece of Danish and dug in.

Sitting beside her on the couch, he said, "I can think of no one else on this planet I would rather be snowbound with."

That snapped her into the present. A smile began to play over her lips. "Truly?"

"Truly." He just hoped he could trust himself now, but the last few weeks had made him believe in his ability to control himself around Kelly. No out-of-control rages, no desires to smash something other than that kidnapping creep. Being around her made him feel centered.

KELLY FELT HER heart skip a few beats, then begin to rise as it hadn't risen much since the disappearance of those girls. Their kidnapping had drained most of the joy from her life, except last night in Al's arms. She wanted to know that feeling again.

Just past him she could see out the windows. He hadn't drawn the heavy curtains yet, and the blizzard was now concealing the whole world. They were locked away together for at least the next day if not longer. Her gaze trailed back to him, and she saw something new in his expression, something she hadn't seen before: hope.

"I know what I told you about me and relationships," he continued. "It might still be true, but there's only one way to find out. I've enjoyed all the time I've spent with you over the last few weeks, and I didn't get triggered, at least not much. So it's possible…if you're willing to try. Kelly, will you date me? Formally. Like movies, and dinners, and maybe…some cohabitation while we try it on?"

As if her face had been frozen for three weeks, she felt a smile crack her cheeks, almost painful in its intensity. "Yes," she said simply.

"Yes to what?"

"To dating, to cohabiting…at least if you think your squirrels can live with my dog."

His face brightened as if the sun was rising on it. Outside a storm raged, but inside peace had settled.

"I think we can all get along. Besides, Regis has his own drey if he doesn't like it here."

She glanced toward the Christmas tree, where about four squirrels seemed to be sleeping. "I think *they* like it here. I know I do."

Then, throwing the stress of weeks, along with all doubts and fears, out into the storm, she wound her arms around him and looked deeply into his eyes. "You won't escape easily, Carstairs."

"I don't want to, Noveno."

Then they dissolved into laughter and fell on the floor, rolling together and hanging on tightly. The animals left them alone.

It was happy time for people.

* * * * *

Addison Fox is a lifelong romance reader, addicted to happy-ever-afters. After discovering she found as much joy writing about romance as she did reading it, she's never looked back. Addison lives in New York with an apartment full of books, a laptop that's rarely out of sight and a wily beagle who keeps her running. You can find her at her home on the web at www.addisonfox.com or on Facebook (Facebook.com/addisonfoxauthor) and Twitter (@addisonfox).

Books by Addison Fox

Harlequin Romantic Suspense

The Coltons of Mustang Valley

Deadly Colton Search

The Coltons of Roaring Springs

The Colton Sheriff

Midnight Pass, Texas

The Cowboy's Deadly Mission
Special Ops Cowboy

The Coltons of Red Ridge

Colton's Deadly Engagement

The Coltons of Shadow Creek

Cold Case Colton

The Coltons of Texas

Colton's Surprise Heir

Visit the Author Profile page
at Harlequin.com for more titles.

COLTON K-9 COP

Addison Fox

For Max

You came into my life when I least expected it and have colored my world with puppy cuddles, cookie (mis)adventures and joy.

Always joy.

Prologue

Five years ago

She held the garland loosely in her hand as she slowly unwound the bright gold in steady, even rows. Turn by turn,
the empty green branches filled with the shiny, vivid
color as Bellamy Reeves enjoyed watching her handiwork come to life.

Her parents had asked her to work the store this evening, their annual holiday event with the local men's
club a highlight of their year. She'd been happy to do it,
the familiar work of managing the counter and ringing
up purchases at Whisperwood's only corner store something she'd been doing since childhood. It was a far cry
from her work in finance at Lone Star Pharmaceutical
but it kept her in touch with her roots and she enjoyed it.

Add on that it gave her a shot at stringing up the decorations just to her personal specifications, and it was a job she was happy to take on.

Maggie had teased her about risking spinsterhood if she were willing to work the family store on a holiday Saturday night and Bellamy had ignored her. Her sister was fond of quoting all the pithy reasons Bellamy was doomed to a lonely existence and she'd learned to ignore it.

Or, if not ignore it, at least stop caring about it so much.

Her sister was the resident beauty queen of Whisperwood, Texas. She'd had men wrapped around her finger basically since she'd crawled out of the womb and had learned to drape herself over their arms not much longer after that.

Bellamy was different.

She wasn't afraid of men. Nor was she afraid of dating or putting herself out there. She dated regularly but just hadn't found anyone who interested her. Or made her feel special.

She'd spent her life observing her parents' marriage and knew that was the type of love and companionship she sought. A deep, abiding commitment that bonded the two of them together.

Tonight was a perfect example.

Although it was the men's club event, both her parents enjoyed the evening in equal measure. It was *nice*, she mused as she dug in a large plastic container for another string of garland. And while the event might seem simple or unimportant—a dinner dance at the Whisperwood Lodge—it was something they looked forward to and talked about all year long.

The bell over the front door of the store jingled and

Bellamy eyed the entrance as a well-built man pushed his way in, a puppy cradled in his arms. Her father was fairly laid-back about the store, but since they sold food, animals were forbidden unless in service. "I'm sorry, sir, but the dog needs to stay outside."

Dark brows slashed over even darker eyes and the guy juggled the black Lab pup from one well-formed arm to another, his biceps flexing as he shifted the limp bundle. "Believe it or not, he's a service dog. In training," the guy quickly added before reaching into his back pocket and pulling out a badge. "I'm with the Austin PD. I'm his handler."

The sight of the puppy—and the sudden delight she didn't need to kick them out—had her crossing the store to greet them. "He's sweet."

"And sick, I think. He's not very energetic and he won't eat."

"Oh." She reached out to lay a hand on the small head, the fur silky soft over the bony ridges of his skull. He was small, but the large paws that hung over the man's forearms indicated the puppy would be a big guy once fully grown.

"I wanted to pick up some chicken and rice and hoped you'd have what I needed."

"Would you believe me if I told you I had both already cooked in the stockroom?"

"Seriously?"

"Yep. They're my bland leftovers from lunch that I brought along in some vague attempt to offset Christmas cookie consumption."

Although he wasn't inappropriate, his eyes drifted over her body before settling back on her face. "You're dieting?"

Heat burned a path where he'd gazed, that steady appreciation lighting a fire. "I prefer to think of it as holiday calorie management. A goal I'm failing at miserably, seeing as how the bland chicken and even blander rice were horrible."

"Why not toss it?"

"Some vague notion of trying again tomorrow. You know—" she waved a hand as she headed for the back of the store "—to make up for the pizza I ate in its place today."

A hearty laugh followed her through the swinging door into the stockroom and she beelined for the fridge and the leftovers.

Her father's store carried all the basic necessities of a convenience store and boasted a fairly hearty kitchen out front to accommodate the breakfast and lunch crowds who buzzed in for coffee and portable meals. She'd nuke the chicken and rice out at the counter and be able to keep an eye on the front door at the same time.

She could also keep an eye on Officer Hottie.

Wow, the man was good-looking. His body, evident beneath the long-sleeved black T-shirt that seemed sculpted to his shoulders, was strong without being imposing. And the way he cradled the dog had pretty much put her ovaries on high alert.

He was hot *and* a dog lover. Did it get much better?

She pushed through the stockroom door, only to see the back of the guy's head disappear through the front exit. Spears of disappointment layered over the lingering heat until she saw him bend over through the glass, his small charge quivering before him on the sidewalk. She raced to the counter and grabbed a few bottles of water, then headed for the miserable little puppy getting sick on the front parking lot.

"Is he okay?"

The guy glanced up from where he crouched on the ground, his hand on the small black back. "I think so. Or he will be."

She passed down a bottle of water, touched when the guy twisted it open and poured some into his palm. "Come on, Alex. Here you go."

The small head bent toward that cupped hand, the sound of his tongue lapping drifting toward her in the cool night air.

"Poor baby." She didn't miss the three brightly colored plastic pieces that lay in the pile of vomit. "Legos strike again."

"What?"

She pointed toward the small pile. "Looks like a blue vase holding a single plastic flower and a two-piece."

Officer Hottie's gaze zeroed in on the offending irritants, his voice gruff. "Just the pieces my niece mentioned were missing from her masterpiece before we sat down to dinner."

He poured more water into his hand and the Lab lapped it up, the trauma of his ordeal fading as his natural eagerness returned.

"He's looking better already." Bellamy opened the second bottle and poured it over the sidewalk, erasing the evidence and washing the Lego blocks aside. She'd come out later and pick them up with a broom.

Or planned to, until the guy pulled out a hanky from his back pocket and cleaned up the plastic, tossing the entire package into the trash. "That'll teach me to let dog or child out of my sight together again."

"That's wise." She couldn't resist his rueful grin or the clear relief in his dark eyes. Suddenly conscious of standing there staring at him, she shifted her gaze toward Alex's sweet face and the tongue that lolled out the side of his mouth. "Why don't you come back in and we can give him the food?"

"If you're sure?"

She smiled at that. "I'm certainly not going to eat it, no matter how many vows I make to myself. It'll be nice to see it go to a more appreciative recipient. Plus, he should probably go easy on dinner based on his recent Lego binge. The bland food won't hurt him."

The guy followed her back inside and she picked up the discarded container to warm up the leftovers.

"Would you mind if I came behind the counter and washed up?" He pointed to the sink beside her.

"Come on."

"Then I can introduce myself properly and shake your hand." He settled the puppy on the ground, issuing a series of commands that had the small body sitting up straight. The little guy tried to move, his butt squirming on the floor a few times, but ultimately gave in to the firm tone and the unyielding command by sitting where he was told.

"He's good. How old is he?"

"About ten weeks."

"And he can listen already?"

"'Sit' is about all he can listen to, but he's coming along." Hands clean, the guy turned the full force of his attention on her. For the briefest moment, Bellamy could have sworn she saw stars, the sky around his face glowing brighter than the gold of the garland. Quelling the ridiculous impression, she focused on the moment and not making an ass out of herself, especially when that warm, slightly damp palm closed around hers.

"I'm Donovan Colton."

Colton?

The Coltons were well known in Texas; several branches of the family were scattered across the Hill Country. She thought she knew the entire family who lived in Whisperwood, but hadn't placed Donovan when he'd walked in.

Shaking off the sudden awareness when she realized she was standing there, staring at the man, she quickly shook his hand. "Bellamy Reeves."

"Thank you, Bellamy. I appreciate the help."

"I'm happy to help. And I'm glad the little guy's okay."

The microwave pinged and she pulled the food out, then transferred it to a paper plate before handing it over. The moment was oddly domestic, Donovan's close proximity and their joint actions to put food together for the puppy surprisingly intimate.

The bell over the store entrance pinged and she went to help her customer. One of the high school coaches, who came in regularly for his nightly dinner of soda and a meatball sub seemed unphased by the addition of a puppy behind the counter.

"Hey, Bell. Haven't seen you in a few weeks."

"I'm helping my parents out tonight. They're out cutting a rug at the men's club event."

"You doing well?"

"Yep. We're closing out a busy year at work."

"How's Magnolia doing?"

It happened often enough, she wasn't sure why she was surprised any longer. The small talk as a method to ask about her sister. The pretend friendliness that was really just a fishing expedition.

"Maggie's good. She had a hot date tonight so she abandoned me in favor of a night of dinner and dancing."

Bellamy handed over the sub, not surprised when the coach's face fell. And while she'd not-so-delicately delivered news he obviously didn't want to hear, it didn't make the facts of Maggie's plans any less true. The besotted coach paid and was on his way out without saying much more.

"Did he even notice Alex was back here?" Donovan marveled once the guy was gone, the scent of his spicy sub wafting in his wake.

"He deals with teenagers all day. I suspect it takes a lot to rile him."

"Maybe." Donovan bent and took the now-empty paper plate. "Guess Alex got his appetite back."

She dropped to her knee and rubbed the silky head. The puppy's gaze caught on hers, his brown eyes trusting as he stared up at her. "He sure is sweet."

"Don't let him fool you. He's a Lego thief."

Bellamy rubbed a bit harder before laughing when the puppy presented his belly for additional petting. "He's at risk of being spoiled." Pulling her hand back, she realized the potential danger of her lavish affection. "Should I be doing that? Am I going to put his training at risk?"

"There are hard-core guys among my numbers who may not agree with me, but I think part of his training is also knowing there's praise and affection. A few belly rubs after this evening's trauma shouldn't do too much damage."

When Alex's wiggles of ecstasy quickly faded to longer breaths and droopy eyes, she gave him a final pat and stood, coming face-to-face with Donovan.

Goodness, the man was attractive. His dark hair was cut close and showed off a sharply angled face and strong jaw. He was thick in build, but there wasn't an ounce of fat on him. Instead, he looked competent.

Capable.

And no one to mess with.

It made the warm eyes and sexy smile that much more powerful. Like she'd tempted him just the slightest bit to go against character.

"You mentioned closing out a busy year to that guy. You don't work here?"

"This is my parents' store. I grew up working here and can still be counted on to take a shift every now and again."

"This place is a Whisperwood institution."

She laughed at that, the description not quite how she'd have classified a small town corner store. "One they know about all the way up in Austin?"

"My family's here in Whisperwood. I grew up here and Mr. Reeves could always be counted on for a summer popsicle or a late night cup of coffee. I just came down for the evening for a family Christmas party and to put my dog at risk of my niece and her Legos."

She glanced at the clock and thought that eight was awfully early for an evening family party to end, but held the thought. Maybe they started early or maybe the kids had to go to bed. But…it raised questions.

"How long have you been a part of the APD?"

"I went in straight out of college, so a few years now. I've wanted K-9, and Alex is my first opportunity."

She did the quick math, estimating he was about four or five years younger than her. The thought was briefly unsettling—she usually went for older guys—but there was something about him that made the question of age seem more arbitrary than anything else.

Perhaps you've been looking in the wrong places, Bellamy Reeves.

Catching herself staring, she refocused on Alex. "You're responsible for his training?"

"A good part of it. There's a formal program for the entire K-9 team and their handlers, but we're paired. He lives with me and works with me."

She glanced down at the now-sleeping puppy and considered what that must be like. Fun, in a way, but what a responsibility. "What will he be able to do?"

"Once he's fully trained? He'll run the gamut on what he can find, including humans, drugs and bombs."

"Wow."

As she eyed the jean-clad form that even now leaned against her counter, she had to admit Donovan Colton made an impressive figure. And it wasn't just his body, though she could hardly deny that she found him attractive.

Wow was right.

There was an intensity about him. Some indefinable quality that intrigued her.

He was *interesting*. And she'd often found the opposite of attractive men, especially if her sister's long list of past boyfriends was any indication. It was as if somehow masculine features, a firm jaw and a sparkling smile negated any sense of humanity or interest in the world around them.

But not this guy.

"The K-9 team is designed to work across cases so we can go where we're needed. There are six others in the APD. Alex and I will make seven."

"It's impressive. And while he's obviously got great promise, you've got a big year ahead of you. I wish you the best."

"Thanks." Donovan's gaze dropped toward the sleeping puppy before lifting back to her. "So if you don't work here, what do you do?"

"I'm an employee at Lone Star Pharmaceutical. I'm just helping out here since my parents had plans tonight."

"LSP. That's impressive. Are you a chemist or something?"

"No, I'm in finance." Ignoring the whisper through her mind of Maggie's continued admonitions to showcase herself in the best light, Bellamy pressed on. "They're wise to keep me away from beakers. Other than warming things up in a microwave, I avoid anything that involves cooking or open flames."

"Maybe I should consider inviting you to dinner, then, instead of risking you making anything behind that counter for me."

"Maybe."

"What time do you get off tonight?"

"I close up at ten and this is small town Texas. Nothing's open then."

"What about next week?"

"Sure. I—" She broke off when a distracted air came over his face, his hand dropping to the phone clipped at the waist of his jeans.

"I'm sorry. I'm getting a dispatch."

He excused himself and moved around the counter

toward the door, his gaze morphing from friendly and sexy to straight cop.

Alex stirred, his senses on immediate alert at the emotional change in the atmosphere. He was on his feet and scrambling toward Donovan in a heartbeat. When he reached Donovan, he sat immediately, his little body arrow straight.

Bellamy marveled at it, the ease and trust she could already see between the two of them. If the dog was this responsive to training at ten weeks, she couldn't imagine what he'd become once fully grown.

The low tenor of Donovan's voice pulled her from her thoughts. Something had happened. Something bad, if his clipped responses were any indication.

"I'm sorry. I have to go. Can we take a rain check on that dinner?"

"Of course."

The sexy cop and his trusty sidekick were out of the store as fast as they came in and for several moments, Bellamy simply stood and watched the door where they'd disappeared, wondering if the evening had actually happened.

It was only when she got the call a half hour later that she knew the exact accident Donovan Colton was called to. And that the people he'd helped pull from two tons of wreckage were her parents.

Chapter One

The last strains of "Jingle Bells" faded out, giving way to "All I Want for Christmas Is You" as Bellamy Reeves clicked the last email in her inbox. Despite the multicolored lights she'd hung in her office and the music she'd determinedly turned on each morning and kept on low throughout the day, nothing seemed to get her in the holiday spirit.

Losing both parents over the summer had left a hole in her life and in her heart. She'd braced herself, of course, well aware the holidays would be a challenge. But even with the knowledge the season wouldn't be the same, she'd diligently clung to the belief she could find some sense of joy, somewhere.

How wrong she'd been.

The days seemed to drag, no matter how busy she made herself, and her job at Lone Star Pharmaceutical—a job she'd worked hard at for several years—couldn't fill the gaps.

"One more email," she whispered to herself on a resigned sigh. "I'll do the last one and cut out early."

The company was estimated to finish out the year with stellar earnings, and management had given everyone an extra day of comp time as a reward for all the hard work. Most people had used the time to go shopping for presents in nearby Austin or to take in the pretty decorations scattered throughout downtown Whisperwood. She'd done none of those things, not up for walking the sidewalks and making small talk with her fellow townsfolk.

Which had also meant she was still sitting on the extra time. Perhaps an afternoon off would provide a chance to recharge and shake the malaise that seemed determined to hover around her shoulders.

She missed her parents terribly, but it was also the first holiday in more than she could remember that wasn't encumbered by illness. Her father's loss of mobility five years before had taken a toll on all of them and her life had been filled with pill bottles, a wheelchair and ramps throughout the house, and bouts of belligerence that telegraphed DJ Reeves's frustration with his body's betrayal.

It hardly spoke well of her, that she was relieved that stage of life had passed, but in her quiet moments of honest reflection she could admit it was true.

Illness. Suffering. And an endless sort of wasting away that stole the joy out of life. All of it had affected her mother as surely as her father's loss of mobility in the accident had decimated his. Where her mother had once found joy in simple pleasures—gardening or cooking or even a glass of wine—watching her husband deteriorate had caused a matched response. Ginny Reeves had wasted away as surely as her husband had and nothing Bellamy had tried could coax her out of it.

The kidney failure that finally stole him from them in June had been the final straw for her mother. Her mental health had deteriorated rapidly after that, and the heart attack that took her in late July had almost seemed unavoidable.

"And here I am, right back to maudlin and depressed," she whispered to herself as she reached for the bottle of water she kept perpetually refilled on her desk.

The water had been another nod to health, her recognition of mortality—a fact of life with her parents, and an equally relevant fact of life working for a pharmaceutical company. Lone Star Pharmaceutical had hired her out of college and she'd steadily worked her way up through the ranks, responsible for any number of financial projects. For the past two years, she'd been part of the team that managed the costs to bring new drugs to market and had honed her skills around price elasticity, working with insurance companies and ensuring LSP had a place on doctors' prescription lists.

The role had been meant for her, honing her accounting knowledge and expanding her contribution to the overall business and its bottom line. She'd loved LSP already, but coupled with the professional advancement, her employer had also been understanding of her family situation. They'd allowed for flexible scheduling when she'd needed it and hadn't asked her to curtail the care and attention her parents needed.

She'd met enough people in waiting rooms at the hospital to know that flexibility was a gift beyond measure.

The fact she'd also had an opportunity to still be considered for and receive promotions had cemented her sense of loyalty to LSP that was impossible to shake.

The company was a good one, with a focus on making life better for its consumers, its employees and even the community where it made its home—Whisperwood, Texas. Their CEO, Sutton Taylor, was a longtime resident and had stated on many occasions how important it was to him that his company have the same deep roots as he did.

Deep Texas *roots*, he usually clarified with a wink and a smile.

She couldn't hold back a faint smile of her own at the image of Sutton Taylor, standing tall in his suit and cowboy boots, proudly telling the employees how strong their year-end numbers looked. It wouldn't bring her parents back, but she could at least take some small joy in knowing she'd worked hard and contributed to a job well-done.

Satisfied she might leave the office on a glimmer of a bright note, Bellamy returned to her email, determined to tackle the last one before leaving for the afternoon.

The missive still bold because it was unread, Bellamy scanned the subject line, registering the odd description. RE: Vaccine Normalization.

Normalization of what?

The sender said INTERNAL, a company address she didn't immediately recognize, but she clicked anyway. A quick scan of the header information didn't show a named sender, either, nor was there anyone in the "To" list. Intrigued, Bellamy leaned forward, searching for anything that resembled usable details to describe what she was looking at.

Was it a virus?

That subject never failed to make her smile, the fact they had a department that battled real viruses housed in the same location as one who battled the digital kind. The humor quickly gave way to the sobering details that filled the content of the note.

Bellamy caught the subject in snatches, the words practically blurring as she processed the odd, bulleted sentences.

LSP's virus vaccine, AntiFlu, will be distributed in limited quantities, with release schedule held in the strictest confidence.

Quantities are throttled to highest bidder, with market pricing increased to match quantity scarcity.

Management of egg supply has been secured.

If those points weren't bad enough, the closing lines of the email left no question as to what she was reading.

Lone Star Pharma has a zero-tolerance policy for discounted distribution of AntiFlu for the annual flu season. There will be no acceptance of annual contract prices with existing accounts.

Bellamy reread the email once, then again, the various details spiking her thoughts in different directions.

Throttled availability? Controlled pricing? Fixed scarcity?

And the fact there was mention of the egg supply—the incubation engine for production of the vaccine—was shocking.

What was this?

She read the note once more before scrolling back up to review the header details. The sender was veiled, but it did originate from an LSP email address.

Who would send this to her? And worse, why would anyone possibly want to keep the very product they created for the public's good out of that same public's hands? She knew for a fact they had more than enough flu vaccine for the season. She also knew the scientific team had followed the CDC's guidelines for which strains of flu needed to be included.

She scrolled through the details once more, daring the words to change and prove her interpretation incorrect. But one more reread, or one hundred more, wasn't going to change the information housed in the email.

If this email was to be believed, the company she loved and believed in had turned to some dark and illegal practices.

"WELCOME BACK TO WHISPERWOOD, Alex. Quintessential small town Texas, from the tippy top of the big white gazebo smack in the middle of the town square, to the string of shops on Main Street."

Donovan Colton glanced over at his companion as he passed the gazebo and turned from Maple onto Main, unsurprised when he didn't receive a pithy response or even acknowledgment of his comment. As a matter of course, he'd have been more concerned if he *had* received a response.

His large black Lab possessed many talents, but a speaking voice wasn't one of them.

What Alex—short for Alexander the Great—did have was a nose that could sniff out explosive materials and he knew exactly how to translate that knowledge back to Donovan so he could in turn secure help. The fact Alex had several hundred million scent receptors in his nose—and had been trained almost since birth to use them in support of police work—meant Donovan had a powerful partner in their work to capture the bad guys.

It also helped he got along far better with his canine partner than he ever would have with a real live human one.

Donovan had been an animal lover since he was small. His various chores around the Colton ranch never seemed like chores if an animal was involved. Whether it was horse duty, mucking stalls or collecting eggs from the coops, he hadn't cared or seen any of it as work, so long as he got to spend time with the furry and the feathered Coltons who shared space on the large ranch that sprawled at the far west end of Whisperwood.

That love ran ever deeper to any number of mutts who had called the Colton ranch home.

Just like me, Donovan added to himself, the thought a familiar one.

Shaking it off, he focused on the gorgeous dog next to him. Donovan had loved each and every canine that had graced his life, but Alex was something extra special. Alex had been trained since puppyhood for life on a K-9 team; the two of them had bonded quickly, one an extension of the other. Alex looked to him for security, order, discipline and the clear role as alpha of their pack. In return, Donovan stroked, praised, and directed the animal into any number of search and rescue situations, confident his companion could handle the work.

And Alex always did.

From bombs to missing persons, Alex did his job

with dedication, focus and—more often than not—a rapid wag of his tail.

Yep. Donovan would take a four-footed partner over one with two feet any day.

Not that he could technically complain about any of the fine men and women he'd worked with in the past, but something just *fit* with Alex. They had a bond and a way of working that was far easier than talking to someone.

Their trip to Whisperwood had been unusually quiet, he and Alex dispatched to an old warehouse site to confirm the Austin PD hadn't missed any drugs on a raid the prior week. The cache they had discovered had been worth millions and Donovan's captain wanted to ensure they hadn't overlooked anything.

Donovan's thorough site review hadn't revealed any missed stashes but it was Alex's attention to the crime scene that reinforced the fact the initial discovery team had found all there was to find. Donovan would bet his badge on it.

If Alex couldn't find it, it's because it didn't exist.

What it also meant was that his trip to Whisperwood was over far earlier than Donovan had planned.

And disappearing back out of town—especially after greeting the local chief of police at the crime scene—wasn't going to go down very well. If his mother knew he'd come through and hadn't stopped by, no amount of excuses could save him.

"You're just too damn good, Alex."

The dog's tongue lolled happily to the side while he maintained a steady view of the passing scenery outside the car. The use of his name had Alex's ears perking but even the warm tone couldn't distract the dog from the holiday wreaths hanging neatly from each lamp-post in town.

Donovan took in the view, his memories of his home-town not too far off the mark of the real thing. The wreaths came out like clockwork the Monday before Thanksgiving, hanging until precisely the third day after the new year. A town committee changed out the ribbons on each wreath every week so they remained perfectly tied throughout the holiday. Red, green and gold, they alternated in a steady pattern, accompanied by bright, vibrant banners that wished people the hap-piness of the season.

His gaze drifted toward the corner store, an old memory pushing against his thoughts. A night, sev-eral Christmases past, when he'd had a sick little puppy and had flirted with a woman.

She'd been kind, he remembered, and pretty in a way that wasn't flashy, but that intrigued all the same. There was something solid there. Lasting, even. Which was silly, since he hadn't spent more than a half hour in her company before heading out on a call.

He'd thought to go in and ask about her a few times since, but training Alex had provided Donovan with a good excuse to stay out of his hometown; by the time he came back a year and a half later it had seemed lame—and far too late—to stop back in and ask about her.

But he did think of her every now and again. The slender form that filled out a pair of jeans with curves that had made his fingers itch and just enough skin showing at the top of her blouse to shift his thoughts in interesting, heated directions.

Dismissing the vague memory of pretty gray eyes and long, dark hair, he refocused on the pristine streets before him and the large ranch housed at the edge of town.

He needed to go see his mother. If he was lucky, his father would be out for the afternoon and he could avoid the lecture about coming to visit more often. He found it odd—funny, even—that it was his father who was more determined to deliver that particular guilt trip than his mother.

At the edge of the town square, Donovan looked at the large gazebo that dominated the space before putting on his blinker to head toward the Colton ranch. "Pretty as a picture."

At his comment, Alex's ears perked again and he turned from the view out the passenger window, his head tilted slightly toward Donovan.

"You don't miss a trick, do you?"

Donovan took his role as alpha in their relationship seriously, and that meant avoiding tension, anger or panic when speaking and working with Alex. Donovan had always innately understood an animal's poor acceptance of those emotions, but his K-9 training had reinforced it. He needed to stay calm and firm in the face of his furry partner, never allowing random, spiking emotions a place in their partnership.

Which meant the emotions that had the deepest of roots—established in the very foundation of his childhood—needed to be avoided at all costs. Especially if the prospect of visiting the Colton ranch was transmitted by his tone.

Extending a hand, he ruffled Alex's head and ears, scratching the spot he knew was particularly sensitive. A low, happy groan echoed from his partner when Donovan kneaded the small area behind Alex's ears, effectively erasing whatever tension he'd pushed into his police-issued SUV.

And on a resigned sigh, he made the turn that would carry him to the large ranch that sprawled for over a thousand acres deep in the heart of Texas Hill Country.

Home.

BELLAMY FOUGHT THE steady swirl of nerves that coated her stomach, bumping and diving like waves roiling on a winter's day as she walked the long corridor toward the human resources department. Lone Star Pharmaceutical had a sprawling campus and HR was three buildings away from her own, connected through a series of parking lots as well as overhead walkways for when the weather was poor or just too darn hot during a Texas summer.

She'd thought to call ahead and share her concerns but for reasons she couldn't quite explain to herself, ultimately decided on a surprise approach.

Was she even supposed to have the email?

The sender was veiled, but so was the distribution list. She didn't even know why she'd been targeted for such information.

Snatches of the email floated through her mind's eye, each destructive word adding another pitch and roll to those waves.

Limited quantities...throttled to highest bidder... quantity scarcity...

No acceptance of annual contract prices.

Was this the reason for the exceptionally strong year at LSP? Were they all celebrating extra time off and assured holiday bonuses at the expense of human lives?

She'd worked in finance her entire life and monitoring the ebbs and flows of the business was a part of her day to day. She understood balance sheets and marketplace pricing. She understood profit and loss statements. And she understood what it took to run an ethical business that still remained profitable.

And creating a scarcity in the market—*deliberately*—was not legal.

But it could be very, very profitable.

All the drugs LSP produced were essential for the individuals who needed them. They led the market on several fronts, with specialties in diabetes, heart disease and cholesterol reducing medicines. LSP had also done wonders with drugs designed to improve motor skills, several of which had been essential to her father's well-being.

But the flu vaccine was a whole different issue.

For anyone suffering from an illness, access to proper care and medicine was essential, but the flu affected everyone. A bad season could kill a large number of people, especially those at highest risk.

Just like her parents.

Had her father forgone a flu vaccine for the last several years of his life, he'd surely have been at higher risk of dying from the virus. And the fewer people vaccinated, the higher the risk.

Was it really possible LSP was attempting to profit from that?

Technically, they were late in the season to get the vaccine, but even as late as the prior week she'd run the numbers and realized that immunizations were down versus the prior year.

Was that because too many people felt they didn't need protection?

Or because there wasn't any protection in the market?

She tamped down on another wave of bile cresting in her stomach and knocked on the open door of the HR department. She'd been at LSP long enough to know several members of the HR team but wasn't acquainted with the head of HR, Sally Borne.

A light "come in" echoed through the cavernous outer office. Bellamy understood why the voice sounded so far away when she saw only one person seated in what appeared to be a sea of about six desks. She headed for the woman, taking in the office along the way. Decorations celebrating the holiday season peppered the walls and filing cabinets, and a bright string of lights hung from the ceiling over a table that held a pretty menorah as well as a beautifully carved wooden kinara holding the seven candles of Kwanzaa.

This holiday sentiment was matched throughout the five buildings of LSP and reflected Sutton Taylor's stated goals of inclusion and celebration of diversity. It had been yet one more facet of life at LSP and one more reason she loved where she worked.

Could someone who believed so deeply in humanity and culture and individuality be so soulless as to withhold essential drugs for the good of others?

"Can I help you?" The lone woman smiled, her voice kind as she stood behind her desk, effectively welcoming Bellamy in.

"I'd like to speak to Sally Borne."

"What's this regarding?"

"It's a private matter."

There was the briefest flash of awareness in the woman's bright blue eyes before she nodded. "Let me see if Sally has a few minutes in her schedule. I'll be right back."

Pleasant smile for a watchdog, Bellamy thought.

The idea struck swiftly and was at odds with the sense of inclusion that had welcomed her into the human resources department.

The woman disappeared toward a wall of frosted windows that allowed in light but made it impossible to see through. The windows covered what appeared to be one large office that extended across the back of the space. While it was to be expected—Human Resources dealt with any number of private matters—something about the glass made her think of a prison.

Which only reinforced just how far gone her thoughts had traveled since reading the email.

This was Human Resources, for Pete's sake. The department in all of Lone Star Pharmaceutical that was designed to help the employees.

Bellamy had worked with HR during her flex time requests when she was caring for her parents and they'd been kind and deeply understanding. They'd been in a different building then, only recently having moved into this space in the main building that housed the LSP executive staff.

Sally Borne was new to the company, as well. She'd replaced their retiring HR lead in the fall and had already implemented several new hiring initiatives as well as a new employee training program that was rolling out department by department. The woman was a leader and, by all accounts, good for Lone Star Pharmaceutical. Painting her as some fire-breathing dragon behind a retaining wall wasn't going to get Bellamy anywhere.

Especially as those waves in her stomach continued to roil, harder and harder, as she waited for the meeting.

The sensation was so at odds with her normal experience at work. She'd become accustomed to the frustration and fear that came from managing her father's care, but LSP had always been a safe haven. She loved her job and her work and found solace in the routine and the sense of accomplishment. At LSP, she was in control.

So why did she feel so *out* of control since opening that damn email?

"Are you ready?" The lone HR worker reappeared from Sally's office, her smile still firmly intact.

"Thank you."

Bellamy ignored the sense of being watched, and headed for the inner domain, hidden along the back wall. There was neither a fire-breathing dragon nor anything to worry about. *She*'d been sent the suspicious email. Coming to HR was simply about doing her job.

More, it was about being responsible to it.

"Hello." Sally Borne met her at the door, her hand extended and that same bright smile highlighting her face. "I'm Sally."

Bellamy introduced herself, then provided a sense of her role in the company. "I'm part of the financial team that manages the process of bringing new drugs to market."

"Andrew Lucas's team?"

"Yes, Andrew is my boss."

Sally nodded and pursed her lips before extending a hand toward her desk. Bellamy followed her, settling herself in a hard visitor's chair while Sally took her position behind a large oak monstrosity that looked like it belonged in Sutton Taylor's office.

Sally scribbled something on a blank legal pad, her attention focused on the paper. "Is Andrew aware you're here?"

Bellamy forced a small smile, unwilling to have the woman think she was here to complain about her boss. "Andrew's not the reason I'm here."

"But does he know you're here?"

"No."

"How can I help you then, Ms. Reeves?"

The prospect of sharing the details of what she'd discovered had haunted Bellamy throughout the walk from her office to HR, but now that she was here, the reality of what she had to share became stifling. Whether she'd been the intended recipient or not, the information she held was damning in the extreme. Anyone within LSP who would make such a decision or declaration would surely be fired. Worse, the possibility of jail time had to be a distinct consideration. They might be a for-profit company, but they still worked for the public good.

Was she really sure of what she'd come to discuss with HR?

Even as she asked herself the question, the memory of what she had read in the email steeled her resolve.

She was sitting on a problem and rationalizing it away at a personal moment of truth was unfair at best, flat out immoral at worst.

"I received an odd email today and I felt it was important to discuss it with you directly."

"Odd?" Sally's hands remained folded on top of her desk but the vapid smile that had ridden her features faded slightly.

"There wasn't a named sender, for starters."

"We have effective spam filters on our email but things can slip through. Do you think that was it?"

"No, no, I don't. The email just said 'internal.'"

"And no one signed it?"

"No."

Something small yet insistent began to buzz at the base of Bellamy's spine. Unlike the concern and panic that had flooded her system upon realizing what the email held, this was a different sort of discomfort. Like how animals in the forest scented a fire long before it arrived.

A distinct sense of danger began to beat beneath her skin.

"Here. Look at this." Bellamy pulled the printout she'd made out of the folder she'd slipped it into, passing it across the desk. "If you look at the top, you can see it came from the LSP domain."

Sally stared at the note, reading through the contents. Her expression never changed, but neither did that vague sense of menace Bellamy couldn't shake. One that grew darker when Sally laid the paper on her desk, pushing it beneath her keyboard.

"This is a poor joke, Ms. Reeves."

"A joke?"

"You come in here and suggest someone's sending you inappropriate messaging, then you hand me a note that's something out of a paranoid fantasy. What sort of sabotage are you intending to perpetrate against LSP?"

"I'm trying to prevent it."

"By forging a note and tossing it around like you're some affronted party?"

Affronted party? Forgery? The damn thing had popped into *her* inbox a half hour ago.

"This was sent to me."

Even as Bellamy's temperature hit a slow boil, Sally Borne sat across from her as if she were the injured party. "Are you sure about that? It would be easy enough to make a few changes in a photo alteration program and muster this up. Or perhaps you're even more skilled and able to hack into our email servers."

"You can't be serious. I received this email. Pull up the server files yourself if you're so convinced they've been tampered with."

"I'm sure that won't be necessary."

Bellamy sat back, her ire subsiding in the face of an even more unbelievable truth. The director of Human Resources didn't believe her. "You do understand the implications of something like this?"

"I most certainly do."

Although this wasn't the same as losing her parents, Bellamy couldn't fully shake the sadness and, worse, the acute sense of loss at Sally Borne's callous disregard for her word. Her truth. With one last push, she tried to steer the conversation back to steady ground.

"Who could possibly be sending messages like this? What are they trying to accomplish? And who else might have received something like this?"

"You tell me." Sally waved an idle hand in the direction of the email now lodged beneath her keyboard. "You're the one in possession of the mysterious email. No one else has called me or sent me any others to review." Sally's gaze never wavered as she stared back from her side of the large desk, her words landing like shards of ice as they were volleyed across that imposing expanse.

"Which I'm trying to get your help with. Could you imagine if this were really true?" Bellamy asked, willing the woman to understand the gravity of the situation. "We'd be putting millions of lives at risk."

Only when Sally only stared at her, gaze determinedly blank, did the pieces begin to click into place.

"So it's true, then? LSP *is* tampering with vaccines." The words came out on a strangled whisper.

"What's true is that you're a financial leader at this company determined to spread lies and disruption," Sally snapped back.

"I'm not—"

A brisk knock at the door had Bellamy breaking off and turning to see the same woman from the outer office. "Ms. Borne. Here are the details you asked for."

A large file was passed over the desk and Bellamy saw her name emblazoned on the tab of the thick folder.

Her employment file?

"Thank you, Marie." Sally took the folder as the helpful, efficient Marie rushed back out of the office.

It was only when the file was laid down that Bellamy saw a note on top. The writing was neat and precise and easily visible across the desk.

10+ year employee.
Steadfast, determined, orderly.
Both parents died in past year.

She was under evaluation here? And what would her parents' deaths have to do with anything?

Sally tapped the top before opening the manila file. Thirteen years of performance reviews and salary documentation spilled from the edges, but it was that note on top that seemed to echo the truth of her circumstances.

For all her efforts to make a horrible situation right, something had gone terribly wrong.

"Is there a reason you felt the need to pull my personnel file?"

"A matter of routine."

"Oh? What sort of routine?"

"When an employee is behaving in a suspicious manner, I like to understand what I'm dealing with."

"Then you'll quickly understand you're dealing with a highly competent employee who has always received stellar reviews and professional accolades."

Sally flipped back to the cover, her gaze floating once more over the attached note. "I also see a woman who's suffered a terrible loss."

While she'd obviously registered the note about her parents when the file was dropped off, nothing managed to stick when she tried to understand where Sally was going with the information. "I lost my parents earlier this year."

"Both of them."

"Yes."

"Were they in an accident?"

"My father has been ill for many years, the repercussions of a serious accident. My mother's health, unfortunately, deteriorated along with his."

"It's sad." Sally traced the edge of the damn note again, the motion drawing attention to the seemingly random action. "Illness like that takes a toll."

A toll? *Obviously.* "Dying is a difficult thing. Nothing like the slow fading we see on TV."

Sally continued that slow trace of the paper. "It's also an expensive thing."

"You can't possibly think—"

"It's exactly what I think." The steady, even-keeled

woman was nowhere in evidence as Sally stood to her full height, towering over her desk like an avenging cobra. "And you think it, too. You dare to come in here, convinced you can blackmail this company into giving you money for some concocted lie of immense proportions."

"You can't think that."

"I can and I do. And I want you to pack your office immediately. Security will escort you there and off the premises."

"But I—"

Sally pointedly ignored her, tapping on her phone to summon Marie. When the woman scrambled in, Sally didn't even need to speak. Marie beat her to it. "Security will be here momentarily."

"Excellent." Sally shifted her attention once more, her gaze fully trained on Bellamy as she pointed toward the door. "Don't expect a reference."

Dazed, Bellamy stood and moved toward the exit. The meeting had been nothing like what she'd expected. Surreal at best, even as she had to admit it was fast becoming a nightmare.

Lone Star Pharmaceutical had been her professional home for more than thirteen years and in a matter of moments, that home had been reduced to nothing more than rubble and ash.

Chapter Two

Donovan glanced around the large, welcoming, airy living room of the main Colton ranch house as his mother settled two glasses of iced tea on the coffee table. She'd already bustled in with a tray of his favorites—cheese and crackers, a bowl of cashews and a tray of gooey Rice Krispies Treats—and had topped it off with her world famous sweet tea.

Perhaps that was a stretch, but she had brought her tea to every gathering ever held in Whisperwood. Someone had even asked him about it at work one day, rumors of his mother's special recipe having reached as far as Austin. Donovan reached for his glass and took a sip, more than ready to admit every sugary drop deserved its near-reverent reputation.

"I'm so glad you're here." She glanced down at Alex,

her smile indulgent as she pet his head. "Glad you're both here. Though to what do I owe the pleasure?"

"Alex and I had a job that finished early. I thought I'd come over and visit before heading back to Austin."

"I'm glad you did. Our last dinner ended too early. And I—" She broke off, shaking her head. "I'm glad you're here."

Memories of his last dinner with his family still stuck in his gut and Donovan avoided thinking about it. He loved them—he always had—but he couldn't be who they wanted him to be. And he'd long past stopped trying. Their definition of family was different from his and he'd spent a lifetime trying to reconcile that fact.

And was coming up damn short, truth be told.

He reached for a handful of cashews and ignored the guilt that poked beneath his ribs with pointy fingers. He was here, wasn't he? That had to count for something.

Even if his presence was grudging at best.

"He's so good."

His mother's words pulled Donovan from his musings and he glanced over to where she'd settled Alex's head onto her lap, his gaze adoring as he stared up at her. "All this food and he hasn't even looked at it."

"Oh, he's looking. Don't let him fool you."

"But he's so good and doesn't even attempt to make a play for anything. Remember Bugsy. That dog could find food if you wrapped it in plastic and buried it in the back of the pantry. He'd find a way to get to it, too."

Unbidden, memories of the small, crafty mutt they'd had when Donovan was in high school filled his thoughts. Bugsy was a good dog—as friendly as he was tenacious—and his forays into the Colton pantry had become the stuff of family legend. "He didn't miss much."

"I always assumed all dogs were that way, but Alex is amazing. He hasn't moved an inch."

"He's a formally trained police dog. It wouldn't do to have him nosing into pockets at crime scenes or roaming through the pantry on home visits. He's trained to sniff out bomb materials and illegal drugs."

"Yes, he is. A dangerous job for a brave boy." Her attention remained on the dog but Donovan was acutely aware the comment was meant for him.

"When the bad guys stop being bad guys, he can slow down."

"I suppose so." His mother patted Alex's head. "But for the record, I am all for a dog being a dog. I did enjoy documenting some of Bugsy's escapades."

"There aren't many like him."

"Remember that Christmas he ate all the cookies? Oh boy, was that dog sick."

Donovan remembered that holiday—along with the mess the dog vomited up in the barn later that morning—but true to form Bugsy had been back in business in no time. The wily dog raided the bacon and black-eyed peas on New Year's Day, barely a week later.

"He was a character."

The shift to a safe topic put them back on neutral ground and they fell silent again, his mother's soft smile focused on Alex and the large black head snuggled in her lap. She might not be his biological mother, but Donovan had always known he'd gotten his love of animals from Josephine Colton. Her gentle nature and genuine pleasure with the furry or the feathered had always been a hallmark of her personality.

His mother had never met a stray she didn't love or an animal she couldn't whisper sweet nothings to. And since he'd been a stray himself, Donovan had innately understood the value in that personality trait.

"Dad keeping busy?"

"As much as the doctor allows. Your father is frustrated he can't do the things he used to."

"There's no shame in asking for help."

His mother sighed, trouble flashing in her warm brown eyes before she dropped her gaze back to Alex. "There is, apparently, when your name is Hays Colton."

"He comes by that one honestly, don't you think? In fact, I'd say he comes from a very long line of stubborn Coltons, starting with Uncle Joe and working his way down."

The words were enough to vanquish the spot of trouble in her eyes and she smiled at that. "For someone who claims they can't remember the names of so many aunts, uncles and cousins, you sure can pull them out readily enough when making a point."

"The beauty of a large family." *An adopted one*, Donovan added to himself. He'd managed to hold those words back this time. Coupled with the fact that he and his mother were having a cordial afternoon, Donovan figured he might actually get out of his childhood home without offending anyone or causing a fresh bout of tears.

Because, try as he might, there wasn't any amount of love or extended family or years-old shared stories that could change one fundamental fact: Josephine and Hays Colton weren't actually his parents.

And while Donovan would be eternally grateful for their care, their upbringing and their name, he'd never quite gotten past the circumstances that had put him in their barn one cold Christmas morning, abandoned and alone.

BELLAMY MARCHED THE return trip back to her office building from the human resources department. The walk had been long enough that she'd already worked her way through the first stage of grief—denial—and was fast barreling toward number two.

Anger.

How dare they? Or how dare *she*? Despite the reputation that had spread quickly about Sally Borne's competence since her arrival at LSP, Bellamy still couldn't get over the woman's gall. Nor could she see past the horrifying thought that Sally thought she was somehow responsible for that awful note.

"Are you okay, Ms. Reeves?"

She turned at the sweet voice of Gus Sanger, doing his level best to keep up with her long strides through the above-ground corridors that connected the buildings.

"I'm fine."

"I've known you a long time, young lady. You're not fine. And that was no simple visit to HR."

"It's a private matter."

"Meetings in HR usually are." Gus tugged at his ear, but kept pace next to her now that they'd slowed a bit. "I've known you since you were small. Your parents' store was a key stop for me every morning on my drive to LSP and more often than not, you'd find your way behind that counter, fixing me a coffee and a muffin. You're a good girl, Bellamy Reeves, and whatever that private matter was about, you don't deserve an escort off the grounds."

The tears that had prickled the backs of her eyes intermittently since leaving Sally's office spiked once more but she held them back. She'd cried enough tears for a lifetime the past six months and refused to shed the same emotion over a situation that she hadn't caused, nor was she responsible for.

"Thanks, Gus."

"I don't care what HR says about me watching you like a common criminal. You go back to your office and take a few minutes to pack up. I'll wait for you in the lobby. It'll give me a chance to get some coffee."

"But what if HR catches you? Won't you get in trouble?"

Gus waved a hand. "If HR has a problem with me, they're going to have to go through Sutton. He may have his moments, acting like a damn fool ladies' man, but he and I went fishing in Whisperwood Creek when we were both seven years old. Been fishing there off and on ever since together. No one's firing me."

Bellamy smiled at the image—the grizzled Gus and the erudite Sutton Taylor, casting lines off the side of the creek. The "ladies' man" comment was a bit bold, even for Gus, but Bellamy was hardly unaware of Taylor's reputation.

"You've known each other a long time."

"A lifetime. All it would take is a few words to him and we can fix this."

"No, Gus." She shook her head before gentling her tone at the sincere offer of help. "I can't tell you how much I appreciate it, but I need to take care of this myself."

"If you're sure?"

"I'm sure. I'll find a way to fix this. To fix it all."

Gus nodded before using his badge to open the door to Bellamy's building. "Okay, then. I'll get my coffee and wait here. You take your time."

"Thank you."

A large staircase rose out of the lobby toward the second floor and Bellamy started up the stairs toward her office, another one of her daily concessions to health and wellness. The hallways were even emptier than when she'd left for Human Resources—had it really only been an hour?—and she passed a few pockets of conversation and could hear one of her colleagues talking in muted tones from inside his office.

What would they tell Andrew?

She liked her boss. They'd worked well since she'd been put on his team two years prior and she'd like to tell him in person what was going on. Share her side of the story. But he'd already departed a few weeks early for the holidays, taking his family on a long-planned trip to Hawaii.

The fleeting thought of texting him faded as she imagined what she'd even try to say.

Sorry to bother you on vacation. I just got fired because we're tampering with the flu vaccine supply chain here at LSP.

No way.

Even if she did want to bother him, what would he do from four thousand miles away? What she needed to do was take stock and evaluate what had happened. Then she could decide the best course of action. She was a well-respected employee at LSP and a member of the community. She'd find a way through this.

Even if Sally's comments at the end had taken a toll. Bellamy's father's accident and subsequent financial troubles weren't exactly a secret. She'd even had to sell the family business—the long-standing corner store her father had opened in his twenties—to pay for his medical bills.

No matter how sympathetic or understanding people might have been, it wasn't a far leap to think they'd believe Sally's innuendo.

It's sad.

Illness like that takes a toll.

It's also an expensive thing.

Each miserable word had stamped itself in her mind and Bellamy was hard-pressed to see how she'd come out in the best light should Sally decide to spread those rumors.

On a resigned sigh, she reached for the box Gus had handed her before departing for his coffee. Thirteen years, and she was left with a brown box and the few items she could stow inside.

The photo of her parents out front of the store—one of her favorites—came off her credenza first, followed by her calendar, a silly glass elf she'd purchased a few years before and the small radio that was still playing Christmas songs. She added a personnel file she'd kept her records in, a handful of cards given from coworkers through the years and, last, a few copies of the email she'd printed for herself.

Although she suspected even the affable Gus would have to take back any files she attempted to remove from her desk, she did a quick sweep of her files to make sure she hadn't missed anything.

And saw the framed photo of her sister, Maggie,

she'd shoved in the bottom drawer. A dazzling smile reflected back at her, the remembered warmth there stabbing into Bellamy's heart.

She missed her sister. Desperately. And far more than she probably should, even as she blamed Maggie for all that had gone wrong over the past five years.

Her sister's abandonment had stung, but it was the cold shoulder Maggie had given her at their parents' funerals that had hurt the most. When had her bright, beautiful, vibrant sister become such a cold witch?

The urge to toss the photo into the garbage, along with a few of the folders that held out-of-date information or pamphlets on some of their older drug introductions, was strong, but in the end familial loyalty won out and she shoved the frame facedown on top of the small pile of items in her cardboard box. If she was going to toss the picture, she could do it properly at home, not in a snit in what was soon to be someone else's office.

Shaking off the personal reminder of her relationship with her sister, Bellamy finished placing the last few items in the box. The printouts of the email that had started it all were the last to go in and, on impulse, she took the printouts from the box and secured them in her purse. "At least I have something."

The copy wasn't much but it did have a time and date stamp on it, and if she were able to secure a legal representative who could subpoena the company's electronic records, she might be able to prove the fact the email had been sent to her and was not a result of her own tampering.

With a hard tug on the closure of her purse, Bellamy stopped herself and fell into her chair.

Subpoena? Electronic records? Legal representation?

How had she gone from a fiercely loyal employee to someone ready to instigate legal action in a matter of minutes?

The vibration of her phone caught her moments before the ringer went off, her best friend Rae's name and picture filling the screen. She toyed with not answering when the overwhelming urge to talk to someone who believed her struck hard.

"Hey there."

"What's wrong? You sound upset."

Bellamy smiled despite the horrible weight that had pressed on her chest since leaving Sally Borne's office. The quick response after a simple greeting was straight-up Rae and at that moment, Bellamy couldn't have been more grateful.

"Well. Um." The tears that had threatened on the walk back tightened her throat once more. "I'm packing my office."

"What? Why?" The noise of the Whisperwood General Store echoed in the background, but nothing in the noise could dim Rae's concern. "Who would do that? You're one of their best employees."

"As of a half hour ago, they began treating me like Enemy Number One."

"What? Wait—" Rae broke off, the din in the background fading even as she hollered at someone to come help her at the counter. "Okay. I'm in my office. Talk to me."

Bellamy laid it all out—the email, the walk to HR and the weird meeting, even Gus's kindness in letting her have a few minutes.

"Gus'll give Sutton Taylor what for. Why don't you let him?"

"I need to process this. Something's going on and the faster I figure out what it is, the faster I can get my job back." *If I even want it.*

The thought was so foreign—and such a departure from who she'd been for the past thirteen years—Bellamy nearly repeated the words out loud.

Was it possible the damage of an afternoon could remove the goodwill of nearly a decade and a half?

"Who do you think did it?" Rae's question interrupted the wending of Bellamy's thoughts.

"I wish I knew. It's dangerous, Rae. If it's a joke it's a horrific slander on the company. And if it's true—" Bellamy stopped, barely able to finish the thought. "If it's true, it's a problem beyond measure. We serve the public good. We can't take that good away from them, especially in flu season."

"I've already had a few people in complaining about it. I'm tempted to drag on a surgical mask each morning before I open up."

Rae would do it, too, Bellamy thought with a smile. That and a whole lot more, she had to admit.

"Look, Rae. I need you to keep this to yourself until I understand what's going on."

"Bell, come on, you have to tell someone."

"I will. But. Well. Look, just don't say anything, okay? Please promise me."

The quiet was nearly deafening before she heard her friend acquiesce through the phone. "Okay. I'll hold my tongue for now."

"Thank you. Let me get my feet under me and I can figure out what comes next."

"So long as it entails a visit to the police at some point."

Since her thoughts hadn't been too far from the same, Bellamy had to admit Rae had a point. "I'll call you later. I need to finish packing up and get out of here. Even with Gus's willingness to give me time, the dragon in HR is going to expect me off the grounds."

"Okay. Call me later."

They hung up with a promise to do a good raging girls' night, complete with margaritas and a gallon of ice cream. It couldn't erase her day, but as promises went it was certainly something to look forward to.

Bellamy glanced down at her box, her meager possessions all she had as evidence of her time at Lone Star Pharmaceutical.

Securing the lid, she took a deep breath and pulled her purse over her arm.

She'd already lived through the loss of her family, both through death and through abandonment. She would survive this.

Resolved, Bellamy picked up the box and walked out of her office. She refused to look back.

THE MID-DECEMBER AFTERNOON light was fading as Bellamy trudged toward her car. She'd snagged a spot in the far back parking lot, beneath an old willow that she loved for its sun protection and the added benefit of more daily steps, to and from the front door. Now it just seemed like more punishment as she put one foot in front of the other, her box completing the professional walk of shame.

Thankfully, the parking lot was rather empty, the impending holiday and the general spirit of celebration and success at LSP pushing even more people than she'd expected to knock off early.

Gus had been kind when he met her in the lobby, his expression sorrowful as he took her badge and her corporate credit card. Sally Borne hadn't shown up for the proceedings but her office lackey, Marie, had been there to take the badge and credit card before bustling off back where she'd come from.

It was unkind, but Bellamy hadn't been able to dismiss the image of a small crab scuttling back to its sandy burrow the way the woman rushed off.

And then it had just been awkward with Gus, so she'd given him a quick kiss on the cheek and a warm hug, promising to visit with him in town at the annual tree lighting in the town square the following week. She'd already committed to Rae that she'd go and she'd be damned if she was going to hide in her home like the same crab she'd mentally accused Marie of being.

Shifting the box in her arms, Bellamy laid it on her rear bumper as she dug for her keys. After unlocking the car, then pressing the button for her trunk, she juggled the box into the gaping maw of her sedan, only to fumble it as she attempted to settle it with one hand while her other held her purse in place.

A steady stream of expletives fell from her lips when a brisk wind whipped up, catching the now-loose box lid and flinging it from the trunk.

"Damn it!"

The temptation to leave the lid to fly from one end of the parking lot to the other was great, but she dutifully trudged off to snag it where it drifted over the concrete. She might be persona non grata but she wouldn't add litterbug to the litany of sudden crimes she'd apparently perpetrated against LSP. Nor would she put someone at risk of tripping on it inadvertently.

Box lid in hand, she crossed back to the car, dropping into the driver's seat and turning on the ignition. The car caught for the briefest moment, then rumbled to life. She put her foot on the brake, about to shift into reverse, when her gaze caught on the rearview mirror and her still-open trunk.

Resigned, she opened the door once more and crossed back to the trunk. That damn cardboard box stared up at her, the lonely receptacle of her professional life and—finally—she let the tears she'd fought all afternoon fall.

Lost job. Lost family. Hell, even a holiday that was shaping up to be a lost cause. All of it seemed to conspire against her until all she could see or think or feel was an overwhelming sense of loss.

Frustrated, Bellamy stepped back and slammed the lid.

Instantly, a wall of heat flared up, consuming her before she felt her body lifted off the ground and thrown across the parking lot.

DONOVAN WAS MIDWAY down his parents' stone-covered driveway when the call from Dispatch came in. He answered immediately, responding with his badge number and his location.

"We have a bomb called in at Lone Star Pharmaceutical. Your location indicates you're closest to the site."

LSP?

An image of the imposing corporate park on the edge of Whisperwood filled his thoughts, along with the pretty woman he'd met a million years ago who worked there. Who was bombing the town's largest employer? And why?

"I am," Donovan confirmed. "I can be to the site in three minutes. What are the known details?"

"LSP security called it in. Initial report says a car on fire and a woman shaky but standing."

"She walked away from a car bomb?"

"Reports say she was outside it and tossed back by the blast."

"I'm on my way."

"Thanks, Officer. Backup will meet you there."

Donovan took a left out of his parents' driveway instead of the right he'd planned. Flipping on his lights he headed out over the two-lane Farm to Market road that lead back into town and on toward the corporate headquarters that stood at the opposite edge of Whisperwood.

He'd already spent the morning with the town's chief of police and now it looked like he'd spend his evening with him, as well. The town was big enough to keep a sizable force, but they had to tap into the Austin PD for specialties like bomb squad support. As LSP had grown along with the town, Donovan had often wondered why the local PD hadn't been given more resources, but knew that wasn't always an easy battle.

It was one that big companies readily fought when they preferred to employ their own security.

Perhaps that folly had come back to bite them?

By all accounts LSP's owner was a local maverick who was as delighted to be a pillar of the community as he was to rub the town's noses in it when he wanted to do things his way. Bold and daring, Sutton Taylor had favored the town he'd grown up in to set up his world-renowned pharmaceutical company.

Donovan turned onto Lone Star Boulevard, the well-paved road that ran in front of LSP's headquarters. The scrub grass and occasional ruts that made up the drive across town vanished as he came onto LSP land.

The guards at the main entrance waved him through the gates before he'd barely flashed his badge and Donovan headed straight for the billowing smoke still evident at the back of the parking lot. Alex sat sentinel beside him, his body strung tight as a bow as he waited for his orders.

Even from a distance, Donovan could tell the scene was contained. Two LSP security vehicles were parked near the still-smoldering car and a crowd had gathered at the edge of the parking lot, obviously evacuated from the building. The security team seemed to have it under control, the individuals corralled far enough back to avoid any additional fallout from the wrecked car. With the destruction already wrought on the burning sedan, the car was the least likely source of any remaining danger.

Instead, he and Alex would go to work on the scattered vehicles still in the lot.

He parked, his already alert partner rising farther up on his seat. Within a few moments, he had Alex at his side, leashed and ready for duty. One of the security guards moved away from a huddled woman and walked toward him. The man was grizzled, his body stiff with age, but his clear blue eyes were bright and alert.

Sharp.

The man nodded. "Officer. I'm Gus Sanger. I'm in Security here at LSP."

"Donovan Colton. This is Alex." He motioned for Alex to sit beside him, the move designed to show his control over the animal yet ensure no one missed the dog's imposing presence.

"You got here fast. K-9's out of the Austin PD."

"I was in Whisperwood on another assignment." Donovan shook the proffered hand before pointing toward a pretty woman covered in soot. "Is she hurt?"

"Claims she isn't. That's Ms. Reeves. Bellamy Reeves. She's banged up and has a few scratches on her elbows and a bigger gash on her arm the EMTs bandaged up, but I'd say lucky all in all."

At the utterance of her name, Donovan stilled. Although he hoped it didn't show to Sanger, Alex recognized it immediately, shifting against his side.

Bellamy Reeves? The same woman he'd spoken to so many years ago in the Whisperwood corner store…

"Do you mind if I go talk to her?"

Sanger nodded, his gaze dropping to Alex. "Does he go everywhere with you?"

"Everywhere."

"Good."

Donovan walked to the woman, taking her in as he went. She was turned, her gaze focused on her car, but he could make out her profile and basic build. Same long legs. Same sweep of dark hair. And when she finally turned, he saw those same alert gray eyes, that were mysterious and generous, all at the same time.

She was still pretty, even beneath a layer of dirt and grime from whatever happened to her car. Which he'd get to in a moment. First, he wanted to see to her.

"Ms. Reeves?"

She had her arms crossed, the bandage Gus mentioned evident on her forearm and her hands cradled against her ribs as if hugging herself. She was drawn in—scared, by his estimation—and doing her level best to hide it. "Officer?"

He ordered Alex to heel at his side, then extended his hand. "I'm Officer Colton. This is Alex. We're here to help you."

Whether it was the use of their names or the fading shock of the moment, her eyes widened. "You."

"It's me. How are you, Bellamy?"

Those pretty eyes widened, then dropped to Alex. "He's so big. Just like I knew he would be." She instinctively reached for Alex before pulling her hand back.

"You can pet him if you'd like. He's not formally working yet."

She bent, her gaze on Alex as her hands went to cup the Lab's head and ears. Donovan didn't miss how they trembled or what a calming effect Alex seemed to have on her as she petted that soft expanse of fur. "You grew just as big as I knew you would. But I hope you've learned some restraint around plastic toys."

"Grudgingly." Donovan smiled when she glanced back up at him, pleased that she'd remembered them. "We nearly had a repeat incident with a few Barbie high heels but I managed to recover them before he swallowed them."

"He's a little thief."

"One who fortunately matured out of the impulse."

She stood back upright but kept a slightly less shaky hand on Alex's head. "You're here because of this?"

"I was in town on another assignment today and hadn't left yet. Are you okay?" The assignment was a bit of a stretch but somehow, saying he had to visit his mother or risk her wrath didn't seem like the most comforting comment.

"I'm fine. Gus looked at me quickly and I don't feel hurt other than the scrapes. Shaken and sort of wobbly, but nothing hurts too bad or feels broken."

"How close were you to the car?"

"I'd gotten in and realized I hadn't closed the trunk. I was behind the car when it just—" She broke off, the disbelief still clear in her eyes. "When it just exploded."

"We're going to take a look at it but first I need Alex to sniff the rest of the cars that are still here so we can get these people out of here. Can you wait for me?"

"Where else am I going to go?"

For reasons Donovan couldn't explain, he sensed there was something more in her comment. Something that went well beyond a car bomb or the shaky aftereffects of surviving a crime.

Something terrible had taken the light out of her beautiful gray eyes.

And he was determined to find out why.

Chapter Three

Bellamy stood to the side and watched the chaos that had overtaken the parking lot. Several cop cars had arrived shortly after Donovan and Alex as well as two fire trucks and the EMTs. At one point she'd estimated half of Whisperwood's law enforcement had found its way to LSP. The scene was well controlled and she'd been happy to see how the local police handled the press who were already sniffing around for a story. They were currently corralled on the far edge of the property, clamoring for whatever scraps they could get.

She'd ignored them, even as one had somehow secured her cell phone number and had already dialed her three times. It was probably only the start and she'd finally turned off the ringer. There would be time enough to deal with the fallout once she knew what she was actually dealing with.

And it might be to her advantage to have a working relationship with someone from the press if she needed to tell her side of the story.

If? Or when? a small voice inside prompted.

Sighing, she let her gaze wander back over the assembled crowd of law enforcement. Would they help her if she truly needed it? Or would they bow to whatever pressure LSP might put on them?

Like a bucket of errant Ping-Pong balls, the thoughts winged around in her mind, volleying for position and prominence.

She'd already taken the proffered water and over-the-counter pain meds from the EMT attendant and had finally begun to feel their effect. The pain in her arm had subsided to a dull throb and the headache that had accompanied her since the accident had begun to fade, as well. But the endless questions in her mind continued.

The EMTs had pressed repeatedly to take her to the hospital for additional observation but she'd finally managed to push them off after submitting to several rounds of "follow the light" as they looked into her eyes, searching for a possible concussion. It had only been Donovan's input—and assurances that he'd keep a watch on her—that had finally quelled the discussion about removing her from the premises.

Not that she exactly wanted to stand around and watch her car smolder in a pile of burned-out metal. Or question who might have wanted to harm her enough to put it in that condition.

It had taken her quite a while to come up with that conclusion, but once she did the sentiment wouldn't shake.

Someone had done this.

Cars didn't just explode when the ignition turned

over. And innocent people didn't just get fired from jobs they were good at and loyal to.

So what was going on and what mess had she fallen into? And had she really left her home that very morning thinking it was just another day?

And how was it that Donovan Colton was the one who arrived to rescue her?

She'd thought of him intermittently over the past five years. Most of the time it was a good memory—a sweet, flirty interlude with an attractive man. But there were other moments—when the memory stung and instead of leaving her with a smile it left her with a strange ache. The painful reminder of what she'd lost that night that went beyond a lost date.

Could things have been different?

In the end it hadn't mattered. If she were honest with herself, it still didn't. Her father was horribly injured that night and her life—all their lives—had irrevocably changed.

"Bellamy?" Gus shuffled up to her, his bright blue eyes hazed with concern. "You've been awfully quiet standing here all by yourself. Are you sure you don't need to go to the emergency room?"

"I'm sure. I'm made of sturdier stuff."

"If you're sure?"

"I'm sure." She glanced at the dissipating crowd. "Did they find any other bombs?"

"It doesn't appear so. The damage from this hooligan seems confined to your car."

Hooligan?

While she had no wish to alarm an old man—and she suspected his use of the word was meant to comfort—the casual term wasn't nearly the correct one for what had happened to her. This wasn't a prank. Or a sick joke. Someone had attempted to kill her. And the sooner she got off of LSP property, the better she'd feel.

"Will I be allowed to go home soon?"

"I overheard Officer Colton talking with the chief. You should be able to get out of here right soon."

"Thanks."

Since her purse had been on her arm when she'd gotten out of the car to close the trunk, she still had many of her personal items. Best of all, she'd been pleased to find her cell phone undamaged where she'd had it zipped in a side pocket. The purse was ripped and headed for the trash but the fact it protected the rest of her personal items was the only saving grace of the evening. Especially seeing as how the car and her small box of memories were destroyed.

"Ms. Reeves?"

Donovan Colton took a commanding spot beside her and Gus, Alex immediately sitting at his side. There was something comforting about the presence of both of them and Bellamy felt a small bit of the stress and strain of the day ebb. "Yes."

"I'd like to ask you a few questions but perhaps you'd prefer to answer them after you've had a chance to clean up. Or maybe eat?"

"You can decide that? I mean, I can leave here."

The edges of his eyes crinkled in a small smile before he nodded. "I think I'm allowed to take you to a more comfortable place and out of the increasing cold. It may be Texas, but it's still December."

She had gotten chilled, the air growing cool once the sun set. "I didn't have lunch and now that you mention it, I am hungry."

"Why don't we leave, then?" Donovan turned to Gus and shook his hand. "You and your team have been incredibly helpful here. Thank you for keeping everyone at the edges and not allowing anyone else to leave until we had a chance to check their cars."

Gus stood taller, his chest puffing just like the dog's. "Of course."

"I'll see that Ms. Reeves is escorted home now. I'll be back tomorrow to finish a review of the site with the chief."

"We'll be waiting for you."

Now that she'd given her agreement to leave, there was little keeping her and Donovan on the property. In a matter of moments, he had her in his SUV and was driving them toward the exit on the back side of the property, in the opposite direction from the press. She wasn't sure if the strategy would work, but refused to turn around to find out.

"I'm sorry for the dog hair. Alex usually sits on the front seat."

A strained giggle crawled up her throat, at odds with the exhaustion that racked her shoulders the moment she sat down. "I think a few stray dog hairs are the least of my worries right now. And since I don't mind them on a good day, it's no bother."

"Are you warm enough?" The heater was on full blast, rapidly warming the car as they drove toward the center of town.

"I'm getting there." As days went, December in central Texas was often mild bordering on warm. She was rarely cold, but since being tossed from the car she'd had a weird, aching numbness that had settled in her bones and refused to let go.

"You're probably dealing with the lingering effects of shock. I should have thought of this sooner. Here." He pulled to the side of the road and shrugged out of his coat, handing it over. "Put this on."

The jacket enveloped her, a mix of body heat and a scent that was distinctly male. She could still smell the cold air that had wrapped around them in the parking lot, only instead of being tinged with the lingering, acrid taste of smoke and burned-out car, in its place was a musky, pleasing warmth. She also caught the faintest whisper of dog and smiled to herself.

Clearly Alex wasn't at a loss for hugs and affection.

That thought warmed her beyond the car or the coat, filling her with that years-old memory of a large man cradling a sick puppy in his arms. Her father had always told her you could tell a man's character by the way he treated animals and in the case of Donovan Colton, she had to admit the expression was spot on the mark.

"How are you feeling?"

"Better. Warmer." She took in his profile, not wanting to stare but unable to fully look away.

Goodness, was he handsome. She'd thought so that night in her parents' store and saw it even more now. The firm jawline. The close-cropped dark hair. And the thick, corded forearm muscles now visible where he gripped the steering wheel.

"Make a right when you get to the stop sign at the end of this road."

"That's not the way to the diner."

"You don't need to take me to dinner. Home's fine."

"I promised you a meal and I aim to deliver. In fact—" his gaze flashed toward hers before he resumed his focus on the road "—I believe I promised you dinner some time ago."

"That's not... I mean—" She broke off, feeling silly. "I'm covered in parking lot dirt and smell like the undercarriage of a car. Home's fine."

"I'll take you home but I'm not going to leave you right now. You've had an ordeal and I'd like to stick around for a bit."

"I know you have to question me. Can we just do it at my house?"

He frowned before reaching out a hand to lay over hers. "This isn't about questioning you. You're not a criminal, Bellamy. But I will respect your wishes and take you home on one condition."

"What's that?"

"You let me order a pizza from Chuck's."

"How DID A scrappy little guy from Brooklyn end up in Whisperwood, Texas?" Donovan peeked inside the oversize cardboard box of pizza before dropping the lid into place. He'd called in the order as they drove, hoping to minimize their time in town. In retrospect, the decision was a good one when he'd seen a local TV news truck wending its way down Main Street as he pulled away from Chuck's parking lot.

It was too much to hope she wouldn't be found by the press—or worse, whomever had put the bomb in her car—but if he could give her even an evening's peace, then he wanted to do it.

What he hadn't fully reconciled was how much he was looking forward to having dinner with her.

His offered dinner invitation had gone unfulfilled for so many years, it was humbling to realize how anxious he was to see it through. Which was ridiculous because she was now on his caseload and dealing with a horrific trauma.

Bellamy glanced over her shoulder as she grabbed sodas from the fridge before hip bumping the door closed. "Thank Cupid. Chuck met his wife, Maria, on a cruise and decided he couldn't live without her. New York's loss is Whisperwood's gain."

"And Maria's, obviously," Donovan added.

"You seem familiar with the pizza?"

"I'm from here originally. And you don't have to spend much time in Whisperwood before someone makes sure you have a pizza from Chuck's."

While technically true, his mother preferred food cooked in the Colton kitchens by her extensive staff instead of ordering in. Chuck's pizza had been a fortuitous accident one early evening after he'd ducked out of his parents' house and headed home to Austin. Since then, even though he avoided spending a lot of time in Whisperwood, he'd stop off at the small pizzeria after his sporadic visits to his parents' house. He could always make room for a fresh slice and the pizza was almost better the next day, cold, when it came straight out of the fridge.

A small, amused smile tilted Bellamy's lips. "Plates are in the cabinet above the sink."

She stood by her small kitchen table, her dark hair damp from the quick shower he'd encouraged her to take. She was fully dressed, an oversize long-sleeved T-shirt falling over jeans, but something about the look had him doing a double take. There was something fresh about her.

He'd noticed it five years before and was struck anew by that same fact. Even with the horrible events she'd experienced that day, there was a light in her. It had been dampened since their first meeting, but it was still there. Hovering.

Hoping.

Which made the situation she found herself in that much worse. Although he and Alex would go back tomorrow and do a more thorough search of her car, his initial take was that, while deliberate, the bomb had been planted with a degree of amateur crudeness. Crude or not, the work had been effective, the one who planted it only miscalculating the timing device.

And Bellamy's extraordinarily lucky miss by not closing the trunk.

He buried the thought that she was only standing there by the grace of an accident and finished his quick perusal of her, head to toe. It was a skill he'd honed on the job and he used it to his advantage before his gaze alighted on her bare feet. Where he'd have expected her socks to be a soft pink or maybe even a fun red, the distinct shade of burnt orange that covered her toes had him smiling.

"What's that look for?"

He let his gaze linger one more moment on her toes before meeting her eyes. He owed it to her to apprise her of his thoughts on what she was really dealing with, but he wanted time.

Just a bit of time with her.

"It looks like someone's a Longhorn fan."

"As every good graduate of the University of Texas should be." She wiggled the toes on one foot, followed by the other. "I bleed orange, if you must know."

"A pastime around here."

"Pretty much." The mention of her alma mater had her standing a bit straighter and he was pleased to see a smile persisting on her lips as she crossed the small expanse to the stove. She lifted the lid on the pizza and bent closer to inhale the scent before nodding her head. "Oh yeah. Brooklyn's loss is definitely our gain."

They fixed plates and Bellamy grabbed the two sodas from the counter on their way to a dining alcove just outside the kitchen. The house was modest in size, but cozy, and it was easy to see that she'd made a life for herself here. Her taste wasn't flashy, but he caught subtle hints of whimsy in her home. A superhero cookie jar on the kitchen counter added to the decor and her dining room tablecloth had penguins around the rim.

Alex had laid guard outside the kitchen while they fixed their plates and then repositioned himself after they settled at the table.

"He's so good around food."

"Part of his job."

"It's amazing, though." She shook her head. "I had a dog growing up that made it his business to eat anything he could find, scrounge or flat out steal."

"I had a similar conversation with my mother earlier. I grew up with one of those, too. Alex is special, though. He knows his job and with it, his place."

The flow of casual conversation seemed to do its job. Their easy tumble from topic to topic, from Chuck's love life to the discussion of the Longhorns to ravenous dogs, had left that small, persistent smile on her face.

"Will he eat tonight?"

"I'll feed him when we're done. I keep food in the car because I never know if we'll be out late. He's working now so he can eat once I'm done."

"Working?"

"Absolutely. You're in his care now. He hasn't taken his eyes off of you."

She laid down her pizza and turned her full attention toward the dog. Although Alex never moved, the tip of his tail started to thump against the floor. "He's watching over me?"

"Yes. Has been ever since we walked over to you in the LSP parking lot. He's going to protect you." *And so am I.*

The thought rang so clearly in his mind he nearly dropped his pizza. Of course it was his job, and by taking the call Bellamy Reeves had absolutely become his responsibility.

But something else called to him.

He had thought about her through the years. The easy moments they'd shared in her parents' store that lone December evening. The sweet way she had with Alex and the quick way she'd leaped to help them.

He'd remembered.

And he'd thought of her every time he'd passed the corner store on his way out of town.

The store had changed hands since then. He was curious about it and was about to ask when she interjected a fresh thought into the conversation.

"I think we get the better end of the deal."

"Of what deal?"

"The human and pet deal. They give us so much and we just sort of take it." As soon as the words were out, she seemed to catch herself. "Not that you treat him poorly—that's not what I meant. But they give from a special place. It's one I don't know humans have."

"I know what you mean. We think we're superior but there's an awful lot we can learn from animals. They live in the moment. They're loyal. And there's an honesty to them that we can't ever hope to aspire to."

"You're smitten."

"With Alex? Definitely."

"He was such a cute puppy and he's grown into such a handsome dog. Is he good at his job?"

"The best."

"Let me amend my earlier comment. You're smitten *and* biased."

The lightest whisper of heat crawled up his neck. "I suppose I am. He really is good, though. He consistently wins the drills we run across the K-9 teams. And he's got a special sort of alertness. Like now. He looks like he's casually sitting there but he's totally focused on the two of us and on his surroundings."

"What was your takeaway of today?"

The shift in question caught him off guard and Donovan couldn't help thinking that Bellamy Reeves was totally aware of her surroundings, too.

And the danger that threatened her in ways he couldn't begin to imagine.

BELLAMY WANTED TO hover in the warm cocoon of her house and her most comfy clothes and the incredibly able strength of Officer Donovan Colton and his sidekick, Alex. More, she wanted to lose herself in all of it and shut out whatever lurked outside her door.

Which was the very reason she had to ask the question.

And accept that the darkness that came into Donovan's already dark brown gaze had nothing to do with her question and everything to do with the answer.

Something terrible had happened today and pretending it hadn't wasn't going to set her up very well.

Just like her parents.

Where her sister had been insistent in believing

things weren't "that bad" after the accident, Bellamy had pressed on, well aware of what difficult times faced them. Her father's resulting paralysis—and the difficulty of trying to have a seventy-five-year-old body bounce back against that sort of crushing destruction—was nearly impossible.

And she'd met it head-on.

She hadn't hid, nor had she run.

Then why was the urge to do so now so overwhelming and urgent?

And what was she going to do about what she'd found?

"My takeaway?"

She nodded. "I know you haven't written a formal report, but you've obviously done this for some time. What was your initial impression?"

"I still need to question you. I also need to share my thoughts with my commanding officer."

"I see."

And just like that, he went into cop mode, shutting her out of what was clearly her own problem to deal with. Just like the doctors. Just like her sister. Hell, even just like her mother.

Life had careened out of control once again and the only person left to manage it was her.

Standing, she took her empty plate into the kitchen and placed everything in the sink. The rich scents of tomato sauce and cheese still wafted from the closed cardboard but she'd suddenly lost her appetite.

It was unfair to paint Donovan with the same brush as others in her life—she hadn't even told him of the email yet or the events of the day—but his reticence to share with her still stung.

"Bellamy, I'm sorry." She wasn't surprised he'd followed her, but she was stunned to feel the wall of heat that emanated against her back. "I'm not trying to keep you in the dark."

"Spare me."

"It's my job and I need to report my thoughts to my boss. I owe it to him. But that doesn't mean I won't tell you what I know. Nor does it mean I'm going to keep you in the dark. But I need to follow the correct chain of command and management of evidence."

"Evidence?"

"Your car is evidence. That's what I asked the chief to move into police custody. Alex and I will look at it tomorrow and we'll have a better sense of what we're dealing with."

That wall of heat seemed to grow warmer, if possible, even though he didn't touch her. Despite the lack of contact, she could feel him. Could practically sense the beat of his heart.

And even as she hated being kept in the dark, she couldn't deny how good it felt to have him stand there. To have him in her home, filling up the space.

To have someone nearby.

"I won't keep you in the dark. But please let me do my job."

"I got fired today." The words slipped out, as embarrassing to say them out loud as they'd been to digest in Sally Borne's office.

"What for?"

"Reporting an email I wasn't supposed to have received in the first place." She reached for a nearby dish towel, twisting the material beneath her fingers. "Or maybe I was. Who knows?"

Large hands settled on her shoulders, lingering there

briefly before turning her around. "What's this about? I need you to tell me. Tell me all of it."

She knew this moment was inevitable. Had even expected it as she'd worked to process all that had happened since opening that stupid email earlier.

What she hadn't expected were the tears. Hot and sharp, they filled her eyes and tightened her throat like fingers wrapped around her neck. Worse, once she let them out, there was no way to pull them back.

"I—" She swallowed the hiccup, even as another hard sob swamped her.

And then it didn't matter. There was no need for words or explanations or even apologies as Donovan pulled her against that broad, capable, gloriously strong chest. He held her there, his arms around her and his hand nestled against her head where he stroked her hair, seeing her through the uncontrollable rush of emotion and raw adrenaline that finally had a place to land.

Sobs racked her frame as the hot tears continued to pour, unchecked, from her eyes. Abstractly, she thought to be embarrassed, but the sheer relief of expelling all that pent-up emotion kept her from dwelling on anything for too long.

As the tears finally subsided, those lingering moments of embarrassment bubbled to the surface. On a hiccup, she looked up at him, attempting to slip from his hold. "I am sorry."

He didn't budge, a wall of heat and man and solid strength. "Don't go anywhere."

"I… I mean… I—" A horrified squeak fell from her lips as she realized she stood in her kitchen, crying her eyes out in front of a virtual stranger. "I'm so sorry."

"Don't be sorry. And while you're at it, forget embarrassed, anxious or silly. You had a bad day. A really bad day. This will help you start to feel better."

As pep talks went, his admonishments did the trick. The embarrassment was already fading and in its place came that subtle tug of attraction her body still remembered from all those years ago.

Donovan Colton was an impressive man, and not just for the solid physique and commanding presence. The man had layers. She'd sensed it five years ago and she sensed it now, even as she had no reason for the observation.

Yet something was there.

Her mother had always teased her about being borderline psychic but she'd never paid it much mind. Bellamy had always believed instead it meant taking the time to observe her surroundings. She wasn't shy, per se, but she wasn't the first person to leap in and begin talking. Rather, she appreciated the opportunity to sit and observe before being called on to say anything.

Appreciated the opportunity to get her bearings around people.

The side benefit was that she'd learned to read people. She'd developed a sense of what made them tick and, often, what motivated them.

And that's where Donovan Colton tripped her up. It was obvious he was crazy about his dog. Along with that she took him at face value as a good, honorable cop. Even his reticence to share his thoughts on her case were steeped in following protocol, which she could— and did—respect.

So why the subtle sense that he was almost desperate to prove his place in the world?

She'd thought it earlier when he'd spoken of the

pizza. He might be from Whisperwood but there was a distinct note of dissonance, that he clearly felt he didn't belong here. Nor did he have much love for his hometown. Again, she couldn't define how she knew that, she simply did.

"Are you all right now?" Donovan asked.

"Yeah. I feel better."

"Do you want anything else to eat?"

"No." She rubbed her stomach, the crying jag having left her raw and hollowed out. "I'm good."

"You mind if I feed Alex, then? And we can talk after."

"Go ahead."

Donovan ducked out of the kitchen and after some murmured words to Alex, she heard her front door click shut. Alex trotted into the kitchen in the wake of his master's departure, his tail wagging and his gentle brown eyes alert as he took her in.

"You're such a pretty boy." Bellamy picked up a plastic bowl she'd filled for him earlier and freshened the water. His nails tapped on her hardwood floor as he walked over to the bowl, his gaze on her until he dropped his head to the water and drank his fill.

Even in something so simple and natural, she knew the dog was alert and keen to his surroundings. What fascinated her was how attuned he was to her. It didn't take much to know Donovan's directive to the animal had been to watch over her. What she didn't know was what she was going to do when they had to leave.

Or how she'd fight back against the inevitable threat when it came at her once more.

Chapter Four

While Alex dived into his dinner, Donovan left his partner to his food and walked back into the dining room. Bellamy stood arrow straight, her head slightly bowed as her hands trailed over a small sideboard. She stared down at a series of photos and even from where he stood he could see she focused on one in particular.

"Are those your parents?"

"Yes." She tapped one of the photos. "This was their fiftieth anniversary."

He did the quick math in his head, surprised to realize they had been so old. "Do you have a lot of brothers and sisters?"

"No, just me and my younger sister, Magnolia. Maggie," she quickly added.

"Then your parents were older when they had children? Because there's no way you're close to fifty."

She turned away from the photo, the aimless energy that seemed to grip her at the sideboard fading as he asked her about her life. "Yes. And that photo was taken about six years ago. Before my father—" She hesitated, then continued, "Before his health declined. My mother's followed on the heels of that."

"I'm sorry for that."

And he was. While Donovan took full credit for the personal challenges he had with his own family, he loved them. It had been hard to see his father struggle the past couple of years as he was naturally forced to slow down from his normal routine—racing around the ranch, flying places for his business interests or evenings out entertaining. And his mother, for all her bright and happy chatter, carried the burdens of age, as well. She'd let go of a few commitments over the past few years, preferring events that didn't have her driving at night.

He supposed it was the natural order of things, but it didn't mean it hadn't been a transition.

"What about you?" Bellamy asked. "Any brothers or sisters?"

"Oh, the Colton family is a prolific one. I'm one of four, all older than me, and I come from a family that's even larger."

"That must be nice."

"Most of the time." Donovan avoided mentioning when it wasn't, especially since he had relatives who'd both spent time in jail for heinous crimes. While he knew his extended family didn't reflect on him, he was well aware there were places in Texas and beyond where the Colton name didn't win any fans.

How funny, then, that his parents were the antithesis.

They'd been more than willing to take him in, nearly falling over themselves to make him part of the family. To save him, that poor little abandoned soul, dropped into their midst.

"You don't like coming from a big family?"

I don't like feeling like an outsider with all those eyes watching.

He never had. But like the black sheep branch of his family, he refused to mention anything. Instead, he focused on the positive and the values his mother had impressed upon him.

"It has its moments. I can do without everyone being in each other's business. But it is nice knowing I have so many people to count on."

Her gaze flitted back to the photos at the edge of the sideboard before shifting determinedly back to him. "People to count on. That must be nice."

Alex trotted into the room, his dinner at an end and his guard duties back in place as he took a seat facing the two of them. The overwhelming events of the day— and the danger that lurked beneath—still seemed like a dream. Because she wanted to keep it that way for a few hours more, Bellamy focused on the dog. "I should probably let you both go. I'll be fine for tonight and then I can come in and make a statement tomorrow, if that's okay? I'm suddenly not up for getting into a recounting of my afternoon once again."

Exhaustion rode Bellamy's features, with dark smudges settling beneath her eyes postcrying jag. He didn't want to leave her but he hardly had a reason to stay, either. "I'm scheduled to meet with the chief tomorrow morning at ten. I would like to get your statement before then."

"How about if I come into the station at eight?" A hard laugh escaped her chest. "It's not like I have to go into work, after all."

She'd mentioned the job earlier, right before she was overcome with the emotions of the day. "You sure you don't want to talk about it now?"

"Can it wait? I promise I'll tell you everything. Including anything that may become clearer overnight."

"You have a deal, then."

"Oh. Wait." The bum's rush wasn't lost on him, so he was surprised when she stopped him. "I don't have a car."

"Alex and I can swing by and pick you up. I'll even include a stop at the coffee place in town."

"You don't have to—"

He reached for her hand, the move meant to reassure, but the sudden stop of her words hung heavy between them.

"It's okay. I can give you a hand. And it's not like Whisperwood is this sprawling metropolis. You're like a two-minute detour after I turn into town."

"Okay, then."

In moments she had him bustled out her front door, the rest of the pizza in his hands. As he opened the door of his SUV for Alex to hop in, Donovan couldn't avoid the impressions that had bombarded him over the past few hours. Where he'd initially seen a woman dealing with a difficult circumstance, those moments when she stared at her photos suggested something else.

Something more.

Bellamy Reeves was a lonely woman. And if his instincts were correct, she was dealing with something far beyond her understanding.

Jensen Taylor scrolled impatiently through the news articles on his tablet, hunting for anything that might mention the incident in the parking lot at LSP. His father, Sutton, had been touch and go in the hospital for the past few weeks, a private matter Jensen had deliberately kept from the employees at LSP, but the old man had rallied over the past few days.

He'd inevitably be fielding phone calls if Sutton caught wind of a bomb detonating in the LSP parking lot.

He and his father did well keeping their distance—emotional and, when Jensen could manage it, physical—and the hospital stay had helped that even more. Jensen saw no reason to change that. He played the devoted son when it was warranted and then went about living his life the rest of the time. Now that Jensen's mother was dead, the situation worked well for them both.

Of course, cars blowing up in the LSP parking lot were likely to draw the old man's attention, no matter how poorly he felt. His father had been lingering at a private facility south of Austin, but he hadn't died. Public problems at LSP might give Sutton the ammunition to recover fully and that was the last thing Jensen needed.

All he had to do was convince the old man he had it under control.

It was his only choice.

He had little interest—actually, make that *no* interest—in pharmaceuticals, but he'd be damned if any of his father's bastards would get a piece of his legacy. The old man had already suggested he wanted to open up a new position on the leadership team for the moment one of his brats finished business school.

Oh, that was a big, Texas-sized *hell no*.

This was the only way to manage things and ensure his father's far-too-generous heart didn't ruin Jensen's future.

The entire situation had a funny sort of justice to it. His father had always played the field, his simpering mother just living with it while she flitted around as society matron of their hick town. Then his mother died and instead of publicly playing the field after an appropriate mourning period, poor Sutton was all sick and weak.

Justice at its finest.

LSP might have turned Whisperwood into one of the largest suburbs outside of Austin but it was still central Texas. Small freaking potatoes. But that hadn't stopped his father. The man had worked his playboy magic from one end of the Hill Country to the other. His mother had ignored it all, seeming to believe all that mattered was the large house Sutton had built for her, visible to anyone who drove a few blocks off of Whisperwood's main drag.

They really were a pair.

Jensen hadn't spent much time worrying if the two of them loved each other, but he had taken a few notes for himself on the type of woman who'd make a good partner. He could do with one who had his mother's penchant for living in ignorant bliss. Sadly, the last few women he'd dated hadn't fit the bill.

Resigned to worry about it later, Jensen shot a quick email to his father, assuring him all was well and to continue to rest and focus on getting better.

"Wanted you to hear it from me. Absolutely nothing to worry about. A holiday prank gone bad," Jensen muttered as he typed up a quick note and shot it off. He'd know by morning if the old man had bought it.

In the meantime, he wanted to do a bit of digging. And figure out just what Bellamy Reeves knew.

BELLAMY GATHERED HER hair up in a twist, clipping the dark brown mass. Then she added a few quick swipes of mascara to her eyes for good measure. She'd spent a restless night and was well aware there was no amount of makeup that could cover the bags beneath her eyes.

"More like potato sacks," she acknowledged to herself as she added one last swipe of the mascara wand.

Standing back to assess her image in the mirror, she was pleased to see the mascara had at least made her look a bit more human. Zombie TV shows might be popular but no one wanted a monster walking down the Main Street of Whisperwood at eight in the morning.

The lack of a car was a problem, but she'd deal with that after she made her statement to Donovan. She'd already logged in the night before and started the claim process with her insurance company. The automated email she got back confirmed someone would call her today to keep the process moving.

Making one final effort to look human with a pass of her lip gloss, she grabbed a light jacket from her closet and went to wait in the front room for Donovan. The oppressive weight of the day before faded a bit as she thought about the strong, capable man and his dog.

They were an impressive pair. The dog was both obedient and clearly in love with his master, the big eyes and devoted stare something to see. She couldn't stop the small smile at the image they made, the affection in Donovan's eyes for the large black Lab proof he was equally smitten. It was sweet to see. And made a good-looking man even more attractive.

Along with her dad's advice, she'd also read once on a dating blog that three signs to watch for in a prospective mate were how they behaved with waiters, how they spoke in conflict and how they treated animals. From what she could see, Donovan Colton passed all three tests with flying colors.

It had been one of the things she still remembered about that night so long ago when he'd come into the store with a sweet little puppy. That mix of concern and care for an animal was an obvious clue to his personality.

Unbidden, the rest of that long-ago evening filled her thoughts. The easy conversation and subtle flirtation. Even the clear stamp of interest in his gaze. She'd been more interested than she could describe and had wanted to see him again.

Of course, all that had been forgotten once the news of her parents' accident was delivered. And all that had come after had changed her life in ways she never could have imagined.

So how odd that he was back. That he was the one who'd been in Whisperwood and taken the call for her car. And that he was the one she'd now share her story with.

Engine sounds purred from her driveway and a glance out the front window indicated her chariot had arrived. She picked up her things and let herself out of the house, surprised when either Donovan or Alex were nowhere in sight.

"Donovan?" When he didn't answer she hollered. "Donovan!"

His voice was muffled but came back from the opposite side of the yard. "Be right there! Stay at the door."

She stood still, curious to where he and his K-9 partner vanished to, but willing to follow the direction. She was nearly ready to go looking for them when Donovan reached her just as she was turning the key in the lock.

"Good morning, Bellamy."

"Oh!" She'd expected to meet him at the car, so the large frame and imposing presence was a surprise. "You didn't have to… I mean, I could have come to you."

"This is door-to-door service, ma'am. Even when I make you wait while Alex and I check the perimeter." He smiled and mimed tipping an imaginary hat. "It's part of the Texas gentleman's code."

She swallowed hard around the idea her perimeter even required checking and opted for a shot of dark humor. "The Texas gentleman's code? Is that a euphemism for politely escorting a suspect to the police station?"

The moment the words were out of her mouth, she knew they'd missed the mark. The anxiety that had kept her company throughout a restless night—including the fear that something horrible at LSP was somehow being blamed on her—had taken root and wouldn't let go.

But it was the frown that marred his face—matched to an equally disappointed light in his eyes—that had her rethinking the remark.

"This is nothing but routine."

"It may be for you, but it's not every day my car blows up and I follow it up with a visit to the police to make a statement."

"Did you do it?"

"What?" The sheer shock his question gave her had her mouth dropping, her momentary concern at possibly offending him fading away. "You think I did that? To my car? To my stuff? Why would I do that? And possibly kill myself in the process?"

Donovan had already walked her to his SUV, his expression turning serious as he put his hand on the car door handle. "I don't think anything of the sort. Or I'm trying hard not to, even though my instincts as a cop are to question everything."

"So you do think I did it?" The words came out prim and stiff and she wanted to sink through the driveway at the small shot of hurt that burrowed beneath her breast.

"I'm asking questions. Just like the chief will do. Just like reporters will do. Keep that hot core of righteous anger and you'll be just fine."

Bellamy was about to reply when Donovan pulled the door open. Alex was already in the back seat and she could see the depression marks of a sweeper head over the entire seat, from the back panel to the portion where she'd rest in her neatly pressed clothes. "You vacuumed?"

"Of course. I love Alex but I'm well aware no one wants to wear him."

"But… I mean…" She stopped, the weird conversation and the added awkwardness of her reaction to his questions slowing her down. She climbed into the SUV seat, but laid a hand on his arm before he could close the door. "Why don't I try this again? Good morning, Donovan. It's nice to see you. Thank you for picking me up."

He smiled once more, a small dimple winking in his cheek when the corners of his lips tilted upward into a relaxed grin. "Good morning, Bellamy. It's my pleasure."

He closed the door and she watched him walk around

the front of the SUV, more than willing to look her fill unnoticed. He was still as attractive as that night he'd come into her parents' store, but he'd aged, as well. The rounder cheeks that marked a younger man were gone, replaced with a slight hollowing beneath the bones that set off his features. His jaw seemed harder than she remembered and there was a solidness to his frame that was rougher. Worn.

No, she amended to herself, *experienced*.

Age worked itself on every person in a myriad of ways, but experience left a different sort of mark. It stamped itself on the body by way of bearing and attitude, words and gestures.

He fascinates me.

The words popped into her mind, unbidden, but she gave them room to grow and the space to breathe.

Donovan Colton did fascinate her. He was attractive, obviously, but there was more. And what seemed to tug at her the most was what she sensed lay beneath the surface.

Unaware of her close scrutiny, Donovan hopped into the car and turned toward her. "Coffee first?"

"Sure."

"Then here." He reached behind his seat and pulled a cardboard container from the floor. "I didn't know what you liked but figured I couldn't go wrong with a latte."

"Thanks. And you guessed right."

The scent of coffee drifted from the cup in her hand and she wondered that she hadn't smelled it the moment she got into the car.

"You've been busy this morning. First the vacuum. Then the coffee. Did you catch a few bad guys while you were at it?"

"Alex and I are early risers. And I wanted to beat the traffic out of Austin so it worked."

"You didn't just stay at your parents'?"

"No."

Although she'd fumbled her first few comments, she'd gotten them back on track once she took her seat. For that reason, it was surprising to see his gaze shutter so tightly at the mention of his family. Her mother had always teased her that she was intuitive, but she didn't need a lick of extra awareness to know that there was a no-trespassing sign on Donovan's relationship with his parents.

What she wanted to know was why.

The Coltons were well-known in Whisperwood and throughout the greater Austin area. She had been so busy with her own family the past few years she hadn't paid a ton of attention to community gossip, but she wasn't completely immune, either.

She knew of the Coltons. To Donovan's comments the prior evening, he came from a large clan, with several branches spread across the state. The Colton family had been in the news recently, in fact, when serial criminal Livia Colton had escaped from prison. Public knowledge or not, it seemed bad form to mention that, so she relied on the manners her mother had drilled in from childhood and changed the subject.

"I know Austin's not that far. And it's always nice to sleep in your own bed."

"Exactly."

Donovan started the car, the weird moment seemingly forgotten as he navigated down her street and toward the main road into town. At a loss over what to say, Bellamy twisted in her seat, petting and praising Alex as she told him good morning.

Energy quivered beneath the dog's fur but he held his position in the back seat. She ran her fingers over the extra soft areas behind his ear, finding a sensitive spot that had his eyelids dimming in pleasure.

It was so simple, she marveled to herself. So easy. Alex wanted praise, attention and a reason to give his trust.

As Donovan's evasion over his family ran once more through her mind, she acknowledged to herself that people were far more difficult to figure out.

DONOVAN MADE THE turn into the parking lot at the Whisperwood police station. Bellamy had kept up a steady conversation on the short drive from her house, but quieted as they turned into town. The air seemed to shift and Donovan saw Alex shift with it, his already straight posture going even stiffer where he stood guard in the back seat.

Unable to delay the discussion, Donovan instead chose to treat it with the same casual care he'd managed at her house. This wasn't designed to be an interrogation, but they did need to understand what had happened to her and why Bellamy was targeted. He'd already sent the materials he'd collected on scene at LSP to the bomb squad and would oversee their review personally.

But none of that would assuage her anxiety or make this morning's discussion any easier.

Chief Archer Thompson greeted them personally, authority stamped in his bearing. In moments he had them seated in his office, his own coffee in hand. Donovan liked Archer. He was a good guy, took the law seriously and had always been a collaborative partner. The man reinforced that belief in the way he set up the conversation and explained to Bellamy what they needed to understand.

"Ms. Reeves, thank you for coming in today."

"Of course." She nodded and while her shoulders were still set in a stiff line, her hand no longer clenched her coffee cup in a death grip, which Donovan took for an improvement.

"I'm going to ask you several questions and some of them I'm going to ask more than once to see if you remember things from a different perspective."

"I understand."

With her head nod, Archer started. He took her basic information, even how long she'd been in Whisperwood, peppering in pleasant comments along the way and easing her into the discussion. Although Donovan knew his way around an interview, the ease with which Arch managed the conversation was impressive.

"How long have you been at Lone Star Pharmaceutical?" Archer asked.

"For a little over thirteen years. I started with them out of college."

Donovan digested that point. Thirteen years in her profession put her around thirty-five if she did college in the standard timing. He was thirty-one and had estimated her to be around the same age, so it was intriguing to know she had a few years on him.

You'd do better with an older woman, Donovan. You're far too serious for a younger woman to stay interested.

His sister had said that to him recently and he'd been amused and vaguely offended. Too serious? Since she was kind to a fault, he quickly saw his way past it, but the underlying intention in his sister's thoughts had stuck.

He had dated younger and none of those relationships—for the ones that could even be called a full-on relationship—had had much life in them. He had Alex and his work and while the initial weeks of a relationship went well, the moment things turned serious and his schedule wasn't fully aligned to theirs, the women he dated chose to walk.

Bellamy Reeves didn't strike him as a woman who walked. From what she described of her parents' needs, she had stuck around, taking care of them and seeing to their well-being. She'd been loyal to a job when far more people were jumping from company to company for greener pastures. Even the night they'd met, she'd been at the store helping out.

It was an impressive trait, one he couldn't deny appealed to him.

Hell, Colton, might as well just suck it up and admit it. Everything about the woman appeals to you.

"Did anything unusual stand out about your day yesterday?"

Donovan keyed back into Archer's questions, the basic pleasantries of job history and life in Whisperwood long past.

"The whole day was unusual."

"Did something happen?" Archer leaned forward, his already sharp focus growing visibly more pointed. "Something besides the car?"

"It was… Well, I mean, I found something. On email." Her fingers fumbled as she reached for her purse where she'd set it beside her. "I have an email. I printed a few copies."

Archer kept his cop's eyes focused on her purse, his attention unwavering until she pulled the promised piece of paper from her bag. Although Donovan had no qualms her purse held nothing more than what she'd said, he couldn't blame the man for staying on his guard.

If she sensed the heightened attention, Bellamy never indicated it, instead handing over a piece of paper folded in half. She handed a second copy to Donovan and he quickly read through the terse, telling statements, bulleted out in list form after a cold, lifeless salutation.

Donovan scanned the page again, his gaze going to the header that had printed out along with the content of the note. Her name was printed in the "To" line, along with her full email address, but no named sender was visible in the "From" line, just the word INTERNAL. The date was yesterday, the timing late morning as she'd already shared.

He wasn't an expert in technology and programming, but he had enough working knowledge to know something was manipulated in the note. A masked sender was a problem.

A problem that could be easily created if one simply altered a printout.

The thought struck fast and hard, nearly knocking his breath. His gaze shot to Archer's and he saw the chief had already traveled down that path and fast.

"Ms. Reeves. Tell me a bit more about this email. Do you know if anyone else received one?"

"I think it was only me but I don't know. We're on a lighter work schedule with the holidays so there were fewer people around. Not that it would have mattered." She shrugged, her vivid gray eyes dulled with the troubling memories of the day before. "I didn't go around asking anyone. I thought it was wrong to do that until I'd spoken to Human Resources."

"And what did they say?"

"They fired me."

"Yesterday?" the chief clarified, before pointing to the lone sheet of paper in his hands. "After you reported this email to them?"

"Yes, that's correct."

"Based on what you've described, you're a loyal employee."

"I thought so, too. But I wasn't even given a chance to explain. HR refused to support me or even listen to my side of the story."

"Have you been working on any special projects? Anything that would have given you access to the details in this email?"

"Of course not. That email's about price-fixing, market manipulation and harming our customers. If LSP did that, I'd have quit on my own a long time ago."

"So this is a malicious rumor, then? Something to harm the company."

Bellamy stilled at the suggestion, her eyes going wide. "This is a terrible rumor to go spreading. It could ruin the company."

"I agree," Archer said.

Donovan had remained quiet, allowing the chief to do his work, but he couldn't stay silent any longer. "Do you know who sent this? Someone who had a vendetta against the company? A disgruntled employee or maybe someone else let go recently?"

"I don't know anyone who'd do this. LSP is a reputable company. I've worked in the finance department for thirteen years. We file our reports properly and on time. We manage all government requirements and standards the industry is held to. Nothing about this email, or the practices it suggests, makes any sense. Too many people would know if something like this was happening. LSP provides vaccines to the entire Southwest. You don't just cover up something like this."

"Then it does sound like a vicious rumor designed to seed doubt and destroy the company's reputation."

"Maybe. I don't know."

"Don't you, Ms. Reeves?" Archer left the thought hanging, the impression of an affable, easygoing town leader fading in the space of a heartbeat. "Because it would be easy enough to manipulate a printout like this. Even easier for someone with such a lauded history at the company to whisper to a few people and seed a whole lot of doubt."

"You think I did this? Me?" Her voice squeaked on the last word.

"I have to ask those questions. It's my job."

Whatever nervousness carried her into Archer Thompson's office vanished as Bellamy rose from her chair. She stood tall, her gaze direct as she stared the chief down across his desk.

The same alertness that had filled Archer's eyes returned, matched by Alex's sudden readiness beside Donovan. They all seemed to hang there, the moment stretching out in a weird tableau of mismatched power, authority and frustration.

"I lost my job yesterday, Chief Thompson. In the span of an afternoon, I lost my professional home, my reputation and nearly my life. I don't know what sort of cruel, vicious game someone's playing with me but I did not write this email, nor did I manipulate its contents."

"No one's suggesting you did."

"Oh no? I came in here to freely discuss what happened and in moments, you managed to make me feel as if I was responsible for this." She shook her own copy of the email, the one she'd retained for herself. "I'm lucky I even printed this out, but it was a last-minute thought before I blithely marched down to Human Resources, thinking they could help me. Or at minimum listen to my concerns and give me a fair shot. But they failed me and now so have you." She sat back down, her gaze remaining steady before it flicked over to him. "Both of you."

Donovan wanted to argue but said nothing. She wasn't wrong.

And he had failed her. He'd promised her a safe space and instead had brought her into the lion's den.

Bellamy's gaze returned to the chief, her attention so focused Donovan might have left for all she'd have noticed. That same loneliness he'd sensed the night before was back, her posture shuttered and protective as she turned fully in her chair to face Archer.

"Ask me whatever you want, Chief Thompson. Ask me however many ways you want to. The truth remains the same."

Chapter Five

Bellamy couldn't get out of there fast enough. She'd walked into Chief Thompson's office a trusting soul and walked out disappointed and once again unsure of herself. Why had she even listened to Donovan Colton in the first place? Had she really been taken in by the big, bad protector routine? The hot cop with the cute dog.

Was she really that lame? Or that hard up?

Obviously she was both.

With the interview at an end, she'd already left the chief's office a free woman.

For now, that small, scared voice inside whispered. She'd done her level best to keep it quiet, but she couldn't deny the raw, mind-numbing fear or the surreal nightmare she seemed to have fallen into, like Dorothy into Munchkinland. Why didn't anyone believe her? Or, at minimum, listen to her without judgment?

Was LSP so powerful that no one believed anything could happen there? That an employee could possibly discover something that was at best below standard and at worst, nefarious and deliberate?

Even as she asked herself the questions, she knew the truth. Had it been anyone else, she'd have questioned them, too.

What really stung was Donovan. She'd placed her already fragile trust in him and what had she gotten for it?

Just like Maggie.

Her hands fumbled as she stood in the lobby of the Whisperwood police station, punching a request for a car into an app on her phone.

Like Maggie?

Whatever this situation might be, it was nothing like her relationship with her sister. Nothing at all.

Maggie had left her and their parents when they needed her most. Instead of providing the familial support and understanding their family needed, Maggie had chosen a life with her rich new husband, James, and came around as little as possible.

Bellamy had given Maggie the benefit of the doubt at first. Newlyweds should have a chance to start their marriage off right, spending time with each other and cementing their relationship. She'd said those words to her mother often, especially on the occasions when Maggie turned down invitations to Sunday dinner or couldn't come by the hospital when her father got too sick, disabled beyond her ability to care for him. She'd been adamant that her sister needed that time until the day she realized she was adrift at sea, caring for her parents all by herself.

It had been those times that had created the rift that had never mended.

Get out of there, Bell. They're suffocating you.

They're our parents. How can you even suggest that? Worse, how can you walk away?

I'm not walking away. I'm talking about legitimate care that can handle Dad's needs and whatever it is that's got Mom fading away more and more every day.

They're my parents.

They're my parents, too. Yet you've done nothing I've asked. You refuse to even listen to reason.

The conversation had changed as their father's condition worsened, but only about where her parents should be for the optimal care. As if it mattered. The type of facility her father belonged in wasn't anything they could have afforded, even if they'd wanted to. So Bellamy had scraped together what she could for daytime care and had swallowed her pride and taken her sister's husband's money to fill in the gaps.

And they'd gotten by. Her father might not have had perfect care, but he had his family around him and he'd lived in his own home. The house was small, so it hadn't been too difficult to make the needed changes to help him get around. And they'd all gotten used to the hospital bed in the front room after a while.

The images were still so vivid, yet at times they seemed like another lifetime, they were so distant. The house had become hers after her parents' life insurance settlement and it no longer resembled the home of an invalid. Wheelchairs, hospital beds and the endless rows of pills were long gone. The scent of illness no longer lingered.

At times she was relieved and at others she wished

she could bring it all back, would do whatever it took to have even one more day.

When she went to her last physical in September, her doctor had told her these swings in emotion were the natural cycle of grief. Even knowing that didn't make the days easier or the memories any less weighty.

The ping of her phone announcing the arrival of her driver pulled her from the maudlin thoughts. She'd fought so hard not to be a martyr over her parents, so it was disheartening to realize how quickly those feelings could creep in, especially when she thought about Maggie.

It was negative energy and she didn't want it or need it in her life. Just like she didn't need to be the object of a criminal investigation into why she might have decided to blow herself up.

As if.

Shaking it all off, she got into the car that pulled up to the curb. For as small as they were, even Whisperwood had adopted personalized transportation apps and she'd never been more pleased about that. She'd get home on her own and could assess the damage from her kitchen table.

With the police station firmly behind her, Bellamy focused on the driver's route through town and toward her small home.

Her haven.

She'd hole up and assess the damage.

And then she was going to figure out just what the hell was going on and why she'd somehow been targeted as the one to take the fall.

"THAT WENT WELL." Chief Thompson stared at the closed office door in the direction Bellamy just departed.

"Please tell me that's your special brand of sarcasm." Donovan eyed Alex where he lay on the floor across the room and could have sworn the animal let out a small sniff of displeasure.

"Justice may be blind but I'm not. If that woman's guilty, I'll eat my hat."

Donovan thought the same but was curious about Archer's sudden assessment. "You didn't act like she was innocent."

"Appearances. I can't have my constituents thinking I'm soft or unable to ask the tough questions. But there was some pure, righteous anger there the moment the tone changed. She was well and rightly pissed at both of us and I'm glad. She's going to need that bit of fire to get through whatever is going on here."

"You believe the email?"

"No reason not to."

Donovan glanced down at the paper he still held in a tight grip. "Emails can be doctored."

"Lots of things can be doctored. What I don't see in this situation is why. She's got a good job. She's well liked and well respected. I did some preliminary digging. She's not in debt or trouble and there's nothing to suggest she's got some sort of vendetta and is looking to ruin Lone Star Pharmaceutical. Nothing clicks there."

"No, it doesn't."

It didn't make any more sense an hour later as Donovan worked over Bellamy's car. The chief had had her vehicle towed to a small impound area the man kept for police business and Donovan had gone straight there with Alex after leaving the station. Her gray gaze still haunted him, the whispers of "traitor" and "coconspirator" stamped so clearly in those depths they might as well have been written out.

And hadn't he contributed to that?

He'd brought Bellamy to the station himself, hand delivered to the front door. He'd genuinely believed she was the victim in this situation, but the moment she'd pulled out that email the tenor of the meeting had changed. Archer might be working the bad cop routine but that didn't exactly leave Donovan as good cop.

And he still had questions.

Was Bellamy responsible in any way for what had happened? And if she wasn't, then why was she targeted with such incriminating information?

Worse, what sort of scam was LSP running against the market?

The chief had promised to start looking into those elements, especially since the case was on his turf, but Donovan knew well that wasn't an easy investigation for anyone, let alone a small police department that had grown on the goodwill and funding of the town's largest employer.

Donovan had almost used that level of conflict to transfer the investigation to his own precinct in Austin when Archer took matters into his own hands. The chief sent all notes and information to the Austin PD chief himself, CC-ing Donovan in the process.

Nothing about this situation made any sense. Instead, it felt like mysteries wrapped in mysteries, with no discernable threads or entry points.

By all indications, Bellamy Reeves was a solid, well-respected employee. Responsible, but not a part of the company's upper echelon. And yet she'd somehow been granted access to information that created a quagmire of doubt.

What could she possibly know?

If she were higher up in LSP, he might explore a whistle-blower angle, but she didn't have the power to affect that sort of change.

Shaking his head to dislodge the roiling thoughts, Donovan caught sight of Alex from the corner of his eye. The dog was still seated in the position he'd instructed, his gaze never wavering as Donovan searched the car with a flashlight.

Was that accusation he saw in his partner's eyes?

Alex had been his usual obedient self, but he'd deliberately sniffed the front passenger seat of the car before they climbed in and headed for the impound lot. He'd also taken the back seat, refusing to sit in his normal spot in the front.

Loyalty to Bellamy?

If it was, he'd take Alex's judgment more seriously than many others.

But even with the positive canine reinforcement, it didn't change the situation. Bellamy Reeves was in a heap of trouble.

"It's about damn time you figured out why, Colton."

Whether it was the muttered instructions or the simple twist of a moment, he had no idea, but his flashlight tilted over a quick glint of something lightly colored. Repositioning the light, he searched once more for the source and saw a small, thin button, the sort used on men's fancy dress shirts. He flashed the light fully on the object, a momentary pang that a man might have lost a button in Bellamy's car burning through him like wildfire.

The woman *was* entitled to date. To have relationships. Hell, she could make out in her damn car if she
wanted to, buttons flying in all directions in the heat of
the moment. What business was it of his?

At the bark from behind him, Donovan turned to
see Alex, that firm stare still in place. "Okay, fine. No
jumping to conclusions."

Even as the odd shot of jealousy lingered, Donovan
refocused on the evidence he'd collected. He carefully
picked up the button with his gloved hand, anxious to
preserve whatever prints might be on the flat disc as
part of the investigation. After dropping it into an evidence bag from his field kit, he stood back to assess
the car once more.

With a light pat on his thigh, he motioned Alex closer
and was comforted when that large body scrambled to
join him, resettling himself at Donovan's side. Together
they stared at the remains of the car.

It was a simple, serviceable sedan, about four years
old. Nothing flashy, but it had been kept clean. Even
beneath the grit and residue of the explosion, he could
see there weren't items left scattered throughout the
car like an extra storage space or trash receptacle. He
hadn't even found the normal junk stuffed in the armrest, only the charred edges of a few napkins.

The car was neat and orderly. Just like her home.
And just like the office he suspected he'd find when
he headed over to LSP later.

On a resigned sigh, he continued the review of the
car, layer by layer. He'd need more time to take all the
samples he wanted, but he did have enough to start the
process. He needed to apprise his chief of what he'd discovered so far, so he'd kill two birds and drop the mate-

rials off at the lab himself. Maybe with some space and distance, and the idle time on the drive back to Austin, something would shake loose.

It was only ten minutes later, both he and Alex back in his SUV and headed for the highway, that it hit him. Whatever possible involvement Bellamy had in the situation unfolding at LSP, one thing was clear.

She'd been the target of a car bomb.

And since the perpetrator hadn't been successful, what would stop him from trying again?

Donovan skidded to a stop and took a hard spin on his steering wheel, whipping the car around before heading back into town and in the direction of Bellamy's house. Adrenaline lit him up like the Christmas lights on Main Street as he raced toward the small home.

Why had he let her walk out by herself? Worse, how had he been so blind to the needs of someone on his caseload?

The woman was at risk and in very clear danger.

And he'd been worried about a damn button and who she might be dating.

He pressed harder on the gas, bumping over the slightly uneven road that lead to her home. With yet another hard turn of the wheel, he spun onto her street. Relief punched through the adrenaline when he saw her in the distance, on her knees around the flower beds that surrounded the front porch, a hat on her head.

The scenario of smoke and fire that had accompanied him on the wild drive through town was nowhere in evidence. Instead, all he saw was a pretty woman on a cool Texas afternoon digging in her flower beds.

He'd never been more relieved.

Even as he couldn't shake the hard, insistent slam of his pulse that suggested he'd arrived just in time.

"EVERYTHING'S FINE, DAD. Really, it was nothing. It was an unfortunate accident, is all."

Jensen paced around his office, the faint voice of his father, Sutton Taylor, echoing from the speakerphone on his desk.

And everything *was* fine. Hadn't he been trying to tell the old man for half an hour already? Even confined to a bed, the old man could natter on and on.

"Bombs in cars? In our parking lot at headquarters?"

"An incident, nothing more."

"How can you say that, Jensen? It's an employee in danger. On our property."

In danger because I put her there. Voluntarily.

The retort was so close to the edge of his tongue Jensen nearly had to bite it, but held back. Gloating over his plans would get him nowhere and would prematurely tip his father off before he'd completed the work.

But he satisfied himself with a small smile, pleased that he'd found a way to get exactly what he wanted, all while pinning it on an unsuspecting victim.

Even better, no one would question the line of succession from Sutton to Jensen Taylor when the inevitable handoff of LSP finally came. He was the rightful heir to the Taylor family fortune and to Lone Star Pharmaceutical. His father might have enjoyed sowing every oat he had, but there was no way one of his bastards would get a single piece of what Jensen had worked for.

What he deserved.

"Dad, let the police do their job. Bellamy Reeves has been a loose cannon for some time."

"The sweet girl in finance?"

Jensen had to give his father credit—he did know his employees. Or maybe it was more that his father never forgot a pretty face. Whatever the reason, he'd pegged Jensen's scapegoat with surprising accuracy.

"She might have been sweet once but she's had a rough go these last few years. Her father was the one paralyzed in that accident several years ago."

"I knew Daniel-Justice Reeves, Jensen. I know what happened to the man."

Even with the sickness that had gripped him with increasing severity over the past few weeks, his father's withering voice was as clear as ever.

"Then you know he died a terrible death. Lingered there at the end way too long. That does something to a person, Dad. I don't know what I'd do if I was in the Reeves girl's position. If I lost you that way."

Sutton paused for a moment before continuing on in slightly quieter tones. "You need to help her. Find out who did this."

"Of course."

"And keep me posted. I'm not that far away."

"I know that. I know you can be back at any time." *Any freaking time*, Jensen thought. "I want you to focus on getting better. I'll figure out what's going on here and keep you updated."

"You can still come here for Christmas, you know," Sutton said, his voice quiet. "I'd like to see you."

The comment was almost sweet, for a man who'd never shown a large degree of fatherly care. *Nice time to try and mend fences, dear old Dad.*

But he said none of it. Instead, he forced that calm, capable tone into his voice, his focus on getting through the call. "I know I said I'd cover things through the holidays but that won't keep me from coming down to see you. You can count on me."

"All right. We'll talk tomorrow. Get Chief Thompson on this. I make sure that man has a rock-solid department with all the latest tools and tech for a reason. I want him taking care of this."

"Of course, Dad."

After a few more minutes of blustering, Jensen heard the voice of a nurse who'd puttered in to take Sutton's vitals and his father made excuses to hang up.

Jensen hit the end-call button on the speakerphone and stood there, staring out the window of his office at the view of the parking lot and the hill country beyond. He could still see the spot where Bellamy Reeves's car had been parked the day before, yellow police tape flying from a nearby tree. Even at this distance, a large black spot was visible on the ground from the remnants of the burned-out car.

His clueless little scapegoat.

She was the perfect choice. The absolutely perfect scapegoat for what he needed to do.

LSP would turn a shockingly enormous profit.

His father wouldn't be around to see any of it.

And one lonely, unlucky woman would take the fall before suffering a painful, lonely death.

How could he lose?

BELLAMY HEARD THE bark first, immediately followed by the solid poke of a squishy nose on her hip. She turned to see Alex playfully teasing her, his master standing about six feet away, hands on hips.

Her heart gave an involuntarily hitch at the sight he

made. His thick, powerful shoulders were set off and backlit by the winter sun that rode low in the sky. The light breeze ruffled the edges of his hair, and his eyes were a warm, gooey chocolate-brownie brown as they stared down at her.

"We need to talk. Alex and I will check the grounds again and then we can discuss this morning."

Was that apology she saw reflected there? Remorse? Or neither, she quickly scolded herself as she dropped back on her rear and focused on Alex. Donovan was probably just here so he could scold her again.

"You checked the grounds this morning. Talk to me."

"It's important that I check things out."

"And it's important to me to talk to you."

To punctuate her point, she pulled off her gardening gloves and gave Alex a vigorous pat down, from the top of his head, down over his back and on toward the lower part of his spine as he wiggled in ecstasy. It didn't take much after that to push him to his side so she could give him the added joy of a belly rub.

"Careful. He might quit my team and join yours."

"Then I'd say he's one smart cookie." She patted Alex's chest before giving in and looking back up at Donovan. "I'm not sure I'd want to work for a suspicious brute, either."

"Suspicion comes with the territory. What did I do to get 'brute,' too?"

"You really don't know?"

"I'd rather hear it from your perspective."

Whatever she might suspect in his gaze, it was impossible to miss the sincerity, especially once she matched it to his voice. "You played the whole white knight routine this morning. Picking me up. Bringing me coffee. Even reassuring me it would be okay. And instead I walked into a firing squad."

"Chief Thompson wasn't quite that bad."

"He thinks I'm guilty. And so do you."

"Where'd you get that from?"

"The moment the two of you jumped all over those email printouts. I thought I had evidence of something horrible and all anyone who's looked at them has done is accuse me of doing something wrong. First Human Resources at LSP, right before they fired me. Then the two of you. I received that email and I have no idea who sent it or why."

Donovan dropped onto the grass beside her and reached for one of the garden gloves she'd dragged off to pet Alex. Toying with one finger, he twirled it in his hand and she tried her level best not to imagine him playing with her instead. Her hand inside that glove, her fingers trapped in his.

He would be warm, she imagined. His touch strong and capable. And how nice it would be to hang on in every one of those moments where she had no one to lean on except herself.

It'd be nice to hang on in all the other moments, too.

The thought was a surprise, the warmth that flooded her even more so.

Donovan Colton was the enemy.

Or at bare minimum a wary adversary, working at cross-purposes. There was no way she should even be entertaining thoughts of him in her life. Absolutely no reason at all to give them free rein.

"So talk to me, Bellamy."

"Why? So you can grill me again and make me feel like a common criminal?"

"No. Let's talk it through so we can try and find answers. Both the chief and I heard you today, though I'd like you to tell me again. But when I ask you questions, even the hard ones, don't assume it's because I don't believe you."

That sincerity was back, along with a subtle plea in his voice that tugged at her.

"Where do you want me to start?"

"At the beginning."

THE SUN BEAT down over his back as Donovan held his breath. He had driven over to Bellamy's like a madman, determined to get to her to make sure she was safe. Now that he was here, he'd done nothing but watch her, as smitten as Alex.

What was it about this woman?

She was beautiful, that was without question. Slim and lovely, she had a warmth about her that was hard to resist. It was funny, though, because he suspected if he asked her to describe herself she would outline a much harsher, tougher woman than the one who sat before him.

He imagined she saw herself as hard, maybe, because of the challenges she'd managed the past few years. But where she likely saw rough edges, he saw a diamond.

"What beginning?"

"Wherever you think this starts. You keep saying the email you received yesterday. Do you think that's the right spot?"

"Isn't it?"

"It depends."

"On what?"

Did he tell her what he thought? He was a man who

played his life close to the vest and police work had simply been a natural extension of that. He knew the roots of it all. More, he knew it was laughable how his worldview was steeped in every moment of his childhood. And from his continued embarrassment that he wasn't a true Colton.

He'd made the mistake of letting those feelings slip the year he turned fifteen, when he'd made an unsuccessful attempt to find his birth parents on the internet. Hays and Josephine and his siblings had spent the last sixteen years trying to change his mind.

Attempting to convince him he was as Colton as they come.

Oh, how he wished that were true. But he'd just gotten left in their barn one Christmas morning. Heck, he had better knowledge of Alex's lineage than his own.

"It depends on what, Donovan?"

Bellamy's intense focus and near breathless request caught him up short. This wasn't about him. Nor was it about whatever asinine issues he couldn't get over.

This was about her and her life and whatever lurked in the shadows, seemingly focused on her.

"Okay. Three things come to mind when I read that email. Either you inadvertently got information you shouldn't have or you've got information someone's using to embarrass LSP and were specifically targeted with it. Or you did it."

"I didn't!"

He raised his hands in a stop-don't-shoot gesture. "We're taking that one off the table, okay?"

"Okay." She nodded. "But even if we go with the first two, why do either? The company is a significant employer in this area. Their stock has risen year after year for over a decade. They've been on the leading edge in several health categories." Her gaze drifted to Alex as a small smile edged her lips. "We even have a robust veterinary medicine program in partnership with Texas A&M. I just don't see why the company would manipulate the drug supply or why someone with an intent to do ill would suggest they were. None of it rings true."

"Why not?"

Her eyes widened, the smile fading as her mouth dropped open. "Because it's illegal."

He fought his own smile at her innocence. Legality and illegality were lines far too many crossed easily and with impunity, nonplussed by the risk of consequences. For far too many, illegal activities were framed in one way only—don't get caught.

"Let's also table that it's illegal for now. Why don't either of those options ring true for you?"

She stilled, her eyes drifting over the flower beds as she thought over his question. Alex stared up at her, an enraptured expression on his face when her deep thoughts brought on additional belly rubs.

He seemed even more grateful when the belly rubs continued once she spoke again. "Sutton Taylor is our CEO. He's a good man and a great leader. He's not the sort to fix drug prices and throttle supply. It's just not possible."

Donovan wasn't quite ready to give any CEO such carte blanche for benevolence, but he wasn't ready to debunk her instincts there, either. "Okay. Anyone else?"

"I don't know. A disgruntled employee, maybe?"

"You have layoffs anytime in the recent past? It is the holidays. People out of work at Christmas have a lot of fair and well-aimed anger."

"The company hasn't had a single layoff since we brought a major Alzheimer's drug to market a decade ago."

"Okay. Who else? A landowner or a manufacturer? Maybe a government official? There are any number of worlds LSP plays in during the normal course of business. Lots of places an enemy could be lurking."

"Maybe. I guess." She shrugged at that. "I guess I could see it, but I simply don't have knowledge of all those areas. But—" She broke off, something alighting in her face. "Why would I get the email and be possibly framed if it were an area I had no knowledge of? I don't work in real estate or manufacturing. I don't even manage the finances for that area."

"What areas do you manage?"

"Drug trials, drug launches, go-to-market strategies and the relationships with our supply chain."

"There you go. So you are connected there."

"Connected to the degree that I know how it works. I know the players."

"So if someone were framing you, you'd be a person who others could believe might be involved."

"No!" Her hand stilled where it rested over Alex's fur. "Yes, maybe. I guess."

"That's where we need to focus."

"But who would do that to me?"

"We're going to find out."

A light breeze kicked up and with it, Alex shifted into motion. One moment he was flat on his back, tongue lolling in ecstasy, and the next he was on all fours, his nose buried in the ground as he took off through the grass.

"What's wrong?"

"I don't know." Donovan was up and after Alex, his partner's alert focus and intermittent barking all he needed to know.

Alex had found a scent.

Bellamy's property wasn't large and it didn't take Alex long to cover the ground, stopping before a small toolshed.

"What's wrong with him?" Bellamy nearly ran into his back before she stilled, her hand going to his shoulder to steady herself.

"He's fine. It's what he's found that's not. I need you to move back."

"You think he found something? In my shed?"

Since she hadn't moved, he did it himself, walking her back several steps to stand at the corner of the house.

"When was the last time you were in here?"

"An hour ago. I wanted to get my gardening equipment."

"And you didn't see anything odd or off?"

"No." She let out a long, low sigh. "I'm not sure I'd have seen much. I was angry and…well, I just slammed in and out of there without really looking at anything."

Donovan fought the shudder at what might have happened to her if she'd stepped the wrong place and instead focused on the matter at hand. "I need you to go to my car and get my equipment in the back. I need to make a call."

"For what?"

"Backup in Austin."

"Backup?" Her voice faded on that word, her eyes widening in dawning horror.

"If Alex's nose is right, and it always is, it looks like you've got a bomb in your shed. The last thing we need to do is set it off this close to the house."

Chapter Six

Bellamy fought the rising tide of panic that filled her stomach and crept up her throat.

A bomb?

In her shed?

She'd blithely walked past a few hours before.

A *bomb*.

One discovered by a sweet dog she'd been petting two minutes ago.

The anger and frustration she'd carried home from the police station vanished in full as she stared into the back of Donovan's SUV. Protective gear just as he described it filled the space, and she lifted out the thick jacket and headgear so he would be safe.

For her.

Shivers gripped her at the idea his life was in danger. She had a healthy enough self-image to know that she'd not asked for this or wished it on herself, but it didn't change the fact that Donovan was in danger on her behalf. Alex, too, for that matter.

"Bellamy! Did you find it?"

Her woolgathering at an end, she grabbed the gear and ran back to him. The materials were heavy and she was slightly winded by the time she got to him. "Here."

He took them easily, lifting them from her arms. "Go stand by the car, please."

"I can't leave you here."

"Go now. You can't be here. I'm protected and I know what I'm doing."

"I know, but—"

"I'll send Alex with you. He's good company and can stay with you until backup comes."

"Of course."

He ran a finger down her cheek in one long stroke. "I know what I'm doing. But it's easier to do it without worrying about you."

The movement was so unexpected and so very sweet she went with impulse. Without checking herself, she leaned in and pressed a quick, hard kiss to his lips. "Be careful."

The color of his already dark eyes deepened, drawing her in. "I will."

With quick instructions, Donovan ordered Alex to stay by her side. The black Lab trotted beside her, so close they nearly touched, all the way to the front yard. Sirens echoed in the distance and Bellamy braced herself for what came next.

More danger.

More suspicion.

And even more proof that someone was out to kill her.

DONOVAN HEARD THE sirens in the distance, mentally timing when his backup would arrive. He'd already calculated what might lay beyond the door and took some solace in the fact that she'd already entered and exited the shed once without detonating the device.

Dumb luck?

Or further proof they were dealing with an amateur?

The car bomb had been crude, the lapse in detonation time a pretty solid indicator they weren't dealing with an expert. But lack of skill didn't diminish the risk that the bastard would get lucky at some point.

There was the alternative—that someone was trying to scare Bellamy more than hurt her—but why? Even for experts, bombs were tricky things. If the goal was to frighten, there were a hell of a lot easier ways to accomplish that.

Which took him right back to an amateur, and the question that seemed to swirl at the center of all of this: What was going on at LSP?

The email had been quite clear. LSP was fixing prices and managing the supply of necessary flu vaccine. It seemed like an odd choice—surely there was more money to be made on other drugs. But flu was also ubiquitous. So many took the vaccine that keeping it out of circulation would incite panic.

And where there was panic and chaos, you had the right mix to put an object in demand.

Wasn't that the heart of all supply and demand? Make it seem irresistible and you made the product a must-have.

Only in this case, lives were at stake. The elderly and the infirm and small children all needed the vaccine to prevent an outbreak or to diminish the severity of one. How many people were ultimately protected by vaccines supplied by LSP?

Were there other pharmaceutical companies that could provide the needed supply if Lone Star couldn't?

Donovan didn't know enough about the specifics but made a mental note to ask Bellamy later. If the supply chain really was damaged in all this, there had to be reasons it wasn't simply a matter of changing course and getting more vaccine from someone else.

His questions faded in full as the Whisperwood PD pulled up to Bellamy's house, the fire department in tow. Although they depended on Donovan's team in Austin as well as the K-9 unit for the majority of their bomb works, the local team was trained in basic detonation work and could support him as he walked through the proper procedures.

"What do you have there, Colton?" Chief Thompson hollered the request as he strode across Bellamy's yard.

"A hot one, if Alex's nose is any indication."

"Isn't his nose always an indication?"

"That's why you're here, Chief, while that hot sub you bought for lunch is getting cold on your desk."

"It's a cold sandwich today. It'll keep."

It was dopey banter, but it kept the situation moving forward until Archer could reach him. The man was already in protective gear that matched Donovan's, sans the helmet.

"What do you have?" The question was quiet, not meant for any potential bystanders or the small crowd gathered around Bellamy.

"Not sure yet. I don't think it's tied to the door, as Ms. Reeves went in and out about an hour ago, but I figured I'd wait to test that theory."

The chief nodded before asking a few more questions, then ordered his team forward to help set the scene. The fire department had already run their lines so they could quickly put out any potential blazes and an ambulance was on standby a bit farther down the road.

"It looks like Ms. Reeves is in a heap of trouble." The chief eyed the door before his gaze slipped back toward Bellamy. "A rather big heap."

"Sure seems that way." Donovan agreed.

"It also seems like a lot of trouble for someone to set this little scenario up all on their own."

"I was thinking along the same lines. Especially since she's so pale, it's a wonder she's not reflecting light right now." Donovan avoided turning back to look at that confused face for fear he'd lose his concentration. But even without looking, he knew she was scared.

And alone.

That thought had kept him company since his race across town and his discovery of the lone woman tending her garden. She didn't appear to have a support system, as she'd not mentioned anyone since he discovered her yesterday, huddled in the LSP parking lot staring at her car.

Was it really possible she was that alone?

He'd given her space the night before, even as his instincts kept suggesting she was into something they didn't fully understand.

But was it possible she'd been targeted specifically because she didn't have a support system? Or someone nearby paying close enough attention?

He wasn't exactly the poster child for familial happiness, but he could always count on his parents and siblings if he needed something.

But would you go to them?

The mental intrusion had him fumbling his hold on his helmet and he fought to put it out of his mind as he righted his grip on the face cover.

This wasn't about him and he'd do well to keep his damn head in the damn game.

"So what do you say, Chief? Ready to open this one up?"

"I'd say. That sub's not going to eat itself."

Donovan hollered a few instructions to the assembled team, then reached for the shed door. Like a shiny present sitting under the Christmas tree, a small pressure cooker sat in the far corner of Bellamy's shed, easy to miss if you weren't paying attention.

Which she hadn't because she'd stomped in here, still mad at him and Archer.

A chill ran the length of his spine as he imagined what could have happened if the bomb was attached to the door, but forced it out of his mind. He could worry himself into a cold sweat later.

Right now he needed to get it handled.

The bomb was crude, reinforcing his impression that an amateur had made it. It had the same look and feel as the bombs that had littered news stories over the past decade, especially acts tied to homegrown terrorism. More than that, it was a device someone could easily discover how to build online and hastily put together, with the intention of doing localized harm.

Donovan moved closer, quickly cataloging the device before scanning the detonation mechanism. A small burner cell was wired to the device, its face dimly reflecting the fact that it was on and charged.

"You see the detonator?" Archer's voice was thick behind his mask but Donovan heard him and nodded.

"Yep. Burner cell."

"You know how to manage it?"

"Yep."

"Then let's get to work."

Bellamy stood at the end of her driveway, a crowd of EMS professionals surrounding her, and had never felt so alone or scared in all her life. Even with her parents—even at the very end—she hadn't felt this absolute sense of emptiness.

What had happened to her life?

Had she somehow brought this on herself? Pissed someone off at work so badly that they'd decided to make her pay?

Because whatever this was, it was highly personal. First her car and then her home. Which meant whoever was doing this knew what she drove and where she lived.

Unbidden, an image of Sally Borne's hard face popped into her mind. HR would have access to her personnel files, including her home address. They also knew her license plate because it was needed as part of the documentation to receive a badge to the LSP property.

Alex leaned against her leg, the heavy weight of his body a reassuring comfort as she stood there, puzzling through all the implications. She laid a hand on this head and stroked the soft fur that grew even softer where it ran down the backs of his ears. He seemed to understand what she needed, pressing his head into her hand when she stilled, insisting she keep up with the soothing, steady strokes.

The dog was a marvel. She'd always loved pets but had never found time to own one. In the years before her father's accident she'd been busy with work and never felt she could give an animal the proper attention. And after, once there were pills and wheelchairs and a constant focus on keeping him well, it didn't seem like the right time.

Perhaps that had been more shortsighted than she realized. Her father would have responded well to a pet, a gentle friend to keep him company each day. And for herself, it would be nice to have a companion to come home to now. A warm, furry body who was happy to see her.

Maybe if she had a dog they'd have warned her of whatever was lurking around the house and putting bombs in her shed.

Alex laid his head against her thigh and let out a soft sigh. He was a funny creature, she thought as she took comfort in his large body, with a fierce devotion and gentle personality. It was easy to see what he was thinking and she had no doubt he *was* thinking. It might be veiled through the lens of canine understanding, but there was something going on behind those dark brown eyes.

More, there was a fierce protection there that promised the dog knew his purpose in life and would carry it out without fail.

Purpose.

Understanding settled over her, a soothing balm in the midst of the chaos that surrounded her. She'd had purpose once. A focus on the life that stretched before her and the goals she'd set for herself.

Somewhere along the way, she'd lost that. Yes, her parents had needed care and attention. At times, that had taken precedence over other choices in her life.

But she'd been solely responsible for losing her sense of self. For allowing what was happening around her to take possession of her dreams instead of keeping them firmly in her sights.

Whatever her future held or however long she had, it was time to make a change.

Alex let out a large bark at her side, a funny punctuation mark to the definitiveness of her thoughts. But it was the quivering beneath her hand and the immediate thump of his tail that had her smiling just as Donovan came around the corner of the house.

He held a small silver bowl in his hands that took shape as he got closer. A pressure cooker? She had one herself, buried in the back of the cabinet on the rare occasions she decided to cook rice for a week of meals. What was one doing in her shed?

It was only as she saw the wires dangling from beneath his gloved hands that she understood. That was the bomb. Positioned in her shed and ready to cause irreparable damage.

Ready to kill her.

A wave of nausea flooded her stomach as she took in the innocuous kitchen appliance turned into a device that could end her life.

With a gentle push, she urged Alex forward. "Go see him." The dog seemed to waver only a moment before she patted his back and pressed him forward. "Go!"

He ran to Donovan, his focus on the device in his partner's hands. Donovan bent over, allowing the dog to sniff the contents, praising him for his understanding of the threat. His tail wagged at the praise, and again, Bellamy was amazed at all the animal communicated without words.

Where his tail had thumped with the excitement of seeing his master, now it wagged with the determined understanding of the job they did and the risk to the people around them.

The dog *knew*. He understood on a base level that was fascinating to watch.

But it was the body language of his master that had Bellamy taking a step back. Even encased in the heavy protection gear, she could see the purpose and determination as he walked across her yard. He innately understood the danger in the device in his hands—more, he knew the danger it posed to her—and with that knowledge he carried the responsibility for fixing it.

SALLY BORNE SCANNED the email on her phone before tossing the device onto her desk. "Merry freaking Christmas to me."

What had she gotten herself into? Worse, what sort of ridiculous sweet nothings had Jensen Taylor managed to put into her ear that had made her think any of this was a good idea?

She was smarter than this. Had *always* been smarter than this.

So why had she listened to the little slimeball?

Especially since it had become increasingly obvious his father was neither on the verge of turning over the company nor getting ready to enter into his dotage. Hell, she'd have been better off seducing Sutton Taylor. If she was fifteen years younger, she might have tried, but those rheumy old eyes could still pick out a stacked twenty-five-year old at fifty yards. She had a complaint file from several sales reps in her top drawer to prove it.

Unable to hold back the sneer, she thought of the last one who'd pranced in and complained about Sutton's less-than-subtle attentions.

Ridiculous.

When you had assets, you used them. Those same reps weren't above using a little T & A when they visited doctors, selling in LSP's latest offerings. You'd think they'd be more appreciative when the head of the company appreciated the same thing they were flaunting to fill their pockets.

Brushing it off, she picked up her phone and read the email from the police one more time. The friendships she'd cultivated at the Whisperwood PD had paid off and the update on Bellamy Reeves's visit to the station that morning was detailed and thorough. The little bitch had a copy of the email and had freely handed it off to the chief.

Sally reread the last line of the message, heartened that the ploy might end up working in their favor. The lack of sender and the strange nature of the missive had put some doubt in the chief's mind, suggesting that poor little Bellamy Reeves had gone around the bend and was setting this all up for her own benefit as a way to defraud and manipulate the company.

Curious, Sally sat down and pulled out the Reeves file. She flipped through the personnel records, the praise for Bellamy clear on every review and evaluation as well as the input sheets tied to her past promotions.

The woman had a stellar reputation. She was well liked, kept to herself and avoided causing any drama at work. A model employee.

Of course, there was the matter of her family. A loss like that was something that changed a person. It erupted in the middle of life, taking everything you once knew and turning it upside down.

There was power in that. A story she could weave, tightening the threads until they were impossible to unravel.

Shifting to her laptop, Sally began her reply to the Whisperwood PD. No reason not to seed a bit more doubt about poor, sad Bellamy Reeves, preparing to enter the holiday season all alone.

DONOVAN STRIPPED OFF the protective gear and laid it in the back of his SUV. He'd already turned the evidence over to Archer, tagging it with the necessary markers from his side and calling it in to his own chief to keep the man updated. He'd been given the order to stay in Whisperwood until this was handled, the focus on Lone Star Pharmaceutical ensuring his chief didn't want any blowback from the investigation.

If he hadn't been given the go-ahead to stay, he'd have asked anyway, the risks to Bellamy too concerning to leave her alone. But now that he was here, he needed to figure out how to get her to agree to his plan.

Not only was he not going to leave her alone, but he and Alex would stay to guard her. He'd nearly made up his mind on the drive over, but now it was a done deal, especially when it was more than obvious that whoever had targeted her wasn't above escalating their tactics to her home.

Once again, the crudeness of the bomb struck him as he nestled his gear into its proper place. A pressure cooker bomb? It was far from elegant and the fact that they'd been in the news as incendiary devices gave further credence to an amateur picking up on something and running with it. Easy to purchase and easy to build, it made the perfect device for limited range, deliberate hits.

He and his fellow K-9 team members had seen an increase in the devices and the lunatics who thought a homemade bomb made a nice, clean, easy way to deal with a problem. It was a coward's way to kill, far removed from the point of impact, the perpetrator safe at a distance.

And it was easy because no one had to stick around and face the damage.

Just like your mother, dropping you off in the Colton barn, abandoned on Christmas morning.

His hand shook as he laid his headgear on top of his flak suit, the connection between his own birth and a bomb was one that hit way too close to home. Yet even as he rejected the maudlin thoughts, something about them stuck.

It was easy to do the wrong thing when you didn't have to stick around and face the consequences.

"Donovan? Are you all right?"

He turned to see Bellamy, her hands still against her sides as she took him in. The moment struck him, her slender form clad in a simple T-shirt and yoga pants backlit by the afternoon sun. That same breeze that had tipped Alex off to the bomb in the shed whispered around them once more, a bit cooler as the afternoon edged toward evening, a bit wilder as it blew her hair against her face.

"I'm good."

"How do you do that? You walked in, not knowing what you were going to find."

"It's part of the job description."

"Yes, but it's—" She broke off, her beautiful mouth

dropping down into a frown. "But you didn't know what was behind the door."

"Believe it or not, you inadvertently helped there."

"How?"

"While it gives me the chills to say this, you'd already gone through the door. And even though that wasn't a foolproof method, it did indicate the bomb wasn't pressure sensitive to the opening of the door."

She seemed to shrink in on herself at that and he reached out to take a hand, squeezing the slim fingers. "Thanks for the assist. Try not to do that again, please."

"Okay."

Her hand was cold in his and it dragged at him, twisting him up even further about the fact that something could have happened to her. Without checking the impulse, he tugged on her hand, pulling her forward so she was flush against him. In one long move, he seated himself on the back bumper of the SUV, pulling her between his legs as he dragged her mouth down to his.

His seated position gave her the height advantage, but he had the benefit of surprise. When she'd kissed him in front of the shed earlier, she'd surprised him with the power of the simple gesture.

Something inside of him—something hungry and raw and the slightest bit scared—wanted to feel that again. Wanted to feel the heat and the life and the sheer beauty of her pressed against him.

It was with a hunger for all those things and something even more—something distinctly Bellamy—that had his tongue pressing into her mouth, satisfied as she granted him ready access. If this kiss had surprised her, she'd quickly caught up, her tongue meeting his stroke for luscious stroke.

And then she turned the tables on him, her hands wrapping around his shoulders and neck, her fingers lingering at the base of his neck. What had been cool to the touch heated quickly, those exploring fingers also pressing his head to hers, fusing their mouths as each plundered the other.

His hands moved over her hips, tracing the length of her tantalizing curves as the kiss continued to spin out, a sensual web of feeling. It was erotic, the meeting of tongues, the light winter breeze over their skin and the simple touch of their hands on each other.

Donovan knew he should pull away. Knew even better that this was not only ill-advised, but a massive conflict of interest.

Yet, even with the sense of duty that drummed beneath his skin, he couldn't walk away. Couldn't tear himself back or pull away from something so lovely and tantalizing and *real*.

It was the last that gripped him in tight fists.

She was real. Yes, she was beautiful and sensual and appealing as a woman, but she was so much more. He respected her bravery and her determination. Even more, he valued her belief in her truth and her refusal to back down or be cowed by what was happening around her.

"Donovan." Her whisper against his mouth broke the kiss and he tried to nip her bottom lip once more, unwilling to end the sweetly sensual moment.

"Donovan." She whispered it again, even as her lips curved into a smile.

"What?"

"The chief is still here."

He surfaced quickly at that news, combined with Archer's hard cough as Bellamy slipped out of his arms and moved to stand a few feet away from the SUV.

"Archer."

"Donovan."

Donovan knew the man's blue eyes were twinkling, even though he couldn't see them behind the dark lenses of his sunglasses.

"I think we're wrapped up here," Archer said.

"I thought we already were."

"I'm going to need another statement, but seeing as how I was here as it all unfolded, I think I can write up the majority of what we need for the report. Perhaps you could escort Ms. Reeves to the station tomorrow to provide any needed details."

"That will be fine," Bellamy quickly added from where she stood beside Alex.

Archer obviously sensed his presence was no longer welcome and he made a hasty retreat, a tip of his hat before he took off.

A light flush covered Bellamy's face before following a lovely path down her neck and over her collarbone. "He certainly got here quick."

"Shame he couldn't leave as quickly." Donovan's hands still itched and he heard the hoarse, husky notes in his voice. He'd forgotten where he was. Utterly and completely, as he'd fallen into that kiss.

And Chief Thompson had known it, his eyes twinkling as he'd said his goodbyes.

Twinkling, for Pete's sake.

Donovan glanced at Alex, unsurprised to see a large grin painting his furry face as he panted into the breeze beside Bellamy.

The entire situation would have been funny if he

hadn't diffused a bomb in Bellamy's shed. A point only reinforced by the high-pitched cry of a woman who peeled to a stop in front of the driveway, running toward Bellamy as the car still idled in her wake.

"Are you okay? I just heard the news." The woman was attractive, a tall, thin blonde dressed in needle-sharp heels, elegant black slacks and a silk blouse that likely would cost him a week's salary. It was all set off by flashy jewelry that seemed to drip from her, including a large diamond that lay against her collarbone.

Donovan gave the woman credit—she moved in the heels—and watched as she flung her arms around Bellamy's shoulders, pulling her close. He wouldn't have believed it if he wasn't standing there watching, but Bellamy stiffened up so much she could have been a poker standing beside the small fireplace in her living room.

But it was the ice that dripped from her tone that truly caught him off guard.

"Hi, Maggie. What are you doing here?"

The woman pulled back, her shoulders slumping at the greeting. "I'm your sister. Of course I came. What I don't understand is why you didn't call me right away."

"Because I'm fine."

Fine?

The diffused bomb even now being driven to the Whisperwood police station suggested otherwise, but it was the distinct sense of unease and anger telegraphing from Bellamy's rigid frame that truly pulled him up short.

What was going on here?

And what sort of issue could Bellamy Reeves possibly have with her sister?

Chapter Seven

"I'm fine, Maggie. Really. How many times do I have to say it?"

Bellamy heard the coarse, stilted words that spilled from her lips and wanted to pull them back. She wished that she could find a way to get past the anger and the confusion that marked her relationship with her sister.

It hadn't always been like this. No one had been happier to have a baby sister than her. She'd welcomed sweet little Maggie along with her parents and the two of them had been inseparable as kids, even with a five-year age difference.

Maggie had always seemed so fragile and waifish, and Bellamy had developed a mix of protectiveness and encouragement for her sister that she gave to no one else. That gentle, fragile nature had changed over the years and by the time Bellamy graduated from high school, Maggie was getting ready to enter, already the belle of Whisperwood. People spoke of her beauty and their parents doted on her, willing to give their precious baby anything she wanted.

The sweet little soul Bellamy had cared for and protected suddenly didn't need her any longer and it had hurt to realize, as she went off to college, that she wasn't the center of her sister's world anymore.

It had taken several years and making of new friends with fresh perspectives while she was away at school for Bellamy to realize her sister didn't need a second mother, but a friend. But by the time she'd returned to Whisperwood, Maggie's life had shifted in new directions, including spending time with the popular crowd, riding around town in her convertible and winning the heart of half the boys in school.

She'd been happy for Maggie, even if she was forced to accept that her own life had turned out very differently. The job at LSP had provided another fresh perspective and after immersing herself in work and a new group of friends and colleagues, the distance with Maggie didn't seem to matter so much.

Or maybe she'd just stopped caring any longer if it hurt.

She'd had a life and a job she loved and a future to look forward to. Life was good and if she didn't have a strong relationship with her sister, then it was something she'd live with.

"Bellamy, did you hear me? What is going on around here? First I hear about a bomb that blows up your car and now I hear there's one in the shed, too?" Maggie settled three glasses of iced tea on the small drop leaf table Bellamy kept in the corner of her kitchen, handing one over. "And hurry up and tell me before the always attractive Donovan Colton comes back inside. Goodness, I remember him from high school. He was a year ahead of me but what a looker."

Something in the casual assessment of Donovan spiked her ire once more and Bellamy fought to hold her tongue. Whatever her relationship with Maggie, spitting at her like a she-cat—a *jealous* she-cat—wasn't the way to handle things.

"He's part of the K-9 team out of Austin. He's been assigned to my case."

"He's done well for himself. I'd heard he was getting into K-9 a few years after joining the Austin PD."

"How'd you hear that?"

Maggie shrugged, her perfect blond hair rising and falling with the motion. "The Coltons are always the subject of local gossip. People talk, Bell, you know that."

"Is that all people in this town are to you? Gossip? Is that why you rushed over here? So you'd be in the know."

Maggie's glass stopped halfway to her lips, her mouth drawing down in a frown. Carefully, she set the glass back on the table before shifting her cool blue gaze fully to Bellamy's. "I realize you and I have had our differences, but I don't understand how you could think I don't care about you."

"You've never seemed all that interested in taking part in my life."

"You shut me out! Just because I saw how we should be caring for Mom and Dad differently than you did, doesn't mean I'm some horrible person."

"You wanted to put them in a home."

"No, I wanted them to get the proper care they deserved while taking the burden off of you."

"They're my parents. I did it willingly."

"And are now playing the martyr because you did."

That unpleasant rebuttal settled in the middle of the table between them, an oozing pile of resentment and anger that only seemed to grow bigger and more acidic.

How was it that things had gone so badly between them? They'd barely spent ten minutes with each other and were already fighting. Yet even as it bothered her, she couldn't fully kill the resentment and the anger.

"Why are you really here? I can't imagine James would be happy with you putting yourself in danger by being so close to a crime scene."

"James doesn't much care what I do." Maggie ran a hand over the cold condensation on her glass, her cornflower blue gaze averted. "Our divorce will be final in early January. Just after New Year's Day, as a matter of fact."

"Your what?"

The resentment and anger grew smaller and faded in the face of Maggie's news, before vanishing away as Bellamy moved around the table to take Maggie's hand. "When did this happen?"

"Earlier this year."

"But why? How? I thought you were so happy being married."

"We were married. Happiness wasn't a big part of it. A situation that got worse when he informed me he wasn't interested in having children."

"Oh."

She'd not been a part of her sister's life for some time, but the finality of that statement left its sting, chunking away a bit more of her years-old anger. "I'm sorry, Maggie. Really sorry."

"It's fine. We've said a lot of horrible things to each other and now we've just become numb. The New Year can't get here fast enough."

Bellamy wanted to say more—felt she *should* say more—but had no right. Whatever frustrations she might have over Maggie's behavior the past several years, she wouldn't have wished the dissolution of her marriage on her.

Neither would she ever have suspected there was anything wrong in the first place. James Corgan came from one of the wealthiest families in the state and had always seemed smitten with Maggie. Their marriage had happened quickly, but Bellamy had always assumed it was a love match.

Was she wrong about that? Or had things simply gone wrong, the same way her relationship with Maggie had changed into something neither of them recognized any longer?

"I guess we've both been keeping secrets."

"I'm not keeping secrets."

"Oh no?" Maggie raised a lone, perfect eyebrow. "Then what's going on that has you the target of bombings?"

"I have no idea."

"Come on, Bell. This is real life, not TV. People don't just walk out to their car after work and nearly get blown up."

"I'm well aware of that. It still doesn't mean I have a clue to what's going on."

The lie tripped right on out, practically skipping around the room. For the first time in a long time, she wanted to open up to Maggie—wanted to tell her about the email she'd received—but she had no idea how. If she said something, would she put Maggie in danger, too?

And if she told her, she would also have to admit that she was out of work. She still hadn't figured out how she was going to handle the taxes on the house her parents had left her or what she was going to do about getting a new car. She had a little bit saved, but nothing that was going to see her without a job indefinitely.

Especially if Sally Borne made good on her threat to blackball her from getting another.

"This is ridiculous." Maggie drummed one painted fingernail on the table. "Surely you have to know something. Or we can ask around and find someone who might know what this is about."

"I'm not making my personal life gossip fodder for the town."

"But if someone can help you…"

"No. I will handle this and deal with it myself."

"Just like you always do."

Whatever subtle truce they'd arrived at vanished completely as Bellamy got to her full height. "Yes, Maggie. Just like I always do. I can handle myself and whatever comes my way. I've been doing it for years."

The door to the kitchen opened at that moment, Donovan and Alex barreling into the room in a rush of feet and paws. The echo of Bellamy's retort still hovered but even if Donovan had missed the words, there was no way he missed her standing up, hands fisted at her sides.

"Everything okay?"

"Fine. Absolutely fine." Bellamy stepped away from her seat, extending a hand to Donovan and gesturing him to sit in her place. "Let me just get some fresh water for Alex."

The ploy was either enough to divert attention or Donovan was simply too polite to say otherwise, but he took the offered seat as Maggie thrust his glass of iced tea on him while Bellamy busied herself with some water for Alex.

The awkwardness of the moment was quickly covered up with Maggie's questions, her voice a sensual purr now that she was in the presence of an attractive man. As she listened, settling a large bowl of water on the floor, Bellamy felt herself closing up even further.

It didn't matter how badly she wished things were different with her sister; it wasn't possible.

And just like the loss of her parents, she was simply going to have to find a way to accept it.

DONOVAN PLACED HIS empty glass of iced tea back on the kitchen table and counted off the number of minutes until he could make a polite excuse and leave the room once more. If he'd known what he was walking into, he'd have found a way to stay outside with Alex a bit longer.

But they'd already done two perimeter sweeps of Bellamy's small property line and found nothing. Nor had they found anything else inside the shed, even after Donovan ran Alex through the drill a second and third time. He'd finally given in and gotten a fresh treat out of the car, sorry that he'd put Alex through such rigor over an obviously clean site.

Which was one more proof point that he was too far around the bend over Bellamy Reeves. He trusted Alex implicitly. The dog was well trained and had never let him down. That wasn't about to change.

What he now needed to figure out was how he was

going to get Bellamy to let him stay. There was no way he was heading back to Austin and leaving her alone. He briefly toyed with the idea of leaving her at his parents' home. He would consider it if things went truly sideways, but wasn't quite ready to give in and bring his family into this mess.

Which left him and Alex as her newest houseguests.

He'd met the woman who'd arrived earlier, remembering her after the basic introductions. Maggie Reeves had been a year behind him in high school but he still recalled her reputation as one of the most popular kids. Funny how it hadn't mattered to him then and mattered even less now.

Yet somehow, in looking at Bellamy's sister, he sensed it was deeply important to how she saw herself.

"It's been a long time since I've seen you," Maggie said, her smile broad.

"High school, probably." Donovan nodded after taking a sip of his iced tea. "I haven't spent much time in Whisperwood since then."

"What brings you here now?"

"I'm part of the APD's K-9 unit. We support the surrounding communities in addition to Austin and I'm here to help the chief."

"On Bellamy's case?"

"Among others."

Donovan heard the genuine interest in Maggie's voice, but couldn't shake the underlying tension that hovered in the kitchen. He was the last person to criticize family dynamics, but there was a stiffness to Maggie and Bellamy's relationship that struck him as sad.

Not your business, Colton.

And it wasn't. But knowing what Bellamy had been

through in the past few days, he couldn't understand why she wouldn't lean on her sister.

"What you do must be fascinating. Law enforcement. And working with your sweet dog, too."

Maggie kept her distance from Alex, but Donovan had seen how her gaze kept darting to the large form currently slurping water in the corner of the small kitchen. Even that was curious. Bellamy had warmed to Alex immediately, but Maggie kept looking at him as if he were going to attack her at any moment.

"Alex is my full partner. We work together to find and diffuse bombs as well as missing persons and drugs."

"Wow." Her gaze shifted to the dog once again, but her tension seemed to ebb ever so slightly. "He can do all that?"

"He's pretty amazing. His nose can find far more than we can ever understand. And his training ensures he knows how to tell me what he's found."

Jiggling the ice cubes in his glass, Donovan glanced over at his partner, now seated on his haunches with his tongue lolling. "We're going to leave you two alone. Alex and I have a few more things we need to do outside."

Before anyone could protest, Donovan made his escape, a quick nod all the dog needed to follow along. They weren't outside more than ten minutes when Maggie found her way to the back of his SUV. Donovan finished reordering his gear and turned at her quiet greeting.

"Hello, Ms. Reeves."

"It's Corgan. Maggie Corgan. For at least a little while longer." She muttered that last piece, even as a bright smile remained firmly on her face.

"Of course. What can I do for you?"

"Bell and I have a tough relationship. We haven't agreed on a lot of things for a long time and it's chipped away at what we used to have."

While he couldn't deny his loyalty to Bellamy, something in Maggie's words tugged at him. He knew what it was to have a distance between him and his loved ones. More, he knew what it was to want to close that distance but have no idea where to start.

"I love my sister," Maggie continued. "I care for her very much and I hate to think that she's in danger. Please take care of her. And please keep me posted if there's anything I can do."

"This is an active investigation but I'll do my best."

"Thanks. I guess that's all I can ask."

He watched her walk away, her physical look at odds with what he sensed lay beneath the surface. Maggie Corgan was a beautiful woman. Her hair was perfect, as were her body, her clothes, her car and her jewelry.

Yet beneath it all he sensed a woman who had very little.

As Maggie started her car and drove off, Donovan wondered if Bellamy understood that at all.

BELLAMY PUTTERED AROUND the kitchen, at odds with herself. Donovan and Alex were still outside—his SUV was visible in the driveway—but she didn't want to go out to see what they were doing. Maggie's visit had hit hard and she was still raw over the way they'd left things.

Her sister's news was unsettling, as well. It was the holidays and here Maggie was anticipating a divorce in the next few weeks. A small voice whispered that she should have invited her to spend the holidays together but she'd ignored it. And allowed the years-old anger and pain to prevent her from saying anything.

Wherever she'd once expected to be in life, thirty-five and alone, with no relationship with her sister, was so not it.

Which meant she needed to do something.

She retrieved the empty glasses from the kitchen table and washed them all in the sink, and was drying the last one when Donovan and Alex returned to the kitchen.

"We've swept your yard and shed three times and haven't found anything. You're clean."

Clean? Just like the glasses, only instead of washing out a bit of iced tea, he was hunting for bombs. Items designed to maim and kill. On a hard swallow, Bellamy nodded. "Thank you."

"I'd like to discuss what's going to happen next."

"Of course."

"You can't stay here. Not by yourself."

"Where do you think I'm going to go?"

"Your sister's would be a place to start."

Whatever ideas she had about making things better with Maggie, dragging her into this mess wasn't one of them. Bellamy pushed back from the counter and crossed the kitchen to face Donovan. "Absolutely not."

"She cares for you. And she's worried."

The thick lines of his body projected capable strength and something inside of Bellamy melted. How easy would it be to just move in, wrap her arms around him and sink in? The imprint of his lips lingered on hers, the heady sensation of their kiss still in the forefront of her mind.

But much as she wanted to talk to him and tell him how she felt about her relationship with Maggie and all that she desperately wished she could make right, it wasn't his problem.

None of this was his problem.

And a few kisses couldn't change that.

"I'm not bringing her into this." Bellamy said.

"But we can put protection on you both. Can make sure no one harms either of you."

"I'm staying in my house. That's non-negotiable."

"You can't stay here alone. That's why Alex and I are moving in until this is handled."

"You can't move in." The words came out on a squeak, even as a sly sense of delight curled beneath her skin.

"Since you seem to feel similar about going to your sister's, it's the only way."

Bellamy ignored how neatly Donovan made his argument and searched for some way to push back. "But this is my house. And you're assigned to my case. You can't live here."

"This is Whisperwood. The town is small and I'm from here. The department is well staffed but they don't need to put someone out here full-time. And I can work from here as well as Austin. On the few times I need to head into the city you can come with me."

"You can't upend my life this way."

Donovan glanced down at Alex, his smile broad as he placed a hand on the dog's head. "We just did."

THE UPENDING OF her life began immediately, and with surprising regularity. True to his promise, Donovan and Alex kept close watch on her and their days together had taken on an odd sort of routine.

Four days into life with her new roommates, Bellamy found herself once again heading down I-35 with Donovan and Alex, straight into Austin. The afternoon traffic was thick, with cars bumper-to-bumper as they approached downtown.

"This is ridiculous."

"No more ridiculous than a woman who's fighting off bomb threats to her life."

"I meant the traffic," Bellamy said. "I sort of thought the rest of it all had moved into the realm of the absurd."

His grin was broad as he glanced over at her. "Consider it an absurdity I'm determined to end."

She was grateful for that, the quick confidence that he could fix things going a long way toward soothing the nerves that refused to abate. She'd forget about the situation at LSP and her car and her shed for a few moments, and then it would all come streaming back, like a film on constant replay.

She wanted to believe it was over—a temporary madness that had descended in her life and vanished just as quickly—but the presence of man and dog suggested otherwise.

As did the unshakable feeling that things weren't over, no matter how badly she wanted them to be.

"You really believe you can stop whatever's going on?"

"Of course. That's my job. That, and keeping you safe in the process."

"Isn't that the chief's job?"

"We work together. Archer Thompson's a good man. If it's on his caseload, he's committed to handling things."

"For the biggest employer in Whisperwood. Isn't that a conflict?"

The easy smile vanished. "You always go around accusing the police of being in people's pockets?"

"I'm not—" She broke off, aware that was exactly what she was doing. "No, I'm not trying to suggest that. But I do know that much of his funding comes from the fact that LSP is such a huge business in Whisperwood. The tax contribution alone is significant. It can't be easy for the chief to have to investigate them."

"There's nothing easy about his job. Doesn't mean he can't handle it."

The quiet stretched out between them once more and Bellamy was forced to look at her behavior through Donovan's eyes. What must he see when he looked at her? A lonely woman, living in a small house all by herself. No obvious ties to anyone to speak of, made more evident by what he'd observed between her and Maggie. And now she was going around accusing the Whisperwood police of corruption.

The thought had whispered through her mind more than once over the past few days, but now that it had taken root, something had the words spilling from her lips.

"I wasn't always like this."

"Like what?"

"Suspicious and unkind."

"Is that how you see yourself?" Donovan kept his eyes firmly on the traffic but it took no less power out of his question.

"Some days. Others I feel like I'm drifting through life on autopilot, not sure how I got there."

"You suffered a big loss. You're entitled to grieve."

"Am I? Or has it become a convenient excuse to stop living?"

SOMETHING IN BELLAMY'S words tugged at Donovan. He wouldn't have called her unkind—hadn't even considered her through that lens—but he did see the suspicion and the anger.

And the fear.

How did a person deal with that, day in and day out? Yes, the bomb threats were new, but dealing with ill and infirm parents, then losing them, had been a part of her life for far longer. That sort of pressure would change anyone.

"I'm the last person qualified to answer that question."

"Why?"

"I've lived on autopilot myself for an awfully long time. Gets to a point where you stop noticing it anymore."

He hadn't expected to say that much and the words left a bitter aftertaste on his lips.

Bellamy didn't immediately respond. It was only when he felt the light touch on his hand, where it lay over the center armrest, that she spoke. "What are you running from?"

"The same thing I've been running from my entire life. I'm not a Colton and my family refuses to see that."

"What do you mean, you're not a Colton?"

"I'm not. I was left in the Colton stables Christmas morning thirty-one years ago. Hays and Josephine took me in but I'm not their son."

"Of course you are. They're your family. Adoption or biology doesn't change that."

Her ready defense was sweet but Donovan had lived a lifetime feeling like an imposter. A poser. The truth haunted him and only grew worse this time of year.

"It changes everything. I'm not one of them, no matter how much they want to believe otherwise."

"Biology doesn't dictate your relationships. Look at Maggie and me. We're sisters and we can't seem to find common ground. What matters is the relationships you have. The love you have for each other. The family you make."

"You don't love your sister?"

"Of course I love her."

The emphatic response gave him heart that there was a path for Bellamy to move forward with her sister, but the dichotomy of their familial situations wasn't lost on him.

"So you have a family you can't seem to reconcile with, and I have a family who wants me in it and I keep walking away. Is that it?"

"When you put it like that, I suppose so," she agreed.

"Family's hard. It's messy and emotional. That's why I love animals so much. They take you just the way you are."

"From what you've said, the Coltons took you just the way you were. You're the one who doesn't want to accept that."

Bellamy's words lingered long after they cleared Austin traffic and entered downtown. Donovan didn't want to believe them—didn't want to accept that he was the one who'd rejected his family's love—but the lingering guilt that had accompanied him since he was young glommed on to her statement.

And way down deep inside, he knew she was right.

Chapter Eight

The K-9 training center was quiet for midafternoon, but Donovan hardly noticed it as he unclipped Alex's leash and let him bound off into the large grassy area they used for training. He'd always encouraged Alex's socialization time with the other dogs and smiled as his partner headed toward two other members of K-9 teams. Loud barks and leaps onto each other's backs indicated both greetings and the time to play, and Donovan couldn't help but smile at the happy tail wags of his partner.

It was a huge contrast to his own confusion.

Confusion that sat squarely in the knowing eyes of Bellamy Reeves.

She'd already headed for one of the trainers and a group of puppies scampering around the yard. Her diverted attention gave him the reprieve he needed to analyze his thoughts.

What had happened on the drive down?

He and Alex had been with her for four days. Four agonizing days in which he'd diligently ignored the interest that simmered between them in favor of focusing on the task at hand.

Keeping her safe.

Clearly the sexual tension must have gotten to him because here he was, less than a week in her company, and he was like a singing canary.

He never spoke of his family or his feelings of inadequacy as an adopted member of the Colton clan. Yet there he went, spilling his guts to Bellamy like he'd known her for years.

The Coltons took you just the way you were. You're the one who doesn't want to accept that.

Her words continued to roll through and roil up his thoughts. Was it merely a matter of acceptance? Or was that too convenient an explanation?

No matter how much love his parents had lavished on him, they couldn't change the fact that his biological parents had left him. The people who were supposed to love him most had abandoned him in some rich family's barn, hoping and depending on the kindness of strangers. Wealthy ones, who could easily take on another mouth and who would be unlikely to abandon him a second time.

That wasn't a slight on Hays and Josephine, but a fact of his existence.

So why did it so often feel like punishment to the people who'd promised to love him the most?

Here he was, encouraging Bellamy to take the comfort and help of her sister, yet he'd been unable to do the same. Biological or not, his parents had shown their love in myriad ways since his infancy. The day they'd taken him in and given him a home was only the first.

So how did he begin to change? The helplessness he sensed in Bellamy—that question of where to start with her sister—was the same for him. He'd been distant for so long he had no idea where to close the gaps.

No idea of even where to try.

With one last look at Alex, Donovan headed back into the main building. His desk at the K-9 center had all the same equipment and latest software as police headquarters and he was determined to do some digging on Lone Star Pharmaceutical. The company had an outstanding reputation, but the contents of Bellamy's email continued to nag at him. It was a clue that couldn't be dismissed or ignored.

If the corporation was involved in some bad dealing, he owed it to the investigation to tug that line and tug it hard. Deliberately mismanaging the vital supply of vaccines was a crime and a health hazard and no one, no matter how powerful, should be allowed to get away with that.

Since Bellamy was still in the courtyard, safe with the trainers, he wanted to take a few minutes to tug those lines.

In moments he had several articles pulled up on Lone Star Pharmaceutical and its founder, Sutton Taylor. The man was well-known in and around Whisperwood, and Donovan was humbled to realize he only recognized the man peripherally. That knowledge only reinforced his earlier thoughts of his family, another proof point that he was out of the loop with his hometown news, gossip and local politics.

Donovan scanned article after article, getting a sense of the man, before shifting to some of the more telling websites. Anonymous reviews on those job sites where people said what they really thought of their employer, Austin area gossip sites and even a few posts on *Everything's Blogger in Texas*, a blog that had shown zealous attention to his extended family in the past.

The additional sites provided layers and context to his profile of Sutton Taylor, including a subtle thread of the man as something of a lothario.

He supposed it went with the territory—a powerful man with a powerful job—but it smacked of cliché at the same time. He wasn't a man who'd ever understood the appeal of cheating. You either wanted to be with the person you were with or not. It seemed awfully low to string them along when it was easier just to get out of the relationship and start a fresh one.

Was it pragmatic?

Or maybe it was a sign he thought relationships were too disposable?

Either way, Donovan knew it was how he was wired. He'd had several relationships over the years that had simply run their course. Nowhere during that time did he feel he needed to look elsewhere, but when it was time to leave it was time to leave.

Unbidden, an image of Bellamy the first time he met her filled his mind's eye. Bright-eyed and welcoming, she'd helped him with Alex and had been content to stand there in the general store parking lot as his small puppy had gotten sick. The moments that had followed had been even more special, talking and laughing and getting to know each other. He'd never forgotten that evening, nor the number of times he'd thought of her since.

Maybe it was those moments together that helped him see the person beneath the current pain. Or maybe it was just an attraction that hadn't been dulled by the ensuing years. Either way, he was attracted to her. It was inconvenient and not ideal, seeing as how he was working her case, but he *was* interested.

And he'd like to see where things might go between them.

A flash of awareness skittered through his mind as the night he met Bellamy came fully into focus. He'd been called away at the end to go to a nearby accident scene. Shifting gears on the computer, he minimized the articles on Sutton Taylor and pulled up his case files, logging backward until he found that night five years ago. In moments he had it up, the particulars of the accident coming back to him as he recalled the scene.

A drunk driver racing and swerving home from a holiday party. An older couple returning from an evening out. A small patch of road just off the main highway that lead into Whisperwood.

His gaze scanned the screen but Donovan already knew what he'd find.

Airlifted to Austin Memorial due to severe injuries: Daniel-Justice Reeves. Moved by ambulance to Austin Memorial for minor cuts and scrapes and further evaluation: Virginia Reeves.

He'd left Bellamy that night to go to the scene of her parents' accident. That was why he'd never seen her again.

It was the night her life shattered.

BELLAMY HELD THE now-sleeping puppy in her arms, loathe to let the little guy go. He was a smaller version of Alex, the K-9 facility trainer confirming for her that they had a lot of success with Labradors in the program. They'd rescued this one from a small flop in Austin and decided to raise him as their own. The trainer had already assured her they'd find a home for him if he ended up not being focused enough for the K-9 program and, on impulse, Bellamy had given the woman her phone number.

Her thoughts earlier in the week about having a dog had clearly taken root. She smiled ruefully as she headed into the building to find Donovan, but took joy in the idea that the pup had a future, no matter what happened to his time in K-9 training. They'd already named him Charlie and she thought it fit him to a T. That warm little body cuddled closer into her chest as she rounded the corner toward a large open-office area, and she bent down to smell his sweet little puppy head.

Oh yes, this was the right idea. And if Charlie ended up being a fit for K-9, Bellamy had been promised visiting privileges and the name of a rescue organization in Austin that would love to have another ready adopter on their list.

She entered the staff room and saw Donovan hunched over a desk. Winter sunlight streamed into the room, backlighting his broad frame as he focused on his screen. It made for an odd tableau and something in the set of his shoulders pulled her up short.

"Donovan? Is everything okay?" The puppy stirred lightly at her voice but quickly snuggled back into her arms.

He turned from the screen, his dark eyes shuttered. His expression was enough to have her moving forward. Something *was* wrong.

"What is it?"

"I'm sorry."

"For what? Did something happen?"

The puppy did stir then, either sensing her confusion or from a subtle tightening in her arms. He wriggled as his head lifted and she pulled him close, attempting to soothe him.

Since Donovan's attention had been on his computer, she veered there, surprised when he backed up to give her access to the screen.

"Bellamy, I'm sorry."

She scanned the screen and recognized the words, but didn't understand why Donovan had the record of her parents' accident pulled up. "Why do you have this?"

"It's my case file. That night. The night I met you when Alex got sick. We were talking and then I had to leave abruptly to go to an accident scene."

His words rattled around her brain like a loose pinball racking up points against the bumpers. "You? You were there?"

"I never realized it was your parents."

Her gaze roamed over the words once more, disbelief battling with the facts on the screen.

Drunk driver. Daniel-Justice Reeves. Virginia Reeves. Austin Memorial.

And the date all their lives changed.

Had he never put it together? Donovan had been called out to an accident, which was why he'd needed to rush off. There hadn't been one as massive as her parents' in years.

For the past week she'd simply assumed he knew and didn't want to hurt her by bringing it up.

But he'd had no idea.

She dropped into a nearby seat, the puppy now fully awake and squirming in her arms. He licked her face in obvious concern and she hugged him close, taking the comfort he offered.

"Are you okay?"

"I thought you knew. I took comfort that you were there."

"You did?"

"Of course. You saw them that night."

"Yes."

She'd always had a picture in her mind of what the accident must have been like, but didn't know the reality. She couldn't know what it smelled like or what it sounded like to hit another car with such force. She couldn't even begin to imagine.

For all his injuries, her father had seemingly moved past that point—past those horrid memories—but her mother never did. She'd struggled to sleep ever since the accident, to the point that Bellamy had considered a week with only one nightmare a good week.

And Donovan had been there.

"Did you help them?"

"We did all we could to keep your parents comfortable and steady until ambulance arrived."

"You were there for them."

Donovan only nodded, his lack of words somehow fitting.

What was he supposed to say?

It had been the same with everyone else in her life. People cared—they wanted to help and they definitely wanted to express sympathy—but in the end, there wasn't anything for them to do. Grief left a person helpless, but she'd learned it was no easier to comfort a grieving person. That had been the oddest part of her journey with her parents and had left the largest craters in her heart.

It had also served as the fuel to push others away.

She'd lost contact with her friends. She kept her colleagues at a distance, always claiming an excuse when she couldn't attend a happy hour or an event outside of work. Even her relationship with Maggie had suffered.

Years lost, along with some of the most important relationships in her life.

She hugged Charlie close, her attention shifting to Donovan. She'd been attracted to him five years before and a few days in his presence hadn't changed that. If anything, the concentrated time they'd spent together over the past week had only reinforced that initial attraction.

Was it coincidence that he'd come back into her life at a point where she needed a friend?

More to the point, did she want a friend, or did she want something more?

"Are you okay?" Donovan reached across and ran a finger over the top of Charlie's head. The little guy preened under the additional attention before lifting a paw to swat at Donovan's hand.

"I am. I've had a long time to get used to what happened. On some level, it's comforting to know you were there with them when they needed you. I've seen how capable you are. And I know how good it felt to have you there at LSP when we were dealing with my car." She reached out and laid a hand over his. "I'm glad you were there. Thank you."

"You're welcome."

Their gazes met and locked and Bellamy wondered,

with all that had happened in her life, how the world just fell away. The rest of it—her job, her car, even the threat at the house—it all seemed so far away.

In its place was something real and *present*.

She'd put off having a life for so long, it was startling to realize just how good it felt to be the object of someone's attention. To be the object of Donovan's attention.

"So you're okay?"

"I'm okay," she murmured, already anticipating the feel of his lips pressed to hers as he leaned in closer.

"Who's your friend?" His eyes dipped between them, the perusal intimate.

"You mean Charlie?" Her gaze dropped to the puppy, his excitement at having two humans so close causing him to wriggle even more.

Donovan kept a soothing hand on the dog's head, the steady attention holding him still, the back of his hand tantalizingly close to her breasts. "That's a good name. A good partner's name."

"He's the newest recruit for the K-9 program."

"Can you can give him his first lesson?"

"His lesson?"

Donovan moved even closer, his lips drawing nearer. "You think you can hold him still while I kiss you?"

A shot of heat traveled the length of her spine before spreading through her entire body. "I'll do my best."

The last coherent thought she had was that Donovan Colton was doing *his* best.

The press of lips against hers was both firm and yielding, the perfect mix of give-and-take. He kept a calming hand on the puppy, his other hand settling against her hip. His fingers teased the top of her slacks where her waistband met flesh, a tantalizing brush against her skin.

But his mouth. Oh, the wondrous responses he could create with the greatest of ease.

Bellamy fed on his attentions, the sweet push-pull of desire fueled by their sensual play of tongues and the light moans each drew from the other. His fingers continued to trace light patterns against her skin, featherlight yet deeply powerful as her body heated at the simple touch.

She briefly questioned if her response was tied to how long it had been since her last relationship, but even she wasn't silly enough to think any man could compare to Donovan. Strong. Sure. Safe.

Capable.

Those attributes and so many more.

Charlie had stayed still, somehow sensing the humans needed a moment, but the waiting finally got to him. The combination of active puppy and a body that was going limp from Donovan's sexy ministrations got the better of her and Bellamy stepped back from the kiss before she lost her hold on Charlie.

"Whoa there. Hang on." Donovan took him easily, transferring the bundle of energy into his arms and holding the dog as if he weighed nothing. He lifted him up and stared him in the eye but kept his voice gentle. "Way to ruin the mood, little man."

Charlie only wagged his tail even harder, his tongue lapping into the air as his little body wiggled from his excitement.

"He looks very remorseful." Bellamy giggled, the small, wiggly body too cute to resist.

"I think we may also be getting the universal signal to go outside. I'll be right back. There's something I want to show you anyway."

Bellamy watched Donovan go, struck once again by his gentle nature with animals. Even at the risk of wearing puppy pee or something even less desirable, he had a soothing way about him and kept Charlie close.

She stood there for a few moments, absorbing what had just happened. The intensity of the kiss. And the pure joy of being in Donovan's arms. Even the solicitous way he'd worried over her parents.

The computer screen still had all the information on her parents' accident and Bellamy scanned it again, doing her level best to read it with detachment. She knew the case well, but read through Donovan's impressions of the night and what he'd contributed to the report. His description of the scene matched the final crime report. So did the on-scene reconstruction.

"You sure you're okay with that?"

"I'm good." Bellamy glanced back over her shoulder, pleased to see Donovan was still dry. "No accidents before you got him outside?"

"It was close but Charlie showed admirable control. He also ran off to play with the big guys after doing his business so I'll leave it to Alex to keep an eye on him for a while."

"Alex is good with other dogs."

"He is. The socializing is good for him and so's the time outside. We're lucky to have pretty decent winter months here in Austin but I never take them fully for granted. Every opportunity to get him out here is time well spent for him."

The time at the K-9 facility obviously did Donovan good, too. He was more relaxed here. More at ease. Was that because this was his professional home or was it because he wasn't comfortable in Whisperwood? His earlier comments about his family still lingered, but Bellamy chickened out before she could ask him about them.

There was a sweet vibe between them for the moment, a by-product of the kiss and the puppy, and she was loath to mar that in any way.

"Was there something you wanted to show me?"

"What do you know about Sutton Taylor?"

"The CEO of LSP?"

Donovan dragged over a chair from a nearby desk and pulled it up next to her and took a seat. "The same."

"I know him peripherally. Once a year all the departments present to him. Given how long I've been at LSP, he knows my name. I've had a few encounters with him at annual meetings and at the company picnic and I had to take him through a financial file once all on my own."

"What were your impressions of him?"

"He's incredibly well respected. He built LSP from the ground up, using some seed money he'd made early on in pharmaceutical sales. He's grown the business from there."

"That's good." Donovan nodded. "But what are your impressions of him, who he is as a person?"

"Oh. Well, I'm not sure I ever thought about it." She stopped as one of those rare meetings came back to her. "That's not entirely true. I remember this one time. We were waiting for a meeting to start and several of us were in line to get coffee and breakfast."

Donovan's attention never wavered at what she felt was a silly story. "Go on."

"So we're in line and because I had fiddled with a few pages of my presentation I was at the back of it. And

I could see how Sutton admired one of my colleagues. I know men look at women. Heck, women look at men. It's natural. But most people aren't so—" She did break off then. "Most people aren't so obvious about it. And all I could think was that this was the founder of the company and he was ogling this woman like he was a fifteen-year-old boy."

"Do you think others noticed?"

"If they did, no one said anything. But there was just this quality about it all that I found disappointing. Like he should be above that somehow."

"Do you think he's behind the supply management and price-fixing?"

Bellamy wanted to dismiss it but gave the question her attention. "Why would he do that?"

"One of the two greatest motivators in the world. Money."

"What's the other?" The question was out before she could check it and his answer came winging back on a wry grin.

"Sex."

"Of course."

"Which brings me to my other question about Mr. Sutton Taylor. Take a look at these." Donovan clicked through several browser windows he'd opened, pointing out various elements that had caught his attention on each page with the mouse. "See here and here and here. All suggest, either in a veiled manner or in the case of that blog right out in the open, what a ladies' man he is. All reinforce the story you just shared."

Bellamy considered the assessment, weighing her answer. "I guess others have seen what I have."

"You're not ruining his reputation to answer honestly. Especially not if it will help us get to the bottom of what's going on."

It still felt like a betrayal of some sort, but Bellamy knew he was right. More, she was in the middle of this now whether she liked it or not and she had a right to take care of herself.

"He's very highly regarded for all he's built LSP into, but if I'm being honest, people do talk about his wilder side. Apparently he's had a wandering eye for decades now. His wife passed a little over a year ago, but rumor has been that she always turned a blind eye."

"Behavior like that might be enough to piss someone off."

"And give them access to our drug supply chain?" She shook her head, the notion simply not possible. "No way. There are too many people involved. Too many steps in the process. The sheer amount of government reporting we do on the various drugs we produce makes that virtually impossible."

"So we're back to the email as a way to ruin corporate reputation, not as fact."

She held up a hand. "Wait a minute. There's an easy way to find out if this is reputation or reality. Hang on."

Fifteen minutes later, Bellamy hung up the phone and tapped the notepad she'd scribbled onto. After five calls to pharmacy chains she knew LSP provided flu vaccine for, all confirmed they were out of it.

"Five for five?"

"Yep." She tapped the pad. "No one has the vaccine. Once they got past their initial supplies in September and October, all were asked to pay highway robbery to reorder. And I know there's plenty of vaccine. Our supply is manufactured to ensure it."

"And no one at work has mentioned this?"

Bellamy considered Donovan's question, reviewing it through the new lens uncovered by the calls. "The office has been on a lighter schedule because of the holiday and I didn't give it much thought, but one of my colleagues was complaining in the lunch line a few weeks ago. He mentioned how he'd fielded several calls from field reps complaining about problems with orders. Only when he went back to look at the manifests, everything appeared to have delivered in full."

"So where's the gap?"

"Exactly."

Her gaze drifted back to the computer screen and a small link at the bottom of the article currently facing them from Donovan's screen. "What does that say?" She pointed to the link before reaching for the mouse to click on it.

A new window popped open out of the existing one, a small blurb on the blog they were already looking at.

Sutton Taylor in hospital with mysterious illness. Family worried the Hill Country's most powerful CEO is at death's door.

"Death's door? What?" Bellamy scanned the article quickly, trying to decipher through the gossip and the innuendo to see what she could discover. "It says here he's been ill for some time until being checked into a private facility between Whisperwood and Austin earlier this month."

"This site is known for stretching the truth. Has he been seen at work? Or has anything been mentioned about an illness?"

"Not at all. Last I heard his son was boasting that his father was headed out on a well-deserved Mediterranean vacation for the holidays."

"Could be a cover-up."

"But why hide that from the employees?"

"Maybe they don't want anyone to panic or get upset? Or feel they can get away with anything if the boss is ill."

Bellamy stilled at Donovan's theories. While all were sound, they seemed so foreign.

So at odds with the company she'd known and loved for the past thirteen years.

"Did you remember something?"

"No, it's just that this doesn't seem possible. I've worked there for so many years. Maybe my loyalty to them has blinded me to their possible faults, but what we're talking about…corporate price-fixing? Putting millions of lives at risk? How could I possibly have worked for a company who saw that as a way to turn a profit?"

"I'm sorry, Bellamy. Really, I am. You've lost a lot and this is only adding to that burden."

While she appreciated the sympathy more than she could say, it was way more than a burden. Had she truly spent nearly all of her adult life working for a company that was so profit driven they'd violated the core tenets of their business—to make people well?

"It's a lot to digest, that's all."

"Then why don't we do something to take your mind off of it? Staring at these articles isn't going to bring any answers. Maybe something fun and different would be a better idea."

"Like what?"

"There's a neighborhood down off Lake Travis full of big beautiful homes that's known for their Christmas decorations. They're also known for their friendly neighborhood competition of putting holiday inflatables on the front lawn."

"Sounds classy."

"Apparently it started as a prank from one house to another and morphed into a neighborhood joke. Now that they get over twenty thousand visitors a season, everyone decided to get in the act. Especially when they started charging admission for a local charity."

She hadn't been full of a single drop of holiday cheer this season, but something about the promise of goofy inflatable lawn decorations and bright, shiny lights felt like the right idea.

"Can Alex come along?"

"As if I'd leave him behind. Though I have to warn you, he's a bit of a spoilsport."

"Oh?"

"With all the running around he's done today, he's going to be asleep before we leave the K-9 training center."

"Poor baby. He'll miss all the fun."

Donovan leaned forward, a grin on his face as he whispered in a conspiratorial tone. "Shh. It's probably for the best. There's one house with a decoration of a dog dressed like one of Santa's reindeer that will give him nightmares for a month."

"Then it's good I'm along. I can make sure his eyes are covered from the horror of lawn decorations gone awry."

Chapter Nine

It *was* good she was along. Even better, Donovan thought, it was nice to see a broad smile on Bellamy's face as they drove slowly past the brightly decorated houses and the laughable lawn decorations.

"That is not a pig in angel's wings."

"It most certainly is."

Bellamy's laughter filled the car, a soothing balm to what they'd shared earlier. Even with the difficult discussion of her parents at the K-9 center, she'd kept her equilibrium, but he hadn't heard her laugh. The sound was enticing. Sweet.

And thoroughly enchanting.

Is that what the kids were calling it nowadays, Colton?

Bellamy Reeves might be enchanting, but she was also sexy as hell, a fighter and a woman who had come to occupy far too many of his thoughts in far too short a time.

Had she ever fully left?

That notion had dogged him on and off, taking root fully when he reviewed the case file on her parents. He *had* thought about her over the years. He'd be a liar if he said it was a strong, desperate sort of yearning, but he hadn't forgotten her.

He'd also remembered the easy conversation and sexy chemistry from the night they'd met with a certain sort of fondness. It was a sweet memory and he'd enjoyed pulling it out every so often, polishing it off and reflecting in the glow.

But seeing her again was something else entirely.

She was a beautiful woman and despite the understanding that her life was in tremendous turmoil, he couldn't keep denying his interest.

"There's a Santa decorating a tree in his boxer shorts. And over there is another pig but this one is in reindeer antlers. What is with this neighborhood?"

"I think it's a combination of fierce competition and a lot of money to burn. A lot of these lawn decorations are custom-made. This is one of the wealthiest neighborhoods in Austin."

"It sure is fun." She hesitated for a moment, and he might not have realized it if he weren't stopped behind a line of cars that had already slowed in front of them. "And I don't know. It's frivolous but they're obviously excited to share it with others. I think if you have money it's not so bad if you're willing to share it."

"Not everyone feels that way."

"No, I suppose they don't," she mused. "I'm certainly not wealthy. My parents got by at best and the only reason I have my house is because my parents' insurance settlement paid for it for me. But it seems that if you are fortunate enough to end up provided for, it's only right to share what you have. I love that all this fun also contributes to charity."

They drove on in quiet contemplation, occasionally pointing out a certain house or a specific decoration, but otherwise not speaking. Donovan appreciated that they could spend time together silently, but also wondered what she was thinking.

He waited until they'd cleared the traffic and pulled out onto the road that would lead them back to Whisperwood before speaking again. "I know it's not much, but maybe it is a little burst of Christmas cheer."

"Thanks for that. It was nice to forget for a little while."

"Is that all?" A small shot burrowed beneath his breastbone. He'd hoped to do more than just allow her to forget for a while. Donovan had been intent on helping her make a new memory—something to hold close to her heart—even if the rest of her life still had more holes than she'd ever imagined.

"You know, your life's not over."

"Excuse me?"

"Your life. Your opportunity at happiness. It's not over because your parents died."

The warm moments they'd experienced on the drive through the pretty neighborhood vanished, melting away like ice on a summer Texas afternoon. In its place was a layer of cool that would give that same ice a run for its money.

"Are you actually lecturing me on grief?"

"I'm suggesting you have a right to live. Is that wrong?"

"Not at all. In fact, I think it makes perfect sense coming from you."

Donovan heard the warning signs. They all but leaped out at him, yet he pressed on. "Why's that?"

"Do you honestly think I'd take advice on grief and the loss of my parents, at the holidays no less, from a man who can't be bothered to spend time with his own?"

"My family is my business."

"Yes, they are your business. They're also alive and well and interested in sharing your life, yet you hold them at arm's length."

Again, Donovan saw the red flag waving boldly in front of him and he barreled right on through, heedless of the consequences. "Like your relationship with your sister?"

"Maggie abandoned us."

"I was abandoned!"

The words slipped out, harsh and violent in the closed cabin of his SUV. Up to that moment, Alex had lay sleeping in the back seat, but he sat up at the rising tenor of their words. But it was the harsh emotion that ripped from somewhere around Donovan's stomach that had Alex nosing forward, poking at his triceps where Donovan had his arm resting on the console.

"Shh, buddy. Go back to sleep."

Alex was undeterred and sat straight and tall in the back seat, unwilling to lay down.

Neither he nor Bellamy said a word as he drove steadily on toward Whisperwood, and it was only when they neared the city limits that she finally spoke. "I'm not suggesting your feelings aren't legitimate. You've lived with the knowledge of being left by your biological parents. But what I don't understand is why you punish the family who loves you. They're a gift. And there will come a day when you can't take any of it back. When they won't be here any longer."

"They took me in out of duty."

"Isn't duty a form of love?"

The framing of that caught him up short. Duty as love? "It sounds like a chore."

"Caring for Alex is a duty. Yet you love him and you do it willingly. My parents were infirm and it was my duty to help them. Yet I did it with love. Helping others, taking them in, seeing them through the things that are hard—they're the *duties* we take on for the people we love."

Her words humbled him. All the way down deep, in the places he'd kept buried for so long Donovan had convinced himself they'd finally vanished, was a rising sense of remorse.

Had he been that selfish?

Yes, he had.

Worse, he'd thrown his family's love back in their faces, claiming that it was somehow less than or unworthy. He'd rejected them and they'd done nothing but love him. The knowledge was humbling. But more than that, it was enlightening.

The reality he'd spent his life running from was the one place where he truly belonged.

SUTTON TAYLOR SCROLLED through the news on his iPad and tried to make sense of what he was seeing on the screen. He'd felt like warmed-over bull crap for the past month—a sensation that had only grown worse by the day—but he was determined to rally.

Determined to get some of his damn strength back so he could figure out what was going on at his company. Jensen claimed to have everything under control, but if everything was under such tight reins, why did he have four emails on his personal account from long-time distributors asking where their flu vaccines were?

They'd shipped it months ago, the moment the vaccine came off the lines.

How were people out? Worse, he read the supply details himself. Signed the manifests for the eggs they needed to incubate the virus for the vaccines several months ago. They had *enough*, damn it.

So why was he sitting on multiple emails asking where the supply was? One even complained about pricing, which made no sense. They'd decided that back in March.

Head suddenly fuzzy, Sutton laid his tablet on the rolling tray that had become his constant companion and lay back into the pillows. He was so weak. He had moments of clarity but they were interspersed with long windows of fuzziness when he couldn't seem to grasp anything.

But he needed to grasp this.

Why were there no vaccines? Where had they gone?

Had he asked Jensen about it? The last time they talked—was it yesterday or today?—had he mentioned it to his boy? Or had he decided to keep it to himself?

The questions roiled in his mind, growing fainter like an echo that died out over the rolling Hill Country, but still he tried to hang on to the threads. Maybe he didn't ask the question. Maybe he wanted to see if

Jensen asked him about suppliers calling looking for their vaccine.

Was that right?

The exhaustion that had dogged him for weeks finally gripped him in sharp claws and Sutton gave in.

He'd think about it tomorrow. He had to feel better tomorrow. It would all be clearer tomorrow.

It had to be.

BELLAMY STARED OUT the front window of Donovan's SUV and looked at her house, now lit up as man and dog traipsed through her small haven. Was it safe to go in?

And did she have any choice?

Every time they came home, the routine was the same.

Donovan and Alex had already gotten out to reconfirm the perimeter, then started in on the interior, leaving her with strict instructions to stay inside with locked doors and wait for them to come back. He'd also instructed her to keep her phone in her hand with his number already programmed in and her hand near the horn to quickly alert him to anyone outside.

It was a semicrude warning system, but she figured it would do the job if someone approached.

What she hadn't quite figured out was what had happened earlier. She'd pressed his buttons on their evening jaunt around Austin, that was for sure.

The real question, upon reflection, was why.

His relationship with his parents was none of her business. And even as she knew that—accepted it—she called BS on it, too. He'd started it all, poking around at her grief with an emotional stick. She'd simply defended herself in the age-old technique learned on the playground.

When mud's slung at your head, sling it right on back.

Which said very little about her if she was still employing playground tactics as a grown woman.

Donovan opened the front door and waved at her, hollering for her to stay in the car until he got there. She did as he asked and tried to juxtapose the protector marching toward her with the man who'd frustrated her less than an hour ago.

Your life. Your opportunity at happiness. It's not over because your parents died.

It was the holidays, for heaven's sake. The holidays were supposed to be hard for people who'd lost loved ones, and this was her first time through them without her mother or her father. A few bright lights and goofy lawn decorations couldn't change that.

Even if he'd tried really hard to give her something fun to focus on.

That thought caught her up short and whatever playground mud pie she was about to mentally sling died midtoss.

He'd *tried*.

And didn't that count for something? Something quite special, if she were being honest.

The door clicked open with his keyless remote and he opened her door. She swung her legs over, but stayed put in her seat.

"All clear. You got the Alex sniff of approval."

"Thank you."

"It's what we do."

She got out of the car but took his hand before he

could move on. "For before. Thank you. You tried to show me a fun evening and I repaid you by saying some unkind things. I'm sorry for that."

"You don't have anything to apologize for."

"No, I think I do. The past months have been hard. Way harder than I expected, even, and I had more than enough time to prepare for this. But it was nice to escape for a while. To go see something fun and silly and happy."

The breeze that had swirled all day chose that moment to kick up, a sign that even with the warmer Texas days, it was still winter. She wrapped her arms around her waist at the sudden shot of cold. Donovan took her arms and pulled her close, the heat of his body an immediate balm against the wind. His head bent near hers, not quite touching, and she reveled in the loss of personal space.

A warm, manly scent filled her senses. A bit musky, a bit smoky, it made her think of warm fires on cold nights and she would have happily stood there in his arms for hours, if only for the opportunity to breathe him in.

"I think about the night we met," she murmured. "Not often, but I have thought about it."

"I have, too."

Ribbons of pleasure wrapped around her, delight at his words settling in her chest. "I can still see poor little Alex, sick on a few Legos."

"He did learn his lesson that night. He rarely picks up anything that's not food."

"That's good."

"And ensures far fewer messes in my house."

Once again, Bellamy marveled at how easy and freeing it was to be with Donovan. Their argument in the car had faded, and instead of creating a rift, it gave them another opportunity to connect. One of those small steps that paved the way toward a relationship.

Could something good come out of this confusing time? The small tingle that hovered beneath her skin reinforced just how much she hoped that might be possible.

A whisper of sound echoed from the direction of the darkened street and Donovan shifted, instantly alert. He pressed her back into the open car door before looking around, Alex leaping to attention. When man and dog remained still, neither moving, Bellamy whispered, "What is it?"

"I'm not sure. Let's get inside."

Her home was small, the driveway a modest distance from the front door. She often ran the length when she came home during a rainstorm and unless it was a soaker, rarely got too wet. But suddenly the stretch between the car and the front door seemed endless.

"I'll walk behind you and cover you to the front door."

"You can't—" She stilled at his unyielding gaze.

"Behind you. Let's go."

Bellamy respected his wishes, nerves racing the length of her spine and back again as she moved swiftly toward the front door. If something really was out there, wouldn't Alex have already started barking?

The thought had barely had time to land when a loud clatter cracked through the air, lighting up the night with noise. Donovan crushed her body to his before dropping them to the ground, absorbing the impact with his body.

Her breath whooshed out on a hard burst as Donovan

quickly rolled over her, continuing to shield her with the length of his body. The heavy weight pressed her before it vanished. Then, before she could even register the rapid sensory changes, Donovan hollered instructions as he raced down the driveway, Alex at his heels. "Into the house, Bellamy! Now!"

She did as he asked, even as worry for him and Alex nearly blinded her as she fumbled her way through the front door. The precautions he'd taken to sweep the house upon their return had seemed silly at the time but now gave comfort. Her home was free of traps.

On the inside.

But an intruder lurked outside, and they seemed determined to find her, no matter where she was.

DONOVAN FOLLOWED ALEX, his partner's nose down and his focus solely on the hunt. Donovan kept up a steady stream of instructions to keep Alex focused on the scent, yet by his side. He didn't want to let him go and risk getting his partner shot.

The gunshots had been a surprise and they shouldn't have been. *Nothing* about this situation should be a surprise. Yet for reasons that defied description, the faceless threat to Bellamy continued to catch Donovan off guard.

She'd been targeted by a killer and it was time he not only accepted that fact, but took it for the serious threat it was. The crude construction of the bombs might suggest an amateur, but it also denoted determination, focus and a willingness to get the nefarious job done.

The escalation to gunshots only reinforced that determination.

He'd learned long ago that second-guessing himself in the middle of an op was the quickest way to lose focus, but the recriminations continued to pound in time with his steps. They'd been so focused on understanding why Bellamy was a target and what she might possibly know about the inner workings of LSP that they'd lost sight of the bigger concern.

Maybe she was simply the scapegoat.

The thought chilled him, but as the idea took shape and form in his mind, it grew clearer and more defined. By all accounts, the email that started this all shouldn't have even found its way to her. HR had paid no attention to her claims or even given her the benefit of due process. And perhaps the most telling, the initial attack against her happened on LSP property.

Everything centered on Lone Star Pharmaceutical and someone operating from behind its walls.

The online search earlier around Sutton Taylor played through his mind. Was the founder behind this? He'd built a successful company and could easily be maneuvering something like this from a distance. Money bought influence but it also bought professionals to do your dirty work.

Yet the job had smacked of an amateur from the start.

He paced behind Alex, moving off into the wooded area that surrounded her property line. He'd already reholstered his gun when they'd arrived back at Bellamy's home to do the property sweep and he kept a firm handle on it now. Even with that layer of protection, he was exposed. They'd barely cleared the woods when he called Alex to a halt.

He wanted to find his quarry but he was no good to Bellamy if he and Alex became sitting ducks for someone who saw them far more clearly than they could in return.

Alex stilled immediately, his training outweighing even the lure of the scent. With careful steps, Donovan backed them toward the road, his gaze roaming the area before him. Other than the briefest glimpse of their prey shortly after the gunshots, he had been totally blind to their assailant's whereabouts.

As his foot hit macadam, Donovan gave one final scan of the area. Then he turned and ran, zigzagging across the road to make himself harder to sight.

He didn't stop until he reached Bellamy's front door.

JENSEN LOWERED THE night vision goggles and watched the cop disappear into the night. The other hand that held the gun still trembled at his side, the realization the man had a dog an unexpected development. Those beasts knew scents and now the animal had his.

And that wasn't even his biggest problem. He knew the cop and remembered him from growing up in the same town.

Donovan Colton.

They hadn't been in school together, but everyone in town knew the Coltons. The Colton family regularly competed for their share of Whisperwood headlines, especially because of their black sheep cousins who lived a few towns over in Shadow Creek. Hays Colton had always downplayed that branch of the family, but family was family.

Wasn't that what this was all about, anyway?

He was the rightful heir to LSP. The company was his and nothing would stop him from securing his legacy.

Bellamy Reeves had been the perfect target. But

as he watched Donovan Colton fade into the night, he knew the game had just taken on a new dimension. Cops didn't drive their caseloads around town in their cars. Nor did they hover over them in ways that suggested a far more intimate relationship than that of a protector.

But what were the odds?

The question both amused and frustrated as Jensen considered Donovan Colton. The man was a bright, shining example of why Jensen had started on this path to begin with.

It was time to go to ground, regroup and figure out how to manage this added dimension. He needed more information about Colton.

And then he'd take out the woman and the man who'd become her shadow.

Chapter Ten

Bellamy had hot coffee waiting and about a million questions.

"Are you okay? What happened? Was someone out there? I didn't hear any more gunshots."

Donovan had braced for the questions but hadn't prepared himself for the rush of need that poured through him at the sight of her.

"Donovan? Did you see anyone?"

With careful movements, he ensured his gun was safely holstered and removed the piece, setting it on the middle of her dining room table next to the mug of coffee. He scanned the room, pleased to see the curtains were already drawn on all the windows. Then he released Alex so his partner could get to the water and food that already occupied a place of prominence on Bellamy's kitchen floor.

Only when he'd done all that and realized his blood still pounded and his hands still shook with nervous energy did Donovan take what he needed. On a groan, he reached for her and dragged her close, burying his face in her neck and inhaling her. She was safe. Whole.

Untouched.

"Donovan." His name was a whisper where she brushed her lips against his hair. "You're okay. I'm so glad you're okay."

He moved fast, the moment of comfort flashing over to a desperate, achy need that threatened to consume him as he took her mouth. She matched him, her lips meeting his in immediate surrender. He captured her hands, linking his fingers with hers, and gave the mutual need between them free rein.

There was power in the surrender, he realized as the kiss spun out. A power he'd never known or understood before. Dating. Relationships. All that had come before had been satisfying, yet functional.

But for Bellamy he burned.

Passion flared and Donovan kept his hold tight as he moved them both toward the couch. Dropping to the soft, well-worn cushions, he held her close as he draped her over his body so she straddled his lap. Their bodies pressed together intimately, a sign she was real and gloriously, physically present.

By unspoken agreement they never broke the connection of their lips, even as each explored the other. Her hands roamed over his chest, smoothing the lines of his T-shirt before dipping to pull the material from the waistband of his cargos. It gave easily, slipping over his body as her hands tugged the cotton higher and higher.

They broke the kiss only long enough for her to slip

the shirt over his head, her mouth returning to his as her hands moved unerringly over his skin. Her explorations were tentative at first but grew bolder as the tips of her fingers circled the flat area of his nipples. Shots of heat moved from his chest to his groin, insistent darts of pleasure that both fulfilled even as they demanded more.

He wanted all of her.

But for the moment, he'd settle for touching her, feeling her skin beneath his fingers and pressing her to his chest.

His hands traveled the same path as hers, dragging the silk of her shirt from her slacks before shifting to work the line of buttons. One by one, those small pearls fell away to reveal soft skin. He grazed the swells of her breasts over the cups of her bra, the demands of his body building ever higher, ever tighter.

He wanted her. With everything he was, he wanted this woman who was so warm and responsive in his arms. Yet it was because he wanted her so much that he needed to hold back.

But heaven help him, he couldn't stay away from her.

Just a few minutes more. A bit more time to share what flared to life between them and reassure himself she was safe. A few more touches would hold him.

They'd have to.

His hands roamed over her breasts, the weight of her flesh heavy in his palms. He moved his thumbs over her nipples, the sensual play drawing a moan from deep in her throat.

The knowledge they needed to stop—that whatever flared to life when they were together couldn't be acted on further—nearly vanished like smoke at what pulsed and demanded between them. Donovan nearly gave in—nearly acquiesced to desire—when a loud bark echoed through Bellamy's living room.

Alex's war cry was fierce and immediate, effectively breaking the spell of desire that wound around him and Bellamy.

Need glazed her beautiful gray eyes, but rapidly gave way to the moment as she scrambled off his lap. Her motions were stiff but she moved quickly so he could get to Alex. His partner was already at the door, his bark deep and full as he stood guard.

"Alex." Donovan ordered him to quiet as he crossed to the dining room table and picked up his gun. He briefly thought to grab his shirt but refused to waste the time if their quarry lurked outside the house.

He'd already scoped out safe points in the house on his earlier sweep and knew the walls that framed the edge of the dining room were the most secure place. There were no windows in the room, and the short walls that set off the entrance archway would provide additional protection from the front door.

"Bellamy, please get behind the dining room wall. I'll let you know when it's safe to come out."

"Get behind—"

"Now, please."

The adrenaline that had carried him into the house fewer than twenty minutes before spiked once again, a heady cocktail that fired the blood. Alex had remained in place at the door, a ferocious protector who would go through the entrance first to protect his humans. The thought humbled Donovan as it always did, the animal's courage dwarfing that of many people he knew.

"Colton! It's Archer. Let me in."

The order was clear and at confirmation it was the chief, Bellamy scampered from behind the dining room wall toward her clothes.

"Bellamy—"

"I'm half-naked, Donovan, and the chief is here." She hissed the words, color high on her cheeks, and Donovan couldn't quite hide the grin. She did make an awfully pretty picture, her skin flushed a sweet pink while those gorgeous breasts pushed against the cups of her bra that he hadn't managed to get off.

A quick glance down reminded him of his own decision to forgo his shirt and he pulled the door open to let Archer in before striding back to get his clothes. Archer was a quick study and likely would have known what he and Bellamy had been doing, clothing be damned, and there was no way Donovan was leaving his friend to stand at the front door like a sitting duck.

Archer made a fuss over Alex, his gaze averted as Donovan righted himself. If Bellamy's sudden appearance from the corner of the dining room was at all a surprise, Archer was too big a gentleman to show it.

"A neighbor down the way called in gunshots. You wouldn't know anything about that, now, would you, Colton?"

HEAT RACED FROM her neck to her face and back down in increasing waves of embarrassment as Bellamy smoothed her shirt over her hips. It was bad enough she'd fallen into Donovan's arms like a woman starved, but to be discovered by the chief of police added an extra layer of mortification.

She and Donovan had been shot at and how did she respond? By attacking him like some sex-starved fiend.

Although embarrassing, Chief Thompson's arrival was perfect timing before she'd made an even bigger mistake. She barely knew Donovan Colton. Yes, they'd been thrown into a crazy situation. And yes, there was a base attraction.

But to act on it so quickly?

That was the recipe for a serious heartache once her attacker was caught and life went back to normal. She'd already accepted life had changed with the passing of her parents. Even her job could be overcome as she looked to find a new one.

But getting over Donovan Colton? Somehow she sensed that would be a near impossibility.

The man she'd met five years ago and had hoped to get to know better at the time had grown even more attractive and interesting. But their circumstances made it difficult to tell if there was truly something there or just the heat of close proximity in the midst of danger.

"Ms. Reeves? Are you okay?" Chief Thompson crossed to her, his concern evident. If he did have any thoughts about what she and Donovan had been doing—and she had no doubt he knew *exactly* what they'd been doing—it didn't show.

"I'm fine. Scared, but doing okay."

"Did you see who shot at you?"

"No. After we arrived home earlier, Donovan and Alex did a sweep of the house while I waited in the car. It was only after they came out with the all clear that we were shot at. Donovan took off after the shooter but he was gone."

The chief's attention shifted to Donovan. "Did you see him?"

"Nothing more than a fast-moving silhouette. I held

Alex back as we didn't know what we were dealing with, although the suspect did have a man's build. Alex caught the scent and we'll follow it again in the morning and see what we turn up."

"I'll come back out to help you myself."

"We're leaving at first light."

"I do know how to wake up early, Colton."

Bellamy sensed the tension beneath byplay and knew there was something beyond the words. Donovan was embarrassed that he'd missed his quarry. On a base level, she understood that.

The chief, on the other hand, had increasingly impressed her. She'd believed him insensitive to her situation based on their first meeting, but now realized she'd misjudged his questions during the interview for something other than due diligence.

"I owe you an apology, Chief Thompson."

"Me? Why would you say that?"

"You seem upset about this situation."

"Of course I'm upset. There's a dangerous threat to my town and my people. I take that threat seriously and so does my entire department."

She nodded, her anger from that morning a distant memory. "After you questioned me. I thought you believed I was responsible. Now I see you were doing your job."

"You've come around pretty quickly."

"My father was a simple man, but he was quick to teach my sister and me that if you misread someone you owed it to them to fix the error."

Chief Thompson doffed his hat on a head nod. "Daniel-Justice was one of my favorite people in town. I was sorry when he was no longer able to manage the store and even sorrier when he passed. You have my promise I will do all I can to find who is doing this and to make sure you stay safe."

"I believe you will." Their subtle truce in place, Bellamy extended a hand. "I know it."

Feeling his firm handshake, Bellamy saw the promise in Chief Thompson's eyes matched the solemnity of his words. "Thank you, ma'am."

The chief left as fast as he'd arrived, promising to return at first light to go out with Donovan. He also assured her he'd bring along a deputy to stay with her while he and Donovan hunted for who was responsible. It was only after he'd left that Bellamy was left to face her earlier actions, the heat creeping up her neck once more.

She was alone with Donovan. Again. And while her clothing might be firmly resettled on her body, the memory of their flushed skin pressed intimately together was still fresh in her thoughts.

Too fresh, if the quivers that beat in tempo with her pulse were any indication. "You didn't need to do that. Before."

"Do what before?" Hesitation marked Donovan's tone even as his gaze shifted to the couch where they'd so recently explored each other.

"Racing off. Chasing the shooter. You could have been hurt. Or—" She broke off, the reality of what it meant for him to go off after a threat like he had. "Or worse. You could have been killed."

"I had Alex. We're a pretty good pair."

"Neither of you are a match for a crazy, determined person with a gun." She rubbed her hands over her arms, suddenly cold in a way she'd never experienced before. It pierced her skin and invaded her bones, a bleak sort of chill that made her wonder if she'd ever be warm again.

"That's why we only followed to the edge of the woods beyond your property. I know what I'm doing. And despite the threats so far, I will keep you safe. And myself in the process."

He moved closer as he spoke, each step punctuating his points, but Bellamy moved back in matched time, unwilling to give in to the nearly overpowering desire to return to his arms. She had to be strong—had to stand up and do this on her own. Donovan would catch whoever was doing this—of that she had no doubt. It was what would come after that time that worried her. Donovan would catch the perpetrator and then she'd be alone again.

The nearly desperate need for self-preservation had kicked in and she had to protect herself. When this was all over, Donovan would go back to his life and she to hers. It was time to start focusing on that.

"I, um. I should turn in."

"Of course." The small light in his gaze vanished, replaced with a subtle layer of confusion. "It's been a long day."

Bellamy grasped at the peace offering, clawing to keep her head above water and not come off like the most ungrateful bitch in the world. "Too long."

"I'm not tired yet, so I'll hang out here for a while, if that's all right?"

"Of course. Help yourself to the coffee or anything else you'd like."

"Sure. Thanks."

Then she made a run for it, the short trip to her bedroom seeming endless as she felt Donovan's gaze on her back. It was only when she closed her door and leaned back against it that Bellamy finally let the tears come.

In her entire life, she'd never needed anyone more than she needed Donovan Colton. But that way lay madness.

And a heartache she knew she'd never recover from.

DONOVAN SETTLED DOWN on the couch, Alex hopping up to curl at his side. The large blanket he kept for Alex was spread out beside him and his partner obediently stayed on it, his tail thumping lightly as he stared up at Donovan.

"Busy day, my friend."

The tail thumped a bit harder, whether it was agreement or the simple joy of sharing the day together. Donovan wasn't ever quite sure, but he appreciated the companionship all the same. He scratched Alex behind the ears, the dog's soulful brown eyes nearly rolling back into his head in ecstasy. He added a few additional belly rubs and a neck massage and in moments had a partner who snored like the dead perched beside him on the couch.

"And another one lost to Morpheus's powerful brew."

Donovan snagged his tablet from his bag and did a quick scan of his email, sending in a few updates on two of his cases in progress. His caseload was unusually light and he appreciated the extra time it gave him to watch over Bellamy, even as he struggled to find the right balance with her.

Had he scared her off? Or been too aggressive with the make-out session on the couch? Their stolen moments together had seemed mutual, but then she checked out after Archer had arrived, his tempting companion fading behind a very clear wall.

It served him right. He had no business taking advantage of her at such a vulnerable time and a bit of distance would be good for both of them. He'd allowed himself to think otherwise after spending several days in close proximity and the danger of the moment, but it was good Archer had arrived.

Wasn't it?

Well aware he didn't have the mental energy to figure it out, Donovan focused on the lingering questions that still dogged him about LSP instead. Whatever was going on, it had to be tied to Bellamy's job. The email. The car bomb placed at work. Even the way she was summarily fired without even a moment's consideration for her side of the story from Human Resources. All pointed toward something rotten at Lone Star Pharmaceutical.

Donovan pulled the same articles from earlier on Sutton Taylor, reading through the material, looking for any new insights. The man had helmed LSP for over thirty years. He held numerous patents in the field and was responsible for providing lifesaving drugs throughout the US and globally.

What would he gain from manipulating pricing on one of the most basic vaccines LSP produced?

Opening up a fresh search bar, Donovan tried a new angle. If there weren't overt answers with LSP, maybe there was something in the Sutton Taylor's personal life that would provide better insight. He tapped his way through a few searches before finally hitting pay dirt in an Austin lifestyle magazine article from about ten years before.

Donovan abstractly scratched Alex's head as he read the salient points out loud. "Married to high school sweetheart. One son, arriving later in their marriage. Provided extensive grants to the University of Texas medical school."

He kept scanning, the accolades for Taylor impressive. By all accounts the man was a veritable saint, his insistence on working for the public good a consistent mantra even as LSP accrued massive profits year over year.

Benevolence and profit. Was it really possible to maintain the two?

Donovan had a suspicious nature—he'd always believed it was what made him a good cop—and his senses were on high alert for what Taylor might be hiding. It was only as he clicked on yet another link that he remembered the blog from earlier. Toggling back to the *Everything's Blogger in Texas* post, he read through the list of gossip items that had followed Taylor throughout his professional life. Every article suggested the same thing, and all reinforced Bellamy's impressions, as well.

Sutton Taylor was a womanizer.

The blog was full of his conquests, with names, dates and, where those weren't available, a litany of insinuations. The lists also included three known illegitimate children, all claimed by Sutton Taylor as his own. Donovan read through the details, then clicked on the various links the blog provided. It was that last one that stopped him. An image of Taylor, dressed in a hunting outfit with a dog at his side.

The man's hand settled on the animal's head, his gun held against his hip with the other. The dog stared straight ahead, a faithful companion to his master. While the scene was different, it was such a clear match for his own photo for the K-9 team Donovan could only sit and stare.

Sutton's hair was longer where Donovan kept his short and cropped close to his head, but other than that the stance was the same. The jawline was the same. Even the shape of the man's hand where it cradled the dog's head was the same.

A subtle sense of awareness tightened his gut and Donovan flipped back through the other tabs he already had open, scrambling to find the blog and the list of dates. The tablet bumped against his knee as he swiped through various screens, jittery nerves jumping beneath his skin.

Was it actually possible? Could it be this obvious? Had the mystery of his birth been here in Whisperwood all along?

The blog provided confirmation and details on Taylor's three illegitimate children, all born over a ten-year period during his marriage and all provided for through legal means with a piece of his fortune. His son Jensen was the only child produced during his marriage.

Donovan vaguely remembered Jensen Taylor. The two of them didn't go to school together but Whisperwood was a small town and Taylor may have hung out with Donovan's older brother a time or two. Even with his limited memory, he did remember Jensen Taylor as one of the golden kids. Part of Whisperwood's elite, the younger Taylor had enjoyed the freedom his father's wealth provided and had run with a fast crowd. He and Donovan's brother hadn't stayed friends for long.

Was it possible the man was actually *his* brother?

It was a strange, disturbing punctuation mark to his weird thoughts about Sutton Taylor.

Had the man regretted one more illegitimate child and sought to deal with the problem by disposing of him in the Colton family barn? Even as he toyed with the idea, Donovan couldn't get any real enthusiasm behind it. Sutton Taylor was a powerful, wealthy man. He could do far better for his offspring—even the illegitimate ones—than dropping them off in a barn.

The wealthy had options, from farming unwanted children out to families or disposing of them through private adoption. Regardless of the path chosen, Taylor could have avoided ever having his name associated with an unwanted child—he didn't need to abandon a newborn infant to do it.

Nor did abandoning a baby follow pattern. The articles all reinforced the fact that Sutton Taylor had taken care of the children conceived outside his marriage.

Alex stirred next to him before lifting his head and placing it on Donovan's thigh. Warm brown eyes stared up at him, full of support and a devotion that never failed to humble him.

"Do you think it's possible?" Donovan whispered the question, testing it on his tongue and allowing it to expand and take shape in his mind's eye. Even with all the reasons against it, there was no accounting for human nature. Taylor was a wealthy married man with a reputation to protect. A family of his own he wouldn't want to expose to scorn or ridicule. Even if he hadn't cared for either of those things, thirty-plus years ago Sutton Taylor was still building his empire. It might not have set well with investors if the young owner and businessman couldn't demonstrate even the slightest bit of control to keep his baser needs in his pants.

Hays and Josephine Colton were well-respected

members of the community. They had a young, growing family of their own and were well-known residents of Whisperwood. They'd easily have the financial where-withal to take on another child, and would be local so someone could keep an eye on the baby as it grew up.

Donovan considered the scenarios, testing them out to see what might stick. It wasn't a perfect theory, but it had some weight. Maybe what he needed was a good night's sleep and a fresh perspective after sleeping on it. When he woke up, perhaps he'd have answers. Like whether or not Sutton Taylor was his real father.

The one who'd abandoned him in a barn on Christmas morning, left to be raised by strangers.

Chapter Eleven

Donovan had no more answers at dawn than he'd had when he crawled into the small double bed in Bellamy's spare room six hours before. What he did have was a raging headache after a sleepless night and more questions than answers.

If Sutton Taylor was his father, who was his mother?

And if Sutton had abandoned him, had the woman spent the ensuing years looking for him?

Alternatively, what if Sutton didn't know at all? Maybe his mother had been the one to abandon him, leaving him to his fate in the Colton barn.

"You look like hell, Colton." Archer handed off a steaming to-go cup of coffee, his gaze irritatingly bright for 6:00 a.m.

"Thanks."

"You don't even look like warmed-over hell. You

actually look like that special sort of tired reserved for first-year medical residents and parents of brand-new babies."

Donovan took a long sip of hot coffee and barely winced as the brew scalded his tongue, such was his need for the caffeine. "How would you know about either of those scenarios? Last time I checked you got queasy at the sight of blood and your ugly mug hasn't had a date in a year."

"Six months, but thanks for checking." Archer took a sip of his coffee and glanced toward the woods. He'd already left one of his deputies as backup in a cruiser parked in Bellamy's driveway before reiterating his intention that he wanted to go on the search himself. "I know Alex is good and all, but you think he can catch the scent again?"

"I know he can."

Donovan dropped to a crouch, his gaze level with Alex. "You ready to go to work?"

Alex's thick tail began its fast metronome thump against the ground and Donovan couldn't help but grin up at Archer. "Alex is ready. The real question is if you can keep up."

"Lead the way."

"Let's go get 'em, Alex."

The three of them took off in the direction of the copse of trees that surrounded Bellamy's property. The area was thickly wooded, though not nearly as overgrown as it had looked in the dark. Alex navigated it with surety, trailing over leaves, twigs and the occasional downed log as he pushed them onward, farther into the trees.

Donovan took it in, the air growing quiet as the foliage grew thicker. While a big part of him would have preferred to end this all the night before, he was still sure of the decision to return to Bellamy. Barreling into the trees, heedless of a man with a gun who potentially had a better view on them than they had in return, was a suicide mission.

"You come up with a motive yet?" Archer asked.

Donovan kept tight hold on Alex's leash, his focus on the dog's small signals that confirmed a change in direction or an increase in the intensity of the scent he tracked. His partner saw the world against the dimension of smell and Donovan had learned long ago to let him work against the pictures that world made.

"Money or power's my pick."

"Money's usually a good one. They teach you that at the academy?"

Donovan ran a tired hand over the back of his head. "First day, I think. Funny how it's a lesson that keeps repeating itself."

They tromped in silence for a few minutes, the only sounds Alex's thick sniffs and occasional whines from the back of his throat as he caught a fresh direction.

"I put in a warrant for access to LSP's tech," Archer spoke. "But I am hitting a wall so far. Between the holidays and a 'flimsy case' as Judge Carson told me, I'm not getting very far on diving into the LSP email server."

"Carson's tough."

"Yeah, but he's not wrong. I need something more than a printout of a suspicious email to go on."

"You been looking at anyone else? You and I both know Bellamy Reeves is innocent in all this." It was on the tip of Donovan's tongue to ask about Jensen Taylor but something held him back. His questions from the previous evening and his hunt for information on Sutton Taylor had left him exposed and raw, and Donovan wasn't quite ready to poke around that one.

Especially not with someone as astute as Archer Thompson.

"I've got notes to call Human Resources today. Something about Bellamy's description of her time with the director kept ringing my bell. It feels funny, you know? Who gets fired on the spot for bringing something to HR's attention?"

"A guilty someone?" Donovan asked.

"Guilty on which side is my concern."

Archer's comment pulled Donovan up short and he tugged lightly on Alex's leash to pull him to a stop. "You think HR's got something?"

"I think it's awfully strange that Bellamy goes to HR to make a formal complaint and is not only fired but walks out to an explosive device in her car. I'm not much into coincidences, nor do I like situations where our victim appears to be bullied."

"So why'd you give her a hard time in your office?"

"To make sure she is a victim and not the puppet master behind the scenes."

Donovan chewed on that idea, the opportunity to bounce things off the chief a welcome distraction from his own thoughts. "I'm not a big conspiracy buff but the puppet master angle has legs."

"Don't you mean strings?"

Donovan only shook his head and wouldn't have been surprised to hear Alex groan at that one. "They clearly didn't make you chief on your rockin' sense of humor. But they did make you chief on your nose for bad guys. Who's in a position to pull those strings?"

"Offhand? I'd say bigwigs at LSP. Maybe a few enterprising drug distributors who have some of the biggest accounts in hand and already locked up. Maybe even a disgruntled employee who manages the supply chain high up."

"I've looked but haven't found anything to suggest LSP is in dire financial straits."

"Me, either." Archer crushed his coffee cup in his hand before shoving it into his back pocket. "Wall Street's happy with their quarterly and annual performances and their stock remains strong. Something like this puts that performance at risk instead of enhancing it."

"Not including the profit they might make in the meantime."

Archer shrugged. "Still seems awfully shortsighted. Why ruin the company reputation and long-term health for the sake of a few bucks in the short term? Especially if you're profitable to begin with."

"Back to our original motive?" Donovan asked. "Money."

"Short-term money versus long-term success, aka money. Still seems shortsighted to me."

Shortsighted, illegal and overconfident. Each description fit and suggested a person who had little self-control and more than their fair share of arrogance.

Which only brought Donovan right back to Sutton Taylor. The man had proven himself out of control and arrogant when it came to his personal choices, but in his business, he'd seemingly exercised control and long-term vision.

So why ruin that now?

SUTTON RAN HIS hands over the thin hospital blanket, his fingers tracing the weave over and over. He'd begun counting the interlocking squares, desperate to stay awake and focused. It was so hard to concentrate and he *needed* to concentrate.

Needed to stay alert.

More, he needed to figure out what was wrong.

He'd have windows of time when he understood something was the matter and then would fall back to sleep, groggy and unfocused, his body exhausted from the mere effort of thinking. But it had to stop.

Twelve. Thirteen. Fourteen.

He couldn't afford to sleep anymore. Like last night. What was he thinking about? And what had filled his dreams with oversize cars that floated in the air before exploding, their parts shattering like a firework?

Twenty. Twenty-one. Twenty-two.

Jensen. Wasn't he worried about his son? Sutton tried to focus on that as he kept counting, forcing himself to stay awake with the repetition.

Where was Jensen?

Forty-four. Forty-five. Forty-six.

Jensen was watching over LSP. But why was Jensen in charge? He hadn't shown a great aptitude for the business. In fact, some of his ideas were flat out wrong.

We need to focus on managing our production. Too much product floods the market, Dad. Scarcity is our friend.

We produce the drugs people need to get well. Why would I throttle production? We need to find opportunities to expand. To push past our production limits to get more into supply. To help more people.

Profit. Jensen had slapped him on the back with a barely concealed eye roll. *Profit is why.*

When had they discussed that? A few days ago? Or was it months?

Sutton stopped counting squares, his hands going still on the blanket. It *had* been months. Back in the spring when they were finalizing the formulary and the orders on the flu vaccine.

And now their suppliers didn't have enough vaccine?

Their suppliers. The emails. He'd read the emails last night.

Sutton reached for his phone where it lay on the rolling tray that sat beside the bed. He lifted the device, his hand shaking as he tried to turn it on. Damned phone, what was wrong? His hand shook as he stabbed at the small button at the base, only to see the phone screen black and lifeless.

Out of charge.

His hand shook harder as he tossed the phone back onto the tray. A loud beep started from the machine behind his head as his entire body began to shake. The dim lights in the room quavered, shimmering in and out of focus as several nurses came running through the door.

BELLAMY AVOIDED ONE more look out the front window, well aware of what she'd find. The deputy's car would still be in her driveway, the man perched behind the wheel with his gaze on the road. She was impressed by his diligence, even as she questioned how horribly bored he must be just sitting there.

For her.

Once again, that thought struck her. It had hit hard when she realized how focused Donovan was on keeping her safe and protected, but it extended to the broader Whisperwood police force. So many people trying to keep her safe from a killer.

Would they succeed?

Was it even possible to succeed against someone so determined?

Sick of pacing and worrying, she crossed her arms and tapped her fingers on her biceps. What else could she do? She'd already cleaned up the kitchen and freshened Alex's water and food for when he and Donovan returned. The beds were made and the living room had been straightened up. She'd even toyed with mopping the kitchen floor, which meant her boredom had reached unprecedented heights.

Still, her thoughts flipped and tumbled, one over the other and back again.

Who was behind all of this? And why had they targeted *her*?

When she stopped asking that question through the lens of the victimized—*Why me?*—she'd begun to ask different questions. It was less a question of why was this happening to her and, instead, why had she been targeted.

Did she know something? Or had she been inadvertently exposed to some sort of information that had made her an easy target?

Her laptop was closed and still sitting on the edge of the kitchen counter. She'd nearly glanced past it, her eyes roaming over the floor once more as she considered pulling out the mop when she refocused on the laptop.

Was it possible?

Reaching for it, she opened the lid and waited for

the computer to come out of sleep mode. In moments, she had a browser window open and tapped in the familiar remote address that would put her into the cloud.

And access into her email.

Butterflies dive-bombed her stomach as she walked through each step. Technically she was no longer an employee. Which meant she had no right to log into the system and even less right to hunt through her email.

Which made it all the more imperative that she take what she could while she could.

Her latest password—HOLIDAYSSUCK, all one word—spilled easily from her fingers. She hit the return key, shocked and extraordinarily pleased when her email filled the screen.

She was in!

In HR's rush to fire her, they'd forgotten to go through the proper protocols to turn off her email and remote access. All standard when an employee was terminated.

Yet they'd forgotten to dismantle her accounts.

Well aware diving into her email didn't put her in a good light, Bellamy shrugged it off as the least of her problems. She sorted through the unread emails that had come in over the past few days. She passed notes about the holiday schedule, the latest financial reports for the prior week and even a note about using up benefits before the end of the year, scrolling toward the email that had started it all.

Staring at it with fresh eyes, she noticed there wasn't a named sender in the chronological listing of email. Instead, all she read was the word INTERNAL. Which was odd. She'd been at LSP long enough that she knew the form their email addresses took. There was no sender called INTERNAL.

Of course, no one sent anonymous email detailing corporate greed and illegal behavior, either.

Yet someone had sent this one.

She opened the email again, quickly sending a copy to her personal address before looking once more at the details she'd not paid enough attention to upon first viewing. She was no tech whiz, but she'd used enough software programs throughout her career that she figured the navigation bar at the top was the place to start.

The information command didn't provide any detail beyond the date and time sent. Ticking through the other options, she tried to open the actual sender's email address, only to find a string of gibberish that read like a garbled line of code.

Was there something in that? Something an expert could track back and use?

The peal of her cell phone pulled her from the screen and Bellamy practically dived for the device, desperately hoping it was Donovan telling her he was on his way back. Instead, her friend Rae's name flashed on the screen. They'd texted recently but hadn't spoken. Bellamy regretted her hasty info dump of what had happened the other day and wanted to minimize Rae's involvement in what was going on.

But ignoring her friend wasn't fair, either.

"Hey."

"You're lucky this week's one of the busiest at the store or I'd be camped out on your front lawn as we speak."

"Good morning to you, too."

"Your sister was in here last night. Told me that your car blew up."

"It didn't—"

Before she could protest, Rae pressed on. "Bell. The bomb squad was called and you've got protection detail at your house. What am I missing here?"

"I didn't want to worry you." *Or risk involving you in something that grows more dangerous by the hour.*

"I'm your friend. Of course I'm worried about you. And Maggie is beside herself."

"Maggie already read me the riot act."

"Good for her."

A small gasp caught in Bellamy's throat. "Don't tell me you're on her side."

"In this I am. I don't care what's in the past or how far apart you two have been. She's your sister and she's worried. Rightfully so."

Bellamy toyed with the track pad on her computer, the cursor circling the screen in time to the sweep of her finger. Rae had always been her rock, her supportive champion who was always on her side. To hear her defend Maggie was a major departure from her usual stalwart defense.

"Does the silence mean you're mad at me?"

"Of course not."

And she wasn't. But it did sting to hear her friend so easily defend her sister. She and Maggie had been on opposite sides for so long, it was startling to realize the sands beneath her feet might have shifted.

Did Maggie actually care about her?

She'd believed it once. The baby sister whom she loved and adored could do no wrong and Bellamy had believed their sibling bond would keep them close forever. Then her father had gotten ill and Maggie had grown more and more distant. It was easier to blame her or think poorly of her instead of trying to see her side of things.

And that was on her, Bellamy acknowledged. She had a right to her opinion and an even bigger right to disagree, but her unwillingness to hear Maggie's side sat squarely with her.

"So what's going on?" Rae's question pulled her back from her thoughts, and Bellamy pictured her friend up to her elbows in holiday inventory as she worked to get the general store open for the day.

"I wish I knew, Rae. Really, I wish I did. Things have gotten weird and scary."

"Is Donovan Colton with you?"

"You know about that?" Why did that bother her so much? Donovan wasn't her personal property and it wasn't exactly a secret he was helping her. Even with the pep talk and the silent acknowledgment not to get flustered about it, Bellamy couldn't quite hide her frustration. "Let me guess, Maggie told you."

"I didn't need Maggie to tell me. Marie in HR at LSP was in here yesterday. You were all she could talk about. You and the hot guy helping you."

Bellamy caught on the name, cycling through the people she knew at LSP. Marie was the woman who'd brought her files into Sally's office the day she went to HR.

"You know Marie? Do you know anything about her?"

"No more or less than I know about most people. She and her husband settled in Whisperwood about three years ago."

"And she told you what happened?"

"Quite happily. Told me some stuff had gone down at LSP and that HR took an employee to task. Unfairly, too." Rae's smile traveled through the phone. "I put two and two together that it was you. And when she started telling me about the hot cop seen around town with his dog, I took my two and two and multiplied them even further. Donovan Colton doesn't make it to Whisperwood all that often. The fact that he's stuck around is a testament to you."

"Why me?"

"There's no love lost between him and his family. Most of his trips through town are quick and functional at best. But from the gossip swirling around town, you've given him a new reason to stay."

"That's just silly. He was the one who got the dispatch call on my car and he's been helping me out. Nothing more."

"Are you sure?"

"Of course I'm sure."

"Then why do I hear that funny note in your voice?"

Bellamy flushed any sense of surprise or outrage from her tone, focused on keeping things as nonchalant as possible. "I don't have any funny notes."

"Yes, you do. You're sort of squeaky at the edges, like that time in freshman year you asked Bill Monroe to the Sadie Hawkins dance."

"I do not."

"I heard it again. You squeaked at the end of your protest. Which means you've got something juicy and interesting to share."

It was on the edge of her lips to protest before Bellamy pulled it back. Rae knew her well and would only take joy in continuing to push her buttons. So she switched gears and focused on why she hadn't called in the first place.

"Please promise me you'll be careful. Keep your ears open but don't ask any questions and don't give anyone the idea you and I have spoken."

The laughter that had characterized Rae's voice up to then vanished. "What's going on, Bellamy?"

"Promise me. Please. You need to be careful and you don't need to let on to anyone that we've communicated. Not until this is all taken care of."

"Taken care of? Who's taking care of it?"

"Please, Rae."

"Okay. I promise."

"Thanks. Now go do what you need to do and I'll call you in a few days."

"If you're sure?"

"Positive."

They said a few goodbyes and then hung up. As her phone switched off, Bellamy couldn't hide her concerns. The person who'd targeted her had made it clear they knew what she drove and where she lived. It would stand to reason they'd know who she was friends with, as well. And who her sister was.

Fear struck low in her gut, raw and icy cold. Not seeing eye to eye didn't mean she didn't love her sister. But could she get to Maggie in time? Reaching for her phone once more, she dialed Maggie's number and counted off the rings.

And wondered what it meant when her sister didn't pick up.

DONOVAN TOSSED HIS gear in the back of his SUV, frustrated with the wasted morning. They'd been out for over three hours and, other than going around in circles, Alex hadn't found anything useful. Or more to the point, their quarry had covered his tracks.

Even with a disappointing trek, Alex always got his treat when he was done. Donovan hunted for the container of bones he kept packed in the back of the car and pulled one out for his partner.

"I'm going in to work on the tech angle." Archer looked as frustrated as Donovan felt, and once again, he was struck by the man's commitment to the community of Whisperwood. "I still don't believe we haven't found a thing."

"Me, either." Archer waved his deputy on before crossing Bellamy's driveway to meet him.

"Wait." Donovan patted his gear, suddenly remembering the button he'd found in the sweep of Bellamy's car and tagged in an evidence bag. "I pulled this when I swept her car and tagged it."

"A button?"

"Off a man's shirt. A fancy one, I think."

Archer turned the bag over in his hands, tracing the thin disc. "I don't have the resources to hunt this down but it is another notch in Bellamy's favor. Where'd you find it?"

"Buried beneath the seat. I would have ignored it except for the fact that she was genuinely surprised to see it. Claimed that it didn't match anything she owned."

"You mentioned earlier this felt like an amateur job." The chief eyed the button once more. "Here's one more example that reinforces the point. No one even halfway decent at their job would risk losing something like this."

"It's clumsy. Lazy, too." Donovan nearly mentioned his suspicions about Sutton Taylor but held his tongue at the last minute. He had suspicions and nothing more. You didn't go around accusing men of Sutton Taylor's stature and standing in the community on a hunch.

Nor did you go around suggesting he was your missing father.

So Donovan waved Archer off instead, mulling over all he'd discovered. And while he considered all of it, he had a woman waiting for him.

One who might have the answers to his questions. And one who might help him figure out the mystery of his father. Donovan finished stowing his things when the sound of tires on pavement had him turning to see Maggie Corgan pulling up.

The woman was out of the car and around the hood, her perfect blond hair waving around her face in the morning breeze. "First it's a bomb and then it's gunshots? What is going on, Officer Colton? Who's after my sister?"

Donovan was struck once again by the sincerity in Maggie's eyes. The relationship between her and Bellamy might be strained, but he didn't think it was because Maggie didn't want one with her sister. "I'm working to find that out, ma'am."

"Why has she been targeted? None of this makes sense. She's the kindest, gentlest person. She's a hard worker and she's always loved working for LSP. I hate that she lives out here all by herself, but I know it's what she wanted. It's why—" Maggie broke off, her eyes widening.

"It's why what?"

"Nothing." Maggie waved an airy hand, the motion dismissive. "Nothing at all."

"Ms. Corgan." Donovan moved closer, curious to

see a look of utter defeat in the woman's eyes. "Do you know something?"

Maggie shook her head, her gaze dropping to the sidewalk. "About what's happening to her? No."

"Then what are you talking about?"

"I tried the only way I knew how."

She broke off again, her slim form agitated as she twisted her hands and shifted from one high heel boot to another. "Tried what, Maggie?"

"I tried to marry the right person to have money for my father's treatments. It was the only way I knew how, and I thought James and I would be a good fit. He wanted a trophy wife and I never minded being a trophy all that much." She sighed, brushing her hair back. "I'm butchering this. Why don't I try again?"

Donovan waited as she gathered herself, suddenly curious to see the parallels between Bellamy and her sister. While he wanted to hear the entire story, he'd already sensed where Maggie was going. It was humbling to see what had changed that lone night he went off to an accident scene and all that had played out since. Two sisters, each driven to help their family.

Each stymied by pride.

There's a lesson in there, Colton.

The thought struck hard, an uncomfortable parallel to his own family relationships that he wasn't quite ready to explore.

"Things didn't work out the way I planned and James wasn't all that free with the checkbook. He gave me a bit as an allowance that I could funnel to my family after I bought the requisite clothing and shoes and my mother-in-law took pity and helped a bit once she knew what was going on. It wasn't enough, but it was something. And it gave me enough to get this house for Bellamy. Before it all—" Maggie hesitated again, her gaze roaming toward the house. "Bellamy thinks my parents left this to her, but they didn't. There wasn't any money from their estate left to leave her and I didn't want to take this from her. I know how important this house is to her. How important these memories are. So I worked with the lawyers to make it so."

"Why can't you tell her?"

"Because I can't. And you can't, either. Bellamy isn't interested in what I have to say and I'm not going to grovel for my sister's affection."

If Donovan thought the knowledge would put Bellamy at risk, there was nothing that would keep him silent, but he could hardly fault family relationships or go against them. "I won't."

"Thank you."

"But I do think you should tell her. There's love there. Between the two of you. It'd be a shame to miss an opportunity to build a relationship as adults."

Maggie's eyes narrowed, her mouth firming into a straight line. "I know your sister. She and I both worked on a Junior League project a few years back."

"Oh?"

"She mentioned her family on several occasions while we worked on that project. I know how important her family is to her and how much she'd like adult relationships with her siblings. I got the sense that she had that with all but one of them."

"I don't—"

"Things aren't always as simple." She laid a hand on his arm. "Even when they should be."

Bellamy chose that moment to come outside, her

eyes shielded against the morning sun. Maggie waved at her, her smile bright. "Just catching up with Officer Colton. He's got things well in hand."

She moved back around to her car and climbed in, starting the car and pulling out before Bellamy had even crossed the yard.

"What was that about? Why did she leave?"

"I think she came to visit me. To make sure I'm handling your case well."

"Was she satisfied with what she found out?" Bellamy's gaze remained on the departing car as it sped down the street.

"I have no idea."

Donovan walked Bellamy back to the house, Maggie Corgan's parting words still heavy in his heart.

Things *weren't* always simple.

Even when they should be.

Chapter Twelve

Bellamy left several messages for Maggie over the next few days but hadn't managed to reach her sister. They exchanged a couple of texts every day and she tried to probe what Maggie's holiday plans were, even going so far as to invite her for Christmas dinner, but got a vague excuse about being busy.

Which stung.

She'd tried, hadn't she? Extended the olive branch and attempted to repair things and got a big fat slap in the face for her efforts.

It was one more layer of frustration overtop of the rest of her life. Donovan and Alex had been in her home for nearly a week and they were no closer to finding the person behind the attacks on her than they'd been since man and dog moved in.

Other than the pervasive sense of being watched,

nothing else had happened to justify Donovan and Alex's ongoing presence in her home.

And the lack of information or movement on her case had everyone on edge.

She, Donovan and Alex made daily trips into Austin, spending time at the K-9 center and getting some distance from Whisperwood, but each night they'd return, no further on her case than when they'd started. It was maddening.

Even more frustrating was the fact that each night they went through this weird, awkward good-night that sent her to her room alone while Donovan and Alex headed for her spare room.

Maddening.

Bellamy snapped the lid of her laptop closed. She'd just paid off her last remaining December bill and was angry by the ever-dwindling number in her bank account. She couldn't be without a job forever, nor could she stand sitting around much longer.

But for the moment she was in a holding pattern.

Her LSP email still worked and she and Donovan had explored all they could find from a distance, but the system was fairly locked down in terms of using it as a mechanism into the inner workings of LSP.

Donovan had sent her email to one of their digital forensics experts to work through the signatures that sat behind the data but the woman had found precious little to go on, and without a warrant for LSP's data they didn't get very far. Which only added to the soup of frustration that was her life.

"It's Christmas Eve. Would you like to go look at lights again? I hear they've got a big holiday festival south of Austin as you head toward San Antonio." Donovan padded into the kitchen, his feet bare beneath jeans that hugged his backside and a black T-shirt that made her mouth water. The man had limited tastes and he'd already washed and recycled several T-shirts that hugged his chest, but the jeans were a mainstay.

Which also only added to her general sense of irritability.

The man was mouthwateringly attractive and he hadn't laid a hand on her since their interrupted make-out session on her couch. Where she'd first thought that was a good thing, as each day went by she'd grown less and less convinced.

"I know it's Christmas Eve. And attempting to cheer me up with shiny lights isn't the answer."

"Okay." Donovan shrugged and poured himself a fresh cup of coffee.

"And you can get rid of the attitude while you're at it. I know it's boring as a tomb around here. Why don't you go back to your family or just go home? It's silly for you to sit here day after day. No one's going to attack me for Christmas."

She'd rehearsed the speech in her head, desperate for her life to return to some sense of normalcy, but had to admit to herself that it didn't come out quite as she'd planned. In her mind, it was competent and confident, setting the tone for how they'd move forward. In reality, it had come out edgy and whiny, with a side of bitchy that didn't speak well of her, especially when she'd stood up and fumbled the chair behind her.

No, it didn't speak well of her at all.

"You want me to leave?" Donovan asked.

"Do you really want to stay?"

"I want you to be safe."

"Since the incidents stopped, it's hard to feel like I'm in danger."

"You didn't answer my question." He left his mug on the counter and moved closer, his hands firmly at his side even as he moved up into her space. "Do you want me to leave, Bellamy?"

"I don't—" The words stuck in her throat when his hand lifted to her stomach, the tip of his finger tracing the skin there. The touch was light but it carried the impact of an atom bomb, fanning the flames of attraction that she'd tried desperately to quell over the past week.

Whatever had happened on the couch was a moment in time. A crazy moment of abandon that didn't need to be repeated.

Hadn't she told herself that over and over this past week? More than that, hadn't she seen firsthand how hard Donovan worked and how committed he was to her and to his caseload? He stayed with her, uprooting his own life while still digging into her case. Even with all that, he remained focused on his other responsibilities, as well. Their daily drives to the K-9 center had shown his dedication to Alex and keeping him fit and well trained. Even the things he'd shared with her over coffee each evening had pulled them closer.

He'd opened up about his family a bit more, usually in the guise of probing her about Maggie, but it was sharing all the same. And a few nights before he'd blown her mind when he shared his theories about Sutton Taylor. His comments hadn't moved far from her thoughts, the image of the man she knew as leader of LSP as Donovan's biological father. She struggled to put the two together, yet as she listened to his points, had to admit his theory had merit.

The fact they couldn't find Sutton Taylor to speak to the man directly had only added to the questions around LSP's leader. The chief's inquiries to Lone Star Pharmaceutical had gone unanswered, Sally Borne's dismissal of requests growing increasingly uncooperative.

Where was the man? Holidays or not, CEOs never went so far away as to be unreachable. Yet the man seemed to be off the grid and every outreach made to local hospitals—even the exclusive ones—hadn't turned up any leads.

All the questions and conversation had brought them closer, yet until this very moment, Donovan hadn't so much as touched her. Nor had his dark gaze turned heated, not once. And neither had he attempted to kiss her again.

So what were they doing here?

Yes, she was under his protection, but she'd never heard of anyone getting a personalized police protector who moved in. He'd gone above and beyond and it was getting more and more difficult to understand why.

"What are you doing?"

A small smile tilted his lips as he continued pressing his finger slightly against her stomach. "Nothing."

"Are you bored?"

"You seem to be."

"Are you?"

"Whatever I am, Bellamy, I can assure you it isn't bored."

She lifted his gaze from the mesmerizing play of his finger. "Then what are you?"

"Truth?"

"Of course."

"I want you and I'm not sure I can do the right thing by you any longer."

"You're—"

The right thing? Had he been purposely keeping his distance?

He waited while she worked through the details, punctuating his point when she gazed up at him once again. "You're under my protection. You're my responsibility. It would hardly do to act on our attraction."

"Why not?"

"Because it's unprofessional. And a conflict. And—"

She moved into his body, wrapping her arms around his neck to pull him close. All the confusion and anger and frustration of the past week faded as he opened his arms and pulled her close. "And completely wonderful, Donovan Colton."

"It's nearly killed me this past week. Everywhere I look, there you are." He framed her face with his hands before shifting to push several strands of hair behind her ear. "I want you. And I want to see where this goes. But I know it's a bad time."

"Maybe it's the perfect time."

And as his lips met hers, Bellamy knew she'd never spoken truer words.

It was the perfect time.

DONOVAN PULLED BELLAMY close for a kiss, the motion achingly beautiful. Hadn't he dreamed of doing this for the past week? Every time he looked at her, he imagined her in his arms. He saw himself peeling off her clothing, piece by piece, until there was nothing between them. And then, once they were both naked, satisfying this hunger that had gripped him and refused to let go.

She'd been so brave. He saw the toll the sitting and waiting had taken, yet she'd remained hopeful. Focused on the future and their ability to find whoever was behind the attacks on her. It had only been today, after she'd finished up on the computer, that he'd finally seen the cracks.

And he had more than a few cracks of his own.

He wanted her. He knew there were consequences to taking this leap but heaven help him, he couldn't walk away.

"Donovan?"

"Hmm?" He kissed her again.

"Stop thinking and take me to bed."

He lifted his head then and stared down at her, a seductive smile lighting her up from the inside. "You're sure?"

"I've never been more sure. I want you. And I want to make love with you. Let's take what's between us and not worry about anything else."

Had he ever met anyone so generous? Or wanted a woman more?

All the questions that had swirled around his life for the past week—heck, for the past thirty-one years—seemed to fade in the face of her. She was warm and generous and she took him as he was. That was a gift beyond measure and he swore to himself he wouldn't squander it.

Her home was small and he was grateful for that when they arrived at her bedroom a short while later. They'd stripped each other along the way, a path of shirts and pants and a sexy bra forming a trail from the kitchen to the bedroom. And after he laid her down on the bed, her arms extending to pull him close, he sank into her, reveling in the play of skin against skin, the full press of her breasts against his chest a delicious torment.

Slipping a hand between them, he found the waistband of her panties, the last piece of clothing to come off. The warm heat of her covered his hand and he played with her sensitive flesh, gratified by the sexy moans that spilled from her throat and the gentle writhing of her legs where they pressed to his hips. She was amazing. Warm. Responsive. And as in the moment as he was.

Long, glorious moments spun out between them as the dying afternoon light spilled into the room. They had all they needed there, just the two of them, as their touches grew more urgent. As fewer words were exchanged. As soft sighs expanded, growing longer before cresting on a gentle breath.

They didn't need anything else, Donovan realized as he jumped up on a rush and raced for his discarded jeans. Her light giggle had followed him out of the room as he ran for protection and her smile was pure and golden when she opened her arms for him and welcomed him back to the bed.

Welcome.

The thought struck hard as he rejoined her, making quick work of the condom before fitting himself to her body.

She was the warmest, softest welcome and it nearly killed him to go slow and take his time. To make the moments last between the two of them, as powerful as a tornado, as delicate as spun sugar.

The demands of her body pulled against him as he moved inside of her, her delicate inner walls indicating her release was nearly upon her. He added a firm touch to pull her along, gratified when she crested mere moments before he followed her.

Pure pleasure suffused his body as he wrapped himself up in her. And as he rode out wave after wave, he knew nothing in his life would ever be the same.

Bellamy had changed him.

And he had no desire to go back to the way he'd been.

JENSEN FITTED THE small hunting cabin at the edge of the LSP property with a strip of explosive. He fashioned the claylike material around the needed wires and then worked backward toward the detonation device.

His father had kept this place, private land adjacent to LSP, as a small getaway right in the heart of the Hill Country. How apropos that a place used to destroy God's creatures had become a human hunting ground, as well.

He'd waited for this, carefully mapping out how he'd secure Bellamy Reeves's arrival at the cabin. In the end, he had no idea it would be so easy as snatching her sister as an incentive to come without a fuss.

Maggie Corgan was hot, but damn, the woman was a sad sack. She'd been moping around Whisperwood like a bored prom queen and it had been easy enough to grab her and bring her here. He'd made a point to run into her in town and made a fuss about some details they'd found at LSP on Bellamy's car. Despite the holiday, the woman had practically jumped into his passenger seat, anxious to find the details that would exonerate her sister.

The chloroformed cloth had knocked her out just after they passed the gated entrance to LSP property and she'd been asleep ever since.

"Do you know what you're doing?" Sally's voice echoed from the small front room slash kitchen, her tone growing increasingly naggy and whiny as they got closer to finishing this. He'd seriously misjudged her. He thought he had a partner in his efforts to secure his future—and he was paying her off well enough for that partnership—but she'd gotten increasingly worried over the past few days. She wouldn't stop asking him if he knew how to handle things and she was convinced his old man was going to make a magical recovery from his blood poisoning.

What good was it to own a pharmaceutical company if you couldn't co-op a few of the products for your own use? The chloroform fell into that category. So did the experimental drug he'd used on his father. That had been the easy part.

Setting up Bellamy Reeves to take the fall while he initiated his "brother" Donovan into the family? Now that took real planning.

"It's fine, Sally. I've got it all under control."

"You said that a week ago and since then I've fielded daily calls from the police nosing around. You're lucky I know my rights. They can't get in without a search warrant and so far they can't get one."

"Good."

"So far, Jensen. It's only a matter of time if I keep blocking."

"The problem will be gone by then and you'll be long gone. Calm down."

She gave him a side-eye but marched back into the front room. He was glad to see her go. The nagging was driving him crazy. They said men looked for women like their mothers, and in that respect he had to agree.

His mother might have been a passive soul, but she knew her place and didn't harp and harangue every chance she got.

No, Jensen thought with no small measure of glee. *His* mother had taken notes. Detailed notes she'd left behind for him to find and pore over. She'd not mentioned Donovan Colton by name but it had been easy enough to note the Christmas date and the reference to Sutton's latest "bastard left in the stables across town like a discarded piece of trash."

He'd read that passage more than once, pleased to know his father was oblivious to the brat's existence. It would make it that much easier to ensure Donovan Colton never got a piece of the Taylor inheritance.

Jensen snipped an extra length of wire and tested the hold. It was only a matter of time until Bellamy Reeves showed up, her knight in shining armor in tow.

And then Donovan Colton would understand, once and for all, what a discarded piece of trash he really was.

DONOVAN LEVERED HIS hands behind his head and watched as Bellamy flitted around the room. She was full of nervous energy post-sex that he found incredibly adorable and he was enjoying just watching her. Especially since he felt like every muscle in his body had just had the best, most effective workout. It was a treat to lay back and watch her beautiful frame and whip-quick energy light up the room.

"Maybe I should have gotten a tree? I know I didn't want one, but it'd have been nice to have the color. And the smell. I love that fresh tree smell."

"We can still get one if you'd like one."

She stopped midpace, a hand going to her hip. "You wouldn't mind doing that?"

"Not at all. Let's do it."

She glanced own, her eyes widening. "But we're naked."

"So we'll get dressed and then get naked later."

"Later?"

He smiled at the slight squeak in her voice. "I'd like that, if you would."

Bellamy crossed to the bed, her nervous energy fading as a soft smile spread across her face. "I'd like that, too. Even as crazy and scary as this time has been, I wouldn't change it."

"Me, either." Donovan reached for her and pulled her close, nestling her against his chest. "Not one single second."

She pressed her lips against his skin before lifting her head. "I'm glad you're here."

"Me, too." He tickled her before rolling her over on her back. "Let's go buy a tree."

"Now?"

"Maybe in an hour."

And then he proceeded to show her just what he could do with an hour.

BELLAMY PRACTICALLY DANCED through the kitchen, gathering up her purse and her phone where they still lay on the counter. She couldn't believe what a difference an afternoon could make in her spirits and her attitude. She'd spent the morning morose and frustrated and had spent the afternoon in Donovan's arms.

And what an amazing afternoon it had been.

Catching herself before a sigh escaped her lips and

already imagining the cartoon hearts that were floating above her head, she took her phone firmly in hand and hit the home screen out of habit. A text from her sister showed up, followed by a phone number she didn't recognize, along with a voice mail prompt.

She'd been waiting for insurance to call her back about her car and had to catch herself a good ten seconds into the voice mail before she realized the message wasn't from her insurance company at all.

A muffled voice, disguised with some sort of filter, echoed against her ear. "Come to the LSP grounds alone if you want to bring your sister home."

She fumbled the phone and listened to the message once more, a desperate sense of urgency forcing her into action, as the message also outlined an appointed time and meeting place. She had to leave. She had to get to Maggie.

Why hadn't she tried harder to talk to her this week? Instead of being persistent and trying to win her sister back, all she'd done was curl into her usual shell and get angry. It was always someone else's fault. She was never the one to blame.

And where had it gotten her?

With Maggie's life in danger, all because of her.

Donovan's voice rumbled from the hallway, where he talked to Alex, and Bellamy quickly cataloged what to do. Tell him where she was going and put Maggie's life at risk? Or take his car and go alone?

This was about her. For reasons she still didn't understand, she'd been targeted by someone inside LSP and all that had ensued was directed at her.

She needed to be the one to fix it.

Her hand closed over Donovan's keys, where they lay

on the counter near her purse. She had them in hand, their heft and weight firm in her palm. She would do this. She'd face this nameless threat and handle it. She had to.

The door beckoned but Bellamy stilled, her resolve wavering.

She *could* do this. She could do anything she set her mind to.

But she could also use the help. Qualified help from an expert trained in crisis and criminal behavior.

"Donovan!" He and Alex came running the moment she screamed.

And as man and dog rounded the corner into her kitchen, Bellamy took solace that she'd not have to act alone.

THE NERVOUS ENERGY that had carried her from the house to the drive to the far end of LSP's property faded as Bellamy caught sight of Sally Borne in the distance. "She's behind all this?"

Bellamy supposed it wasn't all that big a revelation, yet somehow she hadn't seen Sally at the heart of everything. A lackey, maybe, taking orders from the inside, but not as a mastermind behind what had happened to her or the decision to throttle drug production.

The disguised tones on her voice mail hadn't suggested a woman, either, yet Bellamy couldn't argue with the tall, feminine form traipsing and tromping around outside the small hideaway bordering the edge of the LSP property. It was a hunting cabin, as she recalled. Something Sutton Taylor had used for years as a place to let off steam on the weekends.

"She looks mad," Donovan whispered in her ear as he lowered night vision goggles. "A plan unraveling?"

"Or a crazy person at the end of her rope."

"That, too." Donovan took her hand in his and squeezed. "We'll take her down and we'll get Maggie back."

"You seem awfully sure about this."

"It's my job to be sure. It's also my job to pin criminals in their dens so we can haul them in."

His certainty helped, as did the knowledge that he had been through something like this before. All she could think of was that Maggie was inside the cabin, but Donovan had a broader purview. He knew how to manage an op and he also knew how to take down a criminal.

And he also had backup setting themselves up in the distance. The two of them hadn't walked into this alone, despite the clear warning on the voice mail to do so.

She'd trusted Donovan to do the right thing, but knew it wasn't going to be easy. They'd gotten in but they still needed to get out.

"I don't believe it's Sally. She was unpleasant and dismissed me from the company without giving me the opportunity to defend myself, but I didn't take her for a kidnapper and a killer."

"Maybe she got in over her head," Donovan suggested.

"Or maybe you did." The voice was low and quiet in the winter night, but the click of a cocked gun was unmistakable.

How HAD HE allowed himself to get so distracted?

That thought pounded through Donovan's mind as

he covered the remaining ground from the LSP property to the cabin in the woods. He was responsible for keeping Bellamy safe and there was no way he could do that with a loaded gun at his back.

He hadn't seen his assailant's face, but had to give Bellamy points for gut instinct. She couldn't believe Sally Borne was responsible for what had unfolded, and she wasn't. Sally was in this up to her eyeballs, but she wasn't the mastermind.

Donovan toyed with turning on his assailant, but the proximity made it nearly impossible to get an upper hand. If he was by himself, he'd make the move and worry about any possible consequences in the fight, but with Bellamy by his side, it put her at too much risk. Which only reinforced why she belonged home in the first place.

He'd done his best to convince her to stay behind, but nothing had swayed her.

Including the promise that he'd bring Maggie home.

So he'd listened and believed they could keep her safe anyway, buying into her BS that LSP would only negotiate with her. He'd trusted that Archer and his backup fanning the perimeter would be enough and that he could keep her safe, no matter what.

Now he wasn't so sure.

"Come in, come in." The gun pressed to his back as the jerk marching behind them pushed them inside the front door of the cabin. "We're going to have a family reunion."

Bellamy had stiffened each time the man behind them spoke, but it was only once they were inside the door that she whirled on him. "Jensen Taylor. You're behind all of this?"

Jensen?

Donovan's mind raced over his memories of Jensen Taylor. The paunchy man before him was a genuine surprise and he realized that any of the articles he'd read on the father had limited information about the son.

And old pictures.

Taylor had been a popular, good-looking guy, more than able to get his fair share of dates. But the man that stared back at them had changed. The degree of crazy in his eyes was concerning, but it was something more. He was in his midthirties, but he was already soft, his body doughy and neglected. If it weren't for the gun and Bellamy's close presence, Donovan would have immediately taken his chance at overpowering the man.

"Who were you expecting?" Jensen sneered.

Bellamy shook her head. "I'm not sure but certainly not the heir to the company."

"That's exactly why I'm involved," Jensen said. "I need to make sure I stay that way."

"Stay what way? You're Sutton's son. You already sit in on board meetings and you've got a big position inside LSP."

"It's not big enough. Nor is running distribution a sign that I'm being groomed for the CEO's spot. I decided I need to set up my own plan for upward mobility."

"So you fixed the prices of vaccines?" Bellamy practically spat out the words, her gray eyes nearly black in the soft lighting of the room. "And then tried to blame it on me."

"I did blame it on you. It's just my luck that my little brother over here showed up to play knight in shining armor. He kept rescuing you instead of letting you take the fall."

"Your brother?" Bellamy whispered, her gaze colliding with Donovan's. He saw the awareness there and the subtle agreement that he'd been right with his theory about Sutton Taylor's infidelities.

The question was, how did they all get out of there before his big brother imploded?

BELLAMY KEPT HER gaze on Maggie, willing her sister to wake up. She was tied to a chair, her head lolling at a strange angle from where she'd been knocked out. She wanted to go to her, but Jensen's insistence on keeping the gun cocked and pointed directly at her and Donovan had her staying in place.

They needed to talk him down and give Archer enough time to break in.

And they also needed to keep an eye on Sally. The instability that marked Jensen was nowhere in evidence with her. In fact, the more Jensen railed, the calmer Sally got as she stood there, stoically watching the proceedings.

"Why are you so convinced I'm your brother?" Donovan asked the question, his gaze revealing nothing. "I'm a Colton."

"A Colton discovered in the barn on Christmas morning. The whole town knows."

"It's not a secret I was adopted."

"Adopted because you're some stray they felt sorry for."

"Does Sutton know?"

"About you?" A small corner of spittle filled the edge of Jensen's mouth, his skin turning a ripe shade of pink around his collar. "My mother knew about you. A pithy little story, if you must know. Dear old Dad knocked up his secretary. It was my mother who orchestrated everything, convincing your simpering fool of a mother to hand you over to a family who could really take care of you."

"But does Sutton know?" Donovan insisted.

"No. And that's how it's going to stay. My father has already given enough money to his illegitimate offspring. I'm not losing one more piece of my inheritance to the fact he couldn't keep it zipped."

"Fair point." Donovan nodded, his face drawn in sober lines.

Bellamy watched him, fascinated as he began to subtly control the room. She could only assume he'd received some signal from the chief, because bit by bit, he maneuvered Jensen around the room, drawing the gun off of her and her sister.

"It wouldn't do to have more of your inheritance go to anyone else." Donovan's voice was even and level. Reasonable. "Especially since LSP stock stands to go through the roof with the vaccine price-fixing."

"Exactly."

"You had it all figured out. Work the system, blame it all on Bellamy and then get rid of the evidence."

"Yep." Jensen nodded, the dull red of his skin fading again to a warm pink.

"What about your father?"

"Don't you want to call him Dad?"

It was the first moment Jensen managed to get a rise and the smallest muscle ticked in Donovan's jaw. "Where's Dad in all this?"

"Fighting for his life across town in a quiet little facility that isn't on anyone's radar. He's unknowingly been the recipient of a new drug being developed to treat certain forms of cancer. It's a miracle drug, unless you don't have any cancer to cure."

Bellamy knew what Jensen spoke of and had seen the trial details a few months prior. The drug was powerful and had the potential to be a game changer, but it had to be used properly.

And there he was, poisoning his father with it?

"You're a monster."

"Yeah, sweetheart, I am." Jensen shifted his attention at her outburst, his eyes now wild with whatever madness had gripped him. "But you can take solace in the fact that I'm the last one you're ever going to see."

"You're mad."

"Mad at the world, yes." Jensen's gaze swung toward Donovan before coming firmly to rest on her. "I've spent my life waiting for my turn. To run the company. To earn dear old Dad's respect. To get my shot. Yet I was never good enough."

The roller coaster of the past days seemed to slow in the face of Jensen's anger. It was too simple to think of him as a crazy person to be taken down.

Far too simple.

What she saw instead was a man beyond reason. Whatever he believed was meant to be his—his father's love, his birthright, even the Taylor name—had somehow twisted over time. And as she stared at Jensen, Bellamy had to admit that under different circumstances, that could have been her.

Hadn't she spent the past five years resenting Maggie for choosing to live her life while poor little Bellamy stayed behind taking care of their parents?

And hadn't she buried herself in her job, shunning relationships—heck, even shunning the chance to own a pet—because she'd crawled so far beneath the rock of self-sacrifice?

Looking into Jensen's angry, disillusioned eyes, Bellamy saw it all so clearly. And in that moment, finally understood all she was about to lose.

Donovan and Alex had shown her the way. Even if what was building between her and Donovan still needed time to grow roots, she was grateful for what he'd given her.

For what he'd shown her.

That she had a life and it was time to get living.

How horrifying it was to realize that far too late.

DONOVAN'S FINGERS ITCHED as he held his hands by his side. Brother or not, Jensen Taylor was going down. Assuming he could get them all out of there.

"Nice speech, Jensen."

The words were enough to pull the man's attention off Bellamy and it gave Donovan the briefest moment of relief. If he could keep Jensen's focus diverted, he had a chance of getting Bellamy out alive.

If.

"It's the truth."

"Your truth."

"It is my truth!" Anger spilled from Taylor's lips with a violence that shouldn't have been surprising under the circumstances. "And now it's yours, Colton. You think you've got a way out of here, but you don't. Even with whatever backup you inevitably brought along, I've thought of it all. This place is wired."

While Donovan didn't doubt Jensen's threats, taunting him might get the information he needed to defuse whatever lurked around the cabin.

"Like Bellamy's car? Because you were so good at that. A half-assed explosion rigged by an amateur."

"It was meant to be. It wasn't time to kill her. And if it gave the cops time to wonder why someone suspected of stealing company secrets would make herself look like an accident victim, it was that much better."

"And the bomb at her house?"

"Same. How does it look if the poor little woman peddling company secrets escaped death twice? It would be like a red flag—she's setting herself up."

"So killing her here? All of us here? How's that going to go down?"

"Ah, that's where Sally comes in. She's the one with Bellamy's personnel folder and she's the one who let her go. It stood to reason the stress of getting discovered and fired was the last thing Bellamy Reeves needed before going around the bend."

"All figured out."

"Except for you," Jensen sneered.

And the backup waiting outside the cabin.

Donovan calculated the odds—and the acknowledgment that Jensen Taylor had to have walked in here with a plan B.

"What are you going to do about me?"

"Same thing I'm going to do about all of you. I came out here to counsel a distressed former employee. And I'm going to get out barely alive from the bomb she's planted to blow me to smithereens."

Cold. Impersonal. Distant.

The very reason a bomb made an effective weapon for cowards stood before him.

And in that moment, Donovan knew there was no time to wait.

As he leaped forward, Donovan's momentum was enough to knock Jensen off balance. Donovan slammed Jensen's gun hand on the ground, a harsh cry in his ear proof he'd damaged bone, as well. As soon as the man went still, Donovan was on his feet, moving toward Bellamy.

Jensen's fall must have been what Archer was waiting for. The room erupted in gunfire and smoke, a series of officers rushing the room from outside. Donovan had a split second to register it all before Bellamy's scream had his gaze shifting back toward his half brother. The man lifted a small square no bigger than a lighter from his pocket, his hand flipping the top open.

"Donovan!" Bellamy screamed his name once more, just as Donovan leaped into motion. His hand closed over Jensen's, effectively stopping his brother from taking the final step of blowing up the cottage with all of them in it. Archer was the closest, and he twisted Jensen's wrist to retrieve the device that would no doubt blow them all sky-high.

All noise ceased, everyone in the room going quiet as Archer stepped back, the detonation device in hand.

"Tell me you know what you're doing with that, Thompson." Donovan gritted out the words.

"Underestimating me again, Colton?"

"Never."

"Good." Chief Thompson nodded, his hands calm and still. "Then I can swallow my pride and ask you to come handle this."

"Deal."

DONOVAN TAPPED THE back of the EMT vehicle in a signal that the crew could move on. Sally and Jensen had already been transported in handcuffs and the other EMT team had worked on Maggie, treating her for lingering effects of the chloroform and taking her in for an overnight of observation. The bomb beneath the cabin had already been removed, detonated on the far edge of the property where it couldn't hurt anyone. Archer and his men still worked the scene and they'd already called into the facility where Sutton was to get the doctors diagnosing him with the correct meds to get well.

"I had no idea it was Jensen. I never even considered him." That thought had kept her steady company since Archer's team had cuffed Jensen and even an hour later, she still couldn't believe it was true.

Everything that had happened had been engineered by Sutton's greedy—and clearly unstable—son.

"Archer asked me what I thought the motive was in all that was happening."

Bellamy took in his bedraggled form and the spot of blood that had dried on his cheek where Jensen had nicked him in their fight. "What motive did you give?"

"I went with the old standby. Money and power."

"I'd say you pegged them both."

Donovan pulled her close, folding her up against his chest. "I don't know what I'd have done if something happened to you."

He'd said the same thing off and on since Jensen had been taken away, and each time she'd stood patiently, wrapping her arms around his waist and holding him tight. "I'm okay. We all are."

"I never should have let you come."

"You didn't get much choice in the matter."

He shook his head at that, his warm brown gaze still

bleak from the events of the evening. "I shouldn't have let that matter."

"Is that how it's going to be, Donovan Colton?"

"Be?"

He looked crestfallen as she pulled from his arms, her own hands fisting at her hips. "You tell me what to do and I just do it. I'm not Alex, you know."

"A fact I'm glad about."

"I have my own mind and I make my own decisions. It's why I stopped and told you what was happening instead of harking off on my own. That was big for me." She moved in and pressed a kiss to his chin. "Don't make me regret my decision."

"Why didn't you leave?"

Bellamy knew there were a lot of reasons she'd chosen to go to Donovan instead of heading out on her own, but one had stood out beyond all the rest. "Because it's time to stick."

"To stick?"

"I've been doing everything on my own for far too long. It's time to depend on people. To let people in and to depend on them and the support they can provide."

"Does this mean you want me to stick around?"

So much had happened in such a short time, it seemed nearly impossible to be having this conversation.

Yet here they were.

She'd spent too much time unwilling to voice what she wanted, now that the moment was here, Bellamy was determined not to fumble it. "Yes, I do."

"I'm not in a position to walk away from my job in Austin."

"I'd never ask you to."

"And Alex and I are a package deal."

"I certainly hope so."

"And I'm sort of surly and grumpy in the morning."

She smiled. "Believe it or not, I figured that one out all by myself."

"What else have you figured out?"

"That I want to spend time with you. I like having a surly, grumpy man and his furry best friend in my life. I'm tired of my own company and I'm tired of ignoring all the life going on all around me."

"If you're sure?"

She thought about those scary moments, when she stared at Jensen Taylor and saw the faintest outline of herself.

"I'm absolutely positive."

Donovan bent his head and pressed his lips to hers. The kiss was full of passion and promise and abundant joy. As she wrapped her arms around him and sunk into his kiss, Bellamy knew she'd finally found the partner to share her life with.

Two partners, she silently acknowledged to herself as she added Alex. And she couldn't be happier.

Epilogue

Six weeks later

Bellamy juggled the plate of cake and pot of coffee and headed for the living room. She'd come to look forward to these Saturday afternoons with her sister and was excited to share the recently discovered recipe with Maggie.

"Is that Mom's pound cake?" The words were said in a reverent tone as Maggie leaped off the couch to help her with the plate.

"I found the recipe back in the fall. She had it hoarded in the bottom of her jewelry box."

"Who knew?" Maggie's musical laughter was a balm and Bellamy couldn't deny how nice it was to share something funny about her parents.

"She was so proud of that cake. She preened every time someone commented on it at town events."

Maggie reached for a slice. "Then I'm glad it's not lost to us."

Her sister took a bite, her eyes closing as she chewed, and Bellamy screwed up her courage. She'd wanted to say something for a while now, but had struggled with how to express all she felt. "I'm sorry for all that's happened."

Maggie's eyes popped open. "What do you mean?"

"Mom. Dad. All of it. I was stubborn and unfair to you and I'm sorry. I'm sorrier it took a kidnapping and an attempt on both our lives to realize it."

"I'm sorry, too."

"You don't have to be sorry."

"Yes, actually, I do." Maggie settled her plate back on the coffee table. "I thought I could fix everything. That marrying James would give me the financial tools to fix what was happening. I'm not proud of myself, nor was I fair to James."

"But you loved him first."

"Yes. Maybe." Maggie swiped at a small tear that trailed down her cheek. "It's the 'maybe' that's the problem. For a long time, I enjoyed being with him. And I liked being a Corgan. But I liked those things too much. My husband should have come first."

Since coming back into each other's lives, she and Maggie had danced around the subject of her sister's marriage. It was humbling to realize all that had gone on beneath the surface. "But you did care for each other."

"We did. And I'm glad we finally remembered that, there at the end. But James has moved on and in time, I will, too. And in the meantime, he helped me make sure you've got this great house."

"He… You what?"

A mischievous light filled Maggie's eyes. "You belong here, Bell. And I know it's what Mom and Dad would have wanted."

"But the will. The insurance. The house came from there—" Bellamy broke off. "Didn't it?"

"They actually came courtesy of the Corgan fortune."

A sinking feeling gripped her, and Bellamy felt the coffee she'd sipped curdling in her stomach. "I can't accept that. I mean, it's not my place."

Maggie reached over, her gentle touch stopping the torrent of words. "It's what James and I both wanted. He understood it was important to me and in a lot of ways, it was the final act of kindness that allowed us to let each other go. And we both decided to keep it a secret so you wouldn't say no."

"But I can't take it."

"Actually, you can. We both knew how much you sacrificed for Mom and Dad. More, you deserved something to cement your future. This is your home."

"But—"

"But nothing. I know you love playing the big-sister card, but on this one, I win. It's what I wanted. James, too."

The generosity was nearly overwhelming, but in her sister's words, Bellamy sensed healing, as well. "You're okay with the divorce?"

"It's best for both of us." Maggie reached for her plate again. "Speaking of best, how are things with Donovan Colton?"

She knew her sister, and Bellamy suspected the rapid change in topic was deliberate. But she also understood how important it was to Maggie to stand on her own two feet. Vowing to take the issue of the house up with her later, she let the joy of being with Donovan wash over her.

"Things are good. He's good."

"You're spending a lot of time running back and forth to Austin."

"We're enjoying each other's company."

"First you make her pound cake and now you're using euphemisms like Mom?"

Bellamy swatted at her sister's leg. "I like being with him."

"Then tell me what you're doing for Valentine's Day."

LATER THAT DAY, her earlier conversation with Maggie still lingered in her mind as Bellamy cleaned up the plates and mugs. The time they'd spent together since the holidays was helping to mend their relationship and it was wonderful to have her sister back.

She heard the bark moments before a nose pressed into her hip, a large, wiggly body prancing at her side. Donovan followed behind Alex into the kitchen and Bellamy fought the urge to lay a hand against her heart at the sight of him. She bent to lavish praise on Alex instead, willing her pulse to slow down.

How did the man manage it?

"Where's Maggie?"

"She had a date with a sale at the mall."

He moved in and pulled her close. "And you didn't want to go?"

"I'm getting used to having some money back in my bank account. I'd like to revel in that glow a bit longer."

Concern lined his face. "Sutton's made good on everything that happened at LSP. Your job, your good name *and* a raise."

She wrapped her arms around his waist, unable to hold back the truth. "Okay. I admit it, then. I wanted to stay home and spend the afternoon with you."

The worry faded, replaced with a cocky smile. "Well, then, Ms. Reeves. What did you have in mind?"

"This."

The kiss had her pulse racing again, a wild thrill ride that she couldn't imagine ever tiring of.

How things had changed since December. Her lonely, quiet life had vanished and in its place was something more wonderful than she could have ever imagined.

She was in love.

The thought hit so swiftly—and came from a place so deep—it had Bellamy pulling back from the kiss.

Love?

"Bellamy?"

"I… Um… I…" She grasped at the first thing that came to mind. "Do we need to feed Alex?"

"What?" Confusion furrowed a small line between his eyebrows before Donovan glanced toward Alex, who even now lay curled up on the floor, fast asleep. "He's fine."

"Good."

"And he doesn't eat until six."

"Right."

"It's one."

"Sure." Bellamy silently cursed herself for her inability to think on the fly. "Of course."

"Are you okay?"

"Yeah. Sure. I'm fine." She moved back to the sink and snatching up a dish towel to dry the mugs from earlier.

"What's wrong?"

"Nothing."

"Something's wrong. One moment I'm kissing you and the next you're pulling away like you got burned. What's wrong?"

She dropped the dish towel as the cup banged against the counter with a discordant thud. "I love you."

The words were out before she could check them and it was enough to have her holding her breath. Had she really just told him she loved him?

It was stupid and impulsive and about as well thought out as the "let's feed Alex" line.

"Bellamy."

The second, urgent use of her name had her looking up, turning to face him. To face the reality of her impulsive words. "Look. Just ignore me. That kiss scrambled my brain and I sort of short-circuited. It's noth—"

He laid a finger over her lips. "It's not nothing."

The soft press of his finger turned tantalizing as he ran the pad over her lower lip. "Believe it or not, I have a few thoughts on this subject you seem hesitant to voice, too. It's not particularly original but I think it fits in these circumstances."

"You do?"

"I love you, Bellamy Reeves. I love everything about you. I love that you don't mind my attitude in the morning before coffee. And I love that you've been quietly encouraging me to visit with Sutton *and* my parents. And I love that you're mending fences with your sister."

"Those are good things."

"They are. And they're good because I can share them with you."

Whatever she'd been expecting, a declaration of love

was the farthest thing from her mind. "You love me back?"

"I sure do."

"I love you, Donovan. And I love your furry partner, too."

"Alex is a lot smarter than me. I think he already figured it all out and has been waiting for the two humans to get on board."

The heavy thump of a tail had the two of them turning at the same time. The sleeping lump in front of her fridge was wide-awake, his dark eyes full of knowing and endless wisdom.

Bellamy smiled, surprised at how easy it was to believe the dog knew all. "I guess that means he approves."

As if on cue, Alex leaped up from his favorite spot and jumped up, completing the small circle in Bellamy's kitchen and pressing eager kisses on both of them.

Bellamy laughed as Donovan tightened his hold.

"Oh yeah," Donovan whispered against her ear. "He definitely approves."

* * * * *